The Bachelor Portraits

The Bachelor Portraits

A Novel

James Irwin Kruger

VANTAGE PRESS
New York

This is a work of fiction. Any similarity between
the names, characters, and places in this book and any persons,
living or dead, is purely coincidental

Cover design by Susan Thomas

FIRST EDITION

Published by Vantage Press, Inc.
516 West 34th Street, New York, New York 10001

Manufactured in the United States of America
ISBN: 0-533-14189-3

Library of Congress Catalog Card No.: 02-91918

0 9 8 7 6 5 4 3 2 1

To Polly, who got sand in her shoes while helping me find lost hope.

The Bachelor Portraits

1

They stood on the balcony and watched the fiery whirlwind whip their world to ruin. The haze stung Teddy's eyes, and she shuddered as flames ripped the billowing pall of smoke that covered the city. Her father was dazed, staring blankly at the distant devastation. He swayed slightly as she reached up and brushed a dusting of ash from his shoulder. He was lost to her now. She'd seen him that way once before, just after her mother died. For several days Charles Cullen had managed things in his typical manner, with brusque efficiency. But as they stood at last at her mother's grave, he had wavered ever so slightly as he stared as if into a void. It was then that Teddy knew that he was far, far away, so deep in shock that he was unaware of her presence, so lost in grief that he could not hear, could not see beyond his own despair. It took several weeks for him to recover, and it was a difficult time for a ten-year-old. But that was three years ago. Teddy was grown up now, strong and unafraid. She would take care of him.

"You up there, get out!" shouted a soldier in the street, gesturing with his rifle. "Get a move on. The fire's heading this way. Get out—now!"

She took her father's hand in hers, hoping that somehow she could help him recover quickly from his shock. He had been rock solid at first, shrugging off the massive jolt that threw them from their beds as it rocked the granite foundation of their home. He had rushed into her room to comfort her, reminding her that earthquakes were nothing new to them, although conceding that this one was indeed very powerful. He refused to be rattled, even as they watched their neighbors' wagons clattering down Jackson Street in panicked flight. He was patient and understanding when their cook, anxious about his family, fled on foot to the warrens of Chinatown. He was condescending but generous when Senora Garcia, their housekeeper, begged him to escape with them in the carriage as her husband fought to control Lady, a very frightened mare. He smiled benignly as he stood in the cobblestone driveway to see them off. "Go ahead," he said. "But be sure you take good care of Lady, so she can bring you home again. And don't worry about us. We'll be fine. We'll be here when you return."

He set about immediately to try to bring order out of chaos, sweeping up broken glass, straightening furniture, hanging fallen pictures. But when the flames exploded downtown and began to consume everything in their path, he began to mutter to himself and seemed to be wrestling with his own reason. The fire could never reach them here on the heights; weren't the fire brigades battling heroically? There was no need to fear for their safety; weren't the soldiers patrolling the streets? But as the fire spread and flames crept up Nob Hill and the Bonanza mansions blistered and burst into flame, his composure seemed to dissolve and fear danced in his eyes. It was then that Teddy first felt him slipping away.

"Git, dammit!" the soldier shouted impatiently from the street, now aiming his rifle at them.

She guided her father inside and down the stairs. As they passed the parlor, Mac the Macaw squawked in outrage, reminding her not leave him behind. She murmured reassuringly as she covered the bird's cage against the foul air. She took the small bag they'd packed and handed it to her father to carry, and together they stepped carefully through the front door that hung precariously on twisted hinges. As they passed the soot-smudged soldier he asked, "Everyone out?"

She nodded, and a greedy smile flickered on his lips. There were rumors of drunkenness and thievery among the troops, and the image of looters pawing through their belongings flashed through her mind. But the rifle was pointed at them, and there was nothing they could do but obey. She led her father into the cluttered street and down the hill to Van Ness Avenue. They were rudely shunted around the fire lines and soon found themselves part of the crowd of frightened refugees wending its way through the smoldering hell of Market Street. Near the charred skeleton of the Palace Hotel, her father stumbled. Teddy led him to a wicker settee someone had dragged from the courtyard to safety in the street. As they rested there amid the smoking rubble, Teddy remembered the times they had entered the Palace Court in their carriage and disembarked to enjoy the elegance of the hotel's dining room. This had been her father's favorite place, and with the wisdom of youth, she understood why he had faltered at the sight of these sad ruins.

As she toed the ashes at her feet, she wondered about the fate of all they'd left behind. She thought about her mother's jewelry and the heirlooms passed to her when her mother died, the gifts her father had bestowed on her, especially Molly, the rag doll with the beautifully painted china head that had belonged to his mother. I mustn't worry, she thought. They were just things, precious things, but only things. Her task at the moment was to lead her father to the waterfront to find a boat to carry them across the bay to safety. Gently she tugged him to his feet and rejoined the procession of the dispossessed.

"Step lively, Miss," said a curly-haired youth at the wharf. "There's room for you both and your bag, but you'll have to leave the birdcage behind." Teddy's stricken look melted the stern demeanor of the *Napoli*'s first mate. "Well, here," he relented. "I'll hand it down to you. But you'll have to hold it in your lap."

He helped her mount the ladder and guided her down until her feet found the pitching deck of the small fishing boat. Then he passed her the birdcage as the captain called, "Cast off!" The mate, a lad of no more than seventeen, slipped the mooring line and flung it into the water. He swung about and clambered down the ladder and began dragging the line aboard, coiling it at his feet. Teddy clutched the shrouded cage while her father sat with his chin upon his knees, oblivious to the other passengers and the turmoil all around. The *Napoli* drifted clear of the wharf, her engines rumbled to life, and she chugged into the gray mists. Out on the bay, Teddy lifted the cover to give Mac a breath of fresh air, but it was too late. She uttered a cry and buried her face in her hands.

"Crying won't do any good," said the young mate. "You can always get another bird." Teddy looked up and saw a tear streaking the lad's cheek. He looked very tired. How much sorrow and heartbreak he must have seen, she thought. Yet the death of her bird brought a tear to his eye. She was deeply touched.

"I am sorry," said the youth, cuffing his damp cheek. "It was a beautiful bird, probably the most beautiful bird I've ever seen. But you can always get another."

In her desperation and loneliness he seemed to embody everything that was heroic to a girl of thirteen. In the face of overwhelming tragedy, he was strong and manly, yet kind and understanding of the suffering of a stranger. She dabbed at her tears and smiled, feeling safe and truly at ease for the first time since the earthquake disrupted their lives. He returned her smile and his handsome face and dark curly hair fixed itself indelibly in her memory. She laid her head upon her father's shoulder and fell asleep.

*   *   *

Tom Quinn was wide-eyed as Tony Lazarro counted out ten dollars and gave it to him, saying, "This is for you. We charged a fair price and cheated no one. You worked hard, and you'll need the money. We won't be going to sea for a while."

Tom didn't have to ask why. Telegraph Hill loomed over them, a blackened pile. North Beach was devastated; Chinatown lay in ashes, the Barbary Coast and Montgomery Street were smoldering ruins. The Lazarros were among thousands who had lost everything. Tony's wife Vanna and their two young daughters huddled on the wharf waiting for the *Napoli* to dock.

"My family will live aboard until we can find a place to stay, Tom," Tony explained reluctantly. "Come back in a week. The sea will still be full of fish, and people still must eat. We'll cast our nets again."

"Sure, Tony, and thanks," Tom said, fingering the fistful of coins. He'd never held so much money at one time. "I've got to go look for my mother anyway. See you later."

Tom and his mother lived in a small apartment above Le Coq Rouge, one of the "French restaurants" on Pacific Avenue. They shared the rooms of Professor Hunt, a patent medicine salesman who had taken in the widow Quinn and her son several years earlier when he found himself unable to pay his rent. The professor suffered from a multitude of complaints, although most seemed to stem from his addiction to one of his own potions. Tom grew from boyhood to manhood much too quickly among the denizens of the Barbary Coast—the pimps and prostitutes, gamblers, derelicts, roustabouts, and seamen from all corners of the world. When he turned fourteen, tall and handsome, his mother sent him up Montgomery Street to look for work as a messenger boy, as much to get him away from their seamy neighborhood as for the money he might bring in. But

Tom found himself intimidated by the fancy gentlemen of the financial district and turned his search instead to Fisherman's Wharf, where he felt more at ease.

Tony Lazarro of the *Napoli* was amused at first by the eager, bright-eyed lad whose smooth hands had never known hard labor. Tom's air of confidence reminded Tony of himself twenty years earlier when he, a baker's apprentice from Naples who'd never been to sea, sailed to America and found a job on a boat much like the *Napoli*. Since he had no son of his own to help with the nets, he took Tom aboard. The boy didn't mind getting up in the wee hours of the morning. It got him away from the apartment before his mother came home from work, often with a man on her arm. He would not have to pretend to be asleep as they tiptoed by his cot in the parlor and disappeared into the bedroom. He would not have to lie in the darkness, listening to the hushed voices, wondering at the strange sounds that were all but obscured by the snoring of Professor Hunt asleep in the alcove. It was far better to get away from all that, better to sail into the predawn darkness, to thrill to the beauty of the far horizon in the first light of day. It was better to work in the fresh salt air and to return home exhausted by honest labor in the early afternoon, when he would find his mother bright and cheery. It was their private time together, and she would share with him her dreams of a better life, while he would regale her with tales of his adventures at sea.

He took to sketching scenes for her, to illustrate his stories, and she was quick to recognize and encourage his talent. He made her drawings of the *Napoli* and of the weather-beaten face of Tony Lazarro and of the city skyline as it looked as they sailed in through the Golden Gate. And when his pencil sketches failed to capture the beauty of the setting sun as it glistened on the distant hills or of the brilliantly painted boats as they bobbed on the emerald sea, she bought him colored chalk, and soon the apartment was filled with his drawings. Professor Hunt acclaimed the lad a genius and took several of his pastels with him into the street to see what they might fetch. Tom never saw any money, although the professor usually returned home empty-handed.

Professor Hunt presented himself as a man of culture and refinement, and Tom believed him when he said the widow Quinn was a performer of grace and beauty whose talent far exceeded that of the common run of women employed along the Barbary Coast. Tom himself had never seen her perform and never wanted to. He knew that her specialty was to sing popular songs while swinging in a flowered "birdcage" above the raucous crowd at Le Coq Rouge. But after he left Tony at the wharf and returned "home," he found only a jumble of smoking timbers and a single bitter reminder of his mother amid the ashes—the charred and twisted remains of her empty cage. Inevitably it reminded him of the little girl who wept to find her parrot dead, a lingering memory that still saddened him. He was feeling quite forlorn when he heard a familiar voice.

"It's all gone, Tom. Alas, everything we cherished now is ashes."

"There's nothing here I cherished," Tom said bitterly. "At least my mother won't have to swing in this cage anymore. Where is she? Is she safe?"

"I haven't seen her, my boy. Not a sign of her. I was asleep when God's hand destroyed this building. I found myself atop a pile of rubble with a broken gas line spewing noxious fumes in my face. I counted myself lucky to escape with my life."

"Was she home when it happened?"

"I don't know. I was deep in the throes of one of my seizures and remember little about that fateful moment. Since then I've found neither your dear mother nor, more importantly, my medicine. If I don't find that potion soon, I fear my days are numbered. Where were you, lad, when the great temblor struck?"

"We were off the Farallons when we got the word. We headed straight for port."

"And since then?"

"We've been ferrying folks over to Oakland."

"For three days? You must be exhausted," the professor said gently, "but possibly very rich. I'm sure your good captain charged a handsome fee for his services."

"Fifty cents a head, but you can't get many passengers aboard the *Napoli*. We did pretty well, I guess. Tony gave me ten dollars."

"The flinty wretch could well afford such a trifling sum, I suspect. But ten dollars; it's a goodly sum when one is destitute. We must go immediately in search of your mother that we might share your windfall with her. She's probably safe in one of the refugee encampments. Let me see the coins, let me feel them in the palm of my hand. Our future lies in that fortune of yours."

6

Tom took his scarf from his pocket and unfolded it until the coins appeared, cradled in his hands. The professor carefully took the scarf from him, greedily fondling the shiny treasure.

"Yes, yes," he murmured, "this will go a long way toward a new start, my boy. Your mother will be pleased. Now we must find her so we can pool our resources and see just where we stand."

"You stand in a restricted area," called a gruff voice, "that's where you stand. Don't move or you're a dead man."

Tom whirled to see a soldier approaching with his rifle lowered, its bayonet thrust toward them.

"Let me handle this, my boy," said the professor, pocketing the scarf and coins. "Now, now, Captain, let's be calm. As you can see, we're not scavengers. We are gentlemen and former residents of this unfortunate area, come to tally our losses. Obviously there is nothing here of value."

"Shut up, old man, and let me see what you're hiding there."

"Why, it is this and nothing more," the professor said, snatching the scarf deftly from his coat pocket so that its burden of coins remained behind out of sight.

"Then what's that I hear? It's the clink of coins, or I'm a damned monkey. Give them to me, d'ya hear!"

"But they belong to this young gentleman. I was merely holding them for him—for safekeeping, you understand. Believe me, sir . . ."

"Give me the money, damn you, or I'll run you through!"

The professor edged carefully away from the point of the bayonet while wagging the scarf in front of him to distract the soldier. As he did so, he whispered:

"Get out of here while you can, Tom. I'll handle this."

"Yeah, kid, scat! And don't let me catch you around here again," said the soldier.

Tom stumbled over a smoking timber, caught his balance, and dashed away, leaving the professor to deal with the military menace. At a safe distance he turned and called out.

"I'll be back, Professor. I'll be back for my money."

Tom mingled with the crowd on the wharf, cadging a bit of bread from a vendor friend and watching the setting of the blood-red sun as its rays filtered through the smoky air. Just before dark, he made his way back up to Pacific Avenue. He found the professor dangling from a lamppost, Tom's scarf a noose around his neck. Across his chest hung a crude sign, "LOOTER."

*   *   *

Henry Masters, an officer of the Bank of Oakland and a frequent visitor at the Cullen home, brought his wife to the East Bay waterfront early in the morning, where she worked as a volunteer in a canteen established for refugees. He intended to go from there to the bank, but when he saw the number huddled in the cold morning mists, he stayed to help serve bread and coffee. After more than an hour of monotonous, heartbreaking work, he could no longer look into the faces of the pitiful refugees and focused instead on the trembling hands that reached out to him. Murmured expressions of gratitude went unanswered until he heard his own name.

"Thank you, Mr. Masters."

"Teddy! What on earth . . ."

In a moment, he was helping the girl and her father into his carriage.

"You're soaked to the skin," he exclaimed. "We'll get you into dry clothes, and after a good breakfast . . . well, we'll have the doctor look in on him. How long has he been, uh, unresponsive?"

"Since yesterday," said Teddy.

"And you, my dear, are you all right?"

"I guess so," she said grasping her midsection against a sudden stab of pain.

"Poor child, you must be famished. A hot meal should do it." He snapped the reins and they were off to the Masters home in the Oakland hills. It was two days before a doctor could be found to see them.

"Rest is all he needs," the doctor said to Mrs. Masters. "It will take time to come to terms with his loss. As for the child, she has a slight case of the sniffles and a not unusual problem for a girl her age, of which I'm sure you're aware. Despite what she's been through, she's in surprisingly high spirits."

"She's very brave," said Mrs. Masters. "She shed a few tears when we buried her parrot in the garden, but I simply left her alone there, and soon she was at my side asking to help with dinner. She's a remarkable young lady."

8

"Remarkable indeed," the doctor agreed. "Her father's lucky to have her at a time like this. I'm almost afraid to ask—is there a Mrs. Cullen?"

"Oh, she passed away several years ago. It's a shame she can't be here to help Teddy in her transition to womanhood. I'll do everything I can, of course."

"A sip of gin often helps," the doctor said with a wink. "I'll check back with you in a few days."

"What was that all about?" Masters asked his wife after the doctor left.

"Nothing," she said, "nothing important. It may be the excitement of the past few days, but Teddy's suffering her first cramps. Thank goodness I'm here for her, but a girl really needs her mother at a time like this."

On Sunday, Teddy slept in late, dreaming of a handsome prince who saved her from the deck of a burning ship and married her in a shining cathedral on a distant shore. When she awakened, she found her father standing by her bedroom window, listening to the pealing of church bells. As she went to his side to take his hand in hers, he looked down at her with clear, untroubled eyes. She reached up to hug him and felt the stubble of his beard against her cheek. He seemed strong again as he looked out across the bay to the hills of San Francisco where the gray haze had begun to dissipate.

"It's time we were going home," he said.

*   *   *

Deprived of the means to fight the fire when the great earthquake burst the city's water mains, firefighters challenged the blaze at Van Ness Avenue with explosives. By dynamiting the buildings on the east side of the street, they hoped to destroy the fuel that fed the inferno, and halted its westward advance. Damaged by the quake, but unscathed by the fire, the Cullen home had fallen prey to vandals. Charles sadly made the rounds, taking stock and arriving at last at his daughter's bedroom where he found her in her rocking chair, cradling her china doll.

"I see Molly survived the big shake," he said.

"But everything else is a mess. What did you find?"

"Among other things, I found Chinaboy. He managed to get his family safely out of the path of the fire and came back here to find a gang of thieves looting the house. They had raided the wine cellar and were drunk. He tried to stop them and suffered a beating for his trouble. But he broke away and hid in the carriage house until finally they left. Poor devil is still pretty frightened."

"What all was taken?"

"Everything of value, the silverware, my cash box, everything. What they couldn't carry away, they seemed to have destroyed. Your mother's fine china was smashed to pieces. I just don't understand the mentality . . . Oh, well, it's over now."

"Mother's dressing room?"

"Turned upside down and all her jewelry gone. I'm so sorry, my dear. She wanted you to have it. I should have taken it to the bank long ago and locked it safely away. But I did so enjoy going through it, remembering each piece—when I gave it to her, how beautiful it was when she wore it."

He was getting that faraway look in his eye again, and she felt she had to do something about it. She must not lose him again.

"If it's gone, it's gone, and that's all there is to it," she said, clearly imitating her mother. Samantha Cullen had not been one to despair. Pick up the pieces and move on; that was her way. There were no limits to what one might endure with backbone and perseverance, she often told her daughter. Set aside your problems and get on with life. If you don't like things as you find them, then work for change. Teddy had heard it said since childhood that she had inherited her father's intellect and her mother's beauty, but Teddy knew better. She also inherited her mother's grit and determination. She laid aside her china doll and jumped up to give her father a hug. "Time to count our blessings," she said with a smile. "What has Chinaboy found for supper?"

"Some canned meat and a few potatoes," he said, "things the pillagers left behind. Why don't you run down and see if you can give the poor fellow a hand?"

*   *   *

Charles was a quiet, orderly man, one whose personality seemed reflected in the neat columns of figures that he had made his life's work. He was an accountant turned business consultant, a man of high scruples whose honesty was legendary on Montgomery Street,

10

a place where businessmen either fought corrupt politicians or joined them in the cesspool of bribery land graft. He was not naïve. He knew it was the interaction of business and politics that fired the engines of commerce. But he believed passionately that the public good must not be sacrificed on the altar of capitalism. "Offer a good product, price it fairly, market it honestly, and you will prosper," he advised the clients who laid their ledgers before him and sought his advice. "Follow the straight and narrow path and avoid the shortcut that leads through the swamp of political corruption." In a city run by a political boss, the notorious Abe Ruef, and his hand-picked mayor, Eugene F. Schmitz, Charles's philosophy soon brought him into alliance with the city's Progressives, who were dedicated to combating the pervasive influence of the Southern Pacific Railroad.

Although the Progressives waged their war on a local level, they early on adopted national trust buster Theodore Roosevelt as their spiritual leader. Charles's admiration was so great that on the day the news reached San Francisco of citizen-soldier Roosevelt's heroic charge up Kettle Hill in Cuba, his enthusiasm burst its bounds—he nicknamed his daughter Teddy. After all, reasoned the adoring father, wasn't Theodora a child of strong character, fierce independence, and uncommon courage? Indeed, agreed his wife, if such can reasonably be said of a child only five years old. Teddy may have known nothing of war or politics, but as she grew older, she overhead enough talk at gatherings around the Cullen dinner table to understand that men of power and position in the city looked up to "Teddy" Roosevelt, and that to carry his name was an honor. In 1901, when the tragic assassination of William McKinley elevated Roosevelt to the presidency, she announced to her astonished third-grade teacher that she was henceforth to be addressed as Teddy. Theodora was all but forgotten, relegated to a yellowing page in the family Bible.

Samantha Cullen never sat shyly by during the political discussions that took place in her home. She was a well-known progressive in her own right, having marched under the banner of the suffragettes, lobbied against child labor and in favor the eight-hour day. She even entertained at her table the author John Manchester, despised in the conservative community as an advocate of socialism. When she wasn't parading in the street or bearding political lions in their dens, she became infamous among the city's major publishers as an inveterate writer of letters to the editor, all shockingly outspoken and signed with the nom de plume Sam Cullen, the better to assure their publication. The subterfuge fooled no one, of course, and though Samantha's public antics embarrassed her husband on occasion, the courage and independence they represented made her a heroine to her daughter. Her death reinforced Teddy's determination to be as much like her mother as she could be.

∗   ∗   ∗

The young ladies of Pacific Heights Grammar School spent one afternoon each week as Red Cross volunteers in the Fort Mason relief camp. Teddy saw a young man seated alone at one of the long trestle tables. She watched him as he sopped up the last few drops of his soup with a thick piece of crusty bread, pushed his bowl aside, and began scribbling on a scrap of wrapping paper with a lead pencil. He was working intently when he felt her eyes on him and looked up.

"Sorry," he said. "Am I holding you up?"

"We're in no hurry," Teddy said. "You don't remember me, do you?"

He studied her closely for a moment and shook his head.

"You took my father and me across the bay to safety on your boat."

The dawn of recognition lit his face and he snapped his fingers.

"You're the girl with the birdcage!"

"And a dead bird," she reminded him.

"I guess we all lost something," he said, his smile fading.

"You, too?"

"Yes. My mother."

"Oh, that's terrible," Teddy said. "I know what it's like to lose your mother. I lost mine when I was a little girl."

"I don't mean she's dead," said the youth. "At least I don't think so. I mean she's missing, or I'm missing. I'm looking for her, and I suppose she's looking for me. I still haven't searched the camp out at the park. I look for her name every day on the lists, and I'm sure she's looking for me, too. We'll get together soon."

"I'm sure you will, Mr. . . . ."

"Quinn," the lad said shyly. "Tom Quinn. I'm a fisherman."

12

"I'm Teddy Cullen . . ." Allie nudged her in the ribs ". . . and this is my friend Allie Wheatley. We work here every week."

"Hi!" Allie said brightly.

"Nice to meet you both," Tom said, and suddenly remembering his cap, took it off and spanked it against his leg. When the cloud of dust settled, he said, "I'm sorry. I've been working all morning on a cleanup crew, and it's pretty dirty work."

"That's nothing to apologize for, Mr. Quinn," said Teddy. "You should be proud of helping. There's plenty for everyone to do, as my father says."

"We're Red Cross volunteers," Allie announced.

"So I see," said Tom, averting his eyes self-consciously.

Teddy understood immediately why he was embarrassed. There they stood in their frilly white aprons, all clean and starched, while his clothes were ragged and dirty and he was in desperate need of a bath. *What nonsense,* she thought, *to be ashamed of a little dirt. What utter nonsense.* She looked squarely at him as she spoke.

"Mr. Quinn is a hero, Allie," she said, "and he has no reason to apologize for anything. He saved many people by rescuing them in his boat, and now he's working every day to clean up the city, while we come down here once a week and think we're doing something special. You should be proud, Mr. Quinn, very proud. Good fortune will come to those who do their very best and take pride in their work."

"Well, I do work hard," Tom allowed as he edged away. "Nice to meet you both," he called out before disappearing into the maze of tents.

"Why'd you scare him off?" Allie asked. "He's handsome!"

"He wasn't scared. He was embarrassed, although he had no reason to be. I don't think I could ever frighten him. He's too brave to be afraid of anything, certainly not of me. He's a real hero, Allie. Come on, let's finish this job. It's almost time go."

As they collected the dishes and brushed off the table, Teddy thought of how her father's resolve had faded in the face of extreme adversity. Tom was different. He was strong and courageous, yet sensitive and kind.

"Look," said Allie, handing her the scrap of paper Tom left behind.

It was a drawing of a woman's face, a beautiful face with high cheekbones and large, sad eyes.

"May I keep it?" Teddy asked.

"It's good, isn't it?" Allie said, smiling.

"Yes, it's very good," said Teddy, slipping the drawing into her apron pocket. It was his mother's face, she was sure of it. But it was also an omen. She knew she would see Tom Quinn again someday.

*   *   *

Satisfied that his mother was not among the refugees at Fort Mason, Tom hitched a ride to the sprawling tent village in Golden Gate Park. He signed up for a cot, put his name on the bulletin board, and scanned the lists of the lost and the strayed. But it was all to no avail. He tried to keep up hope, but there were times as he strolled along Ocean Beach amid the thunder of the surf when he sank into a deep melancholy, despairing of ever finding her again and wondering at her fate. As for the girl he had come upon twice in the aftermath of the earthquake and fire, he thought of her often. Once, when his cleanup crew was assigned to Fort Mason to dismantle the refugee tents, he ate his lunch at the same table where she had come upon him several weeks earlier. As he ate, he recalled the feisty Teddy Cullen who assured him that good fortune would surely come to those who worked hard and took pride in their labors. The memory lifted him from his depression, and brought a smile to his face for the first time in days.

He made up his mind to go back to Fisherman's Wharf, find Tony Lazarro, and go to sea again. He wanted to feel the heft of a full net in his hands, wanted to feel money in his pocket. He wanted a room of his own, where he could spend his free hours sketching the scenes that survived so vividly in his memory. He wanted to resurrect it all, the vigor and the squalor of the Barbary Coast, the shadowy world of outlaws and outcasts who took refuge in that sordid ghetto that he remembered so well and that now was gone forever. He felt an overpowering urge to raise it up, to make it live again if only in oil on canvas. He wanted to rekindle the great fire, too, to see the awesome flames curling from the tip of his brush in all their terrible beauty. The scenes of his childhood would exist again—the dark, cramped apartment above the Le Coq Rouge, the dance halls and taverns of lower Pacific Avenue, the pagodas of Chinatown, the shops of North Beach, the bustling wharves, and the fleet of fishing boats on the bay. He would breathe immortal life into the people he knew best—Tony Lazarro, Professor Hunt, the barkeeps and sailors, the fish mongers and vegetable peddlers and painted ladies. And his mother! He would paint her beautiful face just the way he remembered her and loved her best. How proud she would be of him. How wonderful it would be to become an artist!

*   *   *

While Tony was rebuilding his home in North Beach, he set up a temporary shelter for his family on the property and set sail again with Tom at his side.

"It's been a long time," he said happily as the *Napoli* breasted the waves of the Golden Gate and coursed toward the fishing grounds.

"I was getting pretty tired of dust and ashes," Tom agreed, inhaling the fresh air.

"Someday you'll want your own boat," said Tony. "It's a good life."

"It is a good life," Tom agreed, "but not for me. I'm going to be an artist."

"An artist! How can you even think of it? You'll starve. Be a fisherman, and you will never go hungry."

But Tony knew by the glint in Tom's eye that he had made up his mind, and since no argument would dissuade him, he resolved to help him all he could. Although he loved his two little daughters more than life itself, he despaired of not having a son. Vanna's last labor had been long and the birth difficult. Since she could never bear another child, Tony dreamed of someday turning the *Napoli* over to Tom. There was plenty of time. Tom was very young, and Tony was not an old man. He could wait.

A man of frugal habits with a history of regular if modest saving, Tony had no trouble getting a loan to build his new home on Green Street off Columbus. While the earth was still warm, he raked away the ashes and began to construct a three-story building on a concrete foundation. For extra income to help pay off his loan, he designed a building that would house a small restaurant at street level, where

15

Vanna could delight paying customers with the culinary treasures she brought with her from southern Italy. The Lazarro family would make their home on the second floor, while the third would be divided into two small apartments. The rear apartment would be reserved as temporary quarters for new arrivals from the old country. The front studio that caught the intense light of the afternoon sun would be for the budding young artist.

Tom was well pleased. For the first time in his life, he enjoyed the privacy of his own room and the security of being part of a family. He worked diligently to pay his own way. After a long, hard day at sea, he plunged immediately into his second job at *Vanna's Ristorante Italiano*, clearing tables, washing dishes, mopping floors. At first, his savings went for art books, drawing paper, chalk, and water colors. Later every spare penny went for canvas and oils, the medium in which he felt he'd found his true strength. There were no longer enough hours in the day, enough days in the week. He worked as a man possessed. In his mind he heard a voice saying, "Good fortune will come to those who do their very best and take pride in their work."

2

In a few weeks, Chinaboy's cuts and bruises were healed and the Garcias had returned from their place of refuge with relatives on the Peninsula south of the city. The shattered windows were replaced. A new front door was fashioned to fit the slightly skewed opening and hung with massive wrought iron hinges. Senora Garcia and a crew of workers went over every inch of the house to rid it of the dust and debris of the Great Earthquake. The Cullens were ready to open their home again to meetings of the Progressives. Not since Samantha Cullen died nearly four years earlier had so much political rhetoric resounded through the dining room, only now it was Teddy, a mature fourteen, who sat at the foot of the table as hostess.

"We must move on Boss Ruef, and we must move soon," said Fremont Older, the crusading editor of the San Francisco *Bulletin*.

"He's got the city's Republican organization in his grip," said banker Henry Masters, an antirailroad Republican. "There's little doubt now that he'll control the state convention and that Jim Gillette will win the Republican nomination. We simply cannot allow the Southern Pacific's handpicked man to become governor of California."

"But for now we should keep our efforts local," Charles interjected. "We don't have the clout to do battle in Sacramento. The railroaders would steam right over us."

"Charles is right," former Mayor James Phelan, a Democrat, interjected. "We've got to engage these people on our own turf, establish a base and strengthen it before we move on to other arenas."

"These goals are not antithetical," Older noted. "There's no doubt that we have exposed the depth of Ruef's graft, corruption, and fraud. It only remains to present our evidence before the grand jury, and Abe Ruef will be discredited before the world and hopefully convicted and imprisoned."

"It's a lot to hope for," Charles sighed, "and a costly effort."

"It's not beyond our reach," Older said. "I have it on good authority that it will cost $100,000. I've just returned from Washington, D.C., and I'm happy to report that we have the support of the president of the United States."

"By George, you actually got Teddy Roosevelt behind us?" Phelan asked.

"He'll free Francis Heney from his government responsibilities and name him special prosecutor if we can guarantee $100,000 to conduct the case. I told him we could."

"We can all contribute," Masters said.

"You can be sure I'll do my part," said Phelan.

"And none other than Rudolph Spreckels will guarantee any shortfall," Older added. "This will be a truly bipartisan effort with Democrats and Republicans linking arms against the power of the railroad."

"And once we've put Ruef behind bars, we'll have the strength and the credibility we need to move our fight to Sacramento," Charles said. "Then the people will rule this state, and not the Southern Pacific Railroad. The seeds of reform were sown here tonight, gentlemen, and perhaps a new political party as well—the Progressive Party."

"Reform must be the first step," Older cautioned. "But you're right to this extent: If we can't clean up San Francisco, no one will support our efforts at the state level. We have work to do."

"Well, what did you learn tonight, my dear?" Charles asked Teddy after their dinner guests departed.

"I learned that President Roosevelt will help us. And I learned that it costs money to do important things in life, lots of money," Teddy said.

*   *   *

The aggressive Heney, assisted by Detective William J. Burns, went to work immediately. There were cheers from the sidelines as evidence was gathered against Boss Ruef, Mayor Schmitz, and the county supervisors, but when the investigation spread to the business community, the source of the money that fed the corrupt system, there was a huge outcry. Business leaders accustomed to paying tribute in order to do business in the city charged that the prosecutor was a Socialist and that his investigation was a threat to the institution of private property. In the heat of the controversy, one prospective juror became so incensed that he shot prosecutor Heney, severely wounding him. Heney's assistant, young San Francisco attorney Hiram Johnson, took over the prosecution and won conviction of Ruef and Schmitz, thereby becoming the new hero of the city's Progressives.

Even though Mayor Schmitz's conviction was overturned on appeal, Johnson's victory over corruption in San Francisco propelled him to the leadership of the statewide Progressive movement. Despite his reluctance to give up a lucrative law practice and his lack of enthusiasm to return to his birthplace, Sacramento, by 1910 he was carrying the Progressive banner inexorably toward the governor's office. Shortly after his inauguration in January 1911, the legislature was at work on the Progressive agenda, including a suffrage amendment to the state constitution that Johnson signed into law.

Teddy, then a freshman at the University of California at Berkeley, moved quickly from women's suffrage to other causes, most of which seemed to her to be embodied in the writings of John Manchester, the once impoverished young author who had been one of her mother's favorite dinner guests. To Teddy's father, Manchester was anathema.

"When you knew him, he was just getting started," Teddy said defensively. "Since then, his books have become popular around the world. He's won fame as a foreign correspondent. Even you remarked about his dispatches from the Russo-Japanese War."

"He's also become very rich," her father said.

"Deservedly so," Teddy countered.

"He's become a 'silk shirt Socialist.' I hope you aren't confusing reform with revolution, my dear. Manchester has earned a reputation as a left-wing agitator, leading torchlight parades through the streets with a ragtag following of ne'er-do-wells. It's shameful and unnecessary. After all, you didn't have to topple the government or riot in the streets in order win the right to vote, did you?"

"Women's suffrage remains a national issue," Teddy noted. "But there are other causes that require drastic action. The torchlight parade you referred to was a protest march by women cannery workers demanding a safe workplace, decent pay and shorter hours. What's wrong with that?"

"The underlying hypocrisy is what's wrong. This fellow Manchester isn't a poor cannery worker. He's a wealthy author who spends more time carousing than he does creating, according to Archie Hobart, who wrote a column on him the other day. He said Manchester hasn't produced a novel worthy of the name in years. He hides away in that castle of his in the Santa Cruz Mountains and comes to the city only when his bottle runs dry."

"He's a socialist theorist, nevertheless," Teddy insisted, "and a most articulate exponent of our views."

"*Our* views! Surely you don't pretend to be a socialist."

"I find the philosophy fascinating."

"Nonsense! You're an impressionable child who's been taken in by a charlatan."

"That's not true. I've heard you and your Progressive friends talking about the same objectives—an eight-hour day, a forty-eight hour week, a living wage, and the right to organize. I've heard it within these very walls."

"It's one thing for educated men sophisticated in the ways of politics to discuss reform, but when the rabble cries out that it wants to get its hands on the levers of industry, that's quite another story. It's revolutionary and downright dangerous."

"I know," said Teddy, smiling engagingly. "And it's very exciting."

*   *   *

The Progressive movement suffered from internecine battles in the campaign of 1912. Former President Roosevelt, returned from world travels and eager to reenter the political fray, challenged his handpicked successor, William Howard Taft, for the Republican nomination. But their bitter personal attacks culminated in Roosevelt's leading the progressives out of the GOP convention to form the Bull Moose Party, while conservatives handed their banner to Taft. Even though Roosevelt turned to California Governor Johnson, the state's Progressive icon, as his running mate, the Republican split proved fatal, and the United States presidency went to Democrat Woodrow Wilson, known as a moderate Progressive himself. Though not quite old enough to vote, Teddy followed the lead of John Manchester and campaigned for the Social Democratic Party's perennial candidate, Eugene V. Debs.

"We never get everything we want from an election," her father noted philosophically. "And although I'm disappointed that you saw fit not to support your own governor and the Progressives, I hope the election results convince you that socialism has no future in America. That reminds me, I've asked Barron Bachelor to come to dinner Friday. Will you follow up with a formal invitation?"

"That was an interesting leap of logic," Teddy noted, "from socialism to unbridled capitalism. I suppose you've seen his calling cards languishing on the hall table. He's persistent, I'll give him that. Why don't we invite John Manchester, too, just to balance the conversation?"

"Nonsense. That would be scandalous. What would our friends say?"

"Mother found him intriguing."

"He was a nobody then, a precocious innocent. He's a rabble-rouser now."

"You seem to have forgotten that Bachelor Enterprises led the opposition to the Ruef investigation not so long ago. He was the enemy then. What changed your mind?"

"Barron's a fine young man, Teddy. And he's interested in you, that's obvious. I thought you might . . ."

"Give him a tumble? Really, Father!"

"Not my choice of words, my dear, but yours. I simply meant that you're nearly twenty-one years old, you're attractive, and it's time you thought of settling down."

"We have absolutely nothing in common."

"But he wants to meet you. I'm afraid to guess how he knows about you, but I trust you'll be on your best behavior."

"I'll do nothing of the kind. I'll do everything I can to shock him. He represents everything bad about capitalism. I wouldn't be able to face my friends again."

"That's a bonus I hadn't anticipated. Tell me I can count on you."

"If you want to take that chance, fine. But I warn you, I may meet him at the door waving a red banner and shouting, 'Workers of the world arise! You have nothing to lose but your chains!' "

*　　*　　*

Barron Bachelor was indeed the quintessential capitalist. At thirty-five he already headed a conglomerate that touched every facet of life in California—agriculture, mining, manufacturing, shipping, and international trade. And he was in the process of establishing his own banking empire through the acquisition of small, independent banks that had fallen on hard times. He had inherited the nucleus of his empire from his father, rough and tumble miner Billy Bachelor, who had come away from the Comstock Lode with a fortune and a talent for multiplying it. From his father, Barron had inherited a genius for business, and from his mother, a regal bearing and an instinct for the finer things in life. She was the daughter of a New York shipping magnate when she married the rustic from the hills of Nevada, and with her came her father's failing fortunes, which Billy Bachelor quickly reversed. Barron (the old man thought the name sounded suitably authoritative and distinguished) was the child of their later years. His mother's greatest wish was that her son obtain the education and refinement that his father lacked, so she sent Barron to study at Harvard and later at the Sorbonne before allowing him to plunge into the marketplace to sharpen his business skills.

The earthquake and fire, which destroyed millions in Bachelor Enterprise's assets, proved old Billy's undoing. At the height of the great fire, Barron and the family chauffeur caught up with him as he stormed down Nob Hill in full counterattack against the flames. Billy was subdued and spirited away to safety aboard one of his own ships, the *Silverado Queen,* that lay at anchor in the bay. Within a week, Barron assumed control of the family holdings, the *Silverado Queen* slipped mysteriously out the Golden Gate, riding high on an empty hold, and old Billy vanished from public view. Barron maintained that his father and mother spent their final days at the family's wilderness mansion deep in the northern redwood forests and steadfastly denied that the old man was insane. But rumor had it that the *Silverado Queen* had carried the mad magnate on a voyage to nowhere and that he died at sea and was buried beneath the waves only weeks after the fire. What was known for certain was that neither the ship nor old Billy ever returned to San Francisco. More than one seaman later told of seeing the *Silverado Queen* at the height of a Pacific storm, a ghostly figure stalking her decks and raging at the towering seas.

Like his father, Barron was a man who appreciated spunk. He was famous for his inability to abide the sycophants who inhabited so many levels of modern business. He wanted men who had ideas of their own and a penchant for expressing them. The great strength of the nation, he often said, was the American worker.

"Their secret lies in their frontier spirit, their independence and initiative," he said. "It's what made this country great and what will make it even greater as we move further into the Industrial Age. If there's a better way to do something, the American will find it. And once he finds it, you can bet he'll turn a profit from it. Give me a handful of people with ideas, and I will never want for profit."

"I wonder if your employees are so exuberantly capitalistic," Teddy responded. "How well do they profit from their labor in your various enterprises?"

Barron was not the least surprised at her impertinence, since he was familiar with her reputation. He had heard she was bright, charming, rebellious, audacious, and outspoken. She was the center of every social gathering, the life of every party. Though he had never met her, he was intrigued beyond measure. While other young ladies fawned over the handsome and wealthy man-about-town, Teddy ignored him. He sent his car around more than once, but had yet to find her at home. He was reduced to conniving with her father to secure an invitation to dinner. And though there was no escaping him now, Teddy put him immediately at a disadvantage by daring to question how Bachelor Enterprises treated its employees.

"I trust that if our employees were in any way dissatisfied, it would have come to my attention," he responded. "It has not."

"What an excellent employer you must be," Teddy said with an air of disbelief.

"As excellent as you are a hostess, Miss Cullen. Your father is very fortunate."

"I'm really a very poor substitute, Mr. Bachelor. I'm sure he'd be happier with a wife, someone who enjoyed this sort of thing. I don't like it, and I'm not very good at it."

"I think you're a wonderful hostess. You have a way of making your guests feel perfectly at ease."

"I assure you that wasn't my intention."

23

"You mean you intended to make me uncomfortable?"

"I mean I didn't set out to impress you or anyone else. I refuse to be coy or clever just to make a gentleman feel superior. I believe the association of men and women should be free of guile. I will not put on party manners to impress a man. It is just that sort of unnatural behavior that has led to woman's subservient role in our society. I won't be a pawn in ridiculous social games."

"You must realize that your attitude is really your most captivating quality. You're a challenge to any man."

"I'm not interested in captivating anyone, Mr. Bachelor. I believe in the equality of the sexes, and I wouldn't think of using feminine wiles to seduce any man. I would prefer a more serious conversation, a discussion of the unequal status of women in the workplace, for example."

"But the sexes are intrinsically unequal, therefore their status in the workplace cannot be equal. A woman cannot lift a heavy load, nor can a man stitch a seam. Men and women are different, therefore their work is different, and therefore, so is their compensation. It's a corollary to the most basic law of nature."

"Your mistake, Mr. Bachelor, is in assuming that 'different' and 'unequal' are synonymous. I assure you they are not. Inequality can be changed, especially in the workplace; natural differences cannot."

"I am glad you concede that there are natural differences, Miss Cullen. For a moment I had serious concern for the future of the human race."

The dinner guests, who had fallen silent to listen to their exchange, broke into laughter and applause. Teddy blushed.

Later, when Barron strolled out onto the terrace, Teddy followed. She found him slipping his snuffbox into his vest pocket.

"I don't mean to interrupt, but it was unforgivable of you to embarrass me that way," she said.

"Please, don't be angry. You were getting the better of me, and I was desperate."

"Then you admit that my argument had merit."

"Of course I do. We think very much alike, you and I. And I never would have known it if you hadn't invited me tonight."

"I didn't invite you, my father did."

"Then I'll be forever in his debt," he said, his hand brushing hers where it rested on the terrace railing. She pulled it quickly away.

"I wish I didn't make you so nervous. If you'd allow us to become better acquainted, perhaps you'd change your mind about me."

"How do you know I've made up my mind about you? How do you know I think about you at all?"

"You can be brutally frank, can't you?" he chuckled. "I think I've been weighed and found wanting. That makes me suspect there's a young man in your life, which wouldn't surprise me."

"Don't make me blush again. I hate blushing. It's so . . . so girlish."

"I could guard against that if I knew you better. But how can I if you won't let me you? We could have dinner. We could go to the opera. We could sail on the bay or ride in the park."

"You're trying to overwhelm me, and I won't allow it. Why do you think I've ignored your calling cards?"

"They're an amusing convention for a modern-day radical. I think you're really just an old-fashioned girl at heart."

"They provide a convenient way of keeping you at arms' length. Calling cards are easy to ignore."

"Then I accept your challenge. You can't discourage me. I'll inundate you with calling cards and roses and diamonds."

"Teddy," her father called from the doorway. "Some of our guests are leaving."

"And so is Mr. Bachelor," she said with a firm smile.

Later as she lay upon her bed jotting notes in her diary, her father looked in on her.

"Did you enjoy the evening, my dear?"

"Mr. Bachelor certainly made it interesting."

"He's quite taken with you, you know."

"He finds me amusing. I hate that. I won't be some rich man's amusement. He wants an ornament, a pretty young thing on his arm."

"That's nonsense, Teddy. I never would have asked him here if I thought for a moment—why, he's truly fond of you, and he respects you. What more could a young woman ask?"

Teddy laid her diary aside and looked squarely at him. The poor dear, she thought. He had planned this whole evening just for me. She knew he had her happiness at heart, but he was the product of another era. He couldn't possibly understand the need of modern

25

women to make independent choices. In his day, choices were made *for* women and accepted *by* them, but not today.

"What more could I ask, Father? I could ask for a shy, charming boy with dark, curly hair and blue eyes and large, strong hands and a heart as big as this house," she said. "Barron Bachelor is overbearing. He is no longer a boy. He has straight blond hair and daintily manicured nails. And if he has a heart, I'm sure it must be gold plated."

"If anyone could melt that heart, it would be you, Teddy. But have you met some young man? Is there someone you're trying to tell me about?"

She got up from the bed and hugged him tenderly.

"No, Daddy," she said. "Not really."

3

Their busy schedules didn't permit Barron to shower attention on Teddy. He was frequently away on business; she was preoccupied with her education. But he did come to call, usually when she was home from classes at Berkeley. She suspected that a conspiracy involving her father kept Barron apprised of her schedule, but she didn't complain. She began to find Barron intriguing, even attractive. He had done many things and traveled extensively. His friends and acquaintances were much more sophisticated than the youths with whom she associated on campus. So it was with a spirit of adventure that Teddy now and then accepted his invitations to dinner or the theater, but only after he agreed to respect her wish not to become romantically involved. School came first.

One of her favorite lecturers at the university was the author John Manchester. Despite his early successes, he remained the amiable Irishman who had enthralled her mother years earlier. He maintained the air of the "working stiff," as he liked to say, who had suffered under the lash of economic necessity since boyhood, when he was obliged to take his first job in the canneries. As a youth he dreamed of attaining great wealth and was easily lured to the gold fields of the Yukon. But he came away with little to show for the hardships he endured, but an imagination filled to overflowing. Unsophisticated and unschooled, he began to write in a vigorous and direct style that found an instant audience in the daily press. The working class claimed him as its own; the intelligentsia hailed him as a visionary. His yarns, the critics claimed, were not merely thrilling adventure stories, but allegories of mankind in conflict with the Industrial Age and yearning for the simplicity of the natural life. Manchester, once an impoverished laborer, became a wealthy and world-renowned author.

During one of his speeches on campus, Teddy saw him turn an audience of spoiled young hecklers into a cheering section for socialism. She was later to fall under the spell of his rhetoric at a trade union meeting in a produce district warehouse. There, his stirring oratory spurred the workers to unite in their struggle for fair wages, decent working conditions, and the battle cry of the era:

"The eight-hour day! It's not so wild a dream, brothers and sisters!" he cried. "It's your due! Capitalists owe their fortunes to you who create wealth by the strength of your back and the sweat of your brow. Labor is the only true source of wealth, and therein lies your power. Alone you have no choice but to offer your labor for whatever the bosses are willing to pay; organized, you have the power to withhold your labor until you're paid what you're worth. Alone you can't do much but put your shoulders to the wheel of industry, finally to be crushed under its weight; collectively you can sit in the driver's seat, steering that wheel toward the common good. But you must organize, you must stand up for your rights, brothers and sisters! You must stand up now!"

A mighty cheer resounded through the cavernous building as the crowd rose as one, with such a stamping of feet that the building shook and dust sifted from between its bricks and the gas lights flickered. Quickly, before the fever pitch waned, union organizers plunged into the midst of the excited throng with cards and stubby pencils.

"Sign here," they urged the workers. "Sign here for trade unionism. United we'll be masters of our own fate!"

At the side of the crowded room, standing in the shadows with women from the canneries, Teddy felt the strength drain from her body. Her knees were weak and tears rolled down her cheeks. She had never heard anything so stirring as the deep, resonant voice of John Manchester. And there he stood not ten yards away, a holy glow in his eyes, passion still hot in his cheeks. He loomed like a guardian angel as the crowd pressed closer to touch him, as if to absorb the strength he radiated. Teddy was certain she was going to faint.

Once back in the dormitory, she went to work on her term thesis: "Trade Unionism and the Struggle for a More Perfect Society." She wrote until dawn, freshened herself for classes, and that afternoon returned again to her desk. On through the weekend she labored, and when she had finished, she fell exhausted into a deep sleep.

Her paper caused a considerable stir among her professors.

"Colorful," one proclaimed, "but naïve."

"There's a passion here that cannot be denied," said another.

"It's subversive, of course," said a third, asking, "Isn't she Charles Cullen's daughter?"

"Yes," replied the first, "and if you can believe the gossip, she's about to become engaged to none other than Barron Bachelor!"

They all had a good laugh at this incongruity, but they awarded the paper high marks, and Teddy Cullen went on to graduate with honors.

The state legislature, meanwhile, was busy passing bills to improve the lot of the working men and women of California, and Governor Johnson was signing them into law as fast as they reached his desk. Much of the credit for that legislative agenda—or blame, depending on one's political persuasion—belonged to the Progressive movement, of which Teddy considered herself a part.

The small successes of her undergraduate days, however, seemed empty as she packed to leave for home. She wondered if it had been a mistake not to follow the example of her roommate, Allie Wheatley, who was going on to law school.

"Three more years," Teddy sighed. "I don't think I could do it, Allie. I'm just too impatient. There's so much work to be done out there. Still I feel so . . . so inadequate."

"Don't be silly," said Allie. "I can think of a lot of things I could do if the richest man in the world wanted to marry me."

"You know how I feel about Barron. He's very nice, but he's old. He takes naps in the afternoon! And you know very well he's not the richest man in the world."

"No, but he's rich enough, and young enough, too. Face it, Teddy, it takes money to make a mark in this world."

"If I only had your ambition, Allie, and your diligence. You're on the right track—a woman lawyer, maybe even a judge someday. Once you get your degree and pass the state bar, you'll be a woman to be reckoned with. You'll be a trailblazer. Imagine! Someday you may sit on the state supreme court."

"But I know there'll be times when I'd gladly trade a judgeship for a courtship," Allie said wistfully. "Take a plain girl's advice. Marry your rich man. Even your socialist friends will tell you where poor but earnest revolutionaries end up: poorer and much less earnest, maybe even dead."

"And if I do marry, what will I have? A rich husband and dinner guests every Saturday. What a dreadful prospect. I want to do something dramatic—now. I want to break free of woman's traditional role. I want to prove that the world's problems require a woman's touch. I want to show that in a modern industrial society, it is possible to assure the rights of the working class without a bloody revolution. I want to prove that women everywhere deserve the right to vote, and that that right can be won, as it was here in California, without resorting to riots and street demonstrations. I want to protect men and women and, yes, children, too, from exploitation in the workplace. All these things are possible, Allie, and I want to help."

The blast of a motor car's horn interrupted her.

"That would be Barron," Allie noted. "Go to him, Teddy. Tell him you want to use his millions to help destroy capitalism and create a new social order, starting with a matriarchal society. I'm sure he'll understand."

"You see, you don't take me seriously any more than he does."

"I do take you seriously," Allie protested. "Think about what you could do with all that money. I can see the headlines now: 'Bachelor Enterprises Invites Workers to Organize; Women Offered Seats on Board of Directors; Industrial Giant Adds His Clout to Suffrage Movement.' It's not so wild a dream, Teddy. And all you've got to do is marry a devilishly handsome multimillionaire to help make that dream come true."

*   *   *

Teddy didn't love Barron, and they both knew it. Romantic love had never been a part of their relationship. She convinced him that it wasn't necessary for a modern woman to love the man she marries. Marriage, she said, should be more than the selfish fulfillment of personal desires; it should be a union with high goals and strong social purpose. As for the more intimate aspects of marriage, she admitted to herself that she had more than a passing interest in sex. After all, it was she who led the campaign to establish a chapter of the National Birth Control League on campus. It was she who won the class debate on the merits of free love. If men could have mistresses, she argued, why couldn't their wives have lovers? Love should be free, she expounded, and not burdened by antiquated social mores. Even the biological consequences of sex were not abhorrent to her, so long as a man and a woman found it mutually

30

agreeable and were willing to accept the responsibilities of raising a family. But they must be equal partners, and the wife must remain free to make her own decisions.

Barron insisted that he had no intention of trying to stifle her idealism, and so he waited several weeks before he asked if Teddy had reconsidered his proposal of marriage. She admitted that she had and surprised him by promising an answer that very evening. They dined at the Garden Court and went on to the theater to enjoy a musical comedy, *The Honeymoon Express.* Later, as Barron's chauffeured touring car chugged them back to Pacific Heights, Teddy gave him her answer in her own peculiar way.

"There are two things I want from my marriage," she announced.

"And what might they be?" he asked.

"I want children and the right to birth control," she said.

*   *   *

While Teddy was pursuing her formal education, Tom Quinn was teaching himself to be an artist. He went about it systematically, beginning with charcoal sketches of his mother's face from many different perspectives. He began each exercise with a few hard lines scratched on heavy drawing paper, then brushed them with the ball of his hand to soften the edges and create a contrast of light and shadow. He did dozens of sketches, never satisfied with the results. It was the eyes, he decided, that presented the biggest challenge. He had to get the eyes just right. And so he worked for hours drawing eyes, convinced that they were the key to capturing the essence of a face, any face. He drew dozens of pairs of eyes over a period of days, pinning the results on his walls until the entire studio seemed to be staring at him. He did his mother's eyes, Tony's eyes, Vanna's eyes, even the darkly pathetic eyes of Professor Hunt.

From eyes, he to turned to hands and soon became obsessed with them as well. He was struck by their distinctiveness, saw differences in them that he had never seen before. He marveled at how accurately they could reflect character and style of life. When he could not afford drawing paper, he scrounged the ends of paper rolls from Angelo Rossi, the greengrocer, and in the corner of his studio, there soon was a stack of drawings—eyes, hands, lips, ears, noses—until he was confident that he could draw anyone. Then he went on to sketch buildings, first Le Coq Rouge as he remembered it, then the jumbled shacks and elegant pagodas of Chinatown, the clapboard cottages clustered on the slopes of Telegraph Hill before the fire, even the grand homes being rebuilt on Nob Hill. Boats were another great challenge. He lingered at the wharf after a hard day at sea and sketched the trawlers and skiffs, the great sailing ships, the launches and tugs and dinghies. As Tony guided the *Napoli* through the Golden Gate, Tom would brace himself against the hatch, sketch board in his lap, trying to capture the flow of the city's hills, the beauty of its skyline in brilliant sunlight and the shadows that it cast.

When he at last was satisfied with his draftsmanship and had a few dollars put aside, he bought his first canvas, brushes, and tins of pigment, a dozen different colors from which he learned to create hundreds more. He built himself an easel from scrap wood discarded as the Lazarros built their new home. Oblivious to curious onlookers, he went into the street to paint scenes of everyday life in the Italian community in North Beach, the bustling crowds of Chinatown, the waterfront at Fisherman's Wharf. He turned out painting after painting, exploring the mysteries of his art. When his burst of creativity outstripped his pocketbook, he went back and painted over the same canvases two, three, even four times. His quest for proficiency was made without mentor and without critic, but as the months passed, he grew more and more comfortable with his work, and when a painting at last satisfied him in all its facets, he dared to share it with his patrons. Tony invariably greeted each with a "Bravo, bravo!" while Vanna, a culinary artist in her own right, studied the work carefully and offered deeper insight.

"That's Angelo, the greengrocer. I'd know him anywhere," she'd say. "But the awning on his shop is wrong. Look out the window. It's not red like a brick; it's red like a ripe tomato. You see?"

"I painted it in the late afternoon after the sun was low and the street was in shadow. Things take on a different hue in shadow."

"Maybe," she'd concede. "If you say so. I still say the awning should be red like a tomato. But Mr. Rossi! You have done a good job on Mr. Rossi. I knew him right away."

She was quick to grasp the emotion behind his work.

"What a face! She looks so tired, yet so beautiful. I want to take that poor woman in my arms and say, 'There, there, *bella mia,* you must come rest a while.' That's what I want to say to her. Your heart is full, Tom, and I can see it in this picture. It shows, you know what I mean? Your heart shows in this picture and makes it come alive."

The comments pleased him, for it was his mother's face on the canvas, lit by the flickering gaslight that turned the dark stairway to their rooms above Le Coq Rouge into a terrifying tunnel of shadows. Behind her in the picture lurked a dim and ominous presence, the object of his childhood fears and anxieties, her companion of the evening come to invade the apartment where a frightened boy lay in nervous wakefulness, listening to the rustlings of their hurried intimacies. But pleased as he was with this rendering of his deepest secrets and darkest fears, it pained him to look upon his mother's face, and so he hid the painting away, still not knowing whether she was dead or alive, wondering if he would ever see her again.

As the years passed, Tom became adept at capturing small flashes of reality with mere strokes of his brush, but the more he produced, the more he realized he was striving for a goal that might lie beyond his reach. He wouldn't be satisfied unless he had instilled in each work an ember from the creative fires that burned within him. He knew that he must bring to each effort a spark of passion that would burst into flame and transform a painting into a compelling work of art. That, he was certain, was the secret of the masters.

For all her own sensibilities, Giovanna Lazarro could not always tell him when he had achieved that lofty goal. But he could learn from her nevertheless. She was a creative genius, a masterful cook. He tried to bring to each canvas the same unbridled passion that she brought to her creations, and with the same flair, the same verve. To the everlasting gratitude of Tom and a host of their North Beach neighbors, Vanna's creations appealed to both the eye and the palate. From the day Tony hung up a sign announcing *Vanna's Ristorante Italiano,* they never wanted for customers. Such was the caliber of Vanna's art. Asked the secret of her success, she would say with a shrug that she cooked *con amore,* seasoning every course with a generous dash of love, love of good food, love of life. Therein lay the spark of her genius.

Vanna's soon became a neighborhood gathering place, and as its fame spread, it attracted customers from all over the city. Vanna herself presided over all with a boisterous good nature that delighted her patrons. The Lazarro girls, Anna and Andrea, waited on tables. Tom helped keep the dining room and kitchen spotless, and Tony kept the books. But at sundown when the restaurant began to fill, the men would retire for the night, leaving the women to run the business while they rested for the next day's struggle against the sea.

Tom adjusted quickly to the hours of a fisherman, rising in the dark of night six times a week, casting the nets at dawn, hauling them in again and sailing back to the wharf. While Tony sold their catch, Tom would race back to his studio to spend the afternoon at his easel. His output was prodigious, often several paintings a week. Although the Lazarros permitted him to hang some of his work on the restaurant walls, none was ever sold there. It remained for Tom himself to display his paintings on the street on Sunday afternoons at the wharf amid the crab pots and the soft pretzel venders and the fishmongers. Here his work drew some praise, not always for the best of reasons.

"I work for days to get a color just so, and when I'm finally convinced that a painting is the best I can possibly do, someone offers me two dollars for it because it happens to match their drapes. If I didn't need the money I'd tell them all to go to hell."

But the sales, however few, fueled his ego and inspired dreams of greater success, and he'd return to his studio and begin anew. From his early street scenes, Tom moved on to a series of paintings of life in San Francisco as he remembered it before the great earthquake and fire. It began with the haunting picture of his mother into which he poured all the love and longing of an orphaned child. He considered his interpretation of that ravaged face with its vestiges of beauty to be one his best works. But it was so full of personal sorrow that it made him weep to look at it. So it remained forever hidden away, covered with old sheets in a dark corner of his studio.

4

Teddy hadn't been away from campus long before she realized that despite her many acquaintances, she had few close friends. The attributes that attracted people—her vivacity, her beauty, her intelligence—were often the very things that kept them apart. Men who flocked around her at social gatherings were at the same time intimidated by her and seldom lingered long. Women, on the other hand, seemed to view her warily and with unfounded suspicion, as if someone so attractive, with such a radiant personality and ready wit, somehow posed a threat to them. Among the men in her life, only Barron possessed the self-confidence to breach the invisible wall that surrounded her. And among the women she knew, only Allie remained a true friend and confidante.

From grammar school through college, they forged a relationship that was to last a lifetime, a relationship based on mutual respect and understanding and marked by honesty and good humor. It was Allie who protected Teddy from discovery when she sneaked out after curfew to join protest marches or to attend union rallies. It was Allie who guarded the portals during that long weekend as Teddy labored over her thesis, at one point shooing away a motorcar by yelling out the window, "Tell Mr. Bachelor that Teddy's busy redistributing the world's wealth, and he'd better watch his wallet."

Allie was a good-natured soul. A frown seldom crossed her face; a cloud never darkened her spirit. She thrived on laughter, inevitably amused by the foibles of the world, more often than not, her own. Teddy, who took life so seriously, never failed to delight her. Although Allie had few gentlemen friends, she found vicarious pleasure in discussing each of Teddy's casual beaux, of whom there were several during their college days. But what really excited her was Teddy's relationship with Barron. She was thrilled at the news of their engagement.

"You've got to tell me all about it," she squealed, settling herself into a parlor chair. "How perfectly wonderful! Barron must be every girl's dream of a husband. He's so handsome and so very, very rich. Whatever made you change your mind about him? When did you decide he was Prince Charming and not a nasty capitalist grinding the faces of the poor?"

"It didn't just happen, Allie. There was no bolt of lightning. It's just something that evolved out of a long friendship."

"But you do love him, don't you?"

"What is love, after all?" Teddy asked with a touch of world-weariness. "It's a sympathetic understanding, little more. We have that, Barron and I. But if you mean a mad, passionate, romantic love, no, that's never been a part of it. Our relationship has been more cerebral."

"You can't fool me, Teddy. I've heard you expound on free love. I want to hear how he galloped up on a white horse and carried you off to his castle to ravish you on a bed of silken pillows and satin sheets."

"Allie! You're terrible! Although that might have been exciting, Barron's just not the type. He's like me. He would never think such mundane thoughts. He's serious, level-headed."

"And the second biggest liar in town."

They were laughing heartily when Chinaboy came in to announce:

"Tea and cookies, Miss Teddy. Just baked. Hot tea good on rainy day. Warm the insides."

What a coincidence," Allie exclaimed. "We were just talking about warming our insides."

Later they got down to the serious business of planning the wedding, but Allie's teasing set Teddy to thinking: What if she and Barron were incompatible? What if romantic love was indeed the key to a happy relationship? What if, heaven forbid, Barron, with his worldly ways, found her to be a boring, inexperienced child? Despite all her talk of free love, she was just that: a boring, inexperienced child.

"I'm going to do it," she announced.

"Do what?" asked Allie.

"I'm going to seduce him."

"Seduce who?"

"Barron, of course. I don't know if he owns a castle, but he does own a ranch in the Santa Clara Valley. I'll ask him to take me to see it, unchaperoned, of course, and once there . . ."

"Teddy, you wouldn't dare!" Allie screamed. "I'll help you pack."

*　　*　　*

Barron drove the 1911 Cadillac himself, decked out in an elegant duster, a motoring cap and goggles. Teddy sat by his side, her broad-brimmed hat bent like a bonnet by the veil that held it against the wind. Behind them, amid the luggage, Chinaboy sat in wide-eyed terror.

"Too fast, too fast!" he cried.

"Then why don't you jump," Teddy muttered under her breath.

Chinaboy's presence was her father's idea. Barron had told him that the housekeeper at the ranch was an awful cook, and Chinaboy would see to it that they were properly fed.

"Not that it hurts to keep up appearances," he added.

"You know I'm not interested in 'appearances,' Daddy."

"Really! I will bear that in mind when the next bill comes from the dressmaker. Run along now, and have a nice weekend. Chinaboy won't be in the way."

The Bachelor ranch was part of a Spanish land grant, the hacienda and several outbuildings dating back to the days of the Californios. It was a sprawling home with plastered adobe walls, red tiled roof, and heavy redwood rafters turned gray with age. It was nestled against the foothills of the Santa Cruz Mountains, with hundreds of acres of grazing land stretching down the gentle slope to the valley floor. Beyond the pastures lay acres of orchards. From the mountains above the hacienda, a creek tumbled down through an arroyo lined with granite boulders. Near the ridgeline, a grove of towering redwoods snagged the underbelly of passing clouds as they drifted in from the Pacific. In the chill of late afternoon, the hacienda looked warm and inviting. The housekeeper, a red-faced woman who spoke with a heavy Irish brogue, met them at the door and led them into the living room, where oak logs blazed in the fireplace.

"This is wonderful!" Teddy sighed, sinking into the soft fullness of the deerskin-covered couch before the fire. "I got cold over those last few miles."

"Then stay close to the fire. Chinaboy, let me show you the kitchen. You'll want to get dinner started. Molly will help you. Just tell her what you want. She'll keep the kitchen clean for you, but don't let her near the stove. She's a disaster as a cook."

"Don't need kitchen lady," Chinaboy insisted.

"You won't be able to find anything without her. She's neat to a fault. Even I don't know where she hides things. You'll need her, I'm sure. And don't worry about us. We'll pour a glass of sherry and make ourselves comfortable here by the fire."

"I have a doll named Molly," Teddy said. "It belonged to my father's mother. She has a porcelain head and limbs. We survived the earthquake together."

"That's charming. You should have brought her along."

"You talk as if I were a child! I'm not, you know. I'm the woman you're about to marry."

"Don't be angry. No matter how old you are, or how mature, you still have a childlike quality about you that I adore. You wouldn't be Teddy without it. Here, this will warm you."

He poured a dram of sherry and gave it to her. It made her tongue tingle, warmed her throat, and brought a glow to her cheeks. He took her hand in his.

"Tomorrow we'll ride to the summit," he said. "There's a trail through the redwoods that leads to a magnificent outcropping of granite that resembles a castle. From the top of it, you can see the ocean on a clear day. It's a spectacular view."

The clock on the mantle struck four.

"Time to freshen up," Barron said. "Molly has your room made up, if you want to rest before dinner."

"I'll just stay here by the fire," she said. "Are you sure you're feeling all right? You look very tired."

"I am, a little. It's nap time. Let me put another log on the fire before I go."

Once she was alone, Teddy planned the seduction of Barron Bachelor, entertaining thoughts she was sure would bring a blush of delight to Allie's cheeks. Before long, she had dozed off, to be awakened by a gentle nudge just as the clock struck six. Barron looked much better, clear-eyed and relaxed. At a long, rough-hewn table, they dined on beefsteaks and baked potatoes and emptied a bottle of red wine. It had a rich, earthy taste, smooth on her tongue. After dinner, Barron poured them each a snifter of brandy and taught her to cup the glass in her hands to warm it so the powerful fumes would rise. She listened intently as he spun tales of a time gone by when *vaqueros* rode the surrounding hills and the *alcalde* presided at that very table, entertaining travelers along the trail between San Francisco and the Pueblo de San Jose de Guadalupe. She hung on his every word, dewy-eyed and adoring, hoping he would find her irresistible. When their eyes met, she fixed him with a long, passionate gaze.

"Are you all right?" he asked.

"Of course I am. Why?"

"You look as if you're not feeling very well. You're flushed. You must be exhausted. Let me take you to your room."

Her plan was working perfectly, Teddy thought as he helped her from her chair. He put his arm around her shoulder to steady her and guided her down a long hallway to the rear of the hacienda. The heavy wooden door was ajar, and inside a flickering candle chased the shadows into the corners of the room. The bed, with its feather mattress and smooth flannel sheets, had been turned back. A thick quilt had been laid across the foot of the bed.

"It will be cold tonight," he said. "If you need more blankets, you'll find them in the chest under the window. Let's be sure the shutters are tight. There's a chance of rain."

She followed him as he crossed the room and stood by expectantly as he latched the shutters. When he turned, she was so close to him that he couldn't move. He smiled and took her in his arms.

"It's been a long day, and I've kept you up too late," he said. "Are you sure you're feeling all right?"

"I don't know. I've never felt this way before," she said sleepily, tilting her face up to his. He kissed her and held her close, then suddenly swept her up and laid her gently on the bed. She grasped him around the neck and pulled him toward her and kissed him passionately. With some difficulty, he freed himself from her grasp and stood looking down on her.

"You're very beautiful, Teddy, and very, very desirable. But I didn't bring you here to take advantage of you, as much as I might want to at this moment. Don't tempt me, please. I have more than my share of human weaknesses, and it wouldn't take much—"

She sat up, smiling seductively, and began to unbutton her blouse.

"Please, Teddy, don't. I don't want you to do anything you may regret tomorrow." He kissed her again, and she closed her eyes and fainted dead away.

*   *   *

Barron's horse led the way along a well-worn trail into the redwoods where the thick fog left droplets strung like pearls along the boughs. All about them amid the ancient trees flourished rich clusters of woodwardia ferns, accented here and there by the red berries of the toyon. In the clearings where the tree branches separated to reveal the low hanging clouds, the tops of the gigantic trees soared heavenward until they vanished in the mist. Near a rustic bridge a doe lifted its head from the stream and watched with great round eyes as the horses approached with muffled steps along the spongy path. Then it bolted silently, gracefully into the woods. By the time they reached the summit road and turned south, the fog had lifted and a warm sun shone upon them from clear blue skies. At Castle Rock they tethered the horses to a scrub oak and climbed the pile of granite. From its peak they could look across a heavily forested basin to the sea beyond.

"It's breathtakingly beautiful," Teddy exclaimed.

"Not as beautiful as you," he said, taking her in his arms.

"We will be happy, won't we?" she asked. "You won't be sorry, will you?"

"How could I be anything but happy with someone like you?"

"I'm not sure, but it's been troubling me."

"You mustn't let anything trouble you, Teddy. I promise to devote my life to making you happy."

"It wasn't my own happiness I was thinking about, but yours."

"Just being with you makes me happy," he said, searching her eyes to find the meaning behind her words.

"Does it really?" she asked somewhat skeptically.

"I think I know what's troubling you, Teddy. You're feeling embarrassed about last night, and you shouldn't."

"But I should. I behaved very badly."

"On the contrary, you were charming."

"Apparently not charming enough."

"I don't understand."

40

"How do we know we're right for each other?"

"So that's what it was all about. You were trying to seduce me."

"Now you're making fun of me," she pouted, "treating me like a child again."

"I know better, Teddy. It was I who undressed you and tucked you in last night. I know only too well that you are not a child. But you were exhausted and maybe even a little tipsy. How could I possibly take advantage of you?"

"But you've never even told me that you love me."

"Nor have you told me! What of it? Love might strike like lightning for the poet, Teddy, but for sensible people like you and me, it takes time. We know so little about one another. How many engaged couples really do? As time goes by, we'll discover true love, I'm sure of it. Love is learning and growing together, my dear. Only a fool would expect to fall head over heels in love with a woman before he really knew her. You must agree that love can't be rushed."

"Perhaps not," she conceded. "But it can be encouraged." With that, she threw her arms around him and kissed him.

*　　*　　*

They returned to the hacienda in time for Barron's late afternoon nap and met again at five in front of the fire. Teddy declined a glass of sherry before dinner and tasted only a sip of wine during the meal. As they sat alone before the blazing hearth listening to Chinaboy rattling the last pot into the kitchen cupboards, Barron took her hand in his. For a long time they talked quietly until the embers faded to a dim glow in the darkness. Then he took her in his arms and kissed her.

"What is love really like?" she whispered.

"It's like dancing," he said. "You should always let the gentleman lead." Then he arose and guided her down the hall to her room, kissed her again and said, "I'll be back."

With great excitement, but not a whit of trepidation, she undressed, wrapped herself in a warm robe and fussed with her hair at the mirror until she heard him rap softly on the door.

"Come in," she said, rising eagerly to embrace him. Feeling his firm body under a silken robe, she shivered uncontrollably as he kissed her.

"You're cold," he said.

"No, I'm not cold," she insisted, loosening her sash and shrugging her shoulders so that her robe fell to the floor. He stepped back to admire her in the candlelight.

"You're beautiful, Teddy, beautiful," he said. Then he lifted her and carried her to the bed and laid her gently among the quilts. He reached to snuff out the candle, but she caught his hand.

"We must learn all we can about each other," she reminded him.

He slipped out of his robe and slid in beside her, covering her with kisses as his hands delicately explored her body. She responded to his touch, enjoying every sensation, every venture, amazed at how natural it all seemed. Tentatively, at his gentle urging, she tried to reciprocate, tried to return the pleasure he was giving her, until suddenly he was ready and they joined in a rhythmic race to ecstasy. When it was over, she was wet with perspiration, clinging tightly to him to prolong the wondrous sensation. When he pulled away, there were tears in her eyes.

"I haven't hurt you, have I?" he asked.

"No, no," she whispered. "It was wonderful."

*   *   *

He built a mansion for her on the cliffs above the sea overlooking the Golden Gate, but then business beckoned, and Teddy was left to decorate their home. With Allie's help she shopped for carpeting, drapes, and furniture. One outing led them to the wharf, where artists offered their paintings for sale. One in particular caught her eye. It was a picture of a birdcage with its door standing open. On an empty perch fluttered a diaphanous white scarf. In the foreground, a brilliant blue macaw lay dead, while in the background, flames engulfed a city of hills.

"How morbid!" Allie exclaimed. "Who'd want a dead bird hanging on their wall? Look at this one. This street scene is lovely. It's so bright and cheery."

"The lady is right," said a voice behind Teddy. "The street scene is the painting for you, Miss. It's only three dollars, but it will bring you a lifetime of pleasure. Besides, *The Blue Parrot* is not for sale."

Teddy held her breath, turned, and looked into a handsome face with deep blue eyes and a halo of black, curly hair. Her heart leaped.

5

They lingered at *Vanna's* through the afternoon, reliving the events of the past eight years and nibbling on *pizza con funghi*. They spoke as old friends to whom the passage of time was inconsequential.

"I had such a crush on you," Teddy confided with a laugh. "It was years before I would even look at a boy unless he had blue eyes and curly black hair."

"I remember the child with the birdcage," Tom said, blushing, "but I never would have recognized you."

"I don't think a skinny little girl would make much of an impression on a young man," Teddy said tactfully.

"I remember I felt terrible that anything as beautiful as that parrot had to die," Tom said. "I still can't look at *The Blue Parrot* without feeling sad."

"But you can take it to the street to lure buyers," Teddy teased him.

"Probably because the Lazarros didn't want it hanging in the restaurant, where it might spoil someone's appetite," Allie cracked.

"Shame on you, Allie. It's a beautiful painting," said Teddy.

"And it's yours," said Tom. "You must take it. It's as much yours as it is mine—more so, really. I think that's why I've never been able to part with it. It never really belonged to me. Take it. It's my wedding present to you."

"What a beautiful gesture! Isn't he everything I ever said he was, Allie?"

"She's not kidding, Tom. For years she's said that her ideal was a young man with blue eyes, curly black hair, and a heart of gold. So now she's engaged to an old man with brown eyes and blond hair. And if he doesn't have a heart of gold, he's probably got a mine full of it."

"It's awful of you to talk that way," said Teddy. "Barron's a wonderful man, Tom, and I want you to meet him."

"I know that he's the richest man in the world—he has you," Tom said.

"What a beautiful thing to say. I really do hope you'll come to our wedding. It's on June twenty-seventh, just six weeks from now. I'll see that an invitation goes out to you tomorrow."

"I'd be honored to attend," Tom said with a wistful smile.

"Well, this certainly has been an eventful outing," said Allie.

"Thanks to Tom, it has," said Teddy. "But we really ought to be going. If you won't accept payment for *The Blue Parrot*, maybe you'll let us consider some of your other works."

"Come by any time," he said. "There are all these on the walls and more in my studio upstairs." He carried out the painting, loaded it into their automobile, and helped the ladies aboard. As he watched them drive away, Teddy turned to wave good-bye. The memory of her smile and beautiful brown eyes was to linger in his memory.

*　　*　　*

"I don't like it, if you want the truth. What is it?"

"You can see very well what it is."

"All right, it's a dead bird. I certainly don't want it hanging in our front hall."

"It's only temporary, Daddy. After the wedding, Barron and I will take it home with us. I'm going to hang it over the mantle."

"Teddy, for goodness sake, be merciful," said Barron, taking a pinch from his snuffbox. "It's a dreadfully somber work. I know it means a lot to you, but wouldn't you prefer something a bit more, well, more cheery over the mantle? Charles, you must help me convince her."

"Why must I? For better or for worse, you're about to take responsibility for her. You convince her."

"You're both being childish and condescending. This is a work of art. It shows great skill, immense tenderness, a haunting reality."

"Great art is pleasing to the eye," said Barron.

"Like a nice, bloody crucifixion? Or what about Mantegna's *Saint Sebastian*? Is that gore pleasing to your eye?"

"You're comparing this fisherman's dabbling to great works of art?" her father asked. "I think you've let your heart interfere with your sense of beauty, my dear. But I'll have Archie Hobart look at it. If he says it's art, then by God, it's art, and you'll get no quarrel from me. If not, out it goes."

"Agreed," said Teddy. "But Barron must abide by Dr. Hobart's decision, too. And to show you both how confident I am, I'll invite both Tom Quinn and Dr. Hobart to dinner on Saturday. Tom would be delighted to have a respected critic evaluate his work."

"That could get sticky," Barron said. "What if Hobart tells him it's awful?"

"He wouldn't dare!" Teddy gasped.

"Archie's never been shy about giving honest criticism, Teddy. And perhaps that would be for the best. After all, it would be unfair to lead your friend to believe he has talent if, indeed, he has none," said her father.

"Honesty is always the best policy," said Teddy. "I have every confidence in Tom's work. Let's bring on the critic."

Dr. Archibald Hobart of the Hobart Gallery was the sole arbiter of artistic excellence in San Francisco. An outspoken critic of the work of a burgeoning creative community that spread from the craggy cliffs of Mendocino to the white sand beaches of Carmel, his nod could make or break an aspiring artist. Superbly well educated, widely traveled, and the possessor of an unfailing eye and ear, Hobart's praise was highly prized, his rejection much to be feared. His gallery was Valhalla to painters and sculptors throughout the state, while his weekly newspaper column was the dread and the delight of visiting thespians, singers, dancers, and musicians, for he was an acknowledged expert in the performing arts as well. It was rumored that even the great Caruso once came to the city with dread and went before the footlights as a man might walk to his wall of doom, so fearful was he of Hobart's pen. If the critic's reputation was well founded, it also was well deserved. No one applied himself more diligently to the practice of his trade then Hobart did to his study of the arts. When he said Madame Emma Eames missed a note in the third act of *Carmen*, you could trust that he knew not only Bizet's score, but also the French in which it was sung. When he read of a new movement in Europe in which painters were using new techniques and employing a bold use of color to express their visions, he went directly to the art centers of the Old World to study their work himself.

He was no less the thorough researcher when Charles asked him to critique the work of an unknown painter.

"You know how Teddy is, Archie. She brings home writers and radicals of every stripe as one might bring home stray puppies or abandoned cats. Only this time it's an artist whose work is hanging in my front hall, and it threatens to become a permanent decoration in the Bachelors' new home. You could spare us a lot of embarrassment if you'd tell her how really bad it is—before Sunday."

The critic stood in front of the painting, his lips pursed, his hands clasped behind his back. He rocked forward on the balls of his feet, then back on his heels, his brow wrinkled. Stepping first to the left and then to the right, he studied the play of shadow across its surface. Finally he went closer and examined the ridges and the furrows of oil and pigment. Then he stepped back to peer at it over the top of his spectacles.

"Imitative," he muttered. He turned his back to it and strode down the hall, stopping at last by the door and whirling about to peer at it again. "No," he said, striding back to it. "Here, give me a hand, Charles. Let's take it into the sunlight."

They carried the painting out onto the patio and placed it on a bench in full sun. Hobart withdrew a magnifying glass from his coat pocket and examined every inch of it, the brush strokes, the subtle shadings, the bold dashes of color. Then he said it again.

"Imitative."

"You mean he's copied someone else's work?" Charles asked.

"I doubt that. No, the subject matter is unique, very personal. It's unquestionably the product of the artist's own imagination. It's the technique that's imitative. It reminds me of the Fauvists, or more precisely the Expressionists. This young man has studied abroad, probably in Paris. It's good work, very good. The quality leaves nothing to be desired. But it's imitative, and others have done it better. But he's offered nothing new, nothing innovative. It belongs to the new school but probably is not great art, in the historical sense. He's part of a movement, an important movement, but is he an important artist? I can't say; it is but a single painting. In my opinion, he has viewed the work of the Impressionists and he has tried his hand at it. He has done remarkably well, but it's only one painting," Hobart said with a shrug.

"He's done others," Charles said. "Teddy tells me there's a little Italian restaurant in North Beach where the walls are covered with his work. I can tell you nothing of its quality."

"The pasta or the paintings?" Hobart asked with a chuckle. "It's nearly lunch time, let's go find out."

*   *   *

After Teddy's automobile disappeared down the street, Tom went directly to his studio to work, as if afraid the vision might vanish as quickly as she had. He roughed out a sketch on clean canvas. In a few moments, he had shaped the head, the nose, the mouth, and the deep brown eyes. He daubed the viscous pigments on his palette and mixed them carefully, trying to approximate the gold of her hair. It was dark before he finally laid aside his brushes and fell onto his couch in exhaustion. He slept late into the evening and awakened only after the rich aroma of Vanna's cooking wafted into his apartment. Hungry, he went downstairs to the restaurant to eat. He found Vanna in a state of high excitement.

"He was crazy!" she shouted. "He was climbing over the tables."

"Who was?" Tom asked sleepily.

"One of the men. There were two of them."

"He climbed on the tables to look at my paintings?"

"They took some of them into the street. I told them I'd call the police if they didn't bring them back. They were crazy, I tell you."

"Not a single painting missing. I guess they didn't buy anything."

"Not one," said Vanna. "They didn't even ask the prices. They bought only my *calamari fritti*."

"What do you expect of people who eat those ugly squid? It'll come to nothing."

"What's wrong with my calamari?" she demanded.

"Your *maccheroni alla pastora* is much better," he said, holding up a forkful. "The sausage has never been better, and the sauce! You're the true artist here, Giovanna Lazarro."

Two days later when he returned from the sea, he found an envelope waiting. It was a dinner invitation from Teddy Cullen.

"She requests the pleasure of my company 'at dinner Saturday night, April 25, 1914, on the occasion of the unveiling of *The Blue*

Parrot, a painting by Mr. Tom Quinn,' " he cried. "Tony! Giovanna! She's asked me to dinner!"

"I don't approve," Vanna said scornfully.

"But they want to show off my painting."

"It isn't proper," she insisted. "A real lady would never invite a man to dinner. She is no lady, I can tell you that."

"She's very rich," Tom explained. "The rich can do anything they like. Besides, she is not inviting *me*; she is inviting the artist. She is engaged to be married in June."

Vanna gasped and rushed away to the kitchen.

"I'll never understand women," said Tony. "Yours or mine."

*   *   *

The Cullen home was a stony aerie at the corner of Pacific Avenue and Divisadero, more than a twenty-block walk from North Beach, most of it uphill. The irony was not lost on Tom as he turned the corner off Grant Avenue in the heart of Chinatown and began the trek up Pacific. Behind him lay the Barbary Coast, where he had grown to maturity. Far ahead of him lay Pacific Heights and the mansions of the wealthy. They were all on one street, yet a million miles apart. His shirt was newly washed and ironed, his coat well brushed though it exuded the odor of fish.

"It will do," Vanna had said, sniffing it. "Just remember to take it off as soon as you get there. No one will notice."

Tom had shined his high-topped shoes and run his comb several times through his unruly curls before pulling his cap down on his head to hold them in place. The evening was cool, and the fog was already rolling in when he reached Polk Gulch and began the descent to Van Ness. The colder the better, he reasoned: He would not sweat so much. Next came the long climb to the heights, where he passed many elegant homes before he stood at last before the Cullen mansion, invitation in hand. Teddy answered his knock.

"Hi, Tom. Please come in."

She was beautiful, even more beautiful than he remembered. Her eyes, those wonderful deep brown eyes, welcomed him inside. He stepped over the threshold and whipped off his cap allowing his curls to tumble freely around his face.

"Thank you," he said, "I mean, excuse me."

"Relax, Tom," she whispered softly. "You're among friends here. Let me take your coat, and we'll go into the parlor and meet the other guests. You're the last to arrive."

"Sorry I'm late," he said, shucking off his jacket and handing it to her, hoping she wouldn't notice its odor. "The walk took longer than I thought."

"You mean you walked all the way from North Beach? Why, we could have sent a car for you or had one of the other guests pick you up on their way. If I had only known . . ."

"It's nothing. It was a great night for a walk. Please don't say anything about it. It's cool outside and foggy. I like it that way. You look very nice, Teddy."

"You're sweet to say so, Tom. Come along, I want to introduce you. And remember, you and I are old friends, so just relax."

He would have agreed that black was white and up was down, so charmed was he. She was so beautiful! Could he ever really capture that special quality on canvas? He knew he had to try.

"If you please, everyone, this is my friend, Tom Quinn. Tom is the artist in whose honor we've gathered tonight."

The guests nodded as Tom's eyes swept the roomful of friendly faces. Teddy took him by the hand and led him to each person, beginning with her father. The warmth of her touch put him at ease.

"How do you do, sir," said Tom, extending his hand.

"Good evening, young man, and welcome to our home."

"And this is my fiancé, Barron Bachelor. You've met Allie, of course. And this is Mabel Meyer, a dear friend and leader of our local Margaret Higgins Sanger Club. And this is John Manchester. I'm sure you're familiar with his work."

Tom shook Manchester's hand warmly, gratified that he, too, had come without a coat and tie.

"And last but not least, this is Dr. Archibald Hobart of the Hobart Gallery. I'm sure you've read his column in the *Chronicle*."

"Good evening, Mr. Quinn. I am very pleased to meet you."

"And now before we do another thing, let's go into the hall for the unveiling," said Teddy, still leading Tom by the hand. On the wall at the foot of the stairs, Tom's painting was draped in a sheet. Teddy stood beneath it, tugging Tom close to her as she reached up and took hold of the covering. When each guest was positioned just

49

so, she whipped it away, revealing *The Blue Parrot*. There were admiring murmurs. Then John Manchester spoke.

"It's an excellent work, Mr. Quinn," he said in his big, booming voice. "I know very little about painting, but as a fellow working man and an artist, I can appreciate the hours of labor that must have gone into its creation. You are to be congratulated."

"It's very nice, Tom," said Allie with a smile. "These surroundings do something for it, don't you think?"

"Y-yes," he stammered. "The lighting is perfect."

"It's allegorical," Mabel Meyer pronounced with intensity. "In it I see the demise of the nineteeth century. I see cataclysm and death, the dead bird, that ghostly wisp of a veil, the cage sprung open. You're clairvoyant, Mr. Quinn. You see that disaster lies ahead."

"Actually," Tom said haltingly, "I was looking back . . ."

"Yes, just as I said, the death of the old century in all its rich plumage and the birth of the new century that will rise like a phoenix from the ashes of the past."

"But . . ."

"Fine work, m'boy," said Charles. "Fine work, indeed. What say we all go in to dinner."

"You have a rare talent, Mr. Quinn," said Barron as he shook Tom's hand.

"Thank you, Mr. Barron."

"Bachelor," said Teddy helpfully. "Barron Bachelor."

"Perhaps you'll sit across from me, Tom," said Dr. Hobart. "I want to ask about your work before I comment on it. I, too, have been to Paris and am astounded to find an Impressionist right here in our midst." He took Tom by the elbow and guided him into the dining room. "I want to know all about your training."

"There's not much to tell," Tom said. "I taught myself to paint."

"But you must have had some schooling," Hobart suggested.

"I left school at nine, sir. I've worked most of the time since."

"Laudable, Tom," said Manchester. "I may be the only one here who can truly appreciate that. You see, I'm also self-taught. I also went to work at an early age. And I also had to struggle through life without an education. It's a real man who can lift himself above childhood deprivation into a rich, full, creative life."

"I really don't think I was deprived, Mr. Manchester. And I'm sure not rich. What do you do for a living, sir?"

"I write books, Tom," Manchester said humbly, to a chorus of laughter, "and treatises and short stories. I also lecture now and then."

"He'll lecture here tonight, unless I miss my guess," said Hobart amiably. "I'm afraid you've pricked Manchester's balloon, Tom."

"I didn't mean to. I don't have much time for reading."

"But you find time to travel, obviously," said Hobart. "I can see the influence of the Montmartre. You must have spent some time on the Left Bank or in the salons of Paris."

"No, I haven't. I don't know exactly when we came to San Francisco, my mother and I, but the only time I've left the city is to go to sea every day. I'm a fisherman."

"A fisherman!" Hobart exclaimed. "Never left the city! Where in the world did you perfect your skills?"

"In North Beach," said Tom. "I live on Green Street above *Vanna's Ristorante Italiano*. I work aboard Tony Lazarro's boat. Vanna is his wife. She runs the restaurant. I work there sometimes, too. The Lazarros are like family to me."

"It's hard to believe," said Hobart. "You've never studied, never traveled. You work alone in some loft. Then I suspect you spend your leisure with other young artists, discussing your work, sharing your thoughts about painting, delving into the latest trends."

"I see other artists on Sunday at the wharf, but we don't talk much. We go there to sell our work."

"But you examine each other's paintings, you offer comments."

"Not often. We're there trying to make a dollar or two. It costs a lot of money . . ."

The delicate tinkle of a silver bell interrupted them.

"Time to eat," Chinaboy announced. He set aside the little bell and picked up a tray filled with soup bowls. "Asparagus soup," he said as he worked his way around the table. "Very hot. Very hot."

Hobart fell silent as the table conversation shifted from art to social and political matters. He studied Tom closely, weighing his demeanor suspiciously. When their eyes met, he stared as if trying to peer into his soul. It made Tom uneasy, and he looked to Teddy to rescue him. Unfailingly she saved him with a smile, genuinely delighted with his company. She saw that if Tom was uncomfortable with Dr. Hobart's interest in him, he was deeply impressed by Manchester's posturing, just as she had been at first. The author spoke at length on the evils of capitalism, proclaiming that the competition for wealth was about to lead the Western world into a senseless war.

"I have seen war," he said. "It isn't pleasant. Yet civilization is plunging headlong into another conflict. The haves will send the have-nots onto the battlefields to die so that the rich can become even richer. It was ever so, and it will be so again soon if the workers of the world don't rise up and defy their moneyed masters. It's time for the laborer to shrug off the chains that bind him to a feudal existence. It's time for him to build a new social order. His alternative is to be sent off to die for another man's gain."

"That's all very romantic, John," said Barron, taking a pinch from his snuffbox and snapping shut the lid. "But President Wilson has vowed to keep us out of war, and I for one believe him because he's right. This nation should mind its own business, which of course is business. Let the nations of Europe fight among themselves. They'll leave us free to pursue our destiny in the world marketplace. I would remind you, sir, that a nation rich in jobs and income is a nation well able to afford the cash and leisure to read books, including yours."

"War only occurs because workers refuse to organize against their masters," Mabel Meyers said as dessert was served. "They should study the philosophy of trade unionism. They should learn there is strength in numbers. They should realize the power of the strike. Generals cannot conduct a war if conscripts refuse to fight."

"A difficult proposition," Charles said. "You forget the persuasion implicit in the firing squad. I dare say the threat of death is a powerful incentive to fight."

"Executions would be counterproductive," Mabel responded. "Once you begin killing your own soldiers you risk destroying your army."

"Or demoralizing it, weakening it until it's useless in the face of the enemy," Barron agreed. "On the other hand, unless you get soldiers on both sides to agree to strike—a virtual impossibility—you are merely trading one nation's oppression for another's."

"I can't abide talk of war," Teddy said wearily. "This was meant to be a happy occasion. I hope we haven't spoiled your evening, Tom."

"Oh, no!" Tom said, in embarrassment. "It's all very interesting. But I suppose I should be getting along. It was a swell dinner."

"Allow me to give you a lift," said Barron. "I have some business to take care of downtown. You're right on my way."

"And you must come again, Tom," said Teddy. "I promise that next time we'll talk about something other than war."

"It would be a pleasure to come again," said Tom. "It's been swell, really it has. And thanks again for dinner."

"You've been a perfect hostess as usual," said Barron, taking her hand in a courtly manner and kissing it. "I'll see that your guest of honor gets home safely."

Tom watched as the couple lingered at the door, their hands touching. Then he turned and went quickly down to the street. He was ashamed of himself. They had been kind to him, and yet, he was jealous and angry. It was ridiculous to be angry. It had been a productive evening, the stolen glances, the opportunity to study her face. He had the fire now to give life to her portrait. Her face was burned into his memory forever, the clear, perfect skin, the line of her nose, the curve of her lips, the high cheekbones, the eyes. He had immersed himself in the warm depths of her lovely brown eyes and basked in the shimmering glow as the candlelight played upon her golden hair. He would work all night by gaslight, and when the morning came, he would carry his easel up onto the roof to catch the first rays of sunlight. He would labor all day Sunday if necessary, and when he had it all set down perfectly on canvas, she would be with him forever.

6

Charles and Archie Hobart were in the billiard room enjoying a snifter of brandy when the knocker fell.

"I'll get it, Teddy," her father called out as he mounted the stairs to the front hall. "It's Barron. I heard him drive up."

"Did he forget something?" she asked from the dining room where she was putting away the silver.

"No, no, we plan to have a few words."

Curious, she waited for a moment and then went down to the billiard room to see what the mystery was about.

"Come in, Teddy. It's quite all right," said her father. "Just some business we want to discuss, but nothing you shouldn't hear. We would value your opinion, actually."

"I don't suppose you want a brandy," said Barron, who flashed her a knowing smile as he poured himself a drink.

"No, thank you," she said sweetly. "It tends to go to my head."

"Best you remain clear-headed, for we need your advice."

"My advice? What are you three up to?"

"It has to do with Tom Quinn," said Hobart. "He's your discovery, after all. Perhaps you'll be able to answer some questions for us."

"I know very little about him, but I'll tell you what I can."

"Is he what he says he is?" asked her father.

"I'm sure he is. He hasn't a pretentious bone in his body," she replied. "He's exactly what he said, a fisherman who paints pictures, good pictures, in my opinion."

"He lives where he says he lives," Barron added. "I've just dropped him at *Vanna's Ristorante Italiano* on Green Street. Odd duck, if you ask me. He didn't speak a word during our drive."

"I've examined his work carefully," said Hobart, "and I've spent the evening examining him, as best I could. It's my considered opinion that he's a diamond in the rough, an unpolished gem with more facets, artistically speaking, than that lovely engagement ring of yours, Teddy. I hope you'll forgive the comparison, but it's true."

"Why is all this so important?" asked Teddy.

"I've only seen a dozen or so of his paintings, including *The Blue Parrot*, but I've seen at least four separate styles, all distinct and all done with a flair one would expect from an established artist. You've been to the restaurant; you've seen what I've seen."

"But I don't have your expertise," she said.

"Then let me try to explain. First there are his paintings of North Beach, the street scenes. In them he exhibits an uncanny eye for detail and a touch so deft that you half expect the people to walk out of the picture frame to join you at your table. These works are in the Realist tradition, but with none of the romanticism historically associated with that school. These are tough, unvarnished views of life, a mirror held up to society, twentieth-century realism, raw and gripping. And quite good, I should add. Then there are his interpretations of the Barbary Coast that used to be—bold, vivid splashes of color to express his feelings for a vanished but colorful chapter in the city's history. It's Expressionism at its best. He might have learned such a technique on the Left Bank, yet apparently he's never left San Francisco. Closely related, yet different in important respects, are his remembrances of the earthquake and fire, the dark, swirling blacks and browns slashed with streaks of red. No realism here, but still they capture the horror and the devastation better than any work I've seen. Impressionism! And then take *The Blue Parrot,* not a picture at all, but a landscape of the mind. It grips the heart with its sorrow and sense of loss. It is stark, exaggerated, surrealistic. I thought it Expressionistic at first. But it's something more than that. It's new. It's exciting. For the life of me I can't understand how he does it. He's unschooled, untraveled. If I told him what I have told you, he wouldn't know what I was talking about. Or would he? You know him best, Teddy. Is he taking us for fools?"

"The Tom Quinn I know is a kind and decent man. I don't know him all that well, Doctor, but I think he's incapable of deceit. If he's created paintings that suggest these things to you, I'm certain he's done it innocently. I've seen no more of his work than you've seen, but I think he paints what he sees around him in one fashion, and what he sees within himself in another. It seems perfectly logical to me."

"Ah ha, Archie!" Charles exclaimed. "She's reached the same conclusion you reached."

"Only she expressed it much better," Barron added with a wry smile. "I've not examined Quinn's work, as you know, but I fully understand what Teddy is saying. More importantly, I'm prepared to accept her judgment."

"What does all this mean?" Teddy asked. "Are you willing to show his work at your gallery, Doctor?"

"Of course I am, but I would hope to do more, with the concurrence of all present. I propose that we form a syndicate and serve jointly as Quinn's patrons. It would be an excellent investment. His work, properly displayed, advertised, and marketed, has commercial possibilities. In time his paintings could become quite valuable. And without a workaday job, Quinn could be productive for many years."

"But he's also very independent," Teddy pointed out. "He isn't the sort who would sell his soul for money."

"I think I know a way to avoid any objections on his part," said Barron. "We could incorporate ourselves as a museum to accept and display only those works that are distinctly associated with the city. Quinn's output would be the nucleus. We'll ask him to join us, and together we would constitute the board of directors. He'd have a vote in all matters, financial and aesthetic. The articles of incorporation would establish the amount of his income, a percentage of the museum's profit, for example. Periodically, assuming he continues to produce, the board would select certain of his works for sale. All of us, including Quinn, would share in the profits. In that manner no one need sell his soul to anyone else. What do you think?"

"It's more professional than selling his work on the street," Teddy observed.

"I've put money into shakier ventures," Charles conceded. "I suppose it's a step up from the racetrack, because we'll own the horse."

"And the stable and the hay," said Barron. "So long as we control all the elements from production to distribution, we can't go far wrong. I'll see my attorney Monday about drawing up the articles. Teddy, it'll be up to you to convince Quinn."

"Perhaps Allie could help with the legal work," Teddy suggested tentatively.

"You just make sure that Quinn is agreeable, and let me take care of the legal arrangements," said Barron.

"You mean you prefer not to have a woman involved," Teddy said.

"But you already are involved," Barron countered.

"And one woman is quite enough, is that it?"

"Well," said Hobart to end the sudden chill, "I'll prepare a column for next week's Sunday *Chronicle*, extolling the work of a new artist we've discovered in North Beach."

"I suppose I'd better see my banker," said Charles with a sigh. "He's not going to believe this."

*　　*　　*

Teddy took a cab to the wharf next morning to look for Tom, but he was nowhere to be seen. Next she had the driver drop her at *Vanna*'s, but found the restaurant closed. Unwilling to disturb the Lazarros, she went quietly around to the rear of the building and climbed the steps to the third floor. The door to Tom's studio was ajar, but no one answered her knock. She was about the leave, when Tom's head appeared above her.

"Who's there?" he called down.

"Sorry to disturb you, Tom. What are you doing on the roof?"

"I'm working. Come on up. Be careful, the stairs are steep."

The roof of the building was bathed in sunshine. Tom's easel stood in full light. As he helped her over the edge of the roof, she noticed that his canvas was covered with a damp cloth. Tom was unshaven, and his eyes were red with dark circles under them.

"Have you been up all night?" she asked. "Let me see it."

"It's a portrait. I couldn't take a chance on losing it."

"Losing it? What do you mean?"

"The impression was fresh in my mind. I've begun this portrait a dozen times in the past week. This time I wanted to capture it quickly before it disappeared. You have a way of doing that, you know. The last time you disappeared, I didn't see you again for eight years."

"It's a picture of me?"

"I can't show it to you. It's not finished. Bad luck to show it. Anyway, it'll never be anything but a poor imitation of you, Teddy."

"Let me see it, Tom. Please? If you do, I'll give you some very good news."

57

"Does Hobart want to display one of my paintings?"

"I won't tell you unless you show me the portrait."

Reluctantly Tim lifted the cloth.

"Why, Tom, it's very flattering. I'm delighted. But you see more in me than really is there. I'm afraid you've glamorized a very plain girl."

"No, no, it doesn't begin to do you justice," he said. "I could never capture the real you, those perfect features, the inner beauty that shines through those marvelous eyes. This is a poor rendition of reality, Teddy. I could paint you a thousand times and never get it just right."

She looked into his haggard face, the eyes that seemed on the verge of tears, the tousled hair. Impulsively she reached out and touched his cheek. It was an instinctive gesture, almost motherly. She felt an overwhelming urge to hold him close, to convey to him how mistaken he was in his assessment of her but how wildly, wonderfully romantic it was. Tom took her hand in his and kissed it passionately.

"Oh, Tom," she sighed. "You really don't understand the impact of your painting. It's beautiful, no matter how it glamorizes its subject. All of your paintings are wonderful. That's what I've come to tell you. It's not only my judgment. Dr. Hobart is impressed too. That's why I'm here. We have an idea, and I want to discuss it with you. But you're exhausted. I should come another time."

"I could never sleep now, not after having you here so close to me. My heart is pounding. I'm alive, Teddy, really alive. You bring me to life like nothing else could. I can do anything!"

"Could you spend the rest of your life painting? Could you give up your job? Could you make art your life's work?"

"Maybe, when the leaves on the trees turn to dollar bills," he said. "I could never make a living painting pictures, not if I spent every day at the wharf hawking my wares."

"What if people who have faith in your talent offered to support you so you wouldn't have to work. What would you say to that?"

"I would say it was too good to be true. It would be wonderful, of course, but how would I ever repay them?"

"Just by doing what you love most, painting more pictures."

"But painting what they wanted me to paint, right? I would have to give up my freedom."

"No, you wouldn't. You would remain free to paint whatever you wished. There would be no constraints."

Tom walked to the edge of the roof overlooking the street to think it over. Teddy left him alone and looked carefully at the portrait on the easel. It showed her seated at the table and leaning forward so that the candlelight fell on her slightly uplifted features. There was a vitality in the eyes that brought the spark of life to the entire work, as if one might watch closely and see the eyes blink or the lips move. Instead of the modest dress she had worn at the table the night before, the Teddy in the portrait was clad in an elegant gown cut to reveal smooth, velvety shoulders and a daring décolletage. Suddenly he was standing next to her.

"Do you like it?" he asked.

"I love it, Tom. It's so . . . so romantic, I guess. I wish I really looked like this."

"You do to me, Teddy. But I can't go on. I'm very tired. I have to rest. Let's go downstairs, and you can tell me what this is all about. And watch out for the steps."

"I know," she said. "They're steep."

In his studio, Tom drew a basin of water, pulled off his shirt and tried to wash away his fatigue. While he was freshening himself, Teddy told him about the discussion that had taken place the night before, of their willingness to gamble on his talent, of a museum to display local works of art, how his own paintings would serve as a magnet to attract other artists.

"You'd sit on the board of directors," she explained. "You'd have a say in everything. You'd help decide which of your paintings to show, which you would like to sell and for how much."

"It sounds too good to be true," he said. "Just the five of us?"

"Exactly. At first, we would put up the money; you'd put up your talent in exchange for a negotiated living wage. After a period of time the profits from the museum would reimburse us for our investment. Still later, when your income was assured, all five of us would share equally in those profits. I think it sounds exciting."

"I think it sounds like a perfect way to stay close to you," he said. "I can't let you disappear again, not ever. You stir me so, Teddy. You make me feel I could do anything so long as you're there."

"Oh, Tom," she said, reaching out impulsively again and touching his cheek. "You must understand that I have nothing to do with your talent. You would be a great artist even if I never existed. You're a very special person, Tom Quinn, you really are."

She felt irresistibly drawn to him. She wanted him to take her in his arms and never let her go. He was the hero of her girlhood dreams come back to her at last. He could do no wrong. Together they could do no wrong. There was a righteousness about it, a bond that transcended convention. It was perfect and uplifting. As their eyes lingered longingly, she tipped forward on her toes and gave him a kiss on the cheek.

"I must go now. I must go before I melt inside. That's how I feel, Tom, as if I were going to melt. Have you ever felt that way?"

He didn't answer but took her into his arms and kissed her.

"Stay with me, Teddy," he whispered. "With you at my side, I know I could become a great artist."

"I will, Tom. I'll stay at your side. I promise you I will."

"But what about Barron? You're engaged!"

"I know, dear Tom, I know. And I don't care. I love you. But I must go." She tore herself from his arms and went quickly down the stairs and into the street and walked for blocks, her head in a whirl. Conflicting emotions struggled within her. An hour passed before she could collect herself. Then calm, if somewhat confused, she hailed a cab.

*　　*　　*

She thought it over very carefully before making up her mind. In the end, she made only one concession to her mixed emotions; she canceled the arrangements she had made at the new Episcopal cathedral that was taking shape atop Nob Hill and planned instead for a wedding at home. She was not a religious person, she reasoned, nor was Barron. Since it was to be a legal relationship, a civil ceremony would be quite appropriate. Even Barron agreed.

"Whatever you wish, my dear," he said.

She confided her deepest feelings only to Allie, who was thrilled and yet aghast at her daring.

"It's the only rational thing to do," Teddy explained. "This is the twentieth century, after all. We are sophisticated adults, capable of managing our relationships in a mature manner. Someday I may even tell Barron how I feel. I'm sure he would understand. I don't

60

expect him to be a saint, and by his own admission, he isn't one. I'll be a good wife, and someday, I may even fall in love with him. It will be a good, solid marriage, but never a totally exclusive relationship. The human heart is expansive, nonjudgmental. Where is it written that a woman can love only one man? We're not born monogamous. Any man will tell you that. It's thrust upon us by society. In the New Society, marriage may no longer exist. The race will be improved by the mixing of bloodlines; love will have nothing to do with the bearing of children. Nor will permanency. We may live to see the day when children are reared by the state. Women will no longer be enslaved by archaic morality. They'll be free agents allowed to compete openly with man in business, science, and industry."

"And in the boudoir when she wants a little lovin' on the side," Allie added with a laugh.

"Allie, you make it sound cheap, and it isn't. It's not an easy decision for a woman to make."

"I only wish I had such problems," Allie said.

Tom's frequent presence gave Teddy a feeling of giddiness as her wedding date neared. They met with Barron, Hobart, and her father to form a corporation to establish a museum to be housed in an expanded Hobart Gallery and to establish a stipend for Tom. For the time being, he'd remain in his studio in North Beach. He was comfortable there with the Lazarros. Tony accepted his announcement fatalistically, although extracting a promise that Tom would be open to an employment offer during the annual salmon run. At Teddy's urging, Barron offered Tom the use of the barn at his hacienda as an auxiliary studio and approved plans to have the hayloft converted into a large apartment with broad windows and indoor plumbing. The papers were drawn up for all to sign, and less than a week before Teddy and Barron took their marriage vows, Tom found himself legally bound to both of them. He was anything but comfortable with the relationship.

"You can't go through with this, Teddy," he argued in the privacy his studio. She had come in the middle of the afternoon, ostensibly to view the completed *Portrait of Teddy*, "You love me, not Barron. It just isn't right, I don't care what you say."

"It must be this way," she insisted. "It just wouldn't work any other way." She had slipped furtively up the stairs and in through his unlocked door and into his arms. He kissed her and held her tightly.

61

"You can't deny this passion," he whispered. "It was meant to be. I know it. You were meant to be with me, not with him. He can have any woman in the world that he wants. You said he doesn't love you, anyway. But I do love you. There isn't anyone else for me. I could never love anyone else. You know that."

"Yes, yes, I do, and I love you. You've got to understand that my marriage has nothing to do with us. We can go on seeing one another. If our love was meant to be, it will survive. You must believe that. You must believe in the new order of things. I know it's good because I feel so . . . so liberated."

"Teddy, that's crazy! You can't mean what you're saying. I don't believe in your new order of things. I believe in you and in me and in our love, not in some rosy, pie-in-the-sky future where men share their wives with other men. It doesn't make any sense. I don't think you believe in it either. You just can't."

"You make it sound dirty and contemptible. Women aren't objects for men to own. We're individuals, free to make of life what we want to make of it. I see nothing wrong with being devoted to Barron and still madly in love with you. I could never feel towards him the passion I feel toward you. But that doesn't mean we can't create a good life together. Nor does it mean that I must put you out of my life. I see no reason we why we can't pursue a fulfilling relationship."

"God, Teddy, if only I could make sense out of what you're saying. I want you so much. Stay with me, my darling. Stay with me," he pleaded, grasping at her desperately.

"Wait, Tom, wait!" she said. "Will we be safe here?"

"Why do you care?" he stormed, suddenly angry at his own weakness. "Isn't this part of your new social order? Who's to deny you your heart's desire? You're a modern woman! You've as much right to sexual gratification as any man has. To hell with convention! You can't break a vow you've never made."

There was a mad glint in his eye, and she felt powerless in his strong arms. He kissed her violently. She felt his hand upon her breasts, and she clasped her arms around his neck and surrendered to his eager groping. In a moment, he dropped to his knees as he eased her onto his couch. She could see the blood pounding in his temples, his face flushed and hot. She closed her eyes in anticipation and went limp in his arms. But just when she wanted most to feel him close to her, he arose and strode over to the window where her portrait stood in the sunlight. He stared at the painting, his chest heaving, and then buried his face in his hands and wept.

"Go away and leave me alone," he said softly.

*   *   *

The wedding was held in the Cullen parlor on Saturday, June 27, 1914. Tom stood among twenty or more invited guests, watching with studied impassivity as the ceremony bound his love to another. He remained for the reception, immaculate in a new suit and tie purchased in part with the proceeds of his host's patronage, and went through the receiving line with a stony aplomb, congratulating the groom and mumbling a terse, "Every happiness," as he brushed Teddy's cheek with his lips. He stayed on for one glass of champagne and a small piece of wedding cake, then thanked his host and hostess and left. He walked for hours, wending his way slowly through the mansions of Pacific Heights and back at last to North Beach and thence to the Embarcadero.

Teddy and Barron stayed until four, then departed in a shower of rice for the pier where the Bachelor Enterprise's steamship *Maui Maiden* was prepared to sail with the tide, its passenger quarters elegantly outfitted for their honeymoon voyage. Teddy's suite was spacious and richly appointed in an Oriental motif, complete with a Chinese handmaiden to see to her every need. It opened into a common area furnished at one end as a parlor with a fireplace, comfortable furniture, and a small library. At the opposite end of the long room was a dining area with a massive mahogany table in front of a wide floor-to-ceiling window that provided a grand view of the endless, ever-changing sea. Beyond lay Barron's quarters, redesigned for the master and his bride, with a sunken tile bath large enough to swim in and a huge, four-poster bed more than eight feet square with a mountain of down pillows, crisp white sheets, and a silken quilt.

It was late in the evening when the *Maui Maiden* got under way and headed out through the Golden Gate. At her rail, the newlyweds watched the city lights fade away, blissfully certain that they were embarking on a voyage into a new and wondrous life. Among the faceless crowd that gathered to watch the vessel's departure stood a heartbroken young artist, equally certain that his dreams of happiness were gone forever.

63

7

Long after the coastline disappeared, Teddy and Barron lingered at the rail. She was mesmerized by the phosphorescent glow of the *Maui Maiden*'s wake as the ship cut a roiling swath through the sea. Barron found his own enchantment; watching moonlight and passing clouds play shadow tag across her face.

"You're lovely tonight," he said.

"I feel very small," she replied. "The sea makes everything seem so insignificant. The ship churns the water to a froth, yet only moments later there's no sign that we ever passed by."

"But it's like pebbles cast into a pond; the ripples reach out endlessly."

"And ultimately vanish," she noted. "The sea merely tolerates us. Given a chance, it would swallow us up, and no one would ever know we existed. It sends a shiver through me. It proves we're just helpless little boats being tossed about on the sea of life."

"So gloomy and philosophical on your wedding night? This should be our happiest moment. I know it is mine, and it's because of you."

"Is that my fate, to be important only in relation to you? Men are used to being the pebbles cast in the pond, but few women can create such ripples—you in business, my father in finance, Tom in art. It's not like that for women. To us life is as vast and uncompromising as the sea. At every turn, it threatens to drown us. We have to cling to a man simply to keep our heads above water. It isn't fair."

"But it's the way life was intended to be," he said, taking her into his arms and kissing her tenderly. "It's getting cold; let's go inside. I think I have something that will cheer you up."

A fire blazed on the hearth, and its glow soon dispelled their chill. As they basked in its warmth, Barron rang for service, and soon, a steward appeared with a tray with two glasses and a decanter of sherry. Teddy gasped.

"Chinaboy! I can't believe it's you!"

"Mista Cullen say go along, see that Teddy eat. I do. Supper at nine. Very good."

"Barron, why didn't you tell me? You conspirators!"

"If we conspired to bring a smile to your face, we succeeded admirably," he said.

"I'm sorry. You've been wonderful to me, and I've been horrid."

"Nonsense. It's been a long day, and you're exhausted. Let's drink to a lifetime of happiness, Mrs. Bachelor."

Their glasses touched with the delicate ring of fine crystal. Sipping the nutty flavored wine, Teddy noticed that Barron suddenly looked very old.

"I think we're both exhausted," she said.

"Then let's not allow the wine to go to our heads."

"Definitely not tonight," she agreed. "Tonight I want to be wide awake, more alive than I've ever been before."

"And so you shall be," he said. "I've ordered a light supper, a beautiful starlit sky, and a special surprise that is guaranteed to refresh you completely."

"I knew you were a man of influence, but a starlit sky! I am impressed."

They sat at the huge picture window, picking idly at their supper, more absorbed in each other than in the beauty of the moonlight on the sea that stretched endlessly all around them. When at last a yawn escaped from Teddy despite her best efforts to suppress it, Barron took a small package from his coat pocket and handed it to her.

"Not another gift!" she said in surprise. "Haven't you done enough?" She opened the package and gasped as she held aloft a gold chain from which dangled a golden cornucopia embossed with strange pagan designs. "It's lovely, darling."

"It's very old. It was found high in the Andes in the sarcophagus of an ancient king of the Incas. Here, let me show you how to use it." He removed his snuffbox from his vest pocket and opened it, revealing a fine, white powder. "This is an elixir made from the coca leaf. The natives of the Andes have used it for thousands of years as a medicine, a tonic. The natives merely chewed the coca leaves; royalty used it in its refined form. Try it. One pinch and your fatigue will vanish, you will feel invigorated. Let me show you," he said, taking the golden pendant from her. "You place a bit of the powder in the cornucopia like this. Then put the small end to your nose and inhale, like this." He sniffed a bit of the powder. "It will tingle for a moment, and then you'll suddenly experience a great exhilaration. You'll be revitalized. Try it. See what I mean."

Teddy raised the golden horn hesitantly. Then, with Barron's encouragement, she inhaled sharply. The sensation was immediate. A feeling of euphoria came over her such as she had never known.

"It's extraordinary!" she exclaimed.

"I knew you'd like it," he said, taking another pinch from the box and sniffing it as she had seen him do so many times.

"And all the while I thought you were taking snuff," she said with a laugh. "Instead you've been keeping this incredible secret. You're a devil! Why didn't you share it with us?"

"Not everyone understands its beneficial qualities, my dear. Like anything else, it can lead to excess."

She looked closely at him. His features, which only moments before were drawn and old now seemed relaxed, youthful. The magical powder seemed to have transformed him from a tired old man into a vigorous youth. A feeling of elation overwhelmed Teddy.

"I love it!" she cried, rising from her chair and twirling about the room. As she passed his chair, she took his hand and swept him up in her impromptu dance. At the window, they paused to look out over a sea aglow with moonlight from a sky sparkling with millions of stars. They shared a long, passionate kiss and a lingering embrace.

"I'm on a cloud," Teddy whispered. "I never dreamed that anything could be so . . . so deliciously decadent."

"Now go to your dressing room," Barron said. "There you'll find another surprise—your personal maid. Her name is Maiyu. It means beautiful gem, and she is all of that and more. She speaks very little English, but she understands it well enough. She'll prepare you for your marriage bed, where I'll be waiting anxiously for you."

Maiyu greeted her shyly with a low bow. Teddy, no less shy, allowed the handmaiden to undress her, pin up her hair, and guide her gently into a tiled bath filled with warm water from which arose a cloud of aromatic vapors. As Teddy luxuriated in the heady fragrance, Maiyu put away her clothes and laid out a silken robe and slippers. As Teddy emerged modestly from the bath, Maiyu enclosed her in a soft towel. Slowly, sensuously she dried her warm body, then led her to a couch and bid her lie down. With strong, practiced fingers Maiyu massaged her shoulders and back, putting every muscle at ease and setting her mind adrift. When she was thoroughly relaxed, Maiyu opened a vial of fragrant oil and gently caressed Teddy's naked shoulders with it. Next she applied a touch of the scent between her breasts, in the small of her back, along the inside of her thighs and on the soles of her feet. Maiyu's touch was so pleasant, the perfume so intoxicating that Teddy was transported. At last Maiyu wrapped her in a silken robe, helped her on with slippers and guided her to the door beyond which Barron waited. Then she disappeared into the shadows.

"You're even more beautiful," he greeted Teddy, taking her in his arms. "I have never found you more desirable nor wanted you so much."

They stood for a long time before the dying fire, embracing and touching until their robes fell away and she was quivering with desire and he was filled with all the vigor of his newfound youthfulness.

*   *   *

On their third day at sea, Barron brought news from the bridge of the assassination of Austria's Archduke Franz Ferdinand in Sarajevo.

"What does it mean?" asked Teddy, bewildered.

"A European war, probably," Barron said. "And that will mean changes. There'll be new demands in the marketplace. We must stand ready to meet those demands."

"Barron, that's unconscionable! How can you even think of profiting from war?"

"It's not our war, Teddy. There's always a war going on somewhere in the world. Men have fought wars since time began. I'd prefer to do business in a peaceful world, but if nations insist on fighting one another, then I am ready to serve them. They'll want food, arms, equipment, transport. You'll see. I won't seek them out; they'll come to me. I won't refuse them."

As he spoke, he took the little box from his vest pocket and sniffed a pinch of the white powder after offering it to her.

"No, thank you," she said firmly. "I'm afraid of it. I'm not sure I like what it does to me. I wasn't myself."

"It turned you into a goddess of love. I have never been so thrilled, so completely satisfied by anything in my life."

"Or by anyone?"

"Or by anyone," he confessed.

"How did you come across this, this . . ."

"It's cocaine, dear. It was prescribed for me, initially. I was suffering from an ailment, a debilitating ailment, and a physician prescribed cocaine to alleviate my suffering."

"It's very powerful. I don't want to develop a craving for it. Besides, I don't think I need to see it, do you? I didn't take any last night, and I think I performed very well."

"Like an elegant and refined courtesan. A hundred years ago, you could have lined your boudoir with the crowns of kings, or all the ones young enough to appreciate you."

"And talent? Do you think I'm a talented lover?"

"You have a natural talent. You're the quintessential lover. You make the heavens part and the thunder roll."

"It's nothing, really," she said with mock modesty. "Not when you have a servant like Maiyu. She knows all the tricks, and she is very clever. She may not know a word of English, but she's an excellent teacher, as I'm sure you must know."

"Whatever do you mean, my dear?"

"I mean that you're a perfect liar, my dear husband, and I love you for it."

*　　*　　*

The author, the activist, and the artist sat in a booth at *Vanna's*, talking of events in Europe that were spinning out of control. John, a former war correspondent, said a San Francisco newspaper had approached him about going to the front.

"I refused, of course," he said grandly, emptying his wineglass. "I'll have none of it. War is antithetical to the socialist ideal. War is the destruction of labor, not the glorification of it. There is no glory in death, only in life."

"Then go as a pacifist," Mabel urged. "Use your talent to reveal the whole awful truth to the world and help bring the warmongers to their knees."

"The world knows the horrors of war," he said, "yet it revels in it. It's disgusting. Men shout for blood and the jingoists spur them on. I've bared their hypocrisy a thousand times, yet again it comes to this. No, we must direct our efforts toward our own government. We must support Wilson in his determination to remain aloof from this madness. And if he wavers, we must do all we can to hasten the socialist revolution. We must work to overthrow any government that accepts the inevitability of war. We must turn over the reins of government to the men and women who otherwise would be the victims of war. This may be our great opportunity. We may be on the brink of a new world order, my friends. This may be the impetus the social revolution needs."

Tom, greatly impressed by his new friends, quickly took up their cause.

"You'll never find me fighting another man's war," he said soberly. "The kings and the kaisers, the dukes and the emperors don't do the fighting. The fighting and the dying is done by men like me, and if we refuse to fight, there would be no war."

"Well said," observed Mabel, pleased to hear her own words coming from the mouth of a convert. "We must convince the public to apply the methods of trade unionism to international issues of peace and war. An organized opposition to war is the key to peace."

They had read Dr. Hobart's extravagant praise of Tom's work in the *Chronicle* and had come to congratulate him and to view his work. John, in San Francisco to address a labor meeting, was fascinated by the arrangement Tom described for his support. But he warned Tom that he must be on his guard.

"Beware the capitalists, my young friend. They have but one thing in mind—profits. You're but a means to their end. Defy them! Use your talent to glorify working men and women. Let your canvases become a shroud in which to bury capitalism. You have power at your disposal now, Tom, and you must use it wisely. Paint the workers of the world with the brush of righteousness. Show them what the future might be. Show them the beauty of the new order. Let the light of your talent guide them out of darkness and into the path of socialism. Don't knuckle under to the money grubbers, particularly not to that hedonist Bachelor and his crowd."

"What's a hedonist?" Tom asked.

"He's person who lives only to satisfy his selfish desires, who wallows in the excesses of the flesh. He is avaricious and evil. He

69

is addicted to money and to women and worse—to drugs!" John proclaimed, pouring more wine into his glass.

"That's what a hedonist does?"

"That's what Barron Bachelor does," the author explained. "He may be charming, but he's an evil man."

"But he's just married Teddy!" Tom exclaimed. "You both were there. If he's such a . . . a hedonist, why didn't you warn her?"

"She must know," John said. "They've been friends for years."

"She's an intelligent woman," said Mabel. "She knows what she's doing. She's made no secret of it. She'll get her hands on his money and use it to advance the cause of women's rights. And she will. I have faith in her."

"But what a price to pay!" said Tom, aghast. "Her father has money. She didn't have to marry Barron Bachelor."

"Her father's money was someday; the Bachelor fortune was now," Mabel explained.

"But you should have warned her," Tom said dejectedly. "You're her friends; you owed her that much. She's not the firebrand she pretends to be. She's an innocent, and now we've abandoned her. Oh, God!"

*   *   *

After nearly a week at sea, Teddy was thrilled to get her first glimpse of the islands. The sea was calm, the sky clear, and the weather warm as the ship skirted the coast of Maui, heading windward to the Pailolo Channel and thence for the port of Lahaina on the southwestern coast of the island.

"That mountain is Haleakala," Barron said as they sailed by. "It's a dormant volcanos over ten thousand feet high. The natives call it the 'House of the Sun.' Their legend says that a folk hero, Maui, stood atop Haleakala and snared the sun, slowing it in its course. That accounts for the fine weather we'll enjoy here."

"It's so beautiful," she said. "I can't wait to get ashore. I want to be just like the natives. I want to run on the beach in the warm sand and swim in the surf. I can't wait!"

"You'll be the loveliest *wahini* on the island, my dear."

The *Maui Maiden* dropped anchor at Lahaina, and the honeymooners went ashore arm in warm, trailed by Chinaboy and Maiyu and a crew of natives enlisted to carry their luggage. At the foot of the pier, they were met by an open cane wagon drawn by a team of four horses. It was large enough to accommodate the passengers, their entourage and their luggage for the three-mile trip to the Bachelor plantation. The sun was still high when they arrived at "the big house," a sprawling, one-story home with clapboard siding and an open veranda all around.

"It was built by a whaling captain from Massachusetts," Barron said. "It's nearly one hundred years old and sturdy as the day it was completed. Look, from here you can see miles of beach in both directions, and on all sides thousands of acres of sugar cane. It's a working plantation. Beyond that row of coconut palms is a valley where the workers live. There's a mill there where they crush and cook the cane. But we'll see all that tomorrow. For now let's get settled."

The shutters had been flung wide, and warm breezes from the sea wafted through the spotless rooms, which were made all the more inviting by copious quantities of fresh flowers. From the kitchen they could hear a gaggle of giggling girls sent to ready their master's home.

"Go to them," Barron told Chinaboy. "They'll show you and Maiyu to your rooms and acquaint you with the kitchen. I'm sure you'll find all you need to feed us for a few weeks and plenty of advice on how to do it. Anything you need, just ask."

"No help," he said indignantly. "Chinaboy know about kitchen." He picked up his bag and his small travel box and left the room with Maiyu padding along behind him.

Teddy found that the master bedroom had dressing rooms at either side, each outfitted with closets and wardrobes and a contrivance she had not seen before, a metal-lined stall with a nozzle in the ceiling that sprayed water at the pull of a lever. The dressing rooms were furnished with a couch, table and chairs, dressing table, and full-length mirror. The bedroom between them contained only a huge four-poster bed and two upholstered chairs beside a serving table in front of a stone fireplace. Above the mantel hung an array of native artifacts, including hideous masks and several wicked-looking spears. In a teak bowl on the table floated a huge orchid.

"It's early," Barron said after showing Teddy the house. "If you like, I'll have a rig brought around and we'll go exploring. Or, if you're tired, perhaps you'd like to rest."

"I'm much too excited to be tired, but you go in and take your nap. I'll unpack my bags and get acquainted with the staff."

"I could do with a bit of rest," he said. "I'll only be an hour."

Barron retreated to his dressing room, while Teddy went to hers to unpack her trunk and hang up her dresses. When she finished, she stretched out on the couch and fell fast asleep. She was awakened a short time later by the sound of Chinaboy's high-pitched voice. He seemed to be scolding someone severely in Cantonese. Teddy went quickly to the kitchen and found that Maiyu was the victim of Chinaboy's wrath.

"What's going on here?" she demanded.

"No matter, no matter," Chinaboy sputtered, shaking his head. "I take care."

His brow was wet with perspiration, his face red with anger. Maiyu cowered in a corner, her eyes on the large carving knife Chinaboy gripped in his hand. She clutched a black leather case in her arms.

"Put that knife away and tell me exactly what's going on," Teddy insisted.

"No good, no good," Chinaboy said, putting the knife on the table and waving his hands emphatically. "No good. We go."

"That's ridiculous, and you know it," Teddy said sharply. "I don't know why you can't get along. You've frightened poor Maiyu half to death. Maiyu, go to your room. He won't hurt you."

The frightened girl, keeping a close eye on Chinaboy, edged cautiously around the room and dashed out the back door, still clutching the leather case.

"You should be ashamed of yourself," Teddy scolded. "I just hope your shouting hasn't awakened Mr. Bachelor. He won't put up with that temper of yours."

"I don't mind, really," said Barron from the kitchen doorway. "I'm sure it was all a misunderstanding. Right, Chinaboy?"

The cook did not answer, but began dragging out pots and pans and creating enough noise to make discussion impossible.

"It's really my fault, dear," Barron said as he guided her into the quiet of the parlor. "I thought it would be convenient to have both Chinaboy and Maiyu with us. I thought they would get along. Obviously I was wrong. Perhaps it would be better if I let Maiyu go and hired another maid for the rest of our stay."

"That's nonsense! You're not going to fire poor Maiyu just because of that foul-tempered old fool in the kitchen. He knows better, and he ought to be ashamed of himself."

"Then you like Maiyu?"

"Of course I do. She's a treasure."

"I think I know why he's upset. He's probably found out about Maiyu's background."

"You hired her; that should be enough for him."

"That's just it, I didn't hire her. I bought her."

"You what?"

"I bought her. She belonged to a tong chief in Chinatown. She was his concubine. I paid five hundred dollars for her. Chinaboy probably feels that she has disgraced herself and isn't fit to serve you."

"This is unbelievable! In this day and age, men are still buying women as if they were slaves?"

"She was a slave," Barron explained. "I bought her and set her free. She works for me happily. She is paid well, and she knows she is free to leave anytime she wishes. But she also knows there's little else she can do."

"Except be your concubine?" Teddy demanded.

"Not my concubine; your body servant. You must admit she's been helpful. How many other young women have had the luxury of such intimate instruction on their honeymoon?"

The wicked glint in his eye brought a smile to Teddy's face.

"I don't know what I would have done without her," she admitted.

The evening sky was blood red at the horizon, and the sun's rapidly vanishing rays pierced the clouds with shafts of gold. They sat hand in hand in a swing on the veranda watching the sunset and awaiting Chinaboy's call to dinner. The beach already was in shadow and the glistening sea shimmered in the dusk. In the fields that rolled away in every direction, the sugar cane waved gently in the evening breeze.

"It's incredibly beautiful here," she said. "It makes me wonder why you ever return to the mainland."

"Communication," he said simply. "If you feel that you are a million miles from nowhere, it's because you very nearly are. It would be difficult, if not impossible, to tend to business matters. That's why

I like to come here at least once a year just to get away from it all. There's nothing here to disturb us, nothing at all."

"Time to eat," Chinaboy called from the doorway, ringing a tiny dinner bell.

"Well, almost nothing," Teddy laughed.

Dinner was a Polynesian feast—plump filets of ahi, the great Pacific albacore, served on a platter garnished with succulent slices of papaya and broiled plantains, and bowl of steaming rice laced with sweet and juicy chunks of pineapple. When they had finished, they returned to the veranda, where they cuddled on the swing while Barron described the natural beauty of the island, the white sand beaches, the towering volcanic mountains, the deep canyons, and their plunging waterfalls and racing streams.

"Tomorrow we'll begin our tour," he said. "Every day we'll explore a new area. Where do you want to start?"

"At the beach," she said without hesitation. "I want to wrap myself in one of those beautiful native dresses and run barefoot through the sand. I want to play in the surf and lie in the sun with a flower in my hair."

"I believe that's called 'going native,'" he said as he removed the little silver box from his vest pocket. "It sounds delightful, if a bit rigorous. We'd better turn in early."

*   *   *

Barron's cocaine habit worried her, not because it radically changed his personality, but precisely because it didn't. She knew first hand that the white powder had a powerful influence on the mind. Yet he used it constantly and seemed unfazed. It obviously had become a part of his being, a bad habit that must be broken. It should be easy. He was indomitable in every other aspect of his existence, so it was absurd to think that he could be dependent on a sniff of that peculiar elixir. He was simply pushing himself too hard, she concluded, trying to squeeze too much out of life. She would slow him down. This island was the perfect place for it. She would wean him away from it, demonstrate to him that it was unnecessary to their happiness. *She* would invigorate him. *She* would exhilarate him. *She* would inspire him. *She* would become the only opiate he needed in life, beginning tonight.

It was still early. Maiyu had yet to come to her dressing room. No matter, she had learned her handmaiden's lessons well. She quickly bathed and anointed her body with the fragrant oil and brushed her long, blond hair until it glowed. Then she slipped into the silken robe and tiptoed silently into the bedroom to turn back the coverlet. A gentle sea breeze came through the open shutters, and a ray of light shown from under Barron's dressing room door. Expectantly she opened the door—and fell back in shock.

He was seated at his table, the wide sleeve of his robe laid back. Maiyu, caught by surprise at Teddy's sudden entry, froze. She appeared to have been loosening a cord from around Barron's upper arm. On the table was the black leather case she had been carrying in the kitchen during her quarrel with Chinaboy. And on the table among other strange paraphernalia lay a syringe with a long, ugly needle. Barron dabbed at his arm with a linen handkerchief and spoke harshly to Maiyu.

"Take your things and get out of here. You can see we must be alone."

Maiyu fumbled with the cord, finally stuffing it into the case along with the syringe. A heavily scented smoke permeated the room, stirred by Maiyu's hurried exit. Teddy was speechless.

"So, now you know," he said, arising from the chair and working his arm back and forth at the elbow to encourage the flow of drug-laden blood. "I've been meaning to discuss this with you, Teddy, really I have. But a man finds it difficult to discuss his weaknesses. I'm sure you understand."

"What . . . what is it?" she asked.

"A solution of morphine," he said. "Diacetylmorphine, to be pharmacologically correct. Heroin. I suffer from a craving for the damned stuff. I hope you understand that I've tried very hard to break the habit, and to a large extent I have. But the body doesn't always do what the mind tells it to do."

"It's the cocaine," Teddy said, trying to grasp his meaning.

"No, my dear. Cocaine is the medicine I take to lessen the desire for heroin. Believe me, it helps. I've made great strides over time."

She clutched her robe tightly about her as if suddenly standing naked in the presence of a stranger. Her initial shock quickly turned to anger, inflamed by jealousy.

"I see you haven't made those strides alone," she said quietly. "Is that the real reason you brought that Chinese woman along? I can't tell you how . . . how dirty it makes me feel."

"You're being unnecessarily cruel, Teddy. Maiyu was merely doing my bidding. Though it's not impossible, it's difficult to inflict that needle upon oneself. She's an expert at it."

"Another of her assets, is that it? Her departure must have been a great loss for some Oriental den of iniquity. I can understand now the source of her other talents. That's what you called them, didn't you, talents? I wonder how you ranked me in comparison to your . . . your concubine. My inexperience must have given you both a good laugh. I've never felt so humiliated."

She buried her face in her hands, ran back to her dressing room, and fell across the couch, sobbing uncontrollably. Barron followed her into the room and stood over her for a moment. Then he grabbed her by one arm and jerked her to her feet.

"Jealousy is unworthy of you, Teddy," he said, his eyes flashing with anger. "And for one who seemed to enjoy dabbling in cocaine, you show a remarkable lack of understanding for the addict. I don't want your pity, God knows, but as your husband, I do expect your indulgence and your help. Now, if you will stop that infernal blubbering, I'll try to explain."

He led her to the chairs in front of the fireplace, and they sat facing one another, Teddy red-faced and choking back her tears. She knew he was right. She did owe him a hearing and all the help she was capable of giving. The story he told was not a pretty one, but he told it dispassionately, blaming no one but himself. He had experimented with drugs during his college days, he said. Rich, spoiled, away from home, alone for the first time, and with a ready supply of cash, he was an easy mark. His addiction was not an uncommon one. Since the end of the Civil War, he explained, many men suffered from "the soldier's disease." Treated with massive doses of morphine to ease the pain of their wounds, veterans demanded easy access to such drugs, and they were not to be denied. Nor were other people, the ones who suffered no other pain than the pain of boredom. He had been such a person when he was young, he said, eager for each new thrill, ready to try anything, confident that he could control his desires as he controlled everything else in his life. But it was not to be. By the time his father died, Barron was an addict, a habitué of the chic opium dens of Chinatown, at last unable to exist without regular injections of heroin. When it came time to take over his father's business enterprises, he realized he needed help to overcome or, at least, control his habit. He submitted himself to a reputable physician who prescribed a system of treatment designed to wean him away from heroin by the limited use of a popular nostrum, cocaine.

"And it worked, Teddy," he insisted. "I am in control of my life again. I have been for many years now. A little pinch now and then throughout the day, and I can exist without heroin. I limit myself to only one injection a day, no more. And perhaps with your help, with your sympathetic understanding, I can rid myself of the habit entirely. I'll not beg for your help, and I don't want your pity. It's up to you. But please remember that I'm doing everything in my power to quit. Obviously I can't do it alone. You are a grown woman, Teddy, a woman of strength and courage and daring. You had to be, or I never would have asked you to marry me. Now is the time to exercise that strength, that courage and daring."

Her anger subsided. His confession, delivered with an odd sense of pride, suggested he had struggled long and hard and not entirely in vain. He seemed to be saying that he had never surrendered, that the battle was still in progress, and he was determined to fight on. She was touched by his sincerity and ashamed that she had reacted so selfishly.

"If you're as sincere as you appear to be," she said calmly, "you may count on all the help I am capable of giving. But there must be no more secrets, certainly none as dreadful as this. And we must agree to face this problem together, just you and I. Maiyu must be sent away. You said you'd given her freedom. If that's true, then tell her she is free to go wherever she wishes. But she must go."

"I will, my dear," he said, taking her into his arms. "In due time, I will. You must remember that at the moment she's in a strange land surrounded by strange people. She can't speak the language. She has limited skills. Give me time to find a place for her, someone to care for her. Is that asking too much?"

"No, I understand. But you must promise that it will be soon."

"I promise you it will be soon."

8

His name was Yee Dao-chen, and he came from an impoverished village in the Hsin-ning district of Kwangtung Province in the southernmost reaches of the Middle Kingdom. He was the third son of a poor farmer who, like his ancestors for many generations, scratched a meager existence from the high rocky plateau, where the soil was the only thing poorer than the people who tilled it. When the violence of the Taiping revolution reached his village, he fled on foot, just one step ahead of a rebel band that murdered his father and was bent on collecting his head as well. Arriving in Canton with little more than his travel bag and a handful of rice, he soon found himself in a marketplace standing before a lush array of fruits and vegetables. Sick with hunger, he was obsessed by a mad desire to begin at the first basket and eat his way to the last.

It was very early in the morning, but he was not alone on the street. A wealthy man attended by three servants also was inspecting the produce, selecting only the finest for his table. He must have a very large family to carry away so much food, thought Yee Dao-chen. The rich man could not help but notice the malnourished youth and sent one of his servants to him. The servant, haughty now that he was empowered to speak for his master, demanded his name.

"I am Yee Dao-chen of Hsin-ning," he said proudly, for though he was ashamed of his pitiable condition, he was mindful of the honor of his family and reluctant to bring shame upon it.

The servant returned to his master and after a whispered conference came back to Yee Dao-chen and said, "My master will return you to the embrace of your family if you will come with us."

"But our village has been overrun by bandits," Yee Dao-chen protested. "I have no desire to return there."

"Your miserable village is of no consequence. Your family is large and widespread. My master will find a cousin here who will assume responsibility for you."

When the wealthy man finished his shopping, he set off down the street, followed by his heavily burdened servants. Yee Dao-chen fell in behind this procession as it wended its way through the narrow alleyways of the sprawling port city to the bustling waterfront. He was led to a large building filled with the dizzying aroma of good food and filled with tables covered by fine linen and set with delicate porcelain bowls and cups. This grand room must be about to serve a banquet to honor some famous personage, thought Yee Dao-chen as hunger pangs twisted his stomach.

"Take him to the kitchen and feed him," the rich man ordered. "I will come for him shortly."

As Yee Dao-chen was gorging himself on a bowl of rice and bok choy, the rich man returned, accompanied by another to whom he spoke in tones of deep respect. He explained that he had found the starving youth in the marketplace and that his name was Yee Dao-chen. The second man was dressed in opulent robes, leading Yee Dao-chen to believe that he must be a magistrate or, at the very least, an officer of the emperor's guard. He waited fearfully, certain the magistrate would demand his head. But instead, without a word to the frightened youth, the magistrate beckoned Yee Dao-chen to follow him up the street. He brought the wanderer to a large building, where the air was heavy with incense and the halls lined with doors. One door was opened for him, and he was told to enter, to bathe in the tub, and to dress in the clothing he found there. He was then to rest upon the mat until he was summoned. All this he did gratefully, if fearfully.

Late in the day, the man came for him and brought him before a group of elders, who questioned him closely about his family, about the Hsin-ning district, about his life on the barren plateau where he was born, and why he had fled to Canton. At last he was informed that he had been accepted as a member of the family association and that, in exchange for the care and training he would receive, he was expected to forever honor his family name and vow never to bring shame upon it. This was easy for Yee Dao-chen to do, for those demands were the same that his father had made upon him many years before. Yee Dao-chen wondered if his father ever knew just how large the Yee family was or how rich it must be. But he was certain his father knew now and was guiding the fate of his third son from somewhere beyond the Celestial Empire.

Yee Dao-chen prospered under the guidance of the family association, working first in the kitchen of one of its fine restaurants, where one hundred chickens were butchered for a single meal and rice was cooked in vats large enough for a man to live in. From kitchen chores, he was elevated to the position of chef in training. He was a good student, and after several years, he was proclaimed a master cook. As he prospered, he was encouraged to send a portion of his earnings to his widowed mother in the wretched village of his youth.

At length Yee Dao-chen was put in charge of a restaurant, with time to pursue a second vocation. Each member of the family, as circumstances permitted, was encouraged to learn a second skill as a precaution against hard times. Yee Dao-chen thought first of becoming a herbalist, but while pursuing this training, he chanced upon a related discipline that intrigued him even more—the science of the needles. It was a skill that could bring a man into balance with the opposite poles of his being and put him in touch with the very soul of the universe. By the time he was thirty, Yee Dao-chen was much respected within the family association, not only for his mastery of the art of Cantonese cuisine, but also for his skill at acupuncture.

In his restaurant Yee Dao-chen often found himself host to sea captains from the farthest corners of the earth, and it was through them that he confirmed the existence of the fabled Gum Shan, the Mountain of Gold that lay many thousands of miles across the sea. He soon succumbed to the urge to flee the harsh rule of the Manchus and, even under the threat of death, to go in search of the land where the streets were paved with gold. He sent the bulk of his savings to his mother, packed his family papers and his lacquered box of needles into his travel bag, and with but a few gold coins in his pocket, took passage aboard a tall ship along with seventy other sons of the Middle Kingdom.

For nearly three months, the great ship plied the waves, even as food grew scarce and illness thinned the ranks of passengers and crew. The Chinese, treated with suspicion by the sailors, were seldom allowed on deck and soon found themselves virtual prisoners in the hold, living amid filth and disease. Before the ship dropped anchor in the Sandwich Islands, eleven of their number had died of fevers that even the needles could not cure, and their bodies were unceremoniously dumped into the sea. But with stocks of food and water replenished in the islands, the ship proceeded under full sail toward the Mountain of Gold and soon deposited Yee Dao-chen and his fellow passengers on the wharves of San Francisco. By the Christian calendar the year was 1878.

Yee Dao-chen turned immediately to his family's *hui guan,* a mutual aid society not unlike the family association that guided his fortunes in Canton. In a short time, he found a job as a cook in a Chinatown restaurant, and not long thereafter, he also established a modest practice in the science of acupuncture. But for all his hard work and law-abiding behavior, Yee Dao-chen found that many of the city's residents hated him and his fellow countrymen. They called him Chinaboy, a name he found more amusing than offensive, since he still was, and always proudly would be Yee Dao-chen. If the unlearned barbarians refused to recognize his heritage, he could afford to be indulgent and forgiving. But when their suspicion turned to anger and then to violence, he cast about for some means of protection from their bigotry. He was no longer young and his family in Hsin-ning continued to grow. He could ill afford to sit idly by while the city ordered him to lay aside his needles or thugs wrecked his restaurant out of sheer meanness. His only refuge, he concluded, was in the arms of the very race that reviled him. He took a job as cook in the home of a Caucasian, Charles Cullen.

The Cullens lived high on a hill in what impressed Yee Dao-chen as akin to a palace, and they paid him a wage very close to that of a successful restaurateur, but with none of the risk. He spoke very little English, and though he tried to tell the Cullens that his name was Yee Dao-chen and that he came from a very old and honorable family in the Middle Kingdom, they seemed not to care. They found him amusing, and their smiles and laughter were a welcome relief from the hatred and harassment he had known on the city streets. So he willingly accepted the name Chinaboy and gratefully moved into a small room in the basement of their mansion. They paid him well each month, and provided as he was with comfortable quarters and plenty of food, he sent most of his earnings to his family in Hsin-ning. His mother was by now very old, the matriarch of what had become the richest family in the village, thanks to the good fortune of her third son who toiled somewhere deep inside the Mountain of Gold.

*   *   *

Teddy slept alone in her dressing room on the night of Barron's confession, not to punish him so much as to come to grips with a problem that, if left unchallenged, could destroy their marriage. She felt helpless in the face of his drug addiction, yet convinced that she must do something about it. After many restless hours, she arose reinforced in the conviction that love and devotion, all she really had to offer, would be their salvation. Devotion she would give unstintingly. Surely love would follow.

Barron was his usual self at breakfast, youthfully handsome, self-assured, quite as if nothing had happened the night before. He rose to greet her with a gentle embrace as she entered the dining room.

"You're beautiful today, my dear," he said. "I've decided that what we need is to be alone, just the two of us. I've asked Chinaboy to pack a lunch. We'll take a carriage to the beach and spend the day there. What do you think?"

"I think that sounds wonderful," she said, grateful for the opportunity to test her new resolve. It would put time and distance between him and Maiyu and the fateful black case with its ugly needles. She alone would be his opiate for this day.

Not far from the Bachelor plantation was a secluded lagoon, protected from the pounding surf by a ring of coral-encrusted rock. The water, incredibly clear and as warm as a well-tempered bath, was alive with a multitude of fish of brilliant hue. Barron had brought colorful wraparounds for them both, and while he spread a blanket in the shade of a palm tree, Teddy slipped shyly among some ferns to change her clothes. Emerging boldly bare-breasted, she ran to him with girlish glee, relishing the unaccustomed sense of freedom and the feel of the warm sand between her toes.

"Come on," she cried. "Let's go for a swim."

Together they dashed to the lagoon and plunged into the water, Teddy squealing with excitement as the tropical fish darted out of her way. They spent an idyllic day, swimming, splashing each other like giddy children, lying in the sun, and dreaming aloud of happier days to come. At one point, certain of their solitude, they made love there in the shade of the palm trees and, after a period of sweet exhaustion, ran again to frolic in the lagoon, resplendent in their nakedness. As the afternoon wore on, Barron took out his silver box, and Teddy had to remind herself that the cocaine was a form of medication to him. As evening approached and they dressed for the drive home, she could see his discomfort as his heroin withdrawal symptoms set in. He began to sweat profusely as he struggled to resist the craving for a surge of the drug through his veins. But though the cocaine helped ward off the pain for a time, at dinner his stomach tightened and spasms wracked his body.

"It's difficult, Teddy," he gasped. "It's very difficult."

"I know, but you can do it," she said. "I know that together we can do it. You must be strong."

"But the pain," he whispered in a strange, constricted voice. It had begun with a vague aching sensation throughout his whole body, accompanied by heavy perspiration and severe chills. As it worsened, it began to localize, first in the intestines where it seemed to grip his innards and twist them beyond his powers of endurance. He stumbled into the bedroom, moaning quietly as he lay upon the bed, tossing and turning. Then the pain shifted to his head, and he sat upon the edge of the bed, rocking back and forth, his face buried in his hands as if his skull were about to explode. Teddy sat beside him, helpless but holding him closely and whispering encouragement. Next the pain stabbed at his heart, and he fell to the floor, writhing and crying out.

"I'm dying! For God's sake, bring me my case! Have pity on me, please!"

As the pain intensified, he began retching and choking until Teddy feared that the whole of his insides would spill out on the floor and he would die miserably in a puddle of his own vomit. When she could stand it no longer, she ran to the kitchen where Maiyu and Chinaboy stood fearfully silent.

"Help him! For the love of God, help him!" she pleaded.

Maiyu drew herself up, her eyes narrowed. She folded her arms defiantly, refusing to move.

"Chinaboy help," he said simply as he went for his needles.

He found Barron on the floor staring blankly at his demons, looking for all the world like a man already dead. Chinaboy knelt beside him and opened his lacquered box. Barron looked at first relieved as if Chinaboy were about to administer a shot of heroin. But when he saw the nature of the needles, he shrank away with a blood-curdling cry.

"Get him away from me!" he screamed. "Get him away! Oh, God, where's Maiyu? Won't anyone help me? The pain . . . I can't stand the pain. Bring my case or bring me a gun!"

As his patient sank into a fit of weeping, Chinaboy went deliberately about his work. He studied portions of Barron's body carefully, pressing gently with his fingertips. When he was satisfied that he had located a critical point he inserted a needle into the skin, probing gently and pushing until at last he felt he had reached the nerve centers that were producing his patient's pain. Then he began probing again. When he had finished, Barron lay quietly upon the floor, several needles piercing an arm, a leg, and the soft tissue of one ear. The pain, for the moment, seemed to subside. Except for an occasional twitch of a limb and his darting, dilated eyes, Barron lay lifelessly upon the floor, his head cradled in Teddy's lap. Gently she wiped the perspiration from his brow. On looking up, she saw Maiyu standing in the doorway, staring narrowly at her with a cold, hard expression. Teddy knew then that this had been a battle for control of Barron's soul and that Maiyu had nearly won. Her eyes flared in anger.

"Get a mop!" she screamed. "Get a mop and clean up this mess, you she-devil!"

The next day was worse. No amount of cocaine would soothe his fevered brow or relieve the pain in his drug-deprived body. He had become a shivering mass of gray flesh with red-rimmed, protruding eyes and pores that stood out like the cold, clammy skin of a plucked bird. Even Chinaboy's needles failed to arrest the pain or ease the craving for more than a moment at a time. Teddy stayed by his side throughout the day and long into the night before retreating to her dressing room and falling into a sleep of deep exhaustion. In the morning, Barron was only slightly improved. Chinaboy had gotten up early to administer another treatment with his needles, and Barron, lying cadaverously upon the bed, looked like the victim of some awful torture with needles sticking out of his icy, pallid flesh. This can't go on much longer, Teddy told herself as she looked upon that wretched body.

"If we can't cure him," she said to Chinaboy, "I fear that surely we will kill him."

"Chinaboy fix," he insisted. "Take a long time. Maybe he die, maybe not. Chinaboy needles no kill. Mista Bachelor needles, they kill. Long time. Take long time. Very sad."

"Yes, dear Chinaboy. It seems it will take a very long time."

In the corner of the room Maiyu watched contemptuously.

Days passed with little progress, Barron, weakened and ill from his ordeal, lay abed, sniffing doses of cocaine that left him groggy and uncommunicative. Late each afternoon as the time for his regular "nap" drew near, he broke out in a cold sweat and braced for the onslaught of pain. As his crisis approached, Chinaboy appeared with his needles and began his treatment, exploring his patient's body for the nerve endings that would respond to the sharp, shiny probes. There was a pattern to them now, certain places where the needles did their best work, easing Barron's pain and craving and offering hope of a cure. Teddy was greatly relieved at Chinaboy's success.

"It's working," she insisted. "In time these treatments will cure you completely. You must cooperate. You must give yourself a chance."

"It's ridiculous," Barron whispered weakly. "Do you really understand my suffering? I'm not doing this for myself. I'm doing it for you. If I had my way I'd ask Maiyu to fetch my case and I'd end this nonsense once and for all."

"Maiyu's been ordered to stay away from you," she said, confident that he was too weak to carry out his threat without her help. "Don't give up now. You've made some progress. You haven't had to resort to that awful heroin for more than a week."

"What kind of progress is that? I'm not even lucid unless I'm all stuck through with these damned needles. What kind of life is that? The rest of the time I'm so doped up on cocaine I'm in a virtual stupor. I was perfectly happy before all this began. I had achieved a nice balance in my life. I knew just how much of each drug to take to maintain myself and no one was the wiser. Even you didn't know until I told you. What was wrong with that?"

"It was a terrible way to live," Teddy replied, "dependent on chemicals coursing through your blood stream, unable to be happy without a sniff of cocaine or a shot of heroin in your veins."

"But it was my life, and I liked it that way."

"Then you had no right to bring me into that life. It was dishonest. It was selfish. It was cruel. You thought you could marry some inexperienced little twit and lie to her and hide your private vices from her and everything would be just fine. Well, it's not fine. It was fraudulent to even think you could do such a thing and get away with it. I'm not a child. I'm a woman determined to have her husband as a natural, healthy man, not a dope fiend."

"The marriage contract could be dissolved on the basis of that fraud," he said dejectedly, "if that's what you're driving at. But you'd have difficulty proving it. I married a woman I thought was sophisticated and broad-minded enough to accept me despite my faults. Where is my free thinker? What happened to my twentieth-century woman? *You* are a fraud, too, Teddy."

She told herself it was his pain talking, but the words stung. She felt trapped on the island and wished they were back in San Francisco, where they could seek competent medical help. She put her hand briefly on his cold, sweaty forehead, and the expression on her face revealed her true feelings.

"I don't want your damned pity," he swore. "Get out of here and leave me alone." As she turned to leave, he added, "And tell that heathen Chinese to come and get these damned needles out of my body!"

She knew she had lost for the time being and did as she was told, then sat rocking on the veranda, watching the sun go down and contemplating her fate. It had been a terrible mistake to marry Barron, she concluded. It could be the ruin of her life if she allowed it to be. She had to summon all her strength. She had to endure despite her emotional pain. She had made her bed, as the saying went, and now she must lie in it. He couldn't have meant it when he spoke of divorce. He was irrational, not himself. He could be so pleasant when he wanted to be. She recalled their day at the beach, went over every intimate detail time and again so that she would never forget it. It could be that way again. It must be that way again. They were the same two people, and they always would be. Once his system was free of the disease of drugs they *would* be that way again—close, intimate, falling in love as she always hoped they would. And if it took a month or a year or even longer, she was prepared to wait. She vowed to persevere.

Chinaboy fixed her a plate, and she ate alone in the kitchen. He was obviously chagrined that his acupuncture treatments had been rejected. Poor, dear soul, Teddy thought. He had been so kind, tried so hard to be helpful. It was unfair to burden him with her responsibilities. She would have to thank him, not now, but someday when it would be less painful for both of them. She picked half-heartedly at her food and went to bed in her own room just as darkness fell. Later, a rhythmic pounding awakened her from a restless, dreamless sleep. The sound of drums and chanting seemed to be coming from the valley below, through the cane break that led to the workers' village. A celebration, she thought, as she slipped into a robe and went to look in on Barron to see if the noise had awakened him. But he was not there. She went hesitantly out onto the veranda and scanned the darkness, thinking he might have gone to silence the celebrants. She could see nothing but a flickering light as if from a huge bonfire. Although the night was warm, she felt a sudden chill and pulled her robe tightly about her.

"Missy cold," Chinaboy whispered from the shadows, startling her. "No good. Must go back to bed."

"What's going on down there?" she asked. "Where is Barron?"

"No good," he said again. "Must go to bed."

A sense of foreboding came over her as she stepped carefully down the stairs and across the lawn toward the cane break, drawn by the flickering light and the hypnotic beat of the drums. Chinaboy followed at a distance, clucking his disapproval. As she neared the village, she discovered a crowd of native workers gathered in a large ring around the fire, swaying to the rhythm of the musicians who sat upon the ground, beating on drums and chanting in a language both sensuous and compelling. At the edge of the fire, dancing slowly in drugged abandon, was Barron, disheveled and red-faced, Maiyu half-naked in his arms.

*　　*　　*

Teddy's last few days in the islands were hell on earth. Hopelessness and despair weighed heavily on her heart. She felt wounded and dirty, as if she had been ravaged by some evil force, unseen and unspeakable. Her marriage was a mockery. She felt abused and alone. She longed to be home, away from the savagery of the islands whose natural beauty seemed only to conceal the demonic powers that overwhelmed her. Living in the plantation house was a game of cat and mouse. She spent most of her time in her room to avoid confronting Maiyu. When they did suddenly meet, the Asian woman averted her eyes while Teddy glared at her with undisguised hatred. It was she who now shared Barron's bed, Teddy was certain of it. It was she who appeared each afternoon at four at Barron's door, the black leather case tucked under her arm. It was she who must now be gloating over her victory. It was she who was needed by her master, not his wife.

As for Barron, he seemed his old self again, cheerful, confident, handsome, and youthful in appearance. He was the man she had married, the man she thought she would come to love one day. But with bitter irony, she admitted to herself that he was no man at all. He was merely a shell of a man, animated by a witch's brew of chemicals. Between his constant sniffing of the white powder and his so-called late afternoon nap, he exuded good cheer and self-assurance as if confident that she would come to accept him as he was. He honored Teddy's desire not to meet him face to face, but when that was unavoidable, he greeted her politely and did not try to force a conversation. It was as if he expected her to realize the error of her ways and was willing to wait.

It was Chinaboy who shouldered most of the burden of their standoff. Well aware of the circumstances that led to the tension between them, he was quick to place the blame on Maiyu. He banned her from "his" kitchen, spoke sharply to her in their common language whenever their paths crossed, and never dared mention her name in Teddy's presence. He served his mistress her meals alone in her room, tiptoed quietly about in her presence, never intruding, yet always there if she needed him. He was her only link to the life she had known in San Francisco. He was a rock to cling to until the emotional storms had passed and she was safely back in her own home with her father to comfort and console her. But she dreaded facing him, telling him what had happened. Would he understand? Would he be tolerant? Charles Cullen was from another generation, one that looked upon divorce as a disgrace, a generation where women were expected to suffer in silence and bend to the will of their husbands. Could she ever convince him of her desperation?

There was always Allie and their long friendship. Allie would be a lawyer soon. She could arrange a legal separation, then a quiet divorce. Everything would be all right then, if there were no complications. She prayed there would be none, that Barron would not challenge her decision to divorce him. On the day they steamed away from Lahaina, she was relieved to learn with certainty that she was not pregnant. That knowledge gave her strength. A child would have complicated everything. She was safe, unless she had overestimated the limits of Barron's forbearance.

On the first night at sea, she insisted on a cabin near the crew's quarters, but Barron refused, asking that she spare him such an embarrassment.

"We mustn't make a spectacle of ourselves," he explained. "We both would be a laughingstock. If we keep up appearances, we may even find an opportunity to resolve our impasse. You owe me that much."

"I've no desire to make a fool of you," she said. "I pity you, but I won't allow you to hurt me any more. I insist you leave me alone, or I swear I'll seek refuge on the bridge and embarrass you in front of your ship's officers. I'll confine myself to my dressing room by day. I'll dine with you in the evening for the sake of appearances, but at night my door will be locked to you."

"I could demand a husband's rights," he said, "but I will not. I promise to treat you with the greatest respect and to honor your wishes. There's no reason we can't act like civilized human beings."

The arrangement worked on the first night out. Barron's behavior was exemplary. They even managed to engage in polite conversation at the dinner table. But on the second night, it was obvious that he had been drinking, and the combination of alcohol and drugs played havoc with his disposition. He turned sullen and argumentative. He berated her and spoke abusively to Chinaboy. When at last she could stand it no longer, she left the table and locked herself in her room. After an hour of pacing, she fell into a troubled sleep, only to be awakened in the dead of night by a pounding at her door and Barron's voice raging at her and cursing about "that damned Chinaman." She cowered under the sheets, fearing he would smash the door in. Then silence fell, and for a long time she lay there and shuddered, afraid he might return. It was a quiet, gentler knock that came later, then another silence broken only by a low moan and a scratching at the door. She sat up and pulled her robe about her, listening intently. Suddenly she recognized the sound.

"Chinaboy!" she screamed, flinging wide the door. "My God! What has he done to you?"

The aging Chinese, his head brutally battered and bleeding, mumbled apologetically as she helped him rise and led him to her bed. Quickly she locked the door again and set about trying to comfort him. At her commode she poured her basin full and soaked a towel in the water to swathe his head. He opened his eyes but once and smiled weakly as if to thank her.

"You must lie very still," she said tearfully, caressing his thin, wrinkled hands. "Try not to move. Oh, God, what can I do?"

"Chinaboy sorry," he said haltingly. "Chinaboy try to help. Too old, too old."

Then he closed his eyes and died.

9

Charles watched as the *Maui Maiden* docked. On deck he could see his daughter preparing to disembark amid a small mountain of luggage and a confusion of deck hands. As the gangway swung into place, Barron came to the rail, caught his eye, and waved. Teddy began the descent alone, clutching Chinaboy's small travel bag. Her father met her at the foot of the gangway, and she fell into his arms. He signaled Barron that all was well and guided her to a waiting automobile. By now she was sobbing hysterically.

"There, there, my dear," he said as he helped her into the vehicle. "I know how you must feel. Barron sent me a radiogram about Chinaboy's accident. I was shocked, of course. He was such a loyal old fellow. I shall miss him more than you can imagine. I never should have sent him along. In a way, it's all my fault."

Teddy looked at him aghast.

"I know accidents will happen," he continued, "but if I hadn't insisted he go along, he would be alive today. What an awful tumble he must have taken. And how terrible that you had to discover him. It must have been a terrible shock. I'm so sorry."

"Yes," Teddy said bitterly, her anger overwhelming her sorrow. "It *was* a terrible shock. He died in my arms, Father. But I'm sure Barron told you all about it. I suppose there's nothing I can add."

"We agreed it would be best if you avoided discussing it, Teddy. He asked me to take you home while he attends to some business matters. He knows how upset you are and thinks you ought to get some rest. The important thing is not to blame yourself. It was an unfortunate accident. There was nothing you could have done to prevent it. As I understand it, everything was handled properly. I've briefed my lawyer on the details and he has agents afoot in Chinatown at this very moment, trying to locate any survivors. He doubts that an inquiry will be necessary. Burial at sea was perfectly legal under the circumstances, and since there were no witnesses . . ."

"No witnesses, no body, no inquiry."

"Exactly, my dear. Best now if we simply put the whole unfortunate incident behind us and get on with our lives."

Teddy clutched Chinaboy's travel bag. It held all his worldly possessions, she thought, everything in life that he treasured. She took out the beautifully lacquered box containing the needles and clutched it to her bosom. He had tried so hard to help, she thought, and then she began to sob again, unable to bear the sorrow, the bitterness, and the lies any longer. Her father gently put his arm around her.

Hours later she awakened from a deep sleep in her own bed. It was late in the evening, nearly dark. She turned on the small electric lamp at her bedside and cradled Chinaboy's lacquered box in her lap. It was a simple affair with a hinged lid. She took the key that had been found in Chinaboy's pocket on the night of his death and unlocked the box. Inside was a tray containing the needles the old man had used to treat Barron. Under the tray she found a secret compartment with several sections. In one she found a handful of coins and a few crumpled bills. Under the bills lay a frayed envelope containing a bankbook, with all the entries in delicate Chinese calligraphy. In another section was a bundle of yellowed letters, Chinaboy's correspondence from relatives in his homeland. Not much to show for a life, Teddy thought as tears welled up again. She heard the ring of the telephone being cranked and, wiping away her tears, went quietly down to the landing to listen.

"Yes," her father was saying, "she agreed it was best to spend the night here at home, since you couldn't be with her immediately . . . No, she doesn't speak of it at all. But she's very, very upset . . . I told her that accidents will happen. It's as simple as that. Perhaps that's what makes his death so devastating . . . No, of course. Whatever you think is best . . . Yes, I agree. There's no place like home at a time like this . . . No, I don't think she blames you. No, of course not. No, no. I'll tell her. Tomorrow then. Yes, you'll be by tomorrow afternoon to collect her. Yes. Goodnight, Barron."

Teddy went quietly back up the stairs and got into bed. He would never understand, she thought. Only she knew what really happened aboard ship that night. Even though she had not witnessed the crime, she was certain beyond any doubt that her husband was a murderer. He had killed the helpless old man in a drug-induced rage when he tried to intervene to protect her. She had heard it all. He had slammed Chinaboy's head against her door repeatedly and crushed his skull. The man she had married had turned out to be a drug addict, a womanizer, and finally, a brutal murderer, and she was helpless to do anything about it. Tomorrow he would come to take her to their new home, and the thought gave her a feeling of dread. It seemed only a matter of time before she became his next victim. Too frightened to sleep, she lay wide-eyed in her bed, imagining all sorts of brutal fates that might befall her. She closed her eyes when she heard her door open quietly. After a moment it closed again and she heard her father's footsteps on the stairs. Only then did she finally drift into a troubled sleep.

*   *   *

Allie was stunned, cringing as Teddy described the awful thump, thump, thump of Chinaboy's head against her door. But she realized the hopelessness of the situation.

"There's absolutely nothing you can do," she said. "You didn't see what happened. It might have been as you first thought—Barron pounding on your door with his fists. You said you heard him shouting, but you can't prove Chinaboy was even there at the time."

"It was murder, I'm certain of it," Teddy insisted. "I distinctly recall Barron cursing 'that damned Chinaman,' and just before he died Chinaboy told me he'd tried to help me. What other explanation could there be?"

"There could be several possible explanations. But the fact is you didn't witness a murder, and Barron certainly would deny he committed one."

"But those dreadful sounds, Allie. I can still hear that poor old man's head being slammed against my door. There's no mistaking it. He must have come to my defense and Barron throttled him and bashed him against the door. There was blood everywhere!"

"But you said there was a time lapse . . ."

"He was probably beaten unconscious, then knocked on the door when he came around at last," Teddy argued.

"Or he could have suffered a fall and dragged himself to your door," Allie countered. "It's entirely possible, you must admit."

"Allie, I heard it, I tell you!"

"But you didn't *see* it, Teddy. It just isn't enough to file a criminal charge against anyone, let alone your own husband. Your suspicions wouldn't convince a prosecutor or a jury. And with the staff of attorneys at Barron's disposal, he'd have them believing you were crazy for dreaming up such a story."

"Then what am I to do? Right now I'm scared to death to be under the same roof with him. I left home early this morning just to avoid him. He was to come for me this afternoon. If he knew I was telling you all this, he'd kill me, I'm sure of it."

"As soon as I pass the bar examination I can initiate divorce proceedings against him on your behalf. But there could be no reference to murder, because there is no evidence of it. Even if there were, you've got to consider the racial matter. The victim was Chinese, a servant. You'd never get a conviction, not in this day and age. You might win a divorce case on other grounds, but it's not likely. You'd have to prove he hid the fact of his drug addiction, and that therefore the marriage was fraudulent. Do you really think he'd ever let those charges be heard in open court? It's not likely. He could keep you tied in legal knots forever."

"But, Allie, you've got to help me. I'm so afraid."

"I can help you as a friend, Teddy. I can come home with you, stand by you so he wouldn't dare do anything to harm you. But this is something you've got to handle yourself, calmly and rationally. You must sit down with him and discuss things openly. Tell him you're afraid of him. Tell him you can no longer live with him as his wife. Come to some understanding, a legal separation, for example. Look, if he's rational enough to run a business the size of Bachelor Enterprises, he's rational enough to listen to your concerns and maybe do something about them. Your only alternative is to run away and file suit against him and spend the rest of your life trying to get around the legal roadblocks he'll throw in front of you."

"But you will come home with me, won't you?" Teddy pleaded. "You won't make me face him alone."

"Of course I will, if that's what you want."

*   *   *

A cleaning crew was still in the mansion that was permeated by the smell of fresh paint. As empty as it was and only partially furnished, the home still was lavish beyond imagination. Teddy took

Allie on a tour of the three floors of living quarters, and then they went out onto the broad balcony that hung over the cliff. One hundred feet below them, the surf pounded ceaselessly against the stony bastion, its thunder so loud the women failed to hear Barron as he approached. It was Teddy who first caught sight of him, looming in the doorway. A gasp escaped her lips.

"I had hoped to carry you across the threshold, my dear. You must forgive me for not calling for you sooner, but your father said you needed rest."

"I'm sorry," Teddy said meekly. "I should have left word."

"It was my fault," said Allie. "I insisted on seeing this marvelous home. And I thought I could help her unpack. I know this is a terrible intrusion."

"Nonsense, Allie. I'm sure you've been a great comfort to my bride. She's been through quite an ordeal, as you must know."

"Yes, I was saddened to hear the news. But she seems fine now. We were just admiring this spectacular view."

"I'm sorry we can't ask you to stay for dinner," said Barron, "but obviously it will be some time before we are prepared to entertain. I'm sure you understand."

"Yes, Allie," said Teddy. "You'll be our first guest. Meanwhile I'm quite all right now." She looked steadily at Allie so there could be no mistaking her meaning. She wanted to be alone with Barron. She was suddenly furious with herself for being afraid to confront him, and her anger had more than overcome her fears.

"If you're sure you don't need any help, unpacking, I mean," said Allie, "then I guess I'll be getting along. I can find my way out. Give me a call when you're settled, Teddy. We'll have lunch."

"Of course. Good-bye, Allie, and thanks for being so kind."

When she had gone, Barron came down the marble steps in long, graceful strides. How handsome he was, she thought, how cool and controlled. As he drew near, she held her ground, leaning against the railing above the thundering surf, ready to fight back if he should try to throw her into the sea. She stiffened as he grasped her arms and stared into her unblinking eyes.

"Why didn't you wait for me?" he asked.

"Because I was afraid."

"Afraid of me?"

"Yes."

"You still think that I killed Chinaboy?"

"Yes, I do."

"I didn't. It's absurd."

"How can you be sure? You were drugged. You were ranting like a madman. You wouldn't remember whether you killed him or not."

"Believe me, I would remember."

"You're hurting me," she said, twisting out of his grasp. "It's cold out here. The fog is coming in."

He followed her up the stairs and into the parlor. It was cold and dank in the great empty house.

"We can't stay here," he said as she clutched her shawl about her shoulders. "We'll go to my suite at the Palace. I've had our bags delivered there."

She was only half listening, distracted by a painting leaning against the parlor wall. It was *The Blue Parrot*. Somewhere through the dark horrors of the past weeks, a glimmer of hope shown through, lifting her spirits.

"I don't want to stay at the hotel," she said. "If this is to be our home, then this is where I'll stay."

"The beds aren't even made up," he argued.

"I'm not helpless. I can make a bed."

"And dinner?"

"You could take me out to dinner. It would be appropriate for newlyweds to be seen at dinner. It would lend an air of credibility to this emotional chaos we call a marriage. I have no desire to embarrass you or to hurt my father. He'd be shocked and brokenhearted to know how I distrust you. I can live a sham, but I refuse to live in fear. I'll remain in this house unless you make it impossible for me to do so."

"You're being ridiculous, you know."

"You should give me more credit. I'm really being quite courageous. You can go to your hotel if you wish; I'm staying here, in my own bedroom."

*   *   *

During the weeks of Teddy's absence, John Manchester had snatched Tom from the productive isolation of his North Beach garret and dragged him into the limelight of local gin mills. The author's reputation flourished in those low saloons even as it flagged in the salons of the intelligentsia. While his hypocritical harangues were making him the laughingstock among credible social philosophers, the royalties that continued to flow from his early writings were making him a millionaire. While he had long since passed the apex of his creativity, he seemed bound to prevent Tom from ever reaching his. When Archibald Hobart said as much in his weekly newspaper column, John took offense. He fired off a withering blast to the *Chronicle* and, with Tom in tow, retreated to his great stone castle in the Santa Cruz Mountains to salve his wounded ego with fine bourbon and to hold court amid a drove of doting dilettantes.

"Manchester's got him drinking, and he hasn't put a brush to canvas for these many weeks," Hobart complained.

"Then we must speak to him," said Charles. "We'll call him before the board and explain that if he wants our patronage, he must exercise some self-discipline. He is a very young man and too easily swayed. He's being led astray, and if we're to avoid embarrassment ourselves, we'll have to get him back to work. We have a financial interest in him, and he must appreciate that fact."

"Did anyone tell him we were meeting today?" Teddy asked.

"I left word at *Vanna*'s," said Hobart, "but the Lazarros haven't seen him in days. They're as worried about him as we are. Tom's not a drinker. They can't understand what's gotten into him."

"I heard today at lunch that he's spending his time at Manchester's place in the mountains above Los Gatos," Charles said. "He's apparently joined a coterie of ne'er-do-wells that conspires there to change the world. The only time they show up in the city is when the booze runs low. They come here to shop and try to drink the town dry while they're at it."

"I'll go and get him," said Teddy. "I think I can make him listen to reason. I'll leave Friday and spend the weekend. I'll send a note today to announce myself."

"You might tell him this," said Hobart. "We've been approached by the organizing committee for the Panama-Pacific International Exposition. The emphasis of the fair is to be on art, and we've been invited to exhibit a sampling from the museum—Tom's work. It'll be his first opportunity for truly broad recognition. He'd be a fool to continue sullying his reputation just at the moment of achieving his first real success."

"I just can't believe that associating with John would harm Tom's reputation," Teddy said.

"It's John Manchester's association with John Barleycorn that's leading them both to ruin," said Charles. "They say it has attracted all sorts of riffraff to his place. It's become a dangerous den of drinkers and idlers, Teddy. It wouldn't do for you to go amongst them. God forbid that you fall under their spell."

"You've always been suspicious of free thinkers, Daddy. I doubt that they're the devils you make them out to be. But even if they are, I can take care of myself."

"Absolute bacchanals!" Charles elaborated. "Orgies to put the Romans to shame. Cavorting about naked in the woods!"

"I don't know where such stories are coming from," Teddy said, "but I don't drink, and I promise to keep my clothes on. I'll be perfectly safe. It'll give me something to do while Barron's in London."

"I think it's a bad idea," Charles said. "We ought to put it to a vote. Tom Quinn isn't a child, and we shouldn't have to treat him as one. We ought to call him before the board and read him the riot act."

"But he is a member of the board," Hobart pointed out.

"And my plan already has a majority, Daddy. I hold Barron's proxy, and I *know* Dr. Hobart wouldn't vote against me, would you, Doctor? So it's three to one in favor of my getting Tom out of the clutches of John Manchester and back to his easel. I move we adjourn."

*   *   *

Tom met her at the Southern Pacific station in San Jose. He was still the handsome, dark-haired lad who had set her adolescent heart aflutter so many years ago, and the sight of him set her to thinking about what might have been.

"Why did you want to see me?" he asked sullenly.

"Well! What kind of greeting is that? Be kind enough to help me with my bag, will you?"

"It doesn't look as if you've come to stay," he said hefting the overnight case.

"I've just come to check on my investment," she countered.

98

"I'm not an investment, Mrs. Bachelor, I'm an artist. There's no price tag on me. I'm not one to be bought and sold."

"That doesn't sound like Tom Quinn. Those must be John's words I hear. What has he done to turn you against me, besides teaching you the vocabulary of revolution?"

"You're making fun of me."

"I'm terribly curious about his hideaway," she said, cutting him short. "It must be fabulous. Which way is the car?"

"It's not a car, it's a buggy. I don't know how to drive a car, and I refused to let Jack come for you."

"So, it's Jack now."

"He's the only real friend I have. Frankly, I'd rather have him guide my career than a bunch of capitalists."

"Now that *is* John talking. I'd know his words anywhere." Teddy dodged deftly aside as Tom angrily flung her bag into the rig and stalked to the other side to take up the reins. Left to her own devices, she lifted herself aboard and took her seat beside him. As they pulled into the street, a La Salle backfired, and the horse reared. Teddy hung on for her life as Tom struggled to regain control of the frightened horse. When at last he had calmed the animal, he looked to see if Teddy was all right. She caught his worried expression and gave him a smile of reassurance.

"Let's not quarrel, Tom. I'm just interested in what's going on down here. It's the talk of the art world. I'm not here to spy on you. I'm taking advantage of an old friendship to satisfy my curiosity. I've known John since I was a child. He was a hero to me once, as he is to you now. There's nothing wrong with seeing him, is there?"

"I suppose not," he conceded reluctantly. "But what does your husband think about your little adventure?"

"I have no idea. He's off to Europe on business."

"I might have known he'd leave you behind once he smelled profit in the war. Apparently a sniff of cocaine sharpens one's nose for business."

His words struck her like a blow. Even Tom knew what must have been an open secret during Barron's courtship. Why didn't anyone tell her? She fell into a silent fury at his audacity. How dare he say such a thing? How dare he fling in her face the sorrow and pain of her cold and loveless marriage? How dare he be so—so right? Her anger, fueled now by self-pity, brought tears to her eyes. Tom saw them and softened his tone.

"I'm sorry," he said as the buggy wended its way down the road through orchards verdant in the sunlight. "I'm sorry. But I still can't believe that you, of all people, would marry someone you didn't love with all your heart. I would never leave you alone."

"I know you wouldn't, Tom," she said quietly, slipping her arm under his and resting her head on his shoulder. "Let's not quarrel."

"Oh, God, Teddy," he said, growing tearful now himself. "How wonderful it could have been."

*   *   *

Castle Cairn, "my rock pile," as John called it, was a great sprawling fortress built into the side of the mountain. One reached it after a steep climb from the valley floor on a road that wound uphill by switchbacks for three miles before passing through a massive stone archway in which was embedded a brass plaque emblazoned with the letter "M". From there the driveway twisted still higher to a granite outcropping blasted level to receive the structure.

"Build your house upon a rock, sayeth the Good Book," John called out by way of greeting. "What do you think of it, Teddy?"

"Magnificent! I love it," she exclaimed. "Take m'lady's bag to her apartment, Tom, while I show off the place. It's a far cry from the cheap flat on the Oakland waterfront where I grew up, or from my drafty cabin in the Yukon, heh?"

It was a far cry, indeed. The main house was replete with the overstuffed and filigreed elegance of the Victorian Age, the very accoutrements that would have impressed a poor boy from the slums a generation ago. The parlor was crowded with heavy furniture, carpeted with thick Oriental rugs, its walls hung with rich tapestries, and over all, an atmosphere of dark brooding. From the courtyard, a stairway spiraled through a narrow, dank tower that loomed high above the front entrance. At the top, a small room was brightly lit by two large windows and sparsely furnished with a small table and chair, a cot and an open cabinet jammed with books, pamphlets, and newspapers. On the table stood the author's typewriter, a desk lamp, and a neat stack of foolscap. Against the wall was a wire basket surrounded by a pile of crumpled paper tossed by a frustrated writer.

One of the two windows looked out across the valley to a line of hills in the east. The other faced north and overlooked a long, free-form pool fed by a live stream and agitated by a series of fountains that drew the water up and spilled it forth again so that the surface of the pond was in constant motion. A wing of the castle extended the length of the pool, and a dozen oak doors and an equal number of windows set in the thick granite walls marked the guest apartments. Teddy could see Tom emerging from the last door, where he had deposited her bag.

From his high workroom, John escorted Teddy back down the narrow winding stairway and into the kitchen, a large, well-appointed room with all the most modern conveniences, including a large gas range and an electric refrigerator that rumbled ominously in one corner. From the kitchen, a step led down into a grand dining hall, one side of which was made of glass. The view from this long window was framed by a wisteria vine that clung to the outer walls, festooned with rich clumps of lavender flowers. Dominating the dining room was a long table with place settings arranged along one side so that each diner was afforded an unobstructed view of the pool, its fountains, and the tangled woodland beyond.

"We'll have to add a place for you, my dear," John said. "We're to be entertained tonight by one of my guests. But come along, we'll find Tom and take a walk to the meadow. My friends are having a picnic lunch and a poetry reading there. You may want to freshen up and slip into your walking shoes. We'll meet you in the driveway."

They followed a narrow trail that took them beyond the craggy granite cliffs to a mountain meadow bordered by towering redwood trees and carpeted with a rich growth of golden mustard flowers. Some fifty yards from where the trail intruded upon this lush vale, they could see a cluster of figures gathered at the side of a stream. Four were reclining on a blanket around a picnic basket, while a fifth lounged close by in the shade of a flowering plum tree, reading from a wind-rustled sheaf of paper. His rhythmic cadences echoed across the meadow, then halted as he caught sight of them approaching.

"Go on, Gil, go on," John called from a distance. "Don't let us interrupt you. We've come to see if you've left us a bite to eat. I want you all to meet Teddy Bachelor. She's an old friend of mine who's come to visit."

Gilbert Nance tucked the loose papers under his arm with some embarrassment. He was tall, gaunt, and extraordinarily unattractive with a long, narrow face, ruddy and pockmarked, wispy red hair and toothy smile. He grew somewhat flustered when John introduced him as "a poet of some consequence. That's his own work, of course," gesturing to the papers. "Isn't that right, Gil?"

The skinny young fellow nodded shyly to Teddy as John guided her among the others for introductions.

"You know Mabel Meyers of course. I believe she's here to enlist the others in the IWW, although she denies it. And this is Janice Kirk. She's also an aspiring poet when she isn't busy inspiring Gil to new heights of poetical brilliance." Jan might have been Gill's sister, tall and thin, plain featured and dressed incongruously in a flowing white gown and silken slippers, a wild rose tucked fetchingly in her mousy hair.

"And Ellen Davis, dancer and choreographer, and her talented protégé, Lucy Lowenthal. Ladies, meet Teddy Bachelor."

Ellen had stood up as they approached, and at first sight, Teddy took her for a man. She was dressed in breeches and boots and a flannel shirt with a small silk scarf at the throat. She ran one hand through a thatch of close-crooped hair and extended the other, saying, "Glad to meet you."

"*Je m'apple Lucy,*" said her young companion in her best high school French. "*Je suis enchanté.*"

"I'm very pleased to meet all of you," said Teddy. "I'm delighted to be in such creative company. I'm afraid I have little to offer but my admiration of your creative activities. Please go on with your reading, Mr. Nance."

While Gil resumed his reading, John and Tom sat down on the blanket and attacked the picnic basket. Teddy primly refused a chicken leg, devoting her full attention to the poet, or nearly her full attention. She stole an occasional glance at Lucy, a petite child of perhaps sixteen years with a boyish figure and a near-perfect face—clear olive skin, dark eyes, high cheekbones, and an elfin smile that gave her a mischievous look. Lucy seemed to take uninhibited delight in Tom's presence, flashing him flirtatious glances that brought a blush to his cheeks. It was immediately clear to Teddy that it wasn't John Manchester who attracted Tom to Castle Cairn.

10

Teddy wondered why a famous and once prolific author would allow a collection of idle romantics to interfere with his work. It had been months since he had produced anything of importance. John's passion for social justice, once responsible for his greatest stories and novels, had faded. The charismatic orator for trade unionism now could barely summon the inspiration for an occasional tract. The press felt obliged to publish these pathetic works, but they served only to chronicle his decline. One reason was obvious: He was drinking heavily, not only during his sprees in San Francisco but every day, all day, from late morning when he arose to late at night when he staggered drunk to his bed. The hero of her college days had turned into a pitiful wretch, full of bluster and bravado, but an empty shell of his former self, mouthing phrases intended only to shock his followers, content to rest on his laurels, unwilling or unable to move on to greater things. But worse than the distractions he permitted, even encouraged, was the influence he wielded over the once ambitious young painter.

"Did you get any work done today, Tom?" Teddy asked. They had escaped from the cocktail hour and sat alone in the gathering darkness.

"No. But I'm not worried about it. Jack calls this my sabbatical. He says every artist needs a break in his daily routine to renew his soul, cleanse his spirit. It prepares him to go on to his next level of achievement."

"Is that what John is working toward, his next level of achievement? He seems to come here just to loaf and to drink."

"He works every day from one until four, except today. He wanted to greet you and show you around. But usually nothing interferes with those three hours of solitude and labor. I can vouch for that. I've been here several weeks now, and every day it has been the same."

"What does he have to show for such diligence?"

"He doesn't discuss a work in progress. It's a matter of principle with him."

"Tom, he showed me his workroom this afternoon. There was little sign of progress, but there a strong odor of alcohol. That little room smelled like a distillery."

"That's not unusual for a great artist. He claims that drinking releases his demons, clears his mind. I've tried it, but it has the opposite effect on me. It locks in my demons and muddles my mind. It also makes me very ill. Jack says my body chemistry is different and there's nothing I can do about it. So I don't drink much."

"If that's true, then what's keeping you from your work?"

"Inspiration, I guess. I've got some ideas, things I want to do. But I'm just not in the mood. I've been out of sorts lately."

"You seem pretty normal to me. A little testy, perhaps."

"Teddy, you know how I felt about you. You know what your marriage did to me. I was crushed. When you sailed away that day, I was sure I'd never paint another stroke. I couldn't go on without you, I wanted you so much."

"But look at all the wonderful work you produced before you even knew I existed. And as for me, why, I practically threw myself at you, and you rejected me. Have you forgotten?"

"You don't understand. It was too late then. You were about to be married. You weren't mine for the taking. You belonged to someone else. You still belong to someone else, now more than ever."

"I don't belong to anyone, Tom, I never did. Barron doesn't own me. Don't use me as an excuse. I won't take the blame for your indolence. We're each responsible for our own lives. I don't blame anyone but myself for my mistakes, and you shouldn't either. See what you've accomplished; the art museum is a great success, your work is drawing new admirers every day, other artists are beginning to bring their work around. You inspired all that, and you deserve the credit. But you also must accept responsibility for your failures, and you've failed to paint a stroke for weeks."

"Why do you scold me?" he flared. "You have nothing to do with me. We live in different worlds, and I only want to be left alone to find my way by myself."

He got up from the steps where they were seated and walked a few yards away. Teddy hesitated, then followed after him.

"We don't live in different worlds, Tom," she said quietly. "You are a very important part of my world. If I was wrong to offer you advice, perhaps it was because, in truth, I need advice myself."

Gently she turned him about to face her, but he averted his eyes.

"What advice could I possibly offer you?" he asked. "What could I ever do or say that would change anything?"

Suddenly John flung open the front door and a ray of light split the darkness and fell upon them.

"Hello out there!" he called. "It's nearly time for dinner. Come in and we'll have one more drink."

Teddy's face was still in shadow. Tom could not see the tears in her eyes. She wanted desperately to share with him the misfortunes that had befallen her, but she couldn't. As they went up the steps, she dabbed away her tears and put on a bright smile.

Florid-faced and reeling, John was a far cry from the indomitable literary lion Teddy once had known. In his drunkenness, he became again the tough little Irish orphan from the Oakland waterfront, the foul-mouthed deck hand, the rough and tumble laborer lured to the Yukon by a lust for gold. After twenty years of hard knocks, he had found himself driven by an overpowering need to tell the tales jarred loose by his bouts with bitter reality. Now that his work had brought him wealth and adulation and success as measured in modern America, something had gone terribly wrong. Teddy wondered what it was that transformed him into an insensitive drunkard, a barroom bard who abused the sycophants around him, a dull-witted brute incapable of carrying on even an elementary conversation. What happened to the great orator of the union halls, the champion of the poor and the downtrodden? Whatever the cause of his decline, Teddy was determined that the same fate not befall Tom. To that end, she sought to learn all she could about the group gathered at Castle Cairn.

"Your poetry is lovely, Mr. Nance. Has it been published?"

"No," the poet said shyly. "None of it. Not yet."

"What about *Petals in the Wind*?" asked Janice Kirk.

"I paid to have that published," he explained. "I don't think that is what Mrs. Bachelor meant."

"I must have a copy," Teddy said enthusiastically. "I'm sure I'll enjoy it. And would I know your work, Miss Kirk?"

"No, I write only for my own gratification."

"She is a wonderful poet," Gil insisted. "We must encourage her to read for us."

"Never, my dear Gil," Janice said. "Those poems are ours alone."

"Hours!" John exclaimed. "If they're anything like Gil's, they're more like days. Don't get her going, Gil, not tonight."

Mortified, Janice hung her head. Gil, seated next to her on a love seat, gently took her hand in his.

"They are very private poems," he explained to Teddy. "Perhaps later Janice can be persuaded—"

"No," Janice whispered. "It's Lucy's night."

"She'll improvise on a theme from Debussy," Ellen explained. "She's a natural-born dancer. Fortunately I discovered her before some incompetent instructor crushed her spirit. I have set her free."

"I am *not* free," Lucy pouted. "I must do as I'm told, or she'll punish me." Then with a toss of her head and an exaggerated expression of defiance, she left her mentor to the mercy her audience.

"I've never punished her," said Ellen with obvious embarrassment.

"Not in public anyway, heh?" John laughed, slapping Ellen on the buttocks. The woman's thick, muscular fists pumped involuntarily, and her face turned red with anger.

"You're drunk, Jack. Shut up," said Mabel. "Ignore him, Ellen. When he's drunk he doesn't know what he's saying."

"Why not?" John asked. "You claim the world's going to hell in a hand basket, so why not get drunk? Let's drink to the war."

"You don't need another drink," said Mabel. "You'll drown in your soup."

"No, I won't. I want to see Lucy fall in the pool. Let's get the show under way." He lurched into the dining room, stumbled into the table, and muttered a curse. Teddy caught Tom's eye and saw disillusionment there. She took his arm as they entered.

The room was alive with shadows cast by the garden lights reflecting off the fountains and the rippling surface of the pool. Somewhere in a darkened corner, Ellen cranked a Victrola, and soon the strains of Debussy's *L'Apres-Midi d'un faune* drifted softly into the room in all their mystic beauty. Then from the shrubbery beyond the pool, Lucy emerged from the shadows with a cautious, graceful stride, a woodland nymph veiled in a diaphanous gown. As if hypnotized by the music, she fluttered around the pool, her veil billowing and falling away and billowing again as if propelled by a playful zephyr. Her supple body responded fluidly as the music set her to whirling and leaping and alighting again with the weightlessness of a butterfly. As if in sheer delight in the gift of life, she bounded atop the polished granite wall that edged the pool and began a dizzying spin, circuiting the pond, her near-naked form reflected in the shimmering water. At last she leaped to the patio, and in the exhaustion born of ecstasy, she folded her lithe form in sinking repose. Her audience, enthralled, sat for a moment in silence while the last chords of the music faded into the night. Then Lucy arose and vanished into the woodlands from whence she had emerged.

"Stunning!" Teddy gasped.

"Beautiful!" said Janice.

"Remarkable!" said Mabel.

Amid the chorus of admiration, Gil confided that Debussy's work had been inspired by the poetry of Mallarme.

"Marmalade, hell!" wheezed John. "Did you see what I saw? The little widget has no tits!"

Teddy glanced furtively at Tom to check his reaction, but no amount of acclaim or pedantry or drunken vulgarity could disrupt his reverie. He sat mesmerized, staring into the empty courtyard as if reliving Lucy's every magical movement. There was no mistaking it, Teddy decided: Tom was infatuated with Lucy Lowenthal.

*   *   *

Lucy was the only child of a theatrical family. Her father, traumatized by the horrors of a pogrom in Czarist Russia, arrived in the United States at fifteen with little more than a talent for telling stories and a severe stammer that made them all the more hilarious. By eighteen, he had become a star in the Yiddish theater on New York's lower East Side, and at twenty, married a petit Rumanian dancer who affected a French accent. By the time their daughter was three, she had learned a few basic steps and shared the billing with her parents on the borscht circuit. A stage veteran by the time she was nine, Lucy was taken backstage by her mother to meet the fabled Isadora Duncan. At thirteen, she was enrolled in the Duncan school of modern dance at Tarrytown, New York.

With the lean body of an athlete and the grace of a ballet dancer, Lucy quickly caught the eye of Ellen Davis, dancer-turned-choreographer, who was a faculty member at the school. Although she was more than twice Lucy's age, Ellen fell madly in love with her beautiful young student and set out to make her a star. Her protégé had an almost boyish charm, the face of an angel, and a stage presence well beyond her years. Ellen soon convinced the Lowenthals that only she could properly develop their child's artistic talents and guide her along the path to fame and fortune. That path began at Chautauqua Lake and led them eventually to California. There Lucy was "discovered" at a Chautauqua tent show in Los Gatos and invited to perform at the Panama-Pacific International Exposition, then in its planning stages. The impresario who extended that invitation also introduced Ellen and Lucy to John Manchester, who offered them temporary haven at Castle Cairn while San Francisco transformed the bog at the foot of Fillmore Hill into a magical kingdom of the arts.

When Teddy learned that Lucy and Ellen also were awaiting the opening of the exposition, she hit upon a plan to lure Tom back to the city and his easel. Up early next morning, she found him seated at the pool, a sketch board in his lap. Taking shape on the drawing paper was a dancer in mid-leap.

"I see you're not entirely without inspiration," she commented.

"I've done a few sketches. Lucy asked me to design her poster for the exposition. I'm trying a few ideas."

"In that case, your work will be doubly prominent there."

"What do you mean?"

"We've been invited to exhibit the nucleus of the museum's collection—your paintings. Think of it, Tom, thousands of visitors from all over the world will see your work. We accepted, of course, if you don't object."

"Why would I object? I think it's great. But it's all old work. Surely they'll want something new, something to celebrate the exposition."

"Then you'd better come back with me," Teddy said.

He thought for a moment.

"All right, I'll come."

"There's a train tomorrow morning."

"Why wait?" he asked, his enthusiasm growing. "I'll talk Jack into driving up. We'll spend the night in San Francisco, collect my equipment in the morning and be back here tomorrow afternoon."

"Wait, Tom. That's not what I meant."

"I don't understand."

"It's obvious that you can't work here. There are too many distractions. How could you possibly get anything done with that little butterfly flitting around in the altogether?"

"I think you're jealous!" he exclaimed.

"That's ridiculous. Why should I be jealous?"

"Why, indeed, Mrs. Bachelor. There could never be anything between us. You've seen to that."

"Why do you insist on bringing that up?" she snapped.

He was shocked at her anger but noted her sadness, too.

"You're unhappy, aren't you, Teddy?" he said. "It isn't working out, is it? You can't deny it; it shows in your face. You were trying to tell me that last night, but I didn't understand then. I'm very sorry for you, I really am."

"Why should you be sorry? I know what you think. I can always buy happiness, right? With Barron's wealth, I ought to be able to buy all the happiness I'd ever want. I'll go out and buy a little every day and store it away in the attic. And when the attic is full I'll store it in Barron's bedroom. It's always empty anyway. And when the bedroom is full, I'll stack the halls with happiness, and—"

From the village of Los Gatos at the foot of the mountain, the peal of church bells interrupted her. She buried her face in her hands and wept.

"Oh, why did you marry him, Teddy?" Tom asked plaintively. "If only we had met a few months earlier, a few weeks, even a few days. My God, how different everything might have been."

"Don't talk that way," she said through her tears. "My problems aren't the issue. I didn't come here to cry on your shoulder. I came here to tell you that a great opportunity awaits you if only you'll get back to work. Can't you see that these people aren't creating anything? If they choose to let their talents dry up, so be it. But that's not going to happen to you, if I have to drag you back to San Francisco myself."

*   *   *

Teddy tried to be patient, but it was not the best of days. Gil and Janice wandered about like the moonstruck lovers they were, while Lucy spent most of her time flirting with Tom, if only to make Ellen jealous. And Mabel seemed intent on enlisting Teddy in the IWW in order to get her sent off to jail.

"Get involved," she cried. "Get yourself arrested. Bring some meaning into your life. If you got arrested for marching to protest the war, it would make the front pages of every major newspaper in America. 'Wealthy Matron Jailed in War Protest!' Think of the headlines, Teddy. You could strike a blow for peace and freedom."

"By going to jail? You can't possibly believe that."

"Of course I could, and you'd be in good company. The jails are full of Socialists and pacifists crying out against the carnage in France. Why should men go to war? Resist, I say. The IWW's got a plan to end the war. Simply refuse to go. And if you're forced to go, refuse to fight. Instead, enlist your comrades in a strike. If no one will fight, there will be no war!"

"I can't see what good I could do. President Wilson is doing everything in his power to keep us out of war. I'll support the president."

"That's the problem. You're too parochial. You've got to think on a global scale. Just imagine a battlefield revolt. Enlisted men overthrow their officers, and peace comes again to the troubled world."

"You're such an idealist, Mabel. It's not that easy."

"It might be if you'd help. Get arrested. Go to jail. Stand up in court and declare a strike for peace. Become a conduit for socialist ideology. Help spread the word."

"I just don't have your passion and courage. I'll fight for women's rights or the eight-hour day, but the issues of war and peace are much too much for me."

John came down from his workroom promptly at four, somewhat the worse for liquor, and the subject of the war and how to end it dominated the cocktail hour and went on through dinner and into the evening. The only diversion was Lucy's blatant flirtation with Tom and Ellen's growing fury. Ordinarily it would have made Teddy jealous and angry, but tonight it was a welcome relief from the conversation.

"I really must say goodnight, John," she said at last to her host. "I've got to get up early in the morning to catch my train. I've had such a good time and I want to thank you—"

"Forget it!" he said. "Enjoy yourself. I'll take you up to the city myself. I've got an appointment with my publisher."

"How very kind of you. But I really am tired. I hope you'll forgive me, but I must get some sleep."

John shrugged and poured another drink as Teddy made the rounds to bid the others adieu.

"You might consider catching a ride with us," she said pointedly to Tom as she said goodnight.

"I can't. I promised Lucy I'd have some sketches ready before I left. It'll be another day or two before I can get away. I'll be along, you can count on it."

If John wasn't the world's worst driver, he was an easy runner-up. It was after ten o'clock before they got away from Castle Cairn, and the sixty-mile drive up El Camino Real took the better part of the day with a stop for gasoline, another for lunch, and a flat tire just south of the city. The final misfortune cost them an hour as John rolled up his sleeves and met the challenge to his manhood head on. He emerged from the test fuming and covered with grease, but with his manhood intact, give or take a few bloody fingers.

But the day wasn't a total loss. As they passed a country lane that turned westward off El Camino toward the mountains, she caught sight of the road sign: Enterprise Drive. She had been here not so long ago. At the end of the drive stood the seldom-used Bachelor hacienda, a perfect place for Tom to work. Barron had promised it could be transformed into a studio apartment. Its front wall could become a huge window overlooking the orchards that covered the valley. The windows would catch the morning light. It would be quiet, isolated. Tom could work in solitude.

"He was too shy to mention it, but Tom's been invited to exhibit his work at the exposition," she said by way of venting her excitement.

"That's too bad," John replied.

"Whatever do you mean? I think it sounds like a remarkable opportunity. Thousands of people will see his paintings. Tens of thousands, perhaps."

"Hundreds of thousands, more likely," said John. "But to what end? It's more likely to spell trouble and disappointment."

"You're referring to Lucy, aren't you?"

"You're very observant."

"I'd have to be blind not to notice the way she was throwing herself at him."

"And there she'll be at the exposition in full flower."

"I prefer to think that Tom is strong enough to resist her overtures."

"I would certainly hope so, for if not, he's in for the greatest disappointment of his life."

"Whatever do you mean?"

"Lucy is merely toying with him," John said confidently. "You see, she already has a lover, a very jealous lover."

"You'd never know it, the way she acts toward Tom."

"Only to make her lover angry, dear lady, a ploy as old as time."

"But who is it? Certainly not Gilbert Nance."

"Oh, my, no! It's Ellen, of course. I thought you might have noticed. They're different, you see, daughters of Lesbos, and I dread the day Tom discovers it. I imagine it will come as a terrible shock. He isn't very sophisticated about such things, you know."

*   *   *

A cable was waiting when Teddy arrived home. Barron had returned from London aboard the *Maui Maiden* and was attending to some business in New York. Then he would be off to Chicago, something about tinned beef for the war effort. He expected to return to San Francisco, but it might be several weeks. He sent his fondest regards.

She had little time to contemplate more long weeks of loneliness. Archie Hobart saw to that. As the fantastical kingdom took shape in the landfill on the edge of the bay, the preexposition social whirl began with intensity. The Bachelor mansion was the perfect site for dinners to lavish attention on visiting dignitaries and patrons of the arts.

"We can manage it quite well," Hobart assured her, "if you'll accept this poor bachelor as a substitute host for the true Bachelor in your life."

"You're a dear, Archie. Of course I'll accept your help. What is it this weekend?"

"Two Latin-American presidents or prime ministers or junta leaders, I never know which. I'll call on their consulates to be certain they're not at war with one another. I never know who's on speaking terms with whom. I hope we can avoid any skirmishes at your dinner table."

"I don't know what I'd do without you. I only wish Tom were here. It would be so much easier to plan an evening around a guest of honor, and he's the reason we're involved in the first place."

"Have you heard from him? Is he working?"

"I haven't seen him since I left Manchester's hideaway. I don't know where he is or what he's doing."

"Don't blame yourself for not coaxing him back. You did all you could. I don't pretend to understand the artistic temperament. As I see it, Tom's done his part. If he never paints another picture, he's given impetus to a movement that will live long after him. The museum he inspired could take on a life of its own, an ever-changing, ever-vibrant record of a great city told through its native art. I can foresee a huge gallery with constantly changing exhibits, a gallery reflecting all the movements in the world of art, each characteristic of its own period, each work a valuable reflection of its moment in time. It will be the life of San Francisco and California, mirrored in its art. Not just Tom's work, not just paintings, but all artists, all mediums, now and for all time. It will be a panorama of human life as lived in one of the world's greatest metropolitan centers."

"You're quite a visionary, Archie. It's sweet of you to credit Tom, but you're the one who provided the impetus behind the museum. As for Tom . . ."

"We must face the possibility that Tom is but a flash in the pan, Teddy, a prodigy who may never fulfill his destiny. Tom's well of talent could run dry tomorrow, but no matter. His work will live on. Other artists will follow. A concept has been born, and it's alive and kicking. The exposition will be its baptism."

Tom was not a flash in the pan, Teddy thought. His greatest works were still ahead of him. She was convinced of it. He needed discipline. He needed encouragement. She would track him down and do what she could to get him back to work. When she finished shopping the next day, she had her chauffeur drive her around to *Vanna's*. Giovanna Lazarro was relieved to see her.

"Thank the Lord!" she exclaimed. "Maybe you can do something with him."

"You mean he's here?"

"He's been home all week. He won't come down from his studio. He won't eat. I send up a plate of food, and it comes back nibbled. That's what he does, he nibbles. How can a grown man live on nibbles? I don't understand. He respects you. Maybe you can help him. Go up, go up! Tell him he must eat."

Teddy found him standing at his window. Fog had hugged the city all morning, and Tom was staring into the gray mist, unmoving. If he heard Teddy enter, he didn't let on. She closed the door quietly and leaned on it lightly until the latch snapped shut. In the quiet of the studio, it resounded like a thunderclap. He whirled about and glared.

"Have you come to enjoy a good laugh?"

"I came to see how you are. I was worried about you," she said quietly. "I was hoping you'd call."

"You must have known all along what a fool I was making of myself."

"I *didn't* know. I'd never thought about things like that before. I didn't know until we were almost home. John told me. I felt very badly. He might have told you. Any one of them might have told you. Lucy herself should have told you. It was cruel of them all."

His frown melted, and he looked at her sadly with tired, reddened eyes.

"I should have known, I guess. It's not her fault. She was under no obligation to tell me anything. I was nothing to her, a trifle. It amused her to have me around."

"She knew exactly how you felt about her," Teddy said bitterly. "She just kept leading you on."

"That seems to be my fate, doesn't it?"

"Stop feeling sorry for yourself. She's not worth it. And I resent your implication that I was leading you on. I never lied to you, and I never will. I told you exactly how I felt about you and what we could do about it. You rejected me."

"What difference does it make? You're as inaccessible as she is. I always seem to be on the outside looking in."

His eyes darted back and forth, studying her face with an expression of contempt. She looked away at first, then boldly, defiantly met his gaze.

"I am not inaccessible," she said. He shook his head and was about to turn away, but she reached up gently and touched his cheek, forcing him to look at her. In his face she saw an awful desperation, a longing that pulsated so violently that she was caught up in its compelling rhythm, and it set her heart to pounding. Suddenly he clasped her in his arms and held her so very close that their hearts seemed to beat as one. She stroked his hair, and he drew back to look into her eyes. Then he kissed her, long and hard.

11

After months of bloody, inconclusive battles, the war in Europe settled into a stalemate with opposing armies dug into the earth like burrowing rodents. It was Barron's assessment that the conflict would be long and difficult. It would be a war of attrition, even if Britain did throw herself wholeheartedly into the conflict on the side of the French. He knew there was a good deal of money to be made in such a situation, and so he diverted to the Atlantic three ships from his Pacific trade routes, the *Maui Maiden,* the *North Star,* and the *Polynesian.* The demand for food and war materiel could only become more acute as the war dragged on, and he would make it his business to supply his share of it. He began by increasing the size of his New York office staff, then traveled to Chicago to arrange for meat and grain purchases before heading home. It had been three months since their honeymoon ended in a tense chill, and Teddy was shocked to find her husband ensconced in the parlor when she returned from her tryst with Tom.

"I hope I didn't startle you," Barron said, as his wife stood frozen in the doorway. "It was a strange homecoming. I had to introduce myself to our staff."

"We didn't expect you quite so soon. Your cable from Chicago indicated it might be weeks."

"Things went much more rapidly than I anticipated. I should have sent a wire ahead. I was wondering if anything had changed. When I found my room made up, I was grateful. I appreciate your consideration."

"Your room has been made up for weeks. This is your home."

"You're flushed, Teddy. Are you sure I haven't upset you?"

"Quite sure. I'll ask Millie to set another place for dinner."

"I've already taken that liberty."

"Then please excuse me while I go and freshen up. I've had a busy day—shopping."

He hadn't changed. Erect and handsome, his long blond hair neatly brushed, he looked ten years younger. Only the thin lines around his eyes gave him away, those tiny lines and the dull serenity of his countenance. That's what struck fear into her heart, that drug-induced calm. She couldn't shake from her mind the image of his ravaged face during the time of his forced drug deprivation. Nor could she forget that night of drunken fury, the night Chinaboy died in her arms. Under that unruffled facade lurked a monster, and it frightened her. She was certain that if he knew she had spent the afternoon with Tom, he would kill her. She had no doubt of it. She listened politely through dinner while he explained the situation in Europe. She was attentive as he detailed his strategy to capitalize on the war. How cold and calculating he seemed in contrast to the passionate pacifists she met at Castle Cairn. It chilled her to hear him speak dispassionately of the tens of thousands of young men who had died already, the hundreds of thousands he was sure would die before the war came to an end. As he spoke, he slipped his snuff-box from his vest and inhaled a pinch of white powder. She knew it was the cocaine that dulled his conscience to the horrors of war. As he spoke, she studied his cold, dilated eyes and realized that no shred of sympathy remained in her. To live with him in this loveless marriage would engender hatred, and she truly did not want to hate him. She had been a fool to marry him, but it was not too late to save herself. She wanted something more of life. She wanted to live without fear. She wanted a man she could love and respect. She wanted a divorce. She wanted Tom.

Several times during the evening she caught herself rehearsing a little speech. It would be matter-of-fact, devoid of sentimentality. It would be as if she were discussing a business arrangement. She could slip it in somewhere between the tonnage of tinned beef and bushels of wheat. But the perfect moment never came. The speech would have to wait. Perhaps at breakfast she would find the opportunity to say, "It's not working out. I'm not happy and I know I can't make you happy. There's no love between us, nor can there ever be. To remain together will only bring us to hate one another. I don't want that, I really don't. I just want a divorce, just that and nothing more, not a dime, not a brick, not a handful of earth. I only want my freedom." Yes, surely a businessman would look favorably upon such a plea. He had nothing to lose, after all, but a loveless marriage.

Of course he'd agree, but at breakfast, not tonight. The time is just not right.

They went up the stairs together, her anxiety growing with each step. She paused at her bedroom door and he at his. She turned and fixed him with a steady gaze, her hand on the latch. How confident he looked, how self-assured. Could he possibly misread what was in her heart? Would she have to explain to him as if to a callow youth? Suddenly he strode toward her, a knowing smile on his face, his arms outstretched. In a panic, she turned the doorknob and slipped inside, locking the door behind her. She had missed his grasp only by inches. She stepped back and watched the doorknob turn one way, then the other. Remembering the night aboard the *Maui Maiden,* she waited breathlessly for a pounding on the door. But all she heard were his footsteps receding down the stairs. The front door closed with a bang.

*   *   *

"Theodora, I can't tell you how disappointed I am," her father said sternly. He hadn't called her by that name for many years. He was using it now by way of expressing his anger. It meant the suspension of their usually warm relationship, a period of detachment that would prevail until their differences could be ironed out.

"No one is more disappointed than I," she replied. "Divorce is not a matter I enter into lightly."

"Divorce," he spat venomously. "What an ugly word."

"Only when it's draped in nineteenth-century morality, Father. In this modern age, there is no need for a woman to suffer the indignities of virtual bondage to a man she doesn't love."

"I suppose it would be impertinent to ask why, in that case, you married him in the first place."

"Indeed it would."

"Or why you've decided all of a sudden to make this shocking announcement."

"Equally impertinent."

"My God, Teddy, you can be an absolute terror. How can I ever explain this to my friends?"

"It's not your place to explain my actions. It's none of their business. It's between Barron and me. It was a matter of courtesy and my love for you that I told you first."

118

"First? You mean Barron doesn't know?"

"Not yet. Allie is serving him with the papers today."

"Allie! I can't believe it. Then *you* are initiating the suit?"

"Exactly. The law was written for all citizens, wasn't it? Why should divorce be only a man's prerogative?"

"Barron is not a man to take this lying down. You've had no discussion with him at all?"

"It won't come as a surprise. We haven't been enjoying wedded bliss for some weeks."

"It's his travel, I suppose. You must recognize that he has business to conduct. He is a man of no small consequence in the world of trade. I spoke to him only yesterday about his travels—London, Paris, Berlin. He gave no hint of trouble between you two."

"If you must know, we haven't lived together as man and wife since we left Maui. I am suing to sever a legal relationship, nothing more. There are no great emotional ties between us. There apparently never have been."

"Then perhaps a quiet annulment . . ."

"It's too late for that."

"You mean—"

"I mean only what I said. I am suing Barron for divorce on grounds of incompatibility. If worse comes to worst, I'm prepared to amend my suit to bring more serious charges. I hope that won't be necessary."

"Teddy, I don't understand. I just don't understand."

"You don't have to understand. Just accept it. Wait, that must be Allie at the door now."

Flushed and wide-eyed, Allie let herself in virtually on the run. She clattered down the hall and burst into the parlor.

"Good heavens, Allie! What did he do, set the dogs on you?"

"No," she gasped. "He was very gracious, very polite. I couldn't believe it. He read a bit of the suit, laid it on his desk and simply said, 'No.' "

"No?"

"Just 'No.' When I tried to explain that you were suing for divorce, he said, 'Never in a million years. My lawyers will be in touch.' That was it. Oh, I just knew it!"

"I'm glad someone's showing some presence of mind," said Charles. "Barron will put a stop to this foolishness."

119

"They'll eat me alive!" Allie exclaimed. "This is my very first case. I'm no match for Barron's lawyers."

Teddy was furious. Fraud, adultery, drugs, murder—the charges flashed like lighting bolts through her mind. If this matter couldn't be handled discreetly, she was prepared to bring it all into the open, and convention be damned. The ring of the telephone cooled her passions a little. The three looked from one to the other, waiting.

"It's for you, ma'am," said Millie. "Mr. Bachelor on the line."

Nervously, Teddy went into the hall to take the receiver.

"I've read the suit, Teddy," Barron said. "I'm sorry, of course. But emotions aside, let's leave this to our attorneys. There's no reason we can't be friends until this matter is settled, one way or the other."

"What do you mean by that?" she asked suspiciously.

"I mean that I see no reason we can't approach this like sophisticated adults with no unseemly recriminations, no scenes. There is so much good we can still accomplish together—the museum, for example, and the exposition. Why jeopardize the things we both hold dear? Surely we can settle our personal differences without publicity. Look at it this way, we have an opportunity to establish a new norm in civilized behavior between men and women. I'm sure you can appreciate what that would mean to the cause of women's rights."

He's running scared, she thought. He's afraid I'll charge into court and accused him of murdering Chinaboy, of committing adultery with Maiyu, of importing and indulging in the use of illegal drugs. But the logic of his argument appealed to her.

"It isn't my intention to be vicious, vindictive, or greedy," she said. "It's a relatively simple legal matter, and I'm prepared to let the law run its course."

"Then let's give the gossips something positive to talk about. Have lunch with me tomorrow. I want to know everything about the museum and the exposition. I've only had a moment to talk with Archie Hobart and your father. I'd much rather talk to you. As for next Saturday night, why can't we go as a group to the opening? And I really mean all of us—you and I, Archie, your father, and of course young Quinn. You have been in touch with Quinn, haven't you?"

"Why, yes," she said hesitantly.

"Good, then I'll send a car around tomorrow at noon. We'll have lunch at the Palace Court and make our plans for opening night of the exposition. Agreed?"

"Yes, yes, I'll be ready."

*　　*　　*

The fair was intended to mark the completion of the Panama Canal that was to revolutionize world trade. More than that, it celebrated the resurrection of San Francisco. Destroyed by earthquake and fire only nine years before, it now had returned to the ranks of the world's truly great cities. Rebuilt, refurbished and reenergized, it was time to flick on its lights, throw open its doors and invite the world to a re-birthday party.

A marshland on the shores of San Francisco Bay had been filled and graded, and upon this reclaimed site had been built a magical city dedicated to the glorification of the arts, the celebration of industrial progress, and the entertainment of the people of the city and the world. Its magnificent buildings, soaring archways, and broad avenues were to lure more than eighteen million visitors during the year 1915. On opening night, it seemed as if those millions had all come at once. The board of directors of the San Francisco Museum of Contemporary Art dined at the Bachelor residence, then headed for the exposition grounds crowded in Barron's new Phaeton Criterion. They debarked at the Scott Street entrance and made straightaway for the Tower of Jewels that loomed in spectacular luminescence before them. From there they traversed the Avenue of Palms to the Palace of Fine Arts, whose rotunda, bathed in light, seemed to float upon a lagoon.

Dr. Hobart, with Tom at his side, led the way, while Teddy with her husband and father, each at her side, followed a few paces behind. Hobart, resplendent in top hat and tails, regaled the young artist with the wonders that lay before them, while Tom, dressed in Byronic splendor in a billowing white silk shirt with a crimson scarf, nodded appreciatively, saying little.

"He's a handsome young man, isn't he?" Barron observed.

"Quinn? He is indeed," Charles agreed. "He'll set the ladies' hearts to throbbing, mark my words."

"Yes, I do believe he will, don't you agree, my dear?"

121

"Yes, yes, of course," Teddy said impatiently. "But isn't the lighting spectacular? Where is it coming from?"

"From flood lights hidden among the foliage in the gardens. There, you see," said Charles, pointing with his walking stick. "It's amazing, light as an art form. Just look at the interplay of shadows there among the colonnades."

In the gallery, which curved behind the great rotunda, they found many alcoves, each devoted to artistic displays. Prominent among them was the space allotted to their new museum. Tom was genuinely thrilled to see his paintings exhibited in such a grand manner, and suffered willingly through nearly two hours of introductions and greetings from the throngs that came to view his work. But at last he'd had enough.

"I've got to get out of here," he whispered to Teddy. "I'll just slip away. Tell them I've gone out to take in the sights and that I'll be back. Tell them, Teddy, will you?"

"Wait, I'll go with you. If I shake another hand, my own will fall off. Barron!"

"Yes, my dear. I was just admitting to Professor Halstrom that I know little or nothing about art, but I can surely appreciate the enthusiasm we've seen here tonight. Professor, this is my wife, Teddy. I believe you met our guest of honor, Tom Quinn."

"Indeed I have. What a great pleasure to make your acquaintance, Mrs. Bachelor. This is a fine thing you've done here, all of you. You're to be commended."

"Thank you so much. Tom and I were planning to go for an ice cream. Why don't we all walk down to the other end of the fairgrounds?"

"Ah! Off to the amusement area," said Charles. "I understand there's a beer garden there too. I could do with something cool."

"I'm sorry, Charles," said Barron, "but I just told Professor Halstrom we'd accompany him to the university's display. He promised not to talk about endowments, and I promised we'd meet the trustees. Let the young people go for ice cream. We can join them later."

"At the main gate at ten?" Teddy suggested.

"Perfect. We'll be there," said Barron.

"Bring along an ice cream for me," Charles whispered plaintively.

The young lovers strolled back down the Avenue of Palms and stopped at the Tower of Jewels to rest under the tall archways. Before them a fountain in the form of a young girl spilled water into a pool, rippling the surface that glistened in the subdued light. Tom seemed far away.

"She reminds me of Lucy," Teddy said.

"What?"

"The statue, the small, boyish figure. The artist might have used Lucy for his model. I think it's quite a striking resemblance."

"But with Lucy only the heart was made of stone."

"Still so bitter? Why can't you put it behind you?"

"I don't mean to be bitter. It wasn't her fault that I insisted on making a fool of myself. I'll get over it in time."

"I thought I was helping you to forget."

He took her hand and clasped it in both of his.

"You are a great help. It's not as if I were trying to forget a lost love. It was never anything like that. I was running away by running after her. It was easy enough to play the fool under those circumstances."

"Then you're nursing wounded pride, not a broken heart."

"My heart was already broken," he said. "It broke the night I watched your ship sail away. It seems like only yesterday."

"We've got a lifetime of tomorrows, Tom. Let's look ahead, not back."

"Will we ever be free to marry?"

"You know we will. It's only a matter of time. The law will run its course."

"Then he's agreed to a divorce?"

"Not in so many words. He doesn't like to discuss it. He finds it unpleasant. His attorneys are handling everything."

"It can't come too soon."

"In the meantime, we have each other."

"But you still live under his roof, while we live in secrecy, sneaking around just to see one another. It's not what I'd call a perfect romance."

"I think it's exciting."

"Teddy, will you ever change? What if he discovered us?"

"He won't. He's too absorbed in business affairs to even think about me. Do you think he'd send us off alone like this if he suspected anything?"

"He's no fool, Teddy."

"He's agreed to let you use the hacienda. He's allowed the remodeling of the barn. It'll make a perfect studio. It's isolated. It has magnificent views. It's quiet."

"And lonely," Tom added.

"Only as lonely as you wish it to be."

"And when the divorce becomes final, what then?"

"He probably will let you stay on. Why wouldn't he?"

"Even after I marry his ex-wife? I think not. He may not be a jealous man, Teddy, but he's not crazy either."

"Then let's not look so far ahead. It may be months before anything is resolved, and we can't live on what might be. Let's live for the moment. And at the moment I'd like an ice cream."

He laughed, squeezed her hand, and kissed her on the cheek.

"Tom! There are people all around."

"I don't care. I love you, and I just don't care who knows it."

She laughed gaily and dragged him to his feet, and they walked briskly arm in arm to the Joy Zone amusement area. Near the entrance they paused to examine a huge model of the Panama Canal, then made their way down the street, searching for an ice cream parlor. On their way, they ran into a large crowd outside a small theater. Like a pair of curious schoolchildren, they pushed closer to see what the excitement was all about. The advertisement at the door explained it.

"I see your work is on display at this end of the fairgrounds, too," said Teddy.

Inside a glass case was Tom's poster, enlarged several times. It showed a beautiful young girl, wrapped in a diaphanous veil, startled at the sight of a fawn that had paused for a drink at the edge of a woodland pool. Beneath the poster was a message: "Come See Lovely Lucille Perform the Dance of the Woodland Nymph." And in smaller print, "Hear the music of Debussy's 'Afternoon of the Fawn.' Admission twenty-five cents. Adults Only."

"Well!" Teddy exclaimed. "That's the way to pack them in."

*　　*　　*

Several times during the exposition, Tom went secretly to the theater to watch Lucy dance, ever fascinated by her grace and beauty, incredulous that one so desirable could be so utterly unattainable. In time he forgot the humiliation he had suffered at her hands. Alone there in the darkness among strangers, he came to grips with his infatuation. He convinced himself that he was no different from any other man in the audience, for they were all infatuated with her, at least for the brief moments when she held them all enthralled, and titillated. No doubt about it, Lucy's shockingly revealing costume had as much to do with her popularity as did her talent.

Within days, complaints were filed by self-appointed guardians of public morality. Lucy's scanty attire was scandalous, they cried, and her dance erotic and suggestive, obscene, some said. No impressario could have afforded the kind of publicity such charges generated. The little theater in the Joy Zone—which also featured an animal act, a trio of singing sisters, a ragtime pianist, a juggler, and four gymnasts from Hungary known as the Barzo Brothers—was always filled to capacity. But it was Lucy the crowds came to see. The police came to see her, too. At first blush, law enforcement officials found her dance to be an offense to common decency and tried to shut down the act. But when the theater concessionaire appealed to exposition officials, the story exploded onto the front pages of the city's newspapers.

"*Is It Art or Immorality?*" the headlines screamed.

Let the experts decide, officialdom proclaimed. And thus it was that Dr. Archibald Hobart was named to head a special investigative commission charged with viewing Lucy's performance and issuing a report. The members of that distinguished panel, including the famous author John Manchester, visiting composer Camille Saint-Saens, and Edwin Henry Lemare of London, the world's greatest living organist, trekked to the little theater in the Joy Zone, accompanied by the chief of police and an army of newspaper reporters and photographers. The verdict: It was not licentiousness, it was art.

Soon Lucy Lowenthal was whisked from the three-a-day routine of the Joy Zone, where she was paid fifteen dollars a week, to the more respectable surroundings of the Festival Hall, where she danced under the name of Lucille Lowe to the accompaniment of the official exposition orchestra. There she performed only on Friday and Saturday nights before a black-tie audience and the arty set for a reputed one hundred dollars a performance. Soon, movie director D. W.

Griffith came to see her performance. He offered her five hundred dollars a week to appear in a moving picture show.

Tom and Teddy watched it all from the sidelines, bemused by the transformation of this strange but intriguing child from vaudeville brat to international film star. Lucy no longer spoke even to her admirers, but veiled herself in mystic silence and allowed her business manager, Ellen Davis, to do her talking for her. Sought after by crowned prince and capitalist parvenu alike, Lucy's romances became the stuff of tabloids. One wealthy young suitor was restrained from flinging himself into San Francisco Bay the day she finally sailed away aboard a ferry outfitted to resemble Cleopatra's royal barge. It was reported that the Southern Pacific Railway car in which she rode to certain glory into the hills of Hollywood was trimmed in gold and carpeted with mink, the gift of a smitten mogul. While a tremulous public awaited the first glimpse of Lucy's image flickering across the silver screen, it could relish the tales of her outlandish existence in the daily press. Her escapades proved more entertaining than the news of the everyday world, dominated as it was by the European war.

12

"Barbarous!" Barron exclaimed.

"What is?" Teddy asked.

"The Germans and their damned U-boats. They've sunk the *Lusitania*. Imagine! Slithering about under the sea, murdering innocent men, women, and children. Even my own ships are being threatened—and they fly the American flag! What the devil is the world coming to?"

"It sounds pretty dangerous. Of course you'll call your ships home."

"I will not!" he fumed. "I have two ships in the North Atlantic at this very moment, and the *Maui Maiden* is being loaded and prepared to sail within the week. The civilized world must not give in to the barbarians. We must stand up to them, teach them a lesson they'll never forget."

It was not the dinner conversation Teddy anticipated. She had reserved a small corner table in order to discuss their tangled legal affairs away from public scrutiny. But Barron arrived preoccupied, incensed over the *Lusitania* tragedy, and now his outburst focused all eyes on them.

"There's really nothing to be done, is there," Teddy observed calmly. "Best stand aside and let that awful war run its course. There's nothing to be gained by putting the lives of innocent people at risk."

"You're only mouthing the slogans of your pacifist friends. Where's your sense of fair play? Where's your compassion? Tens of thousands of men in the trenches depend upon our ships to provide them with sustenance. We can't just leave them to the mercy of the Huns."

"I hadn't realized what a great humanitarian you were," she said with sarcasm. "Nevertheless, President Wilson says we must remain above the fray, that neutrality is our best course. Would you defy your own president?"

"You're damned right I would. I didn't vote for him."

There was no reasoning with him. He was tired from overwork and travel. But he would only be in town a few days and she had agreed to this meeting out of sheer desperation. His battery of attorneys had poor Allie tied in legal knots, and the divorce was going nowhere. She had come to plead with him, if necessary, to expedite the proceedings. It should be so easy. She wanted nothing but her freedom.

"It's not that simple," he explained patiently. "The mere fact of our marriage complicates things more than you realize, particularly in regard to Bachelor Enterprises. It's not enough to say you want nothing. What's to prevent you from coming back in a year, in ten years, and demanding half of everything? No, everything must be carefully worked out, every exigency covered. All that takes time. Teddy, I have made no demands upon you. I've tried to grant you every wish with this single exception. You must be patient."

"But I have my own life to live!" she said with exasperation. "You have your business affairs to keep you occupied. I have nothing. You're free to come and go as you choose, while I—"

He leaned across the table, his eyes suddenly cold and hard. The intensity of his gaze struck fear in her heart. She could not go on. After his icy stare had dissolved into a wicked smile, he continued her sentence for her: ". . . while I am forced to slink about in back alleyways to meet secretly with my lover. Isn't that what you mean to say? Don't speak to me of affairs, my lovely bride. You seem to keep quite busy with yours. I'm surprised you haven't moved Tom Quinn into our home."

Teddy reddened in fury and embarrassment and pushed her chair away from the table, but he grabbed her wrist and held her fast.

"One thing your bumbling lawyer overlooked, my pet. When you come to plead for compassion under the law, you should come with clean hands. I don't imagine you've bothered to confide in Allie Wheatley, but I assure you my attorneys are well aware of your less than clandestine affair with young Mr. Quinn. They want me to file a countersuit documenting your infidelities as insurance against any future legal demands you might entertain. I have managed to stave them off for now, content with a stalemate. You may get the divorce you so fervently desire, but only when I think you should have it and not a moment before. In the meantime, I think you should be grateful for my forbearance. Against the advice of my attorneys I have been exceedingly generous with you and your lover. I have given you more freedom than you deserve. Do as you like with the hacienda. Make a fool of yourself over Quinn, if you insist. It only strengthens my legal position. But don't presume to lecture me on my freedom. Don't presume to burden me with your hypocrisy. I'll have none of it, do you hear?"

"Yes, I hear," she spat, jerking her wrist from his grasp. "And if you raise your voice any louder, so will everyone else in the restaurant hear. Don't bother getting up. I'll ask the maitre d' to call a cab."

She cast a defiant glance around the room and then stormed into the foyer. In moments, she was huddled low in the seat of a cab, muttering in her fury.

"Where to, Miss?"

Where to indeed, she wondered. Home to the cold, empty halls of the Bachelor mansion? Home to her father who would never understand and surely disapprove? Was there really any choice?

"*Vanna's*," she said quietly. "Green Street at Columbus."

*   *   *

With a regular income from his museum commission, Tom was able to expand his studio into the rear apartment above the Lazarros' living quarters. It was small, barely enough room for his bed, a table and chairs, and a highboy. A kitchen and a small bath occupied nearly a third of the space. The expansion cleared his front studio for a growing collection of paintings and sketches. His rear apartment had a balcony that overlooked Giovanna's lush herb garden and the tightly packed flats that marched like a stairway up the steep slopes of Telegraph Hill. The sun peeked through the kitchen window only briefly each morning, and on this day, Tom waited patiently for the moment it burst into the room to lay a blanket of light across Teddy's naked body. As the sun crept higher, he worked hurriedly with charcoal on his large drawing board, capturing her graceful lines. At the same time, he fixed in his memory the rapidly shifting colors the light produced. When the rays reached Teddy's eyes, she yawned and stretched and ran her fingers through her hair that fell in golden profusion over her shoulders and lightly brushed her breasts. As she blinked awake she saw Tom across the room and reached for the sheets.

129

"Don't move!" he commanded. "Not yet."

She dropped the sheet and lay as still as she could, unashamed, studying him curiously as his eyes darted quickly from her body to the sketch board and back again as he translated his vision through his fingertips and onto the paper. At last, as the sun rose higher and the room fell into shadow, he laid the board aside and stared at her as if mesmerized by her beauty. Brazenly she allowed his eyes to devour her, the glimmer of a smile playing at the corner of her mouth. Impelled by desire, he arose and came to her and took her gently into his arms, so gently that the touch of him aroused her. Even his kiss was soft and sensuous, his tongue delicately tracing the outline of her lips. She clasped his head in her hands and pressed his face against her breasts where he could feel the throb of her heartbeat. In a moment, his hands began an urgent exploration that set her body to heaving rhythmically. A low moan escaped her lips as his hands grasped her hips and their bodies became synchronized in the timeless tempo of love.

Later, when he had kissed away the tears of ecstasy that coursed her cheeks, they lay exhausted, his head upon her breast. She picked idly at his black ringlets, her mind far away. Through the open window they could hear the grating of a shovel as Vanna worked her garden. Occasionally she threw forth greetings in her rich dialect, and her words clattered down the alley like a handful of stones, striking everything in their path and eliciting a chorus of response.

"You'd think they were fighting," Tom said.

"What are they saying?" she asked.

"Good morning, nice day, how's the family . . . but you'd never know it. It sounds like a challenge followed by a stream of insults. What a strange language, like raucous music."

"You like it here, don't you," she said.

"It's comfortable. I feel at home here."

"Would you ever leave? Would you come away with me?"

"I would go anywhere with you. Where would we go?"

"Just a few miles away, down the peninsula to an old hacienda. I'm having the barn remodeled. It will be your studio apartment. It's larger than this, and it overlooks the valley. The morning sun would linger there and not vanish so quickly. I've always imagined you living and working there."

"Barron would appreciate that, I'm sure," he said.

"I don't worry about that. He's never there anyway. But I do worry about taking you away from North Beach. You find so much beauty here. I fear you'll grow bored with the country."

He got up and wrapped himself in a robe and went to the bathroom and turned on the faucet in the tub. When he looked out again, Teddy was still lying naked on the bed.

"If you're there, I'll never want for beauty," he said. She blushed and pulled up the sheet.

"I thought you preferred slimmer women," she teased.

He came over to her and kissed her forehead.

"You are like *Earth,*" he said.

"Earth?"

"The Aitken sculpture in the Court of the Universe at the fair. It reminds me of you, full-bodied, voluptuous."

"You think I'm fat!"

"No. Allie is fat. You are voluptuous."

"At least there's some meat on my bones. Not like that Lucy." She hesitated, fearing her words might hurt him. But he only smiled. "I don't mean to be unkind."

"You could never be unkind. Besides, I'm through mooning over Lucy Lowenthal."

"Lucille Lowe, if you please," she corrected him.

"Whatever name she goes by now. I don't miss her. I have so much more now."

"There! You see. You think I'm fat. I'm going home this instant."

"Wrapped in a sheet? I'm afraid you wouldn't get far. Here, the tub is full. Better have a warm bath while I fix some breakfast."

She got up, trailing the sheet behind her, and kissed him on the check as she passed. He caught her hand, as if to prolong the moment, and noticed that the ring was gone from her finger. She smiled, slipped his grasp, and closed the bathroom door.

*　　*　　*

Following their confrontation in the restaurant, Barron ceased to be a problem. He took an apartment in New York, where most of his business now was conducted, and his visits to California became less frequent. When he did come, he went directly to his suite at the Palace Hotel. They spoke by telephone. They met for lunch, sometimes for dinner. He did not attempt to interfere in any way with Teddy's life. If he was waiting for her affair with Tom to run its course, he never said so. He spoke only of business, of legal matters, of the war. He made no personal demands upon her, and when he left, he telephoned to say good-bye.

Tom agreed not to make an issue of the divorce. It troubled him deeply at first, but Teddy convinced him that she had done all she could to expedite matters, that the legal machinery had been set in motion, and if Barron's attorneys, for whatever reasons, insisted on proceeding slowly and carefully, there was nothing she could do about it. It was nothing personal, she assured him. It had to do with the immense fortune represented by Bachelor Enterprises. It had nothing to do with jealousy. It had nothing to do with their love affair. So long as Barron didn't make an issue of it, they were free to do whatever they wished, except marry. That would come in due time, Teddy promised. Tom accepted her explanation. Whether he believed it or not, she didn't know. So long as it didn't disturb their happiness, she didn't care. She was happy, really happy, for the first time in her life.

While work was under way at the hacienda, she even indulged her passion for political discussion and briefly reestablished her salon in the mansion on the cliffs above the Golden Gate. Mabel was a regular guest. John appeared whenever he was in town. On one occasion he brought along Gil and Janice. Gil had finished a small book of poems and was seeking a publisher. Allie fell madly in love with the gangly poet, much to his lover's chagrin. Allie thrived on the intellectual stimulation provided by Teddy's coterie of friends—socialists, labor leaders, suffragettes, writers and agitators, philosophers and artists. With the issues of war and peace looming large, there was never a dull Saturday night at the Bachelor mansion.

Tom, still under John's spell, sided with labor and the Socialists in the beginning. The winds of political change that were sweeping the country brought new inspiration to the young artist. He took his sketch board to the piers and spent hours capturing the heroic labors of the longshoremen, the vitality of the street-corner orators who railed against the war, the grim foreboding of the labor hall, the cheerless taverns, and the cluttered streets that were the working man's milieu. He found himself growing ever more sympathetic to their plight, particularly to the dilemma the war posed for honest men of good faith. The paintings he produced during this period were bold, muscular works that managed to glorify the contributions of the laboring class while, at the same time, powerfully illustrating its plight. In their stark realism, the paintings, with subtle yet compelling force, cried out for economic justice.

There was no lack of patriotic fervor among the ranks of labor, but there was great division. Patriotism to one working man meant keeping out of the war and spending American money and energy to improve the lot of workers at home. To another it meant honoring the nation's commitment to the defense of democracy, siding with the Allies against the Germans invaders of peaceful European countries. The presidential campaign only served to inflame passions on both sides. Woodrow Wilson's supporters campaigned on the slogan, "He kept us out of war!" And although Wilson was to carry the day, the war's violence still would take a domestic toll.

Tom came early for a curbside seat from which to view the Preparedness Day parade along Market Street. Many of his friends from the wharves marched proudly under labor's banner to urge that the nation not shrink from its moral duty to enter the war. Tom might disagree with their outlook, but he understood what was in their hearts. It never occurred to him that others—anarchists, some said later; antiunionists, said others—were not so charitable.

No one knew where it came from, but suddenly amid the martial music and the pounding of thousands of feet upon the pavement, an explosion ripped the fabric of patriotism and left nine persons dead in the street. Tom was close enough to the blast that it lifted him off the ground and flung him into the street amid the shards of a plate glass window. He arose bloody and shaken, without either his sketch pad or his senses. As he wandered around the fringes of the frantic crowd, he heard someone call out, "That's him! That's the artist from the wharf!" Confused, he wiped away blood that ran into his eyes and staggered away from the dead and the wounded that lay about him in the street. Scuffling broke out in the crowd as some tried to render aid to the fallen, while others sought to collar someone, anyone, to blame for the terrible deed. He tried to make sense of the chaos around him, but the only thing certain was that someone had recognized him and he had to get away before he fell victim to the panic. With great effort, he struggled to the perimeter of the mob and leaned against a building, trying to gather his wits. When his head cleared, he made quickly for Grant Avenue and headed through Chinatown toward North Beach. Teddy found him next day in his studio, still bloody and barely conscious.

"Tom! What in God's name happened? I've got to get you to a doctor."

"No, no, I can't go out. They may be looking for me. Just help me clean up. I'll be all right."

"Why would they be looking for you? You couldn't have had anything to do with the bombing, could you?"

"No, of course not. But someone recognized me. They called out. I don't know who or why. It was absolute chaos. Suddenly police were everywhere. I was afraid they might come after me. I got away as fast as I could. I've never seen anything like it."

"Can you sit up? Here, let me wash your face. There's a bad cut on your forehead," she said, dabbing at his face with a wet towel.

"Glass," he explained. "I was sitting on a curb, sketching the parade. A bomb went off somewhere behind me. It lifted me up and threw me into the street. There was broken glass everywhere, bodies lying about. Everybody was grabbing everyone else. It was insane. Have they arrested anyone yet? Who's getting the blame? Some poor working stiff, I'll bet. And to think it might have been me."

"This settles it," she said. "We're going to get you out of the city. It's just not safe here anymore. The renovation is finished. We'll move down there, away from this madness. You'll be safe. You can paint to your heart's content."

"But I'll miss the city. It's my home. It's all I know."

"It's only forty miles away! We can come back whenever you wish. Come with me, Tom please."

"Ironic, isn't it? Working people fighting each other, killing each other. It's the war, I guess. It's made everyone crazy. Unite for peace? We can't even unite for a parade. The world's turned upside down."

"We can find peace, Tom. We can find it together."

In a matter of days, even before Tom's wound had healed, the police announced arrests in the bombing. One suspect was a labor organizer, Thomas J. Mooney; the other was a young worker, Mooney's friend Warren K. Billings. The labor movement leaped to their defense, while the press cried, "Fiends!" and "Anarchists!" At a party to bid farewell to Tom and Teddy, Charles Cullen assured all that justice would be done.

"It's the American way," he proclaimed. "We are a nation of laws. Our system of justice is inferior to none. If these men are innocent, trust in a jury of their peers to set them free."

"Trust in our corrupt courts to hang 'em in the name of capitalism," John countered, downing another glass of the Lazarros' red. "This isn't a criminal case with a presumption of innocence. It's another battle in the war between the classes. To accuse is to convict. They'll lock them up and throw away the key. It'll be a lesson to other working men—defy the power structure and you will be crushed."

"The workers must unite!" cried Mabel. "It's their only hope, What choice do they have, die in the street or die in the trenches?"

"You can't reduce every social problem to class warfare," Charles argued. "There are legitimate conflicts between management and labor that can be resolved at the bargaining table. But this case goes well beyond a labor dispute. It's an issue of war or peace, an issue that cannot be resolved by terrorism. Stand by your country. Trust the president. Let wiser heads prevail."

"Wiser heads indeed," John scoffed. "Greed and power are the issues here. I deal with those very concepts in my latest book."

"It'll be good to report that you're writing again," said Dr. Hobart.

"I never ceased," John said. "I won't discuss a work in progress. But I'm sure you critics will have a grand time with it. For now, let's drink a toast to our wounded warrior as he leaves the field of battle. Here's to Tom Quinn, may he forever remain a soldier in the war against social injustice."

*   *   *

In its isolation, the hacienda was an island of peace and quiet. Tom went to work immediately with renewed enthusiasm, concentrating first on completing his first nude, based on the sketch he made of Teddy lying in the sunlight amid a jumble of sheets. He captured not only the graceful flow of her body but also the earthy simplicity of his North Beach apartment against an atmosphere suffused with the eerie light of the early morning sun as it spilled through his window. Teddy was embarrassed by the intimacy of the work, the air of total abandon projected by its subject.

"Do I really look like that in the morning?"

"You are beautiful in the morning. That's why I painted you."

"You could call it *A Bad Night at the Bordello*."

"Nonsense, it was a fleeting moment of extraordinary beauty. I'll never forget how you looked that morning. I'll never again be able to look at you without being stirred to the very depths of my soul."

"But this must be ours, Tom, only ours. Promise me that. No one else must ever see it."

"I promise, if it really embarrasses you. I'll bring it back to North Beach and hide it away where no one else will ever find it. I'll try to make the others more discreet."

"You mean you plan to do others?"

"As long as you'll stay to pose for me. I want to do hundreds of them. I want to capture every facet of your being, every nuance of your beauty. I'll make your portrait a celebration of our love, because no man could ever love a woman so much, no other woman could be so beautiful."

"It's wonderful of you to say so, Tom. But next time, let me brush my hair first," she said with a smile.

That was enough to inspire his next portrait of her as she sat nude in front of her bedroom mirror at the hacienda drawing a brush through her long, golden hair. Others followed. On overcast days, he posed her on a stool in the broad window to catch every glimmer of available light, while she watched nervously over her shoulder lest someone drive suddenly up the road and see her there. When the days were warm and sunny, he led her into a nearby meadow where she sat in a field of grass as monarch butterflies fluttered around her. Often they'd climb to the summit, seeking a likely setting among the redwoods. There she might recline upon a bed of moss as sunlight, through the woodland canopy, dappled her velvet skin with shadow. Or she might wade in a shimmering pool among the lily pads or play provocatively beneath a small waterfall, her usually bright hair matted darkly against her wet and sparkling skin. Beyond the trees in the high granite reaches of the mountains, she stretched languorously across a smooth boulder in full sunlight, a Diana fatigued by the hunt. Even at night he painted her. Once he posed her with her chin resting upon her knees while she stared in childlike wonder at the flames in the fireplace, again as she stood goddess-like in the window, gazing longingly at the full moon, the folds of the drapery only half concealing her classic figure.

Teddy tried to look upon the portraits with detachment, appraising them with a studied objectivity. She tried not to see Teddy Bachelor, but an anonymous model. It was the artistry that was important, she convinced herself. But in her heart, she knew that more than art, these paintings were the private diary of their life together, each portrait celebrated with a feast of love. Tom could not look upon her hour after hour without being overwhelmed by desire. And she responded in kind, seeing in each painting the depth of his love for her. In their walks through the woods, they delighted in counting the places where they had made love, while at the same time searching out sites as a backdrop for a new work.

"That would be beautiful in the early evening, don't you think?" she'd ask. "We must come here tomorrow at sunset." And before she could look around, he had taken her in his arms, and sunset had become now, art had become life, and life had become love. They were living an idyll such as few had ever experienced, and with all their hearts, they believed it would never end, that no storm ever could lay waste their Eden.

13

He laid the syringe on the table and picked up the cord. The sea was rough, the swells running thirty feet. The *Maui Maiden* groaned and rocked and suddenly pitched sharply. The syringe of milky liquid began to roll. He snatched it up in panic as it neared the edge of the table. The voyage had been long and lonely. He could ill afford to lose his one true companion. He studied the wicked needle, then nestled the device safely into its case and turned up his sleeve. As he prepared to knot the cord about his upper arm, he paused to look through the large plate glass window at the vast expanse of tormented sea. The storms of March had obliterated the horizon and turned the world into an endless swirl of grays and blacks, relieved only by the white froth of the relentless waves. He closed his eyes and tried to think of something, anything, to steady his hand and take his mind off his unholy craving.

He imagined her across from him, her face smooth and perfect in the candlelight, her brown eyes sparkling with youth and vigor. Idly he rolled the syringe between his fingers. His back stiffened as a surge of desire coursed through his body, and he smiled a bitter smile. "Ah, my mistress," he murmured. "Ever faithful, never fickle. Time for our daily tryst. What would I have done without you all these empty years?" He broke into a cold sweat at the very thought of wielding the needle himself. *It would be so much easier if Maiyu were here,* he thought. As his desire grew more intense, he pumped his fist eagerly, watching the veins swell to the surface. He probed his pallid skin until he found an unscarred point of entry and gently eased the needle into the vein. A tiny spot of blood appeared as he thumbed the plunger down, released it, and collapsed back into his chair. He heard the syringe clatter to the deck and felt the liquid burst into his blood and race toward his brain. In his sudden ecstasy, it seemed to him that the opiate transformed itself into a frothy white trail splitting the dark sea and speeding toward the *Maui Maiden*.

Then the ship shuddered violently, and he clung to the table. It was as if the heroin had just then reached his head and exploded there with the brilliance of a thousand suns.

The force of the impact sent his paraphernalia flying about the salon—the syringe, the spoon, the cord, the fat packet of powder, and the black leather case. He leaped in panic, trying to retrieve the drug, but a second explosion slammed him against the bulkhead. Stunned, he fell to the deck and felt it rise beneath him then slip slowly away at a dizzying angle. He was sliding now, sliding across the deck along with the chairs, plants, lamps, everything that wasn't bolted down. As he slid past the door, he grasped frantically for it. Just then another horrendous blast rent the ship and sent him sprawling out into the storm. The deck was awash, the bow rising precipitously, and the stern sinking quickly beneath the waves. He was dimly aware of panicky seamen scrambling for their lives. As he clung to the rail to keep from being washed into the roiling seas, he suddenly found himself staring into the face of Doom, a face with fiery, desperate eyes and flared nostrils. A heavily muscled arm reached out to seize him, and a deep voice boomed, "Give me your hand."

"No!" he cried in terror, "No! Leave me alone!" Then he lost his grip on the rail and skidded along the wave-swept deck to what would have been certain death. But the black hand of Doom caught his flailing arms and slammed him into a lifeboat just as that fragile craft snapped its lines and plunged headlong into the maw of a huge wave.

"Hang on!" cried Doom as the sea first swallowed their tiny boat, then spat it out again upon the crest of the next monstrous wave. Wind-whipped and lashed by the icy waters, he hung on for his life as the boat pitched wildly into the heart of the storm. Blinded by the frigid torrents that swept over them, he felt Doom's powerful grip and screamed out for deliverance.

"Pull, man, pull!" Doom shouted, dragging him over the gunwales and into the boat again. "Grab my leg, and hang on!"

He lay in the bottom of the boat, clinging to the huge leg, as to the trunk of a tree, while Doom strained at the oars, gradually gaining mastery of the craft in defiance of the elements. Feeling the great muscles flex and then grow slack again, he realized this was no apparition. This was a giant of a man, a crewman he had never seen before. Looking up, he saw the reflected light from a flaming sea flickering over a face rigid with determination.

In a moment of eerie calm, his rescuer spoke softly.

"There she goes." Barron watched as his *Maui Maiden* vanished beneath the sea, leaving behind her a fiery slick and a column of oily smoke. As if appeased by this offering, the seas subsided, tossing gently with debris. The black man pulled on the oars.

"Take the tiller. We'll look for survivors," he ordered.

"I owe you my life," Barron gasped. "What happened?"

"Torpedoes," said the oarsman. "The second one blew the boilers."

They made their way through the slick, peering into the smoke and flame. But they saw no sign of life. Then came a muffled roar, and the sea surged, lifting the lifeboat on a billowing cloud of foam before settling again on the surface.

"What the hell . . . ?"

"The cargo," Barron said, his teeth chattering. "Munitions in the hold."

"Listen," said the oarsman. "What's that?"

In the distance beyond the smoke and haze, they could hear men cheering above the rumble of engines.

"U-boat," said Barron. "She's surfaced."

"Come about!" shouted the black man. "She's our only chance." He strained at the oars while Barron, at the tiller, guided them toward the sound. In a moment, he could discern the submarine's ghostly outline.

"Ahoy, there!" he shouted. "This way! Help."

His savior worked furiously at the oars, eyes alive with hope, while Barron called out again at the cluster of men dimly outlined on the deck of the U-boat.

"Ahoy, there! Throw us line!"

Instead of a lifeline, a red tongue of flame licked toward them, followed by the clatter of a machine gun. Back and forth the flame roved, raking the boat with bullets. The oarsman emitted a loud gasp as the projectiles ripped into his back and burst out his chest. His huge body stiffened, then pitched forward onto Barron's knees, propelled by the violent impact. His massive arms reached up and clutched Barron's shoulders, dragging him down below the gunwales. He lay there in the dead man's grasp as bullets thudded into the boat and slapped the water all around. Then the gun fell silent and Barron could hear laughter and shouting only yards away. Soon the U-boat's hatch clanged shut and its engines roared to life. As it slipped beneath the waves, the lifeboat clattered against the metal hull. Then all was silent.

*   *   *

From his studio window in what had once been the hayloft in the barn, Tom could see the car coming up the road while it was still more than a mile away. It was moving at breakneck speed, trailing a cloud of dust. He laid aside his pallet and went to the window overlooking the driveway, calling out to Teddy, who was working in the primrose patch at the front door.

"There's someone coming up in a big hurry."

She looked down the drive, but a row of eucalyptus blocked her view. She wiped the sweat from her brow with the hem of her apron.

"I wonder who it can be," she said. She went to the pump and washed the dirt from her hands while Tom covered his easel and went down to join her in the drive. As the car came into sight, Teddy recognized it.

"It's John," she said.

"Who's that in the backseat?"

"Gil and Janice—my God, I hope his brakes work."

They both stepped up into the entryway for protection. At a distance of only thirty feet, John slammed on the brakes and skidded to a dusty halt only inches from the front steps. Gil and Janice were white with fear.

"Howdy, neighbors!" John called out. "We've come to bring you to the wake. Drop everything and climb aboard. We're off to the city, and you must join us."

He stumbled as he climbed out from behind the steering wheel, and as Tom lunged forward to catch him, the brake slipped and the car began to roll backward.

"Set the brake!" Teddy screamed.

Gil plunged over the seat, his long legs flailing, and groped frantically for the brake handle. Before he could find it, the car slammed into a fence, knocking one section askew. Janice fainted dead away.

"Nobody can do anything right anymore," John muttered, hanging limply on Tom's shoulder. "At least I know how to set a brake."

"Then you damn well should have set it," Tom said. "They might have been killed."

"Horse pucky!" John cried. "It's the safest car on the road. What have you got to drink? This wake seems to be drying up."

"I . . . I don't know," Teddy stammered. "I think there's some brandy in the parlor. And there's some wine in the cellar. Why don't you come in and make yourself comfortable while I tend to Janice."

She wet her apron at the pump and held it to Janice's brow as she lay sprawled in the open backseat. Gil untangled himself from the steering column and looked anxiously after his unconscious fiancée.

"She'll be all right," Teddy assured him, "if she doesn't die of fright. Why did you let him drive when he's drunk?"

"You can't tell him anything when he's this way," Gil said. "He's been hell on wheels all week, and I'm not referring to his driving."

"What's the trouble?"

"It's his book. It's gotten absolutely terrible reviews. He thinks the whole world is laughing at him. He's vowed never to write another word. John Manchester the author is dead, he says. He's holding his own wake. He hasn't stopped drinking all week."

"What are they saying about his book?"

"Awful things, cruel things. One referred to him as 'the late John Manchester.' When he read that, he literally died inside. Everything is death now. Every day he picks out a new site at Castle Cairn where he wants us to bury him. We don't know what to do. He seems bent on destroying himself."

"Where was he going?"

"To the city for one last fling. He vowed to beat up every critic in town. We were lucky to get him to turn in here. You must help us."

"Of course I will," Teddy said. "There's a roadster in the barn. I'll drive, and we'll all go together. But not today, it's too late. Stay for dinner, and we'll go up in the morning when John's sober."

Janice was coming around, moaning and fluttering her eyelashes.

"Help her to sit upright, Gil, and I'll bring a glass of water."

"That man is insane," Janice sputtered. "He nearly killed us all. He did kill a chicken, maybe several chickens. He drove right into a flock of them. Feathers were flying all over. It was horrible!"

"Yes, but everything is all right now. Help her inside, Gil."

John was lying unconscious on the couch in front of the fireplace.

"I gave him a glass of brandy," Tom said. "He drained it and collapsed."

"Will he be all right?"

"Sure, until he wakes up."

"It's a shame," said Gil. "His book wasn't that bad. It was a painful outpouring of his emotions, but it was powerful, dramatic."

"What was it about?" Teddy asked.

"The decline of an artist, the story of a man destroyed by alcohol, told as only he could tell it. It was a devastating self-portrait, a dreadful look deep into his own soul. I can't imagine the courage it took to reveal such things, and with such great strength and beauty. They had no right to treat him that way. They had the audacity to compare the sick and aging author with the vigorous young writer of twenty years ago. It's not fair. It's cruel. He has never done work like this before and probably never will again. But they're all too stupid to see it."

"What did Dr. Hobart say about it?" Teddy asked.

"He was the least cruel. He recognized it for what it was, a confession, an intellectual mea culpa, and he praised John for his courage in writing it. But even he picked up on the theme of death. The title of his review was 'Requiem.' We did all we could, but John's been a raving maniac, especially after Mabel gave up on him. He was failing the revolution, she said. He was giving socialism a bad name by not blaming the capitalist conspiracy for his antihero's downfall. Then like a good little socialist, she walked out on him!"

"It was the last straw," Janice nodded. "After Mabel left, he became incorrigible. We held our breath every day until he passed out, which he did quite punctuality just before dinner, unfortunately."

"Yes," Gil added ruefully. "His cook wouldn't fix a bite for us to eat. Seems John owed her several months pay. She left in a huff. And Janice, for all her beauty and charm, can't boil water without burning it. We'd be happy to stay for dinner, by the way."

"Last night was the worst," Janice added. "He collapsed into the pond, and Gil had to wade in to fetch him out. He might have drowned."

"Maybe that's what he intended," Tom said. "I can understand how he felt. John never blamed anyone for his drinking but himself and what he called the demons of his creativity. I can imagine the pain he went through, the need to escape, and death the only way out."

"Tom, that's an awful thing to say," said Teddy. "Death and demons! You Irishmen are all alike—mystics. I think you were all born under a cloud of doom."

*　　*　　*

In the months of their idyll, Tom and Teddy were oblivious to the changes taking place in the world. They grew out of touch with the issues that had fired the atmosphere of Teddy's Saturday soirees, so absorbed were they in their own happiness. But the public mood had changed dramatically during the months at the hacienda. The president, who had been reelected on a platform of peace, now was being cheered for leading the nation into war. The cry was for blood, German blood, and the U-boat attacks were the cause of it. Many of the pacifists of 1916 were flocking to the colors in 1917. The passing outrage over the sinking of the *Lusitania* had given way to fervent militarism as more and more vessels went to the bottom of the Atlantic. The lovers' return to San Francisco was to be a rude awakening.

They arrived with John slumped sullenly between Tom and Gil in the backseat and went first to a private hospital, where Teddy arranged admittance for her distraught and ailing friend. On her guarantee of payment, the doctors agreed to attend to him as best they could.

"We can sober him up," they warned her, "but there's no cure for what ails him. He'll get drunk again the moment we release him. However, if you're willing to pay . . . "

Teddy insisted, wrote out a check as a retainer and left orders that she be notified if John needed anything. Then she brought her friends home with her and waited, for what, she wasn't sure. Certainly it wasn't for the telephone call that came from Allie.

"Thank God you're home at last," she cried. "I've been calling you for two days."

"We just got in," said Teddy. "What in the world is it? Has the divorce come through at last?"

144

"I've got to see you, Teddy. I'll be right out. Wait for me."

"I have guests, Allie. Are you at your office? I could come downtown."

"Is Tom with you?"

"Yes, and Gil and Janice."

"Leave them, and meet me right away at your father's."

"Why all the mystery, Allie?"

"I'll tell you when I see you. I'll be there in a half an hour."

Senora Garcia let Teddy in and led her to the parlor, where her father sat with his head in his hands. Allie rose to greet him with a warm embrace. There were tears in her eyes.

"What is it?" Teddy demanded. "What's going on?"

"Teddy, we tried to reach you . . . " her father began, his voice trailing off.

"Your father got a cable," Allie said. "The *Maui Maiden* was lost at sea."

"And Barron, is he all right?"

"He was aboard. They found no survivors."

"It was one of those dastardly U-boats," Charles said bitterly. "I had to tell the board the details this morning, such as we know them. There was no radio signal. It all happened very quickly. A passing freighter came upon an oil slick. Among the debris was a life jacket from the *Maui Maiden.*"

Stunned, Teddy sank into a chair. Barron dead? The thought brought a range of conflicting sensations, despair and relief, and an overpowering sense of guilt. The riot of emotions set her heart to pounding. Her father came to her and put his hand on her shoulder. At his touch, she gasped for air and burst into tears.

"There, there, my dear. We tried to come up with something, but we knew there was no easy way to break this dreadful news. Straightforward, it's the way Barron would have wanted it."

Teddy leaned forward, her elbows on her knees, and pressed her hands to her face. Her tears flooded between her fingers as she sobbed.

"Oh, God, I've been so selfish," she cried. "I'm no sorry, Father, so very, very sorry."

"You must be strong, my dear," he said. "All that is past and is best forgotten. What's important now is to honor his name. None of us can relive the past, as much as we might like to. Look to future, as your mother would say. Look to the future."

But there was no consoling her and no bracing her. She was devastated.

"Leave us alone for a few minutes, will you Mr. Cullen? I'd like a word alone with her," Allie said.

"Yes, of course. I'll be in the library. The board's asked me to look after things until we get official word on . . . well, I'll be in the library."

"Allie, I've never in my life felt so terrible. It's as if it were all my fault somehow," Teddy said, her eyes reddened by crying.

"I understand, dear, but you had nothing to do with it. Barron knew the danger he faced."

"Still, he makes everything I did, everything I said, seem so tawdry. Just when it seemed to be so—"

"If it will make you feel any better, I've withdrawn your divorce petition," Allie said. "The proceedings are halted. I thought it would make things less complicated for you. Your father said Bachelor Enterprises asked him to work closely with attorneys for the estate on your behalf."

"I don't want anything, Allie. I want them to understand that. I realize I may have obligations, but I want nothing for myself. I deserve nothing."

"Don't be so hard on yourself. I understand how you must feel, but none of this is your fault. If Barron hadn't blocked you at every turn, the divorce might have been final by now."

"But all I can think of is the heartless way I treated him, the awful things I said. And now he's dead, Allie, dead! And I —"

"And you have to get on with your life. If he's left you anything, give it to charity if it'll make you feel any better. But don't make any hasty decisions."

"What do you mean?"

"For one thing, there's been no confirmation of Barron's death. Then there's the matter of Chinaboy."

*   *   *

When Teddy returned home, she found that Tom had gone to North Beach to visit the Lazarros and store several paintings he brought with him from the hacienda. He telephoned later.

146

"I've heard the news," he said. "What can I say?"

"There's no need to say anything. How did you find out?"

"I stopped by the museum. Dr. Hobart told me."

"Father must have called him."

There was a long silence, and she began to dread the inevitable.

"Things should be different now, different for us," Tom said.

"I suppose they will."

"I mean, we'll be free to get married."

"Free?" she asked. "What makes you think I'm free, that I'll ever be free?"

Her sharp tone made him wince, and his reply was angry.

"What do you want, a respectable mourning period? Aren't you being a bit hypocritical?"

"Stop it, Tom! I don't want to talk about it. Not now."

"Teddy, I don't understand. You hated the man."

"I didn't hate him. I failed him. He needed help and I failed him. There's so much I might have done for him if only I had tried a little harder. And now he's gone."

"All you failed to do was charge him with murder. Have you thought of that?"

"He was sick, Tom, very sick, and I did little or nothing for him. I did more for John today than I did for my own husband. I never took Barron for professional help."

"You said nothing could be done. You said you did all that was possible. And now it's over. You said you wanted your freedom and now you are free."

"I wonder if I shall ever be free," she said bitterly.

"Well, maybe you'll give me a call, when and if you are."

"Wait, Tom! Don't hang up, please. Believe me when I say that I love you. And trust me. There's so much I have to sort out. Just give me time."

"That's one thing I seem to have plenty of, isn't it?"

"I do love you, Tom—"

But the line was dead.

*　　*　　*

Albert Prudhomme finished the milking, and as he left the barn, he noticed debris being tossed by the surf. It wasn't the first time the detritus of war had crashed toward the rocky shore. With a quick and eager stride he went to investigate.

"What's mine is mine," he puffed as he descended the trail to the beach. "I'm owed as much."

He'd sent his son to Flanders, after all, and worked the farm alone for more than two years. Why not a little booty for his trouble? Although he had yet to salvage anything of value, he was a born optimist, and today his hopes ran high. But on closer inspection, he could see that his haul would be marginal at best.

"A whale of a blast," he muttered, picking through the bobbing debris. And then, at a point where the fog met the surf and curled into an opaque curtain, he saw a dark shadow. It appeared only briefly, then receded behind the pall. He cocked his head, as if by doing so he could see through the impenetrable mists, and studied the spot where the object had vanished. Sure enough, in a moment it reappeared.

"My word," he exclaimed, "it's a dinghy. Ahoy there, this way! You're safely beyond the rocks. Come this way."

When there was no response, he realized that his first salvage of any value lay afloat not thirty meters off shore, its oars flopping free in their locks. He hurried up the beach to the cove, where his own boat was stashed just above the high tide line. In a moment, it was breasting the gentle surf in search of the ghostly craft. When he spotted it again in the swirling fog, it lifted shoreward on the crest of a wave and appeared to be empty. "Bigger than mine," he chuckled in greedy glee, "and just waiting to be plucked from the sea."

He drew as close as he could and snatched up a loose line to take the derelict in tow. He put his back into the job, rowing shoreward with all the strength he could muster. When it was safely beached, he leaped out and peered into his prize.

"Good gracious!" he exclaimed. "She's not empty after all. Damned if there aren't two of 'em. Well, it means an evening's dig, but bless me, they'll not be eaten by the fishes."

As he studied the bloody tangle of arms and legs, the smaller of the two bodies suddenly shuddered violently, causing Albert to spring back in terror.

"Lord preserve us! It's possessed of the devil. Take 'im, Beezlebub. Take 'im, he's yours! I was only havin' a look."

14

Dr. Archibald Hobart was not used to being awakened in the middle of the night, certainly not by a telephone call from the police. His mistake, he knew, was in ever having one of the blasted contraptions installed in his flat. If this was the twentieth century, he'd had his fill of it. The telephone was a bearer of bad tidings, nothing more. As his carriage rattled through the wet city streets toward the Hall of Justice, he marveled at the glitter and bustle of Chinatown. It was going on two in the morning, and Jackson Square looked like Market Street at high noon. What in the world do they find to do at this time of night? he thought as his driver threaded his way carefully through the crowd. They are the inheritors of an ancient civilization, he told himself, cast upon the shores of a strange new land and seemingly intent on recreating the old world here in the new, even if it means working twenty-four hours a day. Much more civilized, he yawned, to be at home in a warm bed at two in the morning, if it weren't for that damned telephone.

"Drunk and disorderly," the desk sergeant began. "Creating a public nuisance, resisting arrest—"

"Yes, yes," Hobart said impatiently. "What I meant was, what are the charges in dollars and cents? We don't want two of the city's most illustrious artists languishing in this wretched place, now do we?"

"Fifty dollars," said an oily little man who had sidled up beside him. "Each."

"And who, might I ask, are you?"

"I, sir, am a bail bondsman," the man explained, touching a finger to his cap. "You pay me a tenth of your friends' bond, and I guarantee their appearance in court."

"And if they don't appear?"

"Then you lose your money."

"That's the long and the short of it," said the desk sergeant. "The drunk tank is filled to overflowing, so let's get on with it."

They had to carry Tom to the carriage. He had passed out over an hour ago, John explained with a grin. "Can't hold his liquor," he confided, "but he's feisty, I'll give him that."

"So it would seem," said Hobart. "I suppose I should feel grateful that he didn't murder anyone."

"He was doing battle with the war mongers," John explained. "A very noble fight."

"No doubt you put him up to it. I can't help but feel you're taking advantage of him."

"Me!" the author sniffed. "And I suppose you're not. You and your wealthy friends flatter his ego and pay him off with peanuts when he might well be making a fortune on his own. But that's not taking advantage of poor Tom Quinn, now, is it?"

"You wouldn't understand our arrangement, Manchester, so I won't try to explain. But I don't think the European war should be fought in the bars of San Francisco and certainly not by the likes of you."

"It's a terrible responsibility," John said, clapping his brawny arm around Hobart's shoulder, "but somebody's got to do it. We're sending the flower of American manhood to the trenches to die for the greater glory of the munitions industry, and I say it's got to stop!"

"You're beginning to sound like a pacifist tract," said Hobart, struggling to get free. "In all fairness, I shall attribute it to strong drink, but you sound remarkably like your most recent novel. Now please don't hang all over me. You're filthy, and you smell of cheap liquor."

"Maybe it's death you smell," John said dramatically. "You who have already published my obituary shouldn't mind rubbing elbows with the corpse. Look upon me as a ghost come to haunt the empty passageways of your mind, perhaps a spector sent to punish you for your arrogance."

At the Bachelor mansion, Hobart lingered only long enough to unload his charges.

"I didn't know what else to do with them, Teddy," he said apologetically. "I know it's a terrible intrusion, but I can't possibly take them in, and I can't ride about all night waiting for them to sober up. At least you have room for them."

His coachman helped Hobart carry Tom to the divan in the parlor, while John helped himself to a brandy and watched the proceedings from behind a silly grin.

"Whatever am I to do with them?" Teddy asked helplessly. "They're like a couple of naughty little boys in need of a good spanking."

"I am not good in a crisis, Teddy, nor can I cope with tragedy. If you wish, I'll call the police and surrender them again to their fates," said Hobart.

"No, I'll handle this," she said wearily. "It will keep my mind off my own troubles."

"Your bravery puts me to shame, but I really must be going. With any luck we'll wake up in the morning and find it was all a bad dream." He hurried by John and went quickly out the front door. The sound of hooves echoed through the darkness.

"The man's from another century," John said disparagingly.

"You owe him your freedom," Teddy said testily as she fussed with Tom's collar. "Look at him. He's been beaten."

"He gave as good as he got," John pronounced grandly. "I've never known an Irishman to let you down in a pinch. Why, if the kaiser himself had been in the bar, the war would be over now. I swear, we were the only ones left standing."

"How did you get out of the hospital? They promised to call me."

"And I'm sure they would, if they only knew."

"Tom got you out?"

"He came to call and suggested we step out for a drink."

"And you got him drunk and involved him in a brawl."

"We didn't start it. They did!" John protested. "We were trying to persuade his friends not to load the ammunition ships. Don't lend your sweat to the war effort, we urged them. Strike! Use the laboring man's ultimate weapon against those who aim to profit from war. Assert your humanity. It's not your war, it's theirs."

"Damn you, John Manchester!" Teddy flared. "It's my war now, too. I have lost my husband."

Stunned into momentary sobriety, John stood speechless.

"Tom must have told me," he managed at last. "But we had been drinking—"

"The Germans sank his ship," she said. She had knelt to wipe Tom's brow and now laid her head upon his breast and wept.

"I'm sorry," John said. "I thought you . . . I thought he—"

151

"Our marriage was a failure," Teddy sobbed, "but that doesn't mean I wished him dead."

"No, of course not. Let me get you a brandy."

"I don't want a drink. I want to be left alone."

John poured himself another glass and walked to the window, muttering:

"So, Barron Bachelor rests beneath the waves. There's poetic justice for you. I still recall the stories of old Billie Bachelor of Gold Rush fame. Legend has it he went mad and spent his last days as a prisoner aboard one of his own ships. And now they share the icy depths together, old Billie and his boy."

"Stop it! Stop it!" Teddy cried. "Go away and leave me alone."

Gil, his skinny legs protruding from an ill-fitting robe, appeared in the doorway. Awakened from a deep sleep, his hair nevertheless was strangely neat, slicked back and glistening as if newly oiled and brushed.

"What are you doing here, John?" he asked, befuddled.

"I came to console a widow in her grief," he lied. "But I fear I've stirred feelings of remorse. Guilt, they say, finds haven in a grieving heart. Or is it grief that finds haven in a guilty heart? It's too late now to care. Come, Gil, let us retire to the billiard room to discuss the dark dreams that inhabit the night, before the sun intrudes upon us with life's painful realities."

*　　*　　*

Albert Prudhomme's family had lived for centuries on Saint Martin's in the Scilly Isles. He was not a man given to ruminating on the past, but if family lore were to be believed, Albert owed his isolated existence to an ancestor of dubious reputation who was put ashore by fellow pirates to guard a hoard of gold from the local inhabitants. The ship then sailed away never to return, while the abandoned pirate Prudhomme and the legend of gold remained to flourish over the years.

Albert was a farmer and a fisherman by season, a widower who had reared two children and now lived alone, having sent a son to the war and a daughter to London to marry a shopkeeper. He had always known that to exist he must cast his nets and till his soil and milk his cow. But that didn't stop him from poking idly through the caves and coves of Saint Martin's for pirate gold or combing the beach for whatever treasure the sea might toss his way. He never did find gold, and now the beach had presented him with only a problem, a severely afflicted human being.

"He must have been a handful," said the vicar.

"I had to subdue him" said Albert. "He was delirious."

"Has he eaten?"

"He'll take nothing."

"How long have you had him?"

"Since Thursday."

"You sent for help?"

"I knew you'd be by today. I waited."

"The man is emaciated and near death."

"I don't know how long he was adrift. He was in high fever and raving when I got him here. He was incoherent and desperate. He looked as if he'd been through hell. His boat was splintered, riddled with bullets. His companion, a huge African, was dead."

"Where is the corpse?"

"I wrapped it in an old sail and tucked it away in the cove. The body was rank and fragile. Their lifeboat's beached nearby."

The vicar, an old man with a furrowed brow and an impatient manner, examined the victim who stared at him with unseeing eyes. Gently he examined the patient, checking his pulse, prodding him here and there, noting his hands with particular interest.

"Not your common seaman," he said.

"How is that so?" asked Albert.

"His hands are as soft as a woman's. I'd be surprised if he'd ever done a lick of work in his life. His lungs are congested, and he's running a high fever, but his delirium is most likely the result of narcotic deprivation. Note the scars along his lower arm. The man is a drug addict."

"Then he'll surely die," Albert surmised. "We have no drugs here."

"He may die, but not any time soon, unless he dies of constriction," said the vicar, loosening the ropes that Albert had used to secure him to the bed.

"He was a danger," Albert explained. "He was weak, but wild. Can we get him to Land's End and a hospital?"

"No. The hospitals are overflowing with war wounded. You'll have to take care of him yourself. It's your Christian duty."

"But—"

"Interesting, isn't it, Albert, that your castaway should wash up on Saint Martin's. God must have special work for him, to put him in the hands of the patron saint of drunkards. Look to it now, for your hands are doing His work. You'd best prepare him some broth. And pray with him, Albert. Pray to Saint Martin, to whom he owes his life. It can't hurt, and it might help. Good day, Albert."

*　　*　　*

Local newspapers were quick to discover John Manchester's name in the police booking records and by morning had traced him to the Bachelor mansion. Reporters telephoned, demanding interviews. Some even tried to force their way in through the door, shouting absurd questions in an effort to elicit a response and generally taking cruel advantage of the author's debilitated condition.

Tom went unrecognized and was able to escape such harassment. Teddy spirited him out a side door and drove him to his apartment, begging him to stay out of sight until the furor subsided.

"It's all my fault," Tom said. "I was a fool to get him drinking again. I wanted to drown my own sorrows, and I took him down with me."

"He would have gone down without your help," she said. "The doctors warned me he would. You mustn't blame yourself, or me."

"Why would I blame you?"

"Because I've been such a disappointment to you. But you've got to understand how I feel. While Barron was alive, it was easy to blame him for standing in the way of our happiness. I was determined to grasp it anyway, no matter what anyone might say or think. I loved you that much. He knew it, and so did you. But he's dead now, and I can see things more clearly. I know I share the blame for what happened to our marriage. I failed him as much as he failed me. I failed as a wife, as a friend, and as a human being. And because of my failure, he still stands between us."

"You mustn't let a ghost deny you happiness. He has no claim on you now."

"And I have no claim to happiness, not yet. I do love you, Tom. Please believe me when I tell you that. But we must wait. This is not our time, though I know our time will come. We must be patient. I've got to put this all behind me. It will take time."

"A week? A month? A year? Teddy, I love you. Even a moment's wait is an eternity."

"Our happiness is worth waiting for, isn't it?"

"Of course. But you can't go on blaming yourself for Barron's death. You had nothing to do with it. You owe him nothing. All he gave you was three years of misery."

"Don't talk that way, Tom. I don't blame myself for his death; I blame myself for not doing more while he was alive. I'm trying very hard to reconcile myself to all that has happened. But it will take time. Please give me time."

He kissed her lightly on the cheek, then looked into her eyes and saw a real sorrow there. In all the hours he had spent gazing at her over the years, he had never seen such sorrow. Her youthful spark was gone. Its light had faded.

"I always seem to be giving you time," he said softly. "I never knew how valuable time was until I began giving it away. I hope we don't regret squandering it as we do."

"Things will get better, my darling. It just takes—"

"I know," he said. "Time."

*　　*　　*

Once the sinking of the *Maui Maiden* was officially confirmed, it was Teddy's turn in the dreaded limelight. Reporters sought her out with the same persistence with which they had dogged John only a few weeks before. Teddy bore their impertinence stoically. The role of grieving widow was difficult, no matter how sincerely played, and for Teddy, it also served to reinforce her feelings of guilt. She accepted the intrusions into her private life as a form of punishment—the endless interviews, the callous questions, the mob scene at Barron's memorial service, with press photographers' flash trays exploding in her face, reporters pushing and shoving and shouting inane questions at her. She wondered ruefully how they would treat her if her affair with Tom came to light.

Her houseguests stood by her during those trying days, but as time passed Gil and Janice grew impatient with her moodiness. When John lost the will to carry on his battle with the critics, he decided to escape to Castle Cairn to begin work on a new book.

"It will be the greatest antiwar story ever told," he vowed. "If it doesn't bring this war to an end, it certainly will assure that it indeed will be the war to end all wars. Keep the faith, my friends. We'll meet again in less troubled times."

Before he left, he generously penned a forward to the manuscript of Gil's first book of poems, confident that the gesture would assure its publication. But even the naïve poets knew they could not cash in on a name so drastically devalued. They decided instead to travel to New York to an art colony off Washington Square. Desperate to be alone, Teddy gladly paid for their train fare, and she and Tom saw them off on their journey to Greenwich Village. After a tearful farewell, Gil hurried aboard, and Janice pressed an envelope into Teddy's hand, kissed her cheek, and fled after him, never looking back. The envelope contained a sonnet she had dedicated to Teddy. It was meant to console her, but even its title, "Sorrow," made her weep.

Tom saw Teddy home, subdued by the tearful farewells. She wanted to have him driven home, but he insisted on walking to North Beach.

"I want to clear my head," he said. "I'm fed up with sadness and gloom. I want to get back to work. There's joy in working. When you're feeling better, I'd like to go back to the hacienda. We were happy there, and I know we can be happy again."

"I believe that with all my heart," she said. "But right now I need to be alone to sort things out. At the moment I'm not fit company for anyone. But I will be, given—"

"I know," he said. "Given time."

*   *   *

The vicar of Saint Martin's called regularly, bringing not only spiritual comfort but also news from the outside world. His attitude toward Albert's houseguest was clinical and compassionate, because, as he explained modestly, "I came late to the cloth and had seen a bit of life before it."

He had indeed. A medical person with the British Army, Peter Pearson had been with the 24th Regiment under Lord Chelmsford during the invasion of Zululand in 1879. As a member of the eighty-man garrison at Rorke's Drift, besieged by four thousand Zulu warriors, he had performed emergency surgery even as the savages set fire to his rude hospital. When a dozen of them burst in upon him, he laid aside his scalpel, snatched up a Martini-Henry rifle and, with bayonet, dispatched three of the invaders while burning roof timbers crashed down around him. His gallantry won him the Victoria Cross and left him with a keen appreciation for life and an aroused sense of the Infinite that led him eventually into the seminary. The Church of England assigned the overaged clergyman to these lonely isles off the Cornwall coast on the theory that a younger man might have difficulty adjusting to the serenity of the place. Not so with Vicar Pearson. He had had his fill of war and death and destruction. Saint Martin's suited him quite nicely.

He cured the shipwrecked sailor's pneumonia by encasing his chest in mustard plaster and steaming it with hot towels. When the fever broke and the shakes returned, the vicar counseled him and prayed over him and told him in the language of the drill field that the only cure for what ailed him was the power of the Almighty coupled with his own free will. And, by God, he had better begin exercising that free will, the vicar said, or he'd fling his arse back into the sea.

For the first time in his life, circumstances were propitious for the castaway to come to grips with his addiction. He was isolated among strong but kindly and understanding men who asked nothing of him but that he help himself. From the monogram on the snuffbox they found in his pocket, he adopted the name Bill Baker. When times were most difficult, when perspiration burst from his brow and the veins in his body ached for lack of narcotics, he would squeeze the box between his hands in a mighty effort of resistance. When Albert came upon him in such straits, he assumed his guest was praying and tiptoed away.

Bill Baker spent the warm spring days working in the fields or giving a hand with the fishnets. Over a period of weeks, color returned to his cheeks, the violent shuddering was reduced to a nervous twitching. For the first time in his adult life, he felt strong enough to resist his craving for heroin. It helped, of course, to know that there was none to be had on the island. But the castaway also drew strength from Albert, who was always at his side with words of encouragement. By the end of summer, the sweat on his brow was more likely to be due to strenuous labor than to drug deprivation. By September, when the bloody battle of the Somme had dragged on inconclusively for months, Vicar Pearson came around for his weekly visit and brought with him an opportunity for Bill Baker to help repay Albert for his unselfishness.

"Sit down, Albert," said the vicar. "I know how difficult it is for you to get in to church this time of year, so I've come to bring you the blessing of the Lord."

"Why do I have to sit down for the blessing of the Lord?" Albert asked, pouring the vicar a cup of tea.

"Because I said so, Albert," the vicar replied sternly. Albert took his own good time nevertheless, and when he finished pouring, he pulled up a chair and raised his eyebrows in a look of defiant innocence. "That's better," the vicar continued, "for I've come to tell you that your son's name is in the lists."

Albert set erect, as if the old soldier's steady gaze had stiffened his spine. At last tears welled in his eyes and he began to sag. Bill Baker came quickly to his side and braced him with an arm around his shoulder. Albert drew a deep breath and let it out with a gasp that had the cutting edge of a cry.

"How did it happen?" he asked.

"You know they don't tell us that. He was killed in action, that's all I know—your boy and I don't know how many hundreds of others," the vicar said bitterly. "They don't fight wars now the way they ought to be fought, I can tell you that much."

"No, I don't suppose they do," Albert said vacantly. He took Bill Baker's hand and gently removed it from his shoulder, smiling sadly at him as he arose from his chair. "You'll have to excuse me," he said, walking to the window and turning his back on them to look out over the fields. Another gasp escaped his lips as if he had seen a boy running in the sunlight and had tried to call out to him to watch his step.

"I'll pray with you, if you like," the vicar said quietly.

Albert's shoulders shook spasmodically.

"Let me handle this," said Bill Baker. "He needs to be alone. When he feels like talking, I'll be here for him."

"That's very decent of you, Bill," whispered the vicar. "I'm not much good at this sort of thing, too gruff by half, I suppose. It's by God's grace that you're here. May His peace be with you both."

15

Tom spent the summer of 1917 on the streets of San Francisco, completing his series of paintings of men and women on the job. The strongest and best of his work was done at the wharves, where longshoremen were busy twenty-four hours a day loading ships bound for England and France. When he wasn't sketching or painting, he tried to advance the cause of peace by urging resistance to the war and to conscription.

"Turn your labors to building a better world, not to destroying it," he preached. And more than once his soapbox orations landed him in jail, where Teddy or her father or Dr. Hobart would find him and bail him out. His efforts were to no avail. Hysteria was sweeping the country, fueled in part by celebrities from the nascent movie industry who appeared at public rallies to extol the cause of freedom and to sell Liberty Bonds. At one such rally in Union Square, Tom joined in an attempt to organize a counter-demonstration and was clubbed into submission by policemen for his trouble. While he lay stunned on the street, the crowds were whipped into a frenzy of patriotism by the likes of Douglas Fairbanks, Charlie Chaplin, Mary Pickford, and Hollywood's new love goddess, the beautiful and mysterious Lucille Lowe.

"Did you have a chance to speak to her?" Teddy asked as she drove him home from the Hall of Justice.

"Are you joking? She would have had me lynched."

Vanna prepared them an elegant feast, and while they ate, Tony regaled them with his own brand of patriotism. He hailed the British-American advance on the Marne, while, at the same time, insisting that it would be his native Italy that would make the crucial difference in the outcome of the war.

"Once the Italians defeat Austria, the war will be over," he assured them. "Germany will collapse, and General Pershing and his doughboys will be home by Christmas."

"I hope you're right, my friend," Tom said. "But I think the war will be long and bloody. Look at the western front. We sacrifice thousands of lives for a few yards of mud, then lose it the next day in a counterattack that claims thousands more. The war is a crime against humanity."

"Keep your voice down," Teddy whispered, "or you'll get into another fight and land in jail again."

After dinner, Tom brought Teddy up to his studio to show her his latest work. They were powerful statements on the dignity of labor and the fierce pride of working people.

"We've got to get these to the museum, Tom. They're marvelous. You've never done better work. You've poured your heart and soul into them."

"No, my heart and soul are in the paintings we left behind at the hacienda. Let's go back, Teddy. You're free now. There's nothing to keep us apart."

He took her into his arms, and she rested her head on his breast, and it was good to feel his strength again. Was it his touch that stirred her so? Was hers but a physical reaction to the strong and handsome young artist? Or was her love inspired by something deeper, the basic decency of the man and her pride in his talent? Whatever it was, she knew for certain that she was in love with him. At his side she could learn to forget the past. Together they could grasp the happiness that had escaped them. Her weeks of suffering and self-reproach were over. Whatever her sins or her shortcomings, she had paid for them by enduring the torment of the damned. Her debt was paid. The slate was clean. She could live comfortably at last with the memory of the husband she had failed. Tom felt her shudder and held her at arms' length. Her eyes were brimming with tears.

"It's time, Teddy," he said. "Our time has come."

"Yes, yes, Tom," she cried as a great surge of relief came over her. For the first time in many long, cold weeks she felt the warm glow of happiness.

*   *   *

They didn't send Geoffrey Prudhomme's body home from France, just a small packet of his personal effects. There was his wallet, a pocket watch with its hands forever stuck at five minutes before two, a tiny Book of Common Prayer, and three letters, two from his father and one the lad himself had begun but never finished.

"I wonder . . . " Albert mused aloud.

"Wonder what?" asked Bill Baker.

"I wonder if it was five minutes before two in the morning or five minutes before two in the afternoon."

"It doesn't make much difference now, does it?" said Bill, a touch of bitterness in his voice. If he had learned one thing about his friend, it was that he responded positively to a practical approach to life. Don't offer sympathy to Albert Prudhomme, thank you, and hold your tears. Saint Martin islanders were an independent lot, and Albert was a man to stand on his own two feet. "Well," said Bill, "are we going to be about our business or are we not?"

"Of course we are," said Albert, laying the watch aside. "Here's a shovel for you, and I'll take the garden fork. The tide's scoured Dead Man's Cove, and the cave's as clean now as it ever will be. This may be our lucky day."

It was their routine on Sunday afternoon to go digging in the sandy-bottomed caves along the rocky coast, seeking the treasure Albert was certain had been buried there two hundred years earlier. It was a harmless pastime and good exercise, now that the fall harvest was in. But it was Bill's last outing. It was time to move on.

"I can't sit out the war on this island," he told his friend. "There's still a lot I could do."

"For a man your age, I'd say you'd done your share already, whatever it was you did aboard that ship."

"It's been good of you not to ask."

"You owe me no explanations," said Albert. "But I admit I have been curious at times. Why is it, I asked myself, that an able-bodied seaman gets blisters just looking at a shovel?"

"I've done my share of hard work," Bill said, "but in recent years I shipped as purser. A man doesn't get calluses pushing a pen."

"Aye, and you're anxious to get back to it. Is that what you're saying? Well, I can take you to Hugh Town whenever you wish, and you can catch the steamer to Penzance. I'll stand you to the fare myself. I guess you've earned that much."

"I don't ask any favors, Albert."

"And I give you none. You'll get your due and not a quid more. Wait, what's this? I've hit something. Let's have a look."

It was only a length of rusty anchor chain, but its discovery renewed Albert's faith in the existence of hidden gold. He'd come again at minus tide, he swore, and someday. . . .

"I'll be on my way in the morning," Bill said. "But mark me, I get a share of the treasure, if you ever find it."

"Don't ever doubt that I'll find it, Bill Baker. And I'll send you a share, all right—in a thimble!"

They shared a good laugh, and the castaway was certain he was going to miss the camaraderie. But it was time to get on with his life. As he looked into the mirror next morning, he saw a much older man that the one who faced death upon the sea many months ago. His hair was white, and it hung to his shoulders. The face that women had found handsome was now leatherlike and deeply lined. But the eyes were clear and bright for the first time in many years. His system was clean. No drugs clouded his reason; no cravings tortured his body. He was free at last. His victory over his addiction gave him the courage to face the world again.

They picked up Vicar Pearson, and the three set sail in Albert's boat. It was a clear, cold October morning, and the skipper sat pensively at the tiller.

"I suppose you're thinking you'll talk me into helping you dig for treasure, now that Bill here is going," said the vicar. "Well, you've got another think coming. I'll not be doing the devil's work."

"My offer stands," Albert replied. "Half of whatever we find goes to the church. My word on it."

"And what would the church do with a bucket of sand, tell me. It'll be a cold day in hell when you catch me out digging for imagined treasure."

"Imagined, is it!"

"Let's get me ashore," Bill interrupted, "then you two can get back to fighting."

Albert let the sail fall slack and guided the boat into the pier and tied her up. Bill shouldered his sack and prepared to disembark, but first he reached into his pocket and took out the monogrammed snuffbox.

"Keep this," he said, handing it to Albert. "It's a token of my gratitude."

"You owe me nothing," said Albert.

"I owe you my life, you and the vicar. Take it for all the good times and the bad. We've got a lot to remember."

"We have at that," said Albert, pocketing the box. "And I thank you."

"You'll be missed, Bill Baker," said the vicar, shaking his hand vigorously. "I'm only sorry I never got you inside the church. Maybe next time."

"I don't need a church to find religion," said Bill. "If ever a man did the work of God—"

"Get on with you," said the old soldier, "or your regiment will sail without you."

Albert followed Bill up the ladder and pointed down the pier.

"Stop by that shack," he said. "They'll see that you get aboard the right vessel. This time, see that you keep your head above water."

"I wish there were some way to properly thank you."

"There is one small favor."

"Anything you ask."

"If you get back into it, give Kaiser Bill a good kick in the backside, not for me, but for Geoffrey."

The castaway smiled and impulsively embraced the big man.

"There now, get on with you," said Albert gruffly. He pushed him away, and as he did so, they could see the tears in each other's eyes. "Off with you now, before we all get to blubbering."

Bill Baker stood on the pier for a long time, waving to them as they sailed back toward Saint Martin's. When their boat was but a dot on the dark sea, he turned and strode confidently down the pier. In the distance, a steamer's whistle beckoned Barron Bachelor back to reality.

*   *   *

Tom was putting finishing touches on *Teddy in Morning Light*. The angle of the sun was perfect for only about two hours each day. Teddy dutifully sat in the broad window, her right hand lying on her lap, the left extended to support herself as she leaned slightly forward to emphasize the fullness of her bosom. It had been difficult the past few weeks not to let her nausea spoil these sittings. But it was too early, she told herself, to tell Tom of her suspicions.

"What day is this?" she asked.

"I don't know. The sixth of October, I think."

"I mean, it isn't Sunday, is it?"

"I don't think so. Why do you ask?"

"There's a buggy coming up the road. It looks like a priest coming to visit."

"A priest?"

"All in black, a white collar—"

"That would be a priest," Tom agreed. "I wonder why he's coming here."

"There's someone with him. A nun. I'd better dress. I can't be sitting here with my blouse in my lap."

"Wait! Give me another minute."

She held her pose, despite another wave of nausea that came over her. She had become quite professional, a good artist's model. She liked the feeling of his eyes on her, relished the excitement her nudity aroused in them both, an excitement at once innocent and deliciously wicked. Except for her morning sickness, she liked posing in the bright sunlight. And October was her favorite month. The morning fog of summer was gone. The sky was clear, and it was warm all day until sunset. The evenings were cool, perfect for sleeping, better for making love. It was no wonder she became pregnant. Everything was perfect. They were deeply in love. But she couldn't tell him yet. She had to be certain. As the thoughts skipped through her mind, Tom's arm came around her and held her gently. It was almost as if he knew without being told. She savored his touch, warm against her skin. She looked up into his eyes, and he kissed her with great passion.

"You are wonderful today," he said. "I love you."

"And I love you. But I must dress. They're coming up the drive."

She slipped into her blouse and buttoned it quickly. Tom went to the window and looked at the approaching rig.

"I wonder what they want," he said. "A fund drive, maybe. They've come for a donation."

"I don't remember how we left the parlor. I hope it isn't a mess."

"Why invite them in? Give them some money and come back. I feel inspired."

"I know you do, but you should be painting."

She brushed his cheek with a kiss and went carefully down the stairs and out the door. The priest had alighted and stepped forward to greet her, while the nun remained in the buggy with her head bowed and a cloak clutched about her face.

"Mrs. Bachelor?" he inquired.

"Yes, I am Mrs. Bachelor."

"I am Father Timothy. I wonder if we might have a word with you, Sister Clare and I. Our business is of a personal nature."

"Whatever might that be?" Teddy asked, trying vainly to get a look at Sister Clare.

"It's about your husband," said the priest.

She could feel the blood rising in her cheeks. Why, she wondered, did this old priest want to talk about Barron now when she was trying so hard to forget the past.

"My husband is dead," she said.

"So we understand," he replied, giving a hand to Sister Clare as she joined them, her head bowed humbly. "Our visit will be brief and, I hope, of some consolation to you. We've come to bring peace to a tortured soul."

"My husband's soul is at rest," she said impatiently. "And so is mine at last. I don't know why—"

"It is Sister Clare's soul at issue here," the priest explained. "You see, she gave me this." He held out a newspaper clipping.

"This is a report of my husband's memorial service last June. I had hoped that that was the end of it."

"The accompanying photograph, Mrs. Bachelor, shows you stepping into a limousine. Sister Clare saw it and recognized you. She asked me to read the report to her. She said she had to see you, and your father told me where we could find you. Sister Clare has come to seek your forgiveness for the death of Yee Dao-chen."

"What do you mean?" Teddy gasped. "Who is this woman?"

"A very contrite and remorseful child of God," said Father Timothy. "You knew her as Maiyu."

"Maiyu! What does she want of me? Why are you doing this?"

"I will try to explain. You see, Maiyu came to Old Saint Mary's several months ago. I had spent my younger days as a missionary in China; I spoke her dialect and became her confessor. She had led a difficult and sinful life. God asks not that we be perfect, but that we confess our sins, repent, and strive to lead a better life. Maiyu is

165

trying to obey God's will. Your husband had been kind to her in his way. She had been a slave, and he purchased her freedom. In exchange she served him as housekeeper and companion. But when your husband died, she was left destitute. The staff of the Palace Hotel found her in his suite, frightened and hungry. They turned her over to your husband's attorneys, and they dismissed her with only a few dollars to her name. Eventually she found her way to us, and we took her in. She now plans to take holy vows. But first she had to confess her sins. Foremost among them was her responsibility in the death of Yee Dao-chin."

"How could that be?" Teddy cried. "Chinaboy died in my arms. He had been beaten to death."

"Not according to Maiyu. She told me he was very angry with her and made her life miserable. He knew she had been a concubine to a very rich and evil Tong leader. But the poor child had been sold into slavery at the age of twelve and sent here against her wishes. She had no control over her fate. Yet he felt she had brought shame upon his family name, for they had shared a common ancestor many generations ago. He constantly berated her and, aboard the ship, discovered she was assisting your husband in the use of drugs. He threatened to kill her and was chasing her along the deck when she came to a dead end. Only a narrow ladder opening stood between them and the main deck. In her panic, she stepped aside as her tormentor lunged past her and plunged head first onto the deck below. Frightened, Maiyu ran away to hide, believing her tormentor was dead."

"Are you saying that is how he came to be at my door?" Teddy asked, aghast.

"In her confession, Sister Clare said that she knew that you blamed your husband for the death of Yee Dao-chin, but she was afraid to come forward with the truth. I brought her here because she wants to ask your forgiveness. Please, Mrs. Bachelor, grant her peace. I am sure God forgives her."

Sister Clare fell to her knees and grasped Teddy's skirt while Teddy looked out over the valley to avoid the repentant woman's eyes. Her thoughts went back to that awful night aboard the *Maui Maiden* that had ended in death and accusations of murder. An intolerable burden weighed down upon her as she realized that she had wrongly accused Barron of a heinous crime and rejected his denial.

And now it was too late. Barron was dead, and she could never ask his forgiveness. It was too late for anything but the unbearable burden of guilt, the unending pain of remorse.

"Did my husband ever learn the truth?" she asked quietly.

"No," said the priest. "Maiyu was too frightened to tell him."

Teddy looked down at the kneeling woman and lifted the cloak that veiled her face. Tears streamed down the penitent's cheeks, as she looked up at Teddy imploringly.

"How I envy you those tears," Teddy said softly. "What a great relief they must be. If only my husband were here so I could weep and plead for his forgiveness. But don't cry anymore. You've suffered enough. I forgive you, and I deeply regret the unhappiness this has brought you." Then, speaking slowly and forming her words carefully, she said again, "I forgive you."

Maiyu grasped her hands and kissed them, and her tears fell upon them. Teddy pulled quickly away and stared in horror at her dampened fingers as if they had been splashed with blood. The priest helped Maiyu to her feet and led her back to the rig.

"We're very grateful, Mrs. Bachelor," he said. "May God's blessing be upon you." He made the sign of the cross, and Teddy cringed.

"Don't!" she cried. "God will *not* bless me, He will *punish* me! He *is* punishing me. *You* are punishing me. Go away!"

The priest shook his head sadly, raised his hand, and muttered a benediction. Teddy fled in horror into the hacienda, fell upon the couch, and wept as the buggy went slowly down the drive.

*   *   *

It had been a satisfying day for Archie Hobart and Charles Cullen. It had begun with an auction of selected works from the museum, Quinns mainly, and the public response had been generous and enthusiastic. In conjunction with the auction, a showing of Tom's new series, entitled "The Laborers," had drawn huge and admiring crowds. The two old friends celebrated with dinner at *Vanna*'s and now as Hobart's carriage lurched through the dark side streets toward Pacific Heights, they looked forward to telephoning the good news to Teddy and Tom at the hacienda.

"We'll call from my flat," said Hobart. "It's about time I used the telephone for good news. It's gotten so that I dread picking up the receiver these days. Come in, Charles. We'll have a brandy to ward off the chill, and then I'll have you driven home."

Charles picked up the early edition of the Sunday *Chronicle* that lay at the door while Hobart fumbled for his keys.

"Hello, what's this?" he said, looking at the front page.

"Don't tell me, another hundred-yard advance on the western front, or is it another hundred-yard retreat?"

"No, it's John Manchester. He's dead."

"Let me see," said Hobart, taking the newspaper to the hall table and spreading it out in the lamplight. "Terrible, terrible. What an awful way to die."

"What is it?" asked Charles. "A fatal brawl?"

"Worse than that. He fell off a parapet at Castle Cairn and landed head first on the stone driveway below."

"My God! Let me see that," said Charles, scanning the news reports. "Apparent suicide . . . no sign of foul play . . . lay there several days . . . remains scattered by animals. Archie, this is disgusting, It's indeed an awful way to go."

"I'll not touch that telephone, Charles. You'll have to tell them."

"I know I must. John's been a friend of Teddy's for years, and Tom will be heartbroken. They were particularly close, you know. Where is your telephone?"

"In the kitchen by the back door. And when you're finished, rip out the cord and throw the damned thing into the yard."

168

16

Teddy was in the grip of a brooding funk, and there was little Tom could do but try to mollify her. As the hours passed, he realized his efforts were in vain. He could not penetrate the pall of irrational guilt under which she cowered. At last his anger flared.

"You're a woman possessed!" he shouted. "You're letting a dead man ruin our lives. What's done is done, for God's sake. There's no way you can make it right with him. It's not as if you had brought murder charges against him. It was nothing more than your suspicions."

"But that's what drove a wedge between us. Don't you see? I accused him and he denied it and I refused to believe him. He died knowing I thought he was a murderer. There's no greater pain than to be wrongly accused, and because of me he took that pain to his grave."

"That's nonsense! There would have been no suspicion and no pain if it weren't for his addiction to drugs. He had no one to blame but himself and his filthy habit. You told me he was a fiend when he was without his drugs. That's what drove you two apart. And it must finally have driven him insane, or why else would he encourage you to spend time with me? He must have known how I felt about you. Everyone must have known."

His argument seemed to ease her anxiety, but it did not persuade her. Her tears stopped, and she proceeded calmly.

"I thought he was just trying to gather evidence of our affair to delay our divorce suit. He told me as much. How do I know he wasn't seeking time to convince me that I was wrong, that he couldn't have killed Chinaboy? But I had already convicted him in my heart. I never gave him that chance. And now he's gone, and God is punishing me. I know He is. I felt it today when that priest made the sign of the cross over me. It filled me with dread and self-loathing. I truly thought I was going to die, and I was afraid, afraid of God's wrath."

Tom tried to control his anger for fear of agitating her.

"Barron was no fool, Teddy," he said softly. "He knew his faults only too well. He didn't want those faults revealed in public. That's why he fought your divorce suit. You're blaming yourself simply because he's dead. But that's not your fault. He died while trying to profit from an ugly and immoral war. It was a business gamble, and he lost. Don't throw away what may be our last chance at happiness on a man like that. Don't let this ghost come between us again, I beg of you."

Tom was exasperated by the change that had come over her. Teddy had always presented herself as the very model of the twentieth-century woman—capable, assertive, disciplined, self-confident—the same traits she had once tried to instill in him. "Your life is what you make of it, Tom," she had told him. "There's nothing that can stand in your way, if you're resolute and strong. With courage, intelligence, and your God-given talent, there is nothing you can't accomplish in this life." What was it, he wondered, that had brought about such a change in her?

The late afternoon fog that drifted in from the Pacific brought a chill to the air. Tom put his around his beloved and led her into the hacienda. He lit a fire and poured them each a small brandy. She was quiet, staring into the flames, her mind far away.

"What are you thinking?" he asked.

"I'm thinking that I'll burn in the fires of hell."

"Nonsense," he said gently. "You once called me a mystical Irishman, but here you are believing in hellfire and ghosts and who knows what all. I know this doesn't have to be. I know I could make you happy again, if only you'd let me. Think of it, Teddy, think of the joy we knew only a few short hours ago. It could be that way again."

"My happiness was part of the problem, Tom. I had no right to it. I stole it. I brought you here and hid away from everything. But then the priest came with Maiyu. God sent them to show me that I can't hide. I could see it in the priest's eyes. He saw my guilt and brought down the wrath of God to punish me. I didn't deserve the happiness we knew, and now I must pay for it."

"There's that mysticism again. You've had a bad shock, nothing more. It's over, Teddy. It's time now to pick up the pieces of our lives and move on. It's no time to quit. Think about it. Maiyu came here to ask for your forgiveness, and you gave it freely. Now it's time for you to forgive yourself."

"If only I could," she sighed. "Everywhere I turn, I see Barron. He's everywhere, and I can't escape him."

"We *can* escape! We can go away. We can go anywhere you choose. We can get married, settle down, raise a family. Let's do it, Teddy. Let's do it now."

She suddenly buried her face in her hands.

"I can't escape, Tom, I can't escape my punishment," she cried.

"All right," he said angrily, "if that's the way you want it. You don't seem to care that you're destroying my happiness, too. Life has always been a game to you. You play at it, but you're afraid to live it. You played at being a champion of the poor and downtrodden, but you lived in comfort and luxury. You played at love, but you married without it. You played at being a wife, but you quit when the going got tough. You played the liberated woman, mocking conventional morality, but you really didn't have the stomach for it or you wouldn't feel the guilt you feel now. Life isn't a game, Teddy. It's real and it's tough and it demands commitment and courage. You can't give up at every setback."

"I know, Tom, I know," she said desperately. "I know I must try. But it will take time. Go back to North Beach. Go back to work. Leave me here so I can come to grips with my life. I shouldn't have rushed into this. I need more time."

"Time!" he shouted. "There is no more time." He got up and tossed the dregs of his brandy into the fire where it exploded with a flash. Teddy recoiled, then got up and ran to her bedroom. Tom heard the door slam, but before he could follow after her, the telephone rang.

"Tom," said the voice on the other end of the line, "is that you? I've got some bad news to report. It's John Manchester, Tom. He's dead. Apparently killed himself, threw himself out of a window at that mountain place of his. He was always a favorite of Teddy's, so break it to her gently, will you? Try not to upset her."

"I understand, Mr. Cullen," he said. "Teddy mustn't be upset." He replaced the receiver quietly and stalked out the front door, snatching up the brandy decanter as he passed.

*   *   *

The letter came from the Archbishop of Canterbury himself, the

171

first such direct correspondence since Peter Pearson became the vicar at Saint Martin. It instructed him to call a vestry meeting for the purpose of engaging an architect to design a war memorial. It was to be erected on a prominent plot of ground easily accessible to the island's population at all times as a place of peace and solemn meditation. The memorial was to include a brass plate inscribed with the names of all those residents of the island who had made the supreme sacrifice in the war. Finally, the plot and the monument were to be maintained in perpetuity by a resident of the island to be nominated by the vicar and approved by the vestry.

A practical man, Vicar Pearson's eye scanned quickly to the last paragraph: "Funds for the land and for the planning, design, materials, and construction of said memorial, including a reasonable stipend for its maintenance, shall be dispersed by the archbishop from an anonymous endowment."

"Fancy that," said Albert, annoyed that the vicar would interrupt his Sunday digging in the cove. "And what's it supposed to mean?"

"It means the donor doesn't want his name known," the vicar said impatiently.

"And why are you telling me?"

"Sometimes you can be as dense as the fog, Albert Prudhomme. Doesn't it seem strange that this letter should arrive only a matter of weeks after the departure of Bill Baker?"

"Bill Baker! You must be daft. Bill Baker didn't have a quid or a purse to carry it in."

"Think about it, Albert. Why else would the archbishop single out this poor parish for such an honor? And who else but you and the widow Lancaster have lost sons in the war? Think of the thousands of men lost and compare that to our contribution. We've lost only two so far. I think it was our friend who called himself Bill Baker. It could be no other, and here's the proof. It says I'm to make the announcement two weeks hence at the donor's behest. And that's Sunday, November 17, 1917."

"What the devil proof is that?" Albert asked contemptuously.

"Why that's Saint Martin's Day, Albert. That was Bill Baker's clue to us, his way of thanking us."

"I think you're daft, and I still don't know why are you telling me all this."

"Because Geoffrey's name will be on that monument."

"And I can give you its proper spelling, and there's little else can I do for you or Bill or the bishop."

"That's the point, Albert. It's not what you can do for Bill, it's what Bill is trying to do for you."

"Daft!" Albert exclaimed in disgust. "Be off with you, and leave me to my digging."

"You can stop digging for treasure, Albert, after what Bill has done. He's left the choice of a caretaker up to me, and who do you think I'd suggest for that position, if not you, who's given a son to the war? Surely not the widow Lancaster. She's much too fragile. I think he knew I'd offer the job to you. It's his way of paying you back. You've cast your bread upon the water, Albert."

"And it's coming back a soggy crust, I'd wager. You take a lot for granted." He jammed his shovel into the sand and leaned on it while musing over the vicar's words. "On the other hand a small stipend would be welcome indeed. I've been thinking of closing down the farm."

"Why, of course! You'd have to move to town to be near the monument. I had in mind that hillock behind the church with the view of the harbor. Geoffrey always liked it there. And young Henry Lancaster would appreciate it, too, I'm sure."

"Oh, I see it all now. You're just trying to get me near the church. This whole elaborate plan, just to rescue one lost sheep? You're a crafty one, you are, vicar."

"Your return to the church would be a bonus," the vicar admitted.

"I'll tell you what," Albert said. "You leave me alone until all's said and done, and I'll come take care of your monument. But the widow Lancaster gets half the stipend or your offer be damned."

*   *   *

Teddy awoke from a deep sleep and pulled the quilt tightly around her. It was very cold in the bedroom and very dark. She could remember being emotionally exhausted and crying herself to sleep. She could easily fall asleep again, but the ancient rafters creaked and something skittered across the roof—leaves, pine needles, tiny feet. A sudden gust of wind caught the shutter and slammed it sharply. What was it, she wondered? Dimly, across the hours, she remembered hearing the telephone ring. Tom had answered it. Was it now his presence she felt in the old hacienda? She slipped into her shoes and tiptoed quietly down the hall. The wind had blown the front door open, and when she went to close it, she saw flames coming from the upstairs window of the barn.

"Tom! Tom!" she screamed as she raced across the driveway and through the door, taking two steps at a time as she rushed up to Tom's studio. She found him beating at the flames with a blanket. Drapes at the window were ablaze, the fire licking up toward the ceiling.

"The heater," he panted. "It ignited the drapes. Give me a hand."

"No, just get out! There's nothing we can do. Go call for help."

He paused and looked at her with a grin.

"It's an omen," he said. "There was fire all around when we met. Do you remember?"

"You're drunk! Just get out of here. I'll try to save what I can."

"My paintings? Let 'em burn. What are they, anyway? The record of a red hot love affair at last gone up in flames."

"Tom, you've got to get out. Look, it's reached the ceiling. Run, Tom, please. Go telephone the operator, please!"

She pushed him toward the stairway and ran back to snatch the canvas on his easel. She ran down the stairs and outside, resting the unfinished painting against the fence and running back toward the door.

"Don't be a fool," Tom said. "They're not worth it. Let 'em burn." Then he staggered to the pump and stuck his head in the catch basin and ran his fingers through his hair. Teddy came down in a moment carrying two more of his paintings.

"For God's sake, ring the operator!" she shouted. "Please hurry, Tom," she said, running back up the stairs into the spreading flames. When she returned again, Tom was sitting on the front steps watching the fire. "Did you ring, Tom? Did you call for help?"

"No answer," he mumbled. "Let 'em burn."

"Here, then, take the car key. Drive down to the caretaker's place and tell him we need help right away."

She watched the automobile careen down the drive then ran back into the house and rang for the operator. A sleepy voice answered.

"Number, please."

"Operator, please help me. My barn is on fire. You must help me. I'm calling from the Bachelor hacienda on Enterprise Road. This is Mrs. Bachelor calling. Please send help quickly."

"Just keep calm, ma'am. Where was that again?"

"The Bachelor hacienda. It's on Enterprise Road about six miles west of El Camino Real. Please hurry."

"Is that in Santa Clara county, ma'am?"

"Yes, yes, for God's sake, please hurry."

Teddy slammed the receiver into its cradle and ran back outside and into the barn. Flames were shooting from the roof, and smoke was pouring from the doorway. She dashed up the stairs, grabbed two more canvases, and ran down again. Time after time, she ran into the blazing barn, up the stairs, and down again with as many paintings as she could carry. When there were but two remaining, she found the stairwell engulfed in flames. She stopped for a moment to douse herself with water from the pump, threw her arms in front of her face and charged once again into the fire, stumbling up the stairs and sprawling head first onto the floor of the studio. Groping her way to the paintings, she snatched them up and plunged down the burning stairs. Her arms badly burned and her face seared, she stumbled into the driveway and fell to her knees.

"No, not yet!" she screamed. "I can't stop now!"

*   *   *

A neighbor attracted by the orange glow in the night sky was the first to arrive. He had come on horseback, picking up his way carefully along a deer trail that meandered across his property and down into the arroyo to the creek and up the slope to the meadow. From there he could see the barn ablaze. He spurred his horse to a gallop and in a moment reached the driveway.

"She was passed out there by the pump," he told the sheriff, "all soaking wet and pretty badly burned on her arms and her face. Her hair was mostly burned off. I went inside and called the operator, but she'd already alerted the authorities. I came out then and just tried to make the little lady comfortable. Funny thing . . . "

"What's that?" asked the sheriff.

"There are tracks going through the house to the kitchen. She must have gone back and forth a dozen times. It smells of wet ashes in there."

"Probably ran in to soak her clothes at the sink and fill her bucket. Spunky lady, fighting that fire all by herself."

"I guess so," said the rancher. "Course there's the pump right here. Curious why she'd—"

"You see the flames, too?" the sheriff asked the caretaker who had come up from the valley.

"No," he said. "I heard a knocking at my door around midnight. I got my shotgun and went to answer it. That's when I saw the fire."

"Who was at the door?"

"Young fellow smelling of liquor. Said the Bachelor place was on fire. I could see that. I tend orchards for the Bachelors. I went inside to pull on my boots, and when I came back, he was gone. I got up here as quick as I could."

"Young fellow was gone?"

"Yup, left the automobile behind, stuck in my fence. He must have lit out on foot. Looked like the Bachelors' roadster."

"She probably sent a hired hand to get help," said the rancher.

"Maybe," said the sheriff. "I'll have to ask Bachelor about him."

"Can't do that," said the caretaker. "Bachelor died in the war a few months ago."

"Then I'll have to talk to Mrs. Bachelor later when she's out of the hospital," said the sheriff. "Meanwhile, leave that automobile where it is. I'll want to look it over. And if that young fellow shows up again, you tell him I want to see him."

17

They gave her a shot to ease her pain, loaded her into the ambulance, and sped toward the city. The last thing she remembered was the prick of the needle in the fleshy part of her upper arm. She winced, then felt the cold liquid being expelled under her skin. It seemed so long ago. Had it been an hour, a day? Dimly, through the bandages that covered most of her face, she could see that she was in a hospital room. She could feel the cold, crisp sheets against her legs and smell the pungent, antiseptic odor. The shot had worn off, leaving her groggy and in severe pain. She could not lift her arms, but she could feel they were smeared with a greasy coat of salve and loosely swathed in gauze, as was her head and face. The piercing pain brought tears to her eyes.

"Awake now, are you?" a woman asked.

"Yes," she said in a very small voice.

"How do you feel?"

"Terrible."

"I'm not surprised. I'll call the doctor."

She lay in agony after the door closed, holding shut her eyelids that were heavy with the thick ointment. Suddenly she felt the chill of a stethoscope against her breast followed by the touch of gentle fingers searching for a pulse at her throat. Then came the cold shock of alcohol being rubbed on her upper arm and a man's voice.

"This won't hurt." She felt the needle puncture her skin. The doctor, speaking softly, said, "She'll be awake for a few moments. Have them come in."

She heard their footsteps and struggled against the sticky salve to open her eyes. At the foot of her bed stood three forms. One she recognized as her father. Another was Archie Hobart. Between them stood a tall man with flowing white hair. Then the sedative began its work, and her vision dimmed, leaving her unable to focus on their faces. They spoke among themselves in muffled voices, then her father and Hobart left. The tall man with the long white hair came to her bedside, leaned down close to her, and whispered.

"I'm so sorry this happened, my dear. But you're going to be all right. I will be here when you need me."

Unable to resist the sedative any longer, she drifted off into a restless sleep. She dreamed she had been called to judgment, and as she stood before a bright throne, she could see a tall figure in flowing robes and long white hair. He raised his hands over her, and she shrank in fear and uttered a cry.

"Teddy," said a whispered voice. "It's all right, dear."

"Daddy?" she asked groggily.

"Yes, my dear. How are you feeling?"

"I'm afraid, Daddy."

"There, there," he said in a soothing voice. "It's all right."

"I dreamed I saw Barron. There was a bright light, and I'm sure I saw Barron. I was afraid."

"That was no dream, Teddy. It was a miracle. Barron has come home alive."

"No, it can't be," she said tremulously.

"Yes, he's come back. He has visited your bedside every day for a week. He's very anxious to talk to you."

"No, no!" she moaned.

"You poor dear, he won't come if you don't feel up to it. He knows what a shock you've been through, and he doesn't want to upset you. He left just a short while ago when you began to stir. He wanted me to see you first to break the news of his return."

"But how—"

"He'll tell you the story. It's amazing. It's in all the newspapers. He'll come to see you whenever you wish. What shall I tell him?"

"Tell him I'm sorry, Daddy," she said as the tears began to flow. "Tell him I'm very, very sorry."

"I'll tell him, my dear. I'll tell him that. And when the doctor says you're strong enough, I'll tell Barron you're ready to see him."

Teddy turned her face away and wept. Nothing seemed real, only the throbbing pain that drained the last of her energy. She drifted again into a restless sleep and dreamed she was a young girl again, running through a grassy field, hand in hand with a handsome young boy. It was a warm and beautiful day, and they paused at the edge of a stream. She could see his face next to hers as they knelt for a cool drink. But as her hand dipped into the water, he vanished in the ripples. Then a cloud of black smoke darkened the sky, and flames burst all around her. She ran toward a towering peak and climbed frantically upward, fire licking at her heels and a hot wind scorching her cheeks. At last she fell exhausted at the base of an escarpment, trapped between the fire below and the summit above. As she struggled to rise, she felt a hand on hers. She opened her eyes to see Barron standing over her. He looked very different, older now with a bronzed and weathered face. His eyes seemed warm with tenderness. It was several moments before he looked up and saw that she was awake.

"I'm sorry, Teddy, if I hurt you," he said, gently removing his hand from hers.

"You're alive . . . when did you come home?" she asked in a whisper as if afraid to dispel a dream. "How long have I been here? How did you—"

"Wait, wait, Teddy. You mustn't excite yourself. You've been here for several weeks. If I had known you needed me, I'd have come much sooner, but I wasn't sure you'd want to see me. But they said you had been badly injured. I came immediately."

"I thought you were dead," she said.

"I know. I wanted you to think that. I wanted to die." He pulled up a chair and sat close to her bedside. "I wanted to die until I looked death in the face, Teddy, and then I was afraid to die. It was in that fear, and with the help of faithful, selfless friends, that I found the courage to live, to get well, to face life again. I'm not cured. I may never be cured. But I am in control of my life, and I intend to remain in control so I can somehow repay you for all the pain I've caused you. I promise to do whatever I can to make you happy. I'll stand by you forever, if you want me to. Or I'll give you the divorce you wanted and never bother you again—whatever will make you happy. If only you'll forgive me."

"No, no! It is I who needs forgiveness. I thank God that you're alive so I can tell you how sorry I am. I've been so wrong about you, about us. I blamed you for Chinaboy's death, but I know now that you were innocent. I blamed you for destroying our marriage, but I know now that I was also at fault. When I thought you were dead and that I could never ask your forgiveness I was devastated."

"Please, Teddy, don't think about that now. Just think about getting well. You must get well soon, because you are facing some difficult decisions, decisions that only you can make. And there is so little time."

He left her bedside, walked to the window, and looked down into the street.

"What is it?" she asked. "Whatever it is, can't it wait?"

"I wish it could," he said without turning to look at her. "Time is important. You must be strong."

"I don't understand."

"Teddy," he said, turning to face her. "I want you to know that I have begun a very discreet search for Tom Quinn. I will do all that I can to find him."

"Why? Where has he gone? I hope he hasn't run away. He probably blames himself for the fire, but it wasn't his fault. It was the heater that set the drapes afire. It was an accident. If he has run away, it's because I hurt him terribly."

"It's not the fire I'm concerned about, Teddy," Barron said. "The doctor spoke to me privately. He said you were delirious when they brought you in, that you were afraid something might have happened . . . to your baby."

Teddy gasped and turned her head away.

"No one else knows," Barron went on, "not even your father. I think enough of Tom Quinn to believe that he's also unaware of your condition, or he surely wouldn't have left you. What's important is that you have someone to stand by you. I'll find Tom, if that's what you want. I'll be here for you no matter what you decide. But it's a decision that only you can make."

*   *   *

Tom left the roadster stuck in the caretaker's fence and wandered through the valley most of the night, finally taking refuge in a culvert against the cold, damp air. When he awoke, he continued his trek, following a country road to Los Gatos and then up the switchbacks to Castle Cairn. There, at a place in the driveway still stained with John's blood, he knelt to reflect upon the fate of the artist in a society that treated rich businessmen, semiliterate athletes, and corrupt politicians with more respect that it accorded its creative geniuses. He was not a man given to prayer, but he swore by the spirit of John Manchester that he would learn from the author's unhappy example. He swore he would never again put a brush to canvas under the aegis of capitalism, that he would fight for the independence of the creative imagination, and that he would work for world peace and the improvement of the condition of all working people.

To that end, and because he was broke and hungry, he found a week's work in the orchards. It was there in the miserable hovels of the fruit pickers that he came across and newspaper containing an item about a memorial service for John. It was to be held in an Oakland warehouse, a site selected to honor the memory of a man who had dedicated his life to the laboring class. He set out next morning, hitching rides when he could, sleeping beside the road at night with discarded newspapers stuffed in his clothing to keep him warm. He arrived at the makeshift tabernacle in time to hear Dr. Archibald Hobart laud the author's artistic virility and the power with which he used the English language to carve a place for himself in the history of American literature. Next at the podium was left-wing gadfly Mabel Meyers, who proclaimed the deceased to be a prophet whose writings paved the way for the worldwide Socialist revolution now getting underway in Russia. She exhorted her listeners to join her in dedicating their lives to that historic movement. Others took their turn—publishers, editors, critics—dragging the body of Manchester's work through the thickets of hypocrisy, much as the wild animals had scattered his moral remains in the mountain wilderness. When Tom could stand no more, he left the building in search of a hot meal, a warm bed, a new path.

It was later in a waterfront flophouse that he spotted a headline in a crumpled newspaper, "Miraculous Return from the Dead." The report told of Barron Bachelor, the famous American industrialist, who was lost at sea and presumed dead. It said he had washed ashore on a lonely island off the English coast, spent months recovering from his ordeal, and finally returned to San Francisco to be reunited with his young bride as she recuperated from injuries suffered in a fire. Dramatic stuff, Tom had to admit, especially when related in the purple prose of the popular press. But for him, it seemed nothing more than an ironic epitaph to his own romantic dream that lay dead in the ashes at the Bachelor hacienda.

It was a bitter path that Tom followed in search of his salvation. He spent Christmas in a rescue mission on Chicago's South Side where he was later arrested for preaching socialism on a street corner. January found him in New York, where a vagrancy arrest saved him from freezing and starving on the streets. Released in the midst of war hysteria, he recalled Mabel Meyers's implausible dream of an army that would bring peace to a war-weary world simply by refusing to fight. Now in tatters, he was willing to trade his desperate condition for a uniform, a warm barracks, and three hot meals a day. He enlisted in the United States Army to fight for peace in his own peculiar way. By late spring, he was knee-deep in mud in the trenches along the Marne, under guard for urging his comrades to lay down their arms, and facing the threat of court-martial and death before a firing squad should anyone be foolish enough to follow his advice. In his despair over the endless and useless killing, he became obsessed with death. He celebrated his thirtieth birthday sketching a dismal battlefield scene in which he himself lay dead in no-man's land.

It was not an improbable fate. His penchant for proselytizing for pacifism earned him a place in a special squad of misfits and malcontents, who invariably were among the first to be ordered "over the top" in an attack. The scream of shells and the stutter of machine guns were all too familiar to him. More than once as he stumbled through the mud and gore and debris of combat, he witnessed the frightening finality of human destruction, knowing full well that some unseen, unheard shell might blast him into eternity. Or perhaps a hand grenade would land at his feet and lift him heavenward to the great beyond. Or a sniper's bullet might snuff him out like the match he held to light his last cigarette. In fact, a more insidious fate awaited him.

It was shortly after the opening of the Meuse-Argonne offensive in late September. Tom's company advanced into the shell-shattered forest in the face of deadly fire from heavily fortified bunkers. By some miracle, he survived the day, and as night fell, he lay frightened and alone in a muddy crater as a light rain began to fall. He spent a miserable and sleepless night, an eerie night, lit by flares and rocked by the explosion of shells, some so close, they showered him with mud. At one point, that rain of terror left a bloody arm lying across his legs. He recoiled in horror, praying that the next shell would take his life and spare him the awful sight of that severed limb. In a way, his prayer was answered. As dawn approached, a barrage began, heralding a German counterattack. A cry came down the line, and he raised his head above the edge of the crater to hear the command. But it was too late. He was instantly engulfed in a greenish mist that issued from canisters that thudded all around him.

"Gas! Gas!" he cried, groping in vain in the semidarkness for his mask and grasping instead the disembodied arm. As he shrank in revulsion, the mist wafted over the edge of the crater. He could feel it sting his skin, feel the fire of it sear his eyes. He threw up his hands and plunged to the bottom of the muddy pit where he doused his face with the putrid water and gore that had settled there. Then the whistles blew and the order came to fix bayonets and prepare to repel a counterattack. But the defense would have to do without him. He was blind and helpless in that hellhole, and there he remained as the fighting raged all around him. When at last the battle subsided, he heard the shuffling of feet and knew that he was no longer alone.

"Give me a hand, will you?" he begged. "Mustard gas. I can't see." He tried to rise, but slipped in the mud and fell backwards.

"*Hände oben*!" shouted his visitor, and Tom felt the point of a bayonet pressing firmly against his throat.

*　　*　　*

Teddy was slow to recover from the multiple shocks that beset her. For several weeks, she lay abed in a daze, allowing her doctor and the nurses to do what they would with her, but with no desire to get well. She had lost her will to live. Tom was gone, perhaps never to return, while each day's bout with morning sickness reminded her that it was his child she carried.

Barron was little solace to her. Magnanimous to a fault, his insistence that he was to blame for the misfortunes that had befallen them only served to deepen her own feelings of guilt, her sense of unworthiness. His very presence intimidated her. His craggy, deeply lined face and the flowing white hair and black suits that he wore as if in penance for a life of sin made him seem like a puritanical patriarch come to punish her for her selfish and adulterous life. It was nothing he did, nothing he said. He never accused her, never raised his voice. He never admonished her, never offered her anything but sympathy and understanding; it was that more than anything else that depressed her. It would have been easier to bear the weight of her wrongdoings if he had held her accountable for them. It would have been easier to endure his wrath than his kindness. It seemed that he had forged an iron will in the fires of war and the heat of his battle against addiction, while she had grown weak in a life of self-indulgence. He exhibited an indomitable spirit, while she lacked the will to go on. If his heart now burned with righteousness, hers lay heavy in her breast, cold and dark with guilt. How could she ever bring a child, Tom's child, into such a forbidding world?

"There's nothing more we can do for her here," her doctor said. "Familiar surroundings might raise her spirits. She needs love and understanding. Take her home. Be patient with her. She'll snap out of it in time. If not, I can suggest a quiet place over in Marin County—"

Barron stood erect and glared at the doctor. There'd be no sanitarium for *his* wife. She was strong. There were wellsprings of endurance yet to be tapped, courage yet to be put to the test. Her father agreed.

"I can still remember the brave little girl who watched her world crumble and burn," said Charles. "She had strength and courage enough for both of us then. I know she still has it in her."

"I'm going to take her home," Barron resolved. "I've never really made a home for her, you know. It's no wonder she turned to Tom Quinn. I was never there for her. What happened to our marriage was my fault, not hers, and I intend to make it up to her."

"She'll forget about Tom," Charles said reassuringly. "She was lonely. If you can forgive her—"

"There's no question about that. I have forgiven her, and she understands that. The problem is that she seems unable to forgive herself. But I believe she will in time, when she realizes Tom is not coming back. I will devote myself entirely to her well-being. I promise you that, Charles. We already have wasted too many years, and if I've learned anything from my experience, it's that life is simply too precious to waste."

Once they had moved back into the mansion on the cliffs above the sea, he made the same pledge to Teddy. It became a time of unburdening, a time to confess to one another in an effort to cleanse their souls. Barron admitted that he had sunk to the depths of degradation before his brush with death frightened him into dealing with his drug addiction. He told her of his months on Saint Martin Island

and how the patience and understanding of his friends there had instilled in him the courage to confront his demons.

"I came back," he said humbly, "convinced that for the first time in my life I might be worthy to be your husband."

Teddy told him how the report of his death had shocked her into seeing that she had failed him, that she knew she should have done more to help him overcome his addiction.

"And when Maiyu told me how Chinaboy really died, I realized how unfair I had been to accuse you, and it was more than I could bear. All those months of suspicion, all the terrible thoughts that left no room in my heart for compassion or forgiveness. You have every right to send me away. I don't deserve your kindness."

"Don't talk that way, Teddy. I flatter myself that for the first time in our lives you may need me. The child you carry must have a father, and since Tom is nowhere to be found, I am prepared to play that role with all the love and dedication I can muster. Parenthood could become the basis of a strong marriage, if you will take me back."

"If Tom knew, he would come," Teddy said. "But I never told him."

"That explains a lot of things," Barron said, "why he ran away, for instance."

"I can't believe he's gone far," Teddy said. "He probably returned to Castle Cairn. He was distraught when I refused to marry him. He needed someone to talk to, and John was like an older brother to him. You'll probably find him with John now."

"But you must know that can't be!" Barron exclaimed.

"Why not? Has anyone thought to call on John?"

"Teddy, we thought you knew. John Manchester is dead. He's been dead these many weeks. Your father called the hacienda on the night of the fire to tell you. Don't you remember?"

She remembered the night very well; she could never forget.

"Maiyu had come that day to ask my forgiveness," she explained. "She told me she was to blame for Chinaboy's death and that you were innocent. I felt so guilty then and grew very upset. Tom got angry and we quarreled. Finally I left him and went to my room. I remember hearing the telephone ring. Tom must have answered. I was too distraught to care what the call was about, and he never told me. There wasn't time. Later I awakened and found the barn on fire. Tom was up in his studio. He had been drinking. I sent him for help and haven't seen him since. Poor Tom, he idolized John."

Barron detected tenderness in her voice when she spoke Tom's name.

"Teddy, Tom must be told about the child," he said. "You owe him that much."

"But I have no idea where he is, unless he's returned to North Beach."

"No. I checked there first. Tony hasn't seen him. And neither has Archie Hobart. Tom hasn't been by the museum."

"Then we must search for him," Teddy said, "although I wouldn't know where to begin looking."

"I know how to find him, Teddy, and I will. But you must tell me one thing. Are you in love with Tom Quinn?"

Her long silence told him all he needed to know, but he listened carefully when finally she replied.

"I was in love with him," she said quietly. "But now I'm not sure anymore. So much has happened. At the moment I'm not really sure I want you to find him. I'm not sure he ought to be told."

*   *   *

Teddy grew more certain as the weeks passed that Tom was gone from her life forever. Barron said nothing more about him, but put a team of private investigators on his trail and ordered them to build a dossier on his movements and activities. As that trail led east from San Francisco to Chicago and New York, he came to the conclusion that Tom had no intention of returning. That made it possible for him to look upon Teddy's pregnancy with as much pride and satisfaction as if the child were his own.

At Christmas, they entertained Allie and Charles and Dr. Hobart. At dinner, the beaming host announced that they were expecting a child come summer. Charles, tears of happiness in his eyes, hugged his daughter gently. Allie screamed in delight, then gave in to tears. Hobart simply fidgeted nervously and wished them well, preoccupied with a silent count of the months since Barron's miraculous return.

Teddy healed quickly. Her hair grew back to its original luxurious beauty within a few months. She affected a coiffure that concealed a reddened area of her brow where the flames had done their worst. The remainder of her face healed well and left no scars to detract from her beauty. Her arms and hands were quite another story, disfigured as they were with ugly red ridges of scar tissue. To conceal those reminders of the fiery end to her romance with Tom, she took to wearing long sleeves and never went abroad in the city without gloves. As fashions moved inexorably toward the 1920s, Teddy looked more like a charming visitor from the Gay Nineties, a beautiful creation of Charles Dana Gibson rather than a modern young woman with short skirts and hair.

When the war ended, Barron announced that he planned to guide Bachelor Enterprises through a transition from privately held company to public corporation and then he was going to retire. Charles would become the chief executive officer, while Barron would assume the title of president emeritus. His next step was to establish the Bachelor Foundation with himself as chief administrator. It would be supported by the earnings from his majority holdings in BE Inc. The foundation would be devoted to philanthropies worldwide.

The Bachelors became what postwar San Francisco considered model citizens. While Barron attended to his philanthropic endeavors, Teddy immersed herself in charitable work. Together they joined the Episcopal Church and never missed a Sunday morning service. They gave generously to the Grace Cathedral building campaign, and Barron sent regular donations to the Archbishop of Canterbury's discretionary fund, telling Teddy it had to do with certain kindnesses extended to him during his long recuperation in the Scilly Isles. On the town, they attracted attention wherever they went, Barron looking stiffly puritanical with his long white hair and black suits he had favored since his return from Europe. Teddy dressed more colorfully, but in the fashion of an earlier generation, intended to cover her scars. They attended the opera and the symphony and opened their home to benefits of all sorts. They promoted the San Francisco Museum of Contemporary Art at every opportunity and delighted in its growth as more and more the city became a lure for young artists. Around the nucleus of Tom's paintings, they assembled an unparalleled collection of contemporary art.

Barron continued to assemble a dossier on Tom. When his operatives reported that Tom had enlisted in the army in January 1918 and that he had been sent overseas as a replacement in the 1st Division of the American Expeditionary Force, Barron felt he should tell Teddy. But he couldn't bring himself to do so. They were happy. Why should he jeopardize that happiness by bringing up her lost love? In the spring, as Teddy's due date approached, his conscience got the better of him.

"I want you to know about this, my dear," he said, showing her a manila envelope thick with papers. "It's a dossier on Tom Quinn and his activities over the past months. It is updated regularly, and I keep it in the bottom of right-hand drawer of my desk in the library. It is always available to you, if you want to read it."

"I can't imagine that I would," she said. "I'm only curious about one thing."

"What is that?"

"Is he painting?"

"No, he is not. He appears to have abandoned his art."

"What a pity. Then nothing else really matters, does it."

As she spoke, she felt the baby stir in her womb, and a profound sadness came over her. But she smiled brightly at her husband.

*   *   *

Cullen St. Martin Bachelor was born on Tuesday, June 18, 1918. He was a robust seven pounds, six ounces and measured eighteen inches. He had the fine black hair and a lusty cry that echoed through the Bachelor mansion.

"I rather fancy becoming a father at my age," Barron admitted to Teddy. "You see I'm exceedingly fond of the child's mother." He kissed her tenderly on the forehead and smiled benevolently at her. But he did not say he loved her. He never used the word love. Nor did she. Occasionally when Teddy held little Cullen in her arms, she would reflect briefly on the handsome young artist and their troubled lives together. But she never went to the desk to look at the investigators' report. And she never mentioned Tom's name. Barron only mentioned it once, and he did so reluctantly. He brought home the latest report on Tom's activities and found Teddy in the bedroom nursing her child.

"I know you don't like to talk about it, my dear, but there's something I must tell you. Tom has been reported missing in action.

Since the armistice and the prisoner exchanges, I'm sure he will turn up sooner or later. We must not give up hope that he's still alive."

Teddy pressed her son closely to her breast as a wave of emotion washed over her. She was silent for a moment, and when she spoke at last, she chose her words carefully so that there could be no mistaking her meaning.

"I have faith that he is indeed alive and well," she said. "When he returns, as I'm sure he will one day, he will be welcome in our home as a friend. I will tell him how proud we are that he served his country in time of war and that we will always value his friendship—you and I and *our* son."

Barron came to her and looked into her eyes. Then he leaned down and kissed her. She could feel his tears warm on her cheek.

18

It was like a bizarre game of blind man's bluff staged by a group of overaged schoolchildren. They stood in a single file, each with his right hand upon the shoulder of the man in front of him, each with makeshift bandages covering his eyes. But there was no gaiety here, no light-heartedness, no laughter. There was a lot of cursing and constant coughing, the rasping, the gagging agony of men with gas-burned lungs, blind men who could not take a breath without convulsing in pain. There was barely time between coughs to spit out a glob of phlegm and an expletive.

"Name and unit, please," said a polite, very British voice.

"I'm only required to give my name, rank, and serial number."

"Do you have any idea how many times I've heard that ridiculous response today?" asked the voice with great irritation. "Now why don't you be cooperative? A lot of these men behind you are in dire need of medical treatment. In order to notify your unit that you're alive, we'd really like to know who you are."

"I am all men."

"Will you spell that for me, please?"

"A-l-l-m-e-n."

"And your Christian name?"

"What makes you think I'm a Christian?"

"If you please, Yank!" said the voice, no longer polite but exasperated.

"Sorry. It's Tom."

"Thomas?"

"If you will."

"What is your unit?"

"Twenty-eighth Infantry Regiment, First Division."

"How long has it been since you were gassed?"

"I don't know. I can barely tell when it's daylight, so I haven't kept track."

"Have you had medical treatment?"

"From the Germans?" he asked scornfully. "They tied this rag around my eyes. Nothing more."

"Take this form," said the voice, pressing the paper into his hand. "The orderly will guide you to a lorry."

The orderly took Tom's hand and placed it on his shoulder, saying, "Step lively, Yank."

He stumbled awkwardly behind his guide for about fifty yards and then was turned over to a sergeant, who took his papers and gave him a boost into the back of a truck.

"Just take your place beside the last man, Private Allmen," said the sergeant. "And try to be patient. We'll be off within an hour."

There amid colleagues only dimly perceived, Tom Quinn vanished and Thomas Allmen angrily wheezed and coughed and cursed his way into existence. At the hospital, he missed no opportunity to assert his independence and made no effort to conceal his irascibility.

"You're a tough one, aren't you," said the nurse. "Can't do a thing for you, can we now."

"You could leave me alone. I don't need your help. Go see to the others if you must be doing something."

"Doctor tells me you might do very well in time," she said, wheeling him suddenly around a corner and into the glare of sunlight. Tom winced and raised a hand to shield his eyes. "There, you see? What did I tell you? Before long you'll be needing smoked glasses!"

"Yes, and a tin cup," he added sullenly. "When can I get out of this damned chair? I can walk perfectly well."

"When you've learned to handle a cane to help you find your way, that's when. And when you can get about without having a coughing fit."

"I don't need a damned cane, unless it's to teach you manners," he groused.

"You're a wild one, you are. I'll be half sorry to see you go."

"Where am I going?"

"Home, of course. The war's over, in case you haven't heard. You Yanks are being collected at the end of the week. Home's the next stop for you."

A captain from Headquarters, First Division, came to interview the wounded. He sat at a table with a stack of records in front of him that he leafed through as he spoke.

"You've lost your army identification, Private Allmen?"

"Yes."

"What happened to it?"

"The Germans took it."

"I've checked the rolls of the 28th Regiment. I can't find your name anywhere."

"I was a recent replacement," Tom said impatiently.

"Your name should be here. I just don't see—"

"Neither do I," Tom said angrily. "Look, do I have to prove to the army that I exist? Why else would I be here? Maybe you ought to just ship me back to France or drop me off somewhere in London. You certainly wouldn't want to bring home a stray."

"I don't like your attitude, private. I have a job to do, like it or not. I see by your hospital records that you're somewhat of a malcontent. Well, let me give you some advice. Cut the bitterness. The war's over. You're one of the lucky ones. You're alive."

"Begging your pardon, sir, but you've got that all wrong. Am I lucky to be blind? I think the lucky ones are dead."

Tom Quinn's name probably was on the regimental list, but he preferred to remain among the missing. It was the perfect way to escape the past. His career as an artist was over, just as surely as his love affair with Teddy was over. Despite the army's suspicions, orders were cut for one "Thomas (NMN) Allmen," legitimizing his existence and granting him space aboard a troopship bound for New York. Less than a month later, he found himself at a rehabilitation center at Fort Dix, from whence he had begun his odyssey one very short lifetime ago. Next stop was a military hospital, where doctors confirmed that his eyes, which once had observed the world with such clarity, were not a total loss. They were damaged, to be sure and exceedingly sensitive to light, but with the help of grotesquely thick, smoked lenses Tom could see well enough to make his way through the gray, shadowy world that was left to him. He would be able to work for a living and not spend his life in dependency. But a close look in the mirror convinced him that his prospects would be limited. The chemicals that seared his eyes also burned his flesh. Ugly scar tissue was forming over the red patches of skin on his face. His hair, once curly and black, was now gray and limp, wilted like a field of grass in a drought. Small patches of it already had fallen out and more came loose with each grooming. His eyes, when not comically magnified by the thick lenses, were milky and washed out. This was no prize to present to a prospective employer, and he knew it.

"You should join us," said the man seated across the table from him in the mess hall. "They'll be taking us into New York soon for training classes. We're going to learn a trade."

"What trade?" he asked.

"Watch repair."

"Swell," Tom scoffed. "I can't even see the face of my watch, let alone the works."

"That's too bad," said the young veteran. "I still have one good eye and two good hands."

"You're not so bad off then," Tom observed. "You ought to be able to find a better job than repairing watches."

"I doubt it," said the youth. "Watch repair is a sit-down job, and I've lost my legs."

"I'm sorry," said Tom. "I didn't notice."

"They'd notice at home, sure enough," said the youth. "Everyone would notice back in Ohio."

"But you'd have your family there to look after you."

"I don't want to be a burden. They don't have much."

"Even so, I'll bet your folks wouldn't look on you as a burden."

"Oh, I'll go home someday when I can take care of myself."

"Sure you will, kid," Tom said quietly. "Good luck to you."

The young fellow had a point, Tom thought. He could never go back to San Francisco either. Sure, Tony would take him in, but it wouldn't be fair. He'd turned his back on the fisherman's life; how could he take advantage of Tony's friendship now? Besides, Teddy was there, and he could never go back to her. She and Barron would be together again, and he had no right to interfere. And John was dead. Tom wondered what his advice would be, and then it came to him.

The war was over, and thousands of veterans would be clamoring for work. Industry would look upon them as a cheap and plentiful supply of labor to fuel the engines of postwar recovery. He remembered the vow he had made at the site of John's bloody death, and suddenly his path lay clear before him. That very night he went "over the hill," taking with him his white cane and still wearing the shabby, ill-fitting uniform in which the government had clothed him. He might be legally blind, but his arms and legs and his back were strong. He would go to New York, walk if he had to. There'd be work on the docks for a man who wasn't afraid to break a sweat. No one there would care how he looked. There was nobility in honest labor, nobility that would help him rise above even the worst the world had to offer. No hardship, no indignity, no pain of rejection could dissuade him from spending the rest of his life trying to improve the lot of the worker.

*　　*　　*

Charles looked upon the postwar years in quite a different light. As president of the board of directors of BE Inc., he envisioned the returning veterans getting jobs, marrying, and raising families, becoming part of America's burgeoning consumer economy. That made each veteran a prospective customer of BE Inc., whether he wanted to buy the goods and services of its subsidiary companies or to purchase stock in the corporation itself. The latter particularly intrigued Charles. Bachelor Enterprises owned three banks when it first issued stock for sale to the public as BE Inc. His first goal was to expand the corporation's financial reach by acquiring more banks, until BE controlled more than fifty nationwide.

Within each bank, he established brokerages, staffing them with a cadre of highly motivated, thoroughly committed salesmen with a single product, common stock. BE brokers were trained to sell shares with the zeal of missionaries. Clients were told they were buying not just a piece of the corporation but a share in America's future. No one had to be rich to take part in the nation's economic expansion. If a customer was short of cash for an investment, he could buy stock on margin, in effect putting down a little of his own money and borrowing the balance from his broker. The broker in turn borrowed from his parent bank, using the purchased stock as collateral for the loan. That cycle, repeated over and over again throughout the nation and touching every imaginable business enterprise, spun onward and upward, creating a soaring stock market that was the envy of the world.

"A man would have to be blind or exceedingly stupid not to grow rich in an economy like ours," Charles was fond of saying. "The stock market has nowhere to go but up."

"One word of caution," said Barron. "The profits look fine on paper. But never forget that they are just that—paper, and nothing more."

"But what is the likelihood that all our investors would sell off their holdings at the same time? About as likely as every depositor of a bank asking to close out his account at the same time. A bank is founded on the premise that money deposited for safe keeping can be safely used to create new wealth. The principle is the same in the stock market. Wealth invested creates more wealth."

"It certainly seems to be working out that way," Teddy agreed.

"So it seems," Barron admitted. "But it sounds to me like the economic equivalent of a perpetual motion machine. It may be running well at the moment, but what if it stops? The inflated value of stock also troubles me. BE is nearing fifty dollars a share, while I calculate it should be closer to twenty-five dollars, based on earnings. Still, it continues to rise. Why?"

"It's the competition for the stock itself," Charles said. "The certificates have become a commodity and are simply responding to the law of supply and demand. If one buyer offers twenty dollars a share and another offers thirty, the stock will sell for thirty."

"Even if the company itself may be faltering," Barron noted. "It doesn't make sense to me. It is a phenomenon I hadn't anticipated when we went public. It's illogical, and I don't approve of it."

"But in addition to filling the company's coffers for things like expansion and equipment replacement, it also provides The Bachelor Foundation with the wherewithal to feed the hungry and clothe the naked," Charles pointed out. "Certainly you approve of that."

Barron did approve. He had put the foundation at the disposal of the American Relief Administration, whose aim it was to help alleviate the starvation and suffering of Europe's millions after the Great War. That alliance brought the administration's chairman, Herbert Clark Hoover, to the Bachelors' dinner table at one point and led eventually to a key role for the foundation in the relief of the Russian famine of 1921. Later Hoover sought Barron's help in relieving the misery caused by a Mississippi River flood. In 1923, it provided vessels and earthquake relief supplies to Japan. No humanitarian task was too large or too small for the foundation to undertake, so long as profits from BE Inc. kept pouring in. Barron's distrust of the system lessened when Hoover's name was mentioned prominently as a Republican candidate for vice-president in 1924. Hoover announced at the time that he saw nothing amiss in the breathtaking upward spiral of the stock market.

"If a major political party will consider him for the vice-president, I see no reason to question his judgment," Barron said. "The man is highly respected around the world. I'm a mere businessman, and retired at that. Far be it from me to challenge his views."

A reluctant nominee at best, Hoover was overwhelmingly rejected by his party at its national convention, but a philosophical soul mate, Calvin Collidge, not only won the presidential nomination but went on to victory in the general election. Barron accepted the party's success as vindication of Charles's business strategy and never again questioned his free-wheeling activities. Further bolstering Barron's confidence, Hoover succeeded Coolidge as GOP standard bearer in 1928, and he, too, went on to the White House. In his inaugural address, Hoover said, "Ours is a land rich in resources. . . . In no nation are the fruits of accomplishment more secure. . . . I have no fear for the future of our country." And the stock market, bellwether of that future, roared recklessly toward the end of the decade.

*   *   *

Teddy wasn't interested in the superficial issues of the 1920s. It mattered not at all whether her hair was bobbed or her hemline rose or fell. Her scars dictated her style of dress and coiffeur. And no power in the world of high fashion could squeeze her womanly figure into the popular boyish styles. As for wild parties, to Teddy they were characterized by a dinner conversation that lasted past nine o'clock and might include a raised voice or two. If the subject was the stock market, she'd rather help clear the table.

The more important issues of the day did engage her attention. Her preoccupation with motherhood left her little time for the radical activism of her college days. But the issues that stirred her youthful passions still brought the blood to her cheeks and a fire to her belly. She wrote numerous letters to recalcitrant congressmen on the issue of woman's suffrage, pointing to her native California as proof that the political world would not turn chaotic if women were allowed to vote. She left the picket lines and the mass arrests to a new era of activists but was satisfied that her small contribution helped pass the 19th Amendment, which marked the beginning of the 1920s. She was thoroughly in sympathy with the rise of trade unionism and the growth of socialism from clandestine neighborhood meetings to full-fledged national political conventions. But given her preoccupation with raising her son, she confined her political efforts to her writing desk. Whereas her late mother had been a literary bee in the bonnets of San Francisco newspaper editors, Teddy went right to the top. Along with many of the country's leading intellectuals, she wrote directly to President Warren G. Harding to plead for the release of Socialist leader Eugene V. Debs from a Florida prison in 1921. The letter-writing campaign was successful, although the president's compassion drew sneers from both her father and her husband. She was not so successful in working for the release of Mooney and Billings, the San Francisco labor martyrs who went to prison for the Preparedness Day bombing that had injured Tom Quinn back in 1917. She also counted Nicola Sacco and Bartolomeo Vanzetti among her lost causes.

Her political involvement was not a topic of dinner table conversation, since it ran contrary to the views of both her husband and her father. Trade unionism, they both believed, was attractive only to lazy malcontents, stirred to action by foreign agitators who brought the plague of Bolshevism to the land of liberty. Immigration must be halted, they argued, if Bolshevism were ever to be stamped out. Teddy ignored their ranting. She wasn't afraid of Bolshevism or the flood of immigrants. Trade unionism sought a fair shake for all workers, regardless of their politics or their country of origin. They were the heroes of the American economy, the men and women who made the wheels of industry turn. They were the heroes and heroines of the books and stories of John Manchester and the paintings of Tom Quinn. No foreign ideology could ever get them to plot the overthrow of the government of the greatest democracy in the world. American workers were not fools. They could not be hoodwinked by an alien philosophy. They were decent people, Teddy was certain, as committed to a free market economy as any capitalist, so long as they were treated fairly. She prayed she would be successful in passing on her views to her son.

The baby's presence in their lives seemed to draw Teddy and

Barron closer, helping to smooth out the rough edges of their relationship. But she could not press the infant's lips against her breast without thinking of the handsome young artist whose blood flowed through his veins. As Cullen St. Martin Bachelor grew to boyhood, she could see Tom Quinn in the child's blue eyes and his curly black hair. He was there, too, in the boy's ready smile and in that faraway look that crossed his face at odd moments, as if he, too, wondered who he was, where he came from, and where he might go.

Not that there was ever a suspicion on the child's part about his parentage. On the contrary, there was an unmistakable bond of love between Barron and the boy. He was simply an introspective lad, a visionary, Teddy believed, with a dark corner in his heart where shadowy images lurked and sometimes came to the fore to leave him spellbound, enchanted for long moments on end. She often dreamed that he would become a famous artist, one who would exorcise his private demons and unleash his personal fantasies on canvas as his natural father had done. He did seem innately fond of the large portrait in the parlor, the highly idealized painting of Teddy, her youthful beauty enhanced by candlelight, the vision that the lovesick Tom Quinn carried away from her table so many years ago.

When he was old enough to ask, Teddy told her son about the painting and about the artist whose genius inspired establishment of the San Francisco Museum of Contemporary Art and whose life and work had been cut short by the war.

"Is he dead, Mama?" the boy asked.

"I don't suppose we'll ever know," she replied. "He went away to war and never returned."

"Then he must be dead," said the boy with a child's simple logic.

She drew him close to her and hugged him, tears welling in her eyes.

"He'll never really be dead," she said. "Not so long as his paintings exist. They came from deep in his soul. He put some of himself into each work of art, and he will live there forever."

"At the museum?" the boy asked.

"And here, too, in that picture of me. Tom Quinn will always be there in spirit."

"Well, his spirit may be there, but he's dead," the child concluded.

Teddy was equally certain that Tom was alive. Why else would he live so vividly in her memory? She could never forget their days of happiness. She knew that someday he would return. She would answer the doorbell, and he would be standing there. What would she say to him? She rehearsed a hundred greetings over the years, although she knew that nothing she could say would convey what she felt in her heart. He would live forever as the hero of her child-hood dreams, the one great love of her life. Surely she would feel it deep inside if Tom were dead.

*   *   *

Tom spent his first night in New York at a Bowery mission, listening to the evening sermon and receiving in exchange a steaming cup of coffee, a hard roll, and a bowl of thin soup to soak it in. When the clock stuck ten, he lined up for a worn blanket that smelled of mothballs and was assigned to a cot in a flea-infested dormitory. There he and an equally miserable company of derelicts received the blessing of God Almighty, administered by a self-righteous little man with a wrinkled nose and a permanent expression of disdain.

"God would'a come hisself," cracked a tubercular old man as the lights clicked off, "but he couldn't stand the smell in this joint!"

Tom and the old man kept up a chorus of coughing long into the night that left them all cursing in frustration. The coughing and the snoring and the mad sleep-talk of men even more desperate than himself kept him awake most of the night. In the frigid predawn, he arose to find the old consumptive dead. He paused only long enough to mutter a few words of pity over the body. Then he snatched the dead man's muffler and headed for the door. As he wrapped the scarf about his own neck, he remembered the drunken professor hanging from a Barbary Coast lamppost many long years ago. It brought a grim smile to his face. Death no longer was the shocking stranger it had been that day; it had become an all too familiar companion since his days in the trenches. It was near him even now, as his hunger pangs reminded him. He shoved his hands deep into his pockets and hit the streets in search of work.

What he found after several days of failure and near starvation was an offer of a dollar and a half a day for a twelve-hour shift working in the hold of a freighter, loading sacks of grain and crates of food bound for Europe's hungry millions. The irony was not lost on him when after five arduous hours, he was near collapse from fatigue and lack of food and facing a lunch break without a bite to eat. As he rested in the dusty bowels of the ship, trying to gather his strength for a long, hard afternoon, a longshoreman nudged him and stuck a cold sausage in his face.

"Eat this," the man said. "and this, too." He handed Tom a half-eaten onion and the remains of a chewy bagel.

"Are you sure you can spare it?" Tom asked.

"Eat," said the man. "You'll never last the afternoon if you don't. And if you don't finish the shift, you don't get paid."

Tom took the remains of the man's lunch and ate it hungrily. His benefactor was a short man with spectacles nearly as thick as his own, a bull-necked little fellow with a huge chest and heavily muscled arms, all carried on thin, misshapen legs that seemed un-equal to the burden of his massive upper body. In the dim light of the hold and with his own eyes as weak as they were, Tom could not make out his face with clarity. But he knew it must be kindly face, for the man had shared his meager meal with a stranger.

"Thanks," Tom said, extending his hand. "I know I'll make it now."

The man slapped at the hand in a good-natured way as if embar-rassed by Tom's gratitude. Then the whistle blew, and the foreman shouted down into the hold to stand by to receive another load. As they took their places, a cargo net laden with sacks of grain was lowered between them. They made a good team, grabbing the ears of each sack and swinging it onto a waiting dolly to be wheeled off and stacked against the bulkhead. All afternoon they worked until even the deck under their feet was carpeted with sacks of grain. As they worked into the evening, the growing load virtually lifted them, sack by sack, toward the opened hatch. When the quitting whistle blew at last, it was very dark and a cold wind whipped in off the river and stirred the grain dust into suffocating clouds. Gratefully the crew rode the last empty net onto the deck and lined up for their pay. Then it was down the gangway into the night.

"You got no place to go, you come with me," said Tom's new friend. "There'll be goulash and bread and a place for you to sleep on the floor."

"I'd be obliged," said Tom, and the two set out down the wharves and into bleak streets lined with tenements.

His name was Lucjan Szydloski, and he lived in a two-room apartment with his wife and three children. His most prized possession was a concertina his father had given him before he set out for America, and after dinner he played the melancholy airs he remembered from his childhood. On Tom's third night in the cramped apartment, his host took him aside and showed him a smudged and wrinkled card that identified him as John S. Loski, a member in good standing of the Industrial Workers of the World.

"There's a meeting tonight," Loski said. "You come. Join us. When we all stand together, the bosses will have to listen to us. We'll tell them we want more money and an eight-hour day. You like that? Then come with me tonight. And don't say nothin' to nobody, understand? Not until we all stand together and are strong."

Tom understood. At the meeting he saw others like himself, still clad in the remnants of their army uniforms, all ragged and destitute, but intent on doing battle against oblivious capitalism for the greater good of the working people of the world. He paid out fifty cents from his earnings and got a card with his name on it and was invited to stay to hear a speaker who had come especially to rally them behind the Socialist party candidate for the presidency of the United States. Eugene V. Debs was counting on the support of working men and women like themselves, said the young speaker, who said he regretted very much that Debs could not be there in person.

"If he wants our vote, he ought to be here," Tom observed.

"He can't be," Loski whispered. "He's in the federal penitentiary down in Atlanta, serving time for speaking against the war."

Tom might have been locked up himself if weren't for a quirk of fate. It was January 2, 1920, and while the local IWW met in secret in the basement of a nearby tenement, federal agents raided the apartment of Lucjan Szydloski, a.k.a. John S. Loski. The raid was part of a Justice Department crackdown on aliens who the government believed were intent on overthrowing the government. Loski's oldest son, a brave lad of nine years, brought his father the news that drove him into hiding. But before he went, Loski bid farewell to Tom.

"You're on your own, now," he said. "Take my advice. Don't go near the docks for awhile. They'll be looking for us. An informant tipped them off. Get away. Go across the country with your card. Look for the hardest, dirtiest jobs around. Go into the mines and into the mills. Go into the lumber camps and join the railroad gangs. Go where workers have to sweat for a living. Go and organize them. Tell them that together they can be strong. And good luck to you, Tom Allmen."

Tom often thought about John Loski during the hard years that followed, years spent as an itinerant labor organizer. He thought of him as he was being chased out of the migrant camps of Florida at harvest time. He thought of him as he lay semiconscious in a dank jail cell in a Colorado mining town, with an angry mob outside screaming for his blood. He thought of him as he viewed with disgust the beaten and burned body of a brother organizer as it dangled from a railroad trestle along an Arizona right-of-way. And he thought of him late in that troubled decade as he sat upon the dais in a Los Angeles union hall as the local chapter of the International Long-shoreman's Association invested its officers. Long after he had turned into a respectable trade unionist, long after the IWW membership card had become a relic of a bygone day, Tom thought of the un-selfish kindness of John Loski. To Tom, he represented the best of the labor movement, the pioneer who was willing to sacrifice every-thing to win the battle to better the lot of the working class. Loski never heard the social theories that fell so glibly from the lips of John Manchester or the drawing-room rhetoric of Mabel Meyers. Loski was a front-line hero of the labor wars and as such, he always had a special place in Tom's heart.

As he left the union hall and rode the trolley out to the cottage he rented on the outskirts of the city, Tom wondered what became of Loski. Caught, finally, he supposed. Caught and deported during the Red scares that marked the decade. It was a long, lonely ride by trolley and, as usual, his thoughts roamed the green, sunlit meadows and the sun-dappled woodlands where he had spent so many happy hours with Teddy. She, too, was always with him. She was a warm memory on a cold night, a beautiful presence in a world of ugliness, a dream of love amid a nightmare of hatred and rejection. He walked the last two blocks to his cottage and went inside. He took a bottle of near-beer from the refrigerator, spiked it with a shot of grain alcohol and sat alone at the table to drink it. He noted the date on which his brothers had elected him secretary of their still-unrecognized local—October 23, 1929. Teddy might have been proud of him. His wandering days were over. He had settled down. The cottage was comfortable, if lonely. He wondered if she still lived in the mansion overlooking the Golden Gate. He could imagine her now as she was during those weeks of love at the hacienda. His damaged eyes now saw only in shades of gray, but in his memory she lived in vivid color. How beautiful she was, how he longed to be near her again. As the clock struck midnight, he laid his head upon his arms and cried himself to sleep.

19

The stock market opened firm in heavy trading, to Charles's immense gratification. It was a miracle that never ceased to enthrall him. There was a buyer for every seller on Wall Street. It was the miracle that sustained his banks and his brokerage houses and those of the entire nation. Barron's reservations to the contrary, it was the closest man would ever come to perpetual motion, of this he was certain. It was worth arising before dawn each weekday just to be in the office to catch the opening reports from the New York Stock Exchange.

The three-hour time differential suited him perfectly. He could test the pulse of the market before most of his world was awake. Over his first cup of coffee, he could pore over the charts and graphs and portfolios strewn across his desk. By eight, he could stand at his window high above Montgomery Street and look down upon the scurrying crowd, satisfied that he had already made decisions that would help fuel the mighty engines of commerce for the remainder of the day.

He was not a cocky man. He didn't put on his air of confidence each day as he put on his trousers. Rather he build that confidence with a combination of ritual and reaction. The ritual involved snapping on the tickertape at precisely six thirty, allowing it to advance until it touched the carpet. He then retrieved it and ran it between his fingertips in a sensual manner as his practiced eye scanned the figures and symbols that the little machine stamped out. His reaction was more of an intellectual exercise. As his eyes fell upon each successive group of figures, he knew immediately which demanded a response from him and, more than likely, just what that response should be. At each point of reaction, he snipped the tape and skewered it on a slim spike that protruded from the wall. Then his fingers resumed the ritualistic massaging of the endlessly flowing tape.

Soon he was busily reaffirming his initial responses, studying earnings reports, performance charts, and news clippings from financial journals. Next step was to communicate by telephone with

BE brokerage houses in every major city in the United States, advising them on what to buy and what to sell during the business day. His commands were issued in a firm, calm voice, "Buy AT&T, sell Magneto Electric, margin call on Florida Beachcomber Inc." These were the marching orders for an army of brokers, the front line troops in his battle to make BE Inc. the greatest corporation in the nation.

On this day, October 24, 1929, confidence had been a little slow in coming. Since the market suffered a major downturn on September 5, Charles had been troubled by the doomsayers, that minority of analysts who predicted calamity around every corner. Their cautions lingered in the back of his mind like those of a fundamentalist preacher warning of the wages of sin. Yet nearly every day for many weeks, the market had demonstrated a remarkable underlying strength. The foundations of the economy was rock-solid, no doubt about it. Although he did have a doubt now and then, when the tickertape clicked to life, he was easily lulled by the tale it told.

It had been ten years since he took over the day-to-day operation of BE Inc. While Barron devoted himself to family and the good works of the Bachelor Foundation, Charles worked to turn an already huge and successful conglomerate into a commercial colossus. Steamship lines, railroads, banks, construction, land and lumber companies, automobile manufacturers, publishing houses, and a multitude of businesses were sheltered and nurtured under the broad umbrella of BE Inc.

As the corporation grew, stock was issued for public sale, slowly and cautiously at first, then in larger and larger blocks. The board of directors' most recent offering was two million shares at twenty dollars a share. The same board, then sitting as directors of BE Securities, a subsidiary of Enterprise Bank, which they also controlled, voted to purchase one million of those shares for future delivery at the twenty-dollar offering price. The issue was an immediate success. At the end of the first day of frenzied trading, it closed at thirty dollars a share. BE's own brokers were selling it on margin, with purchasers putting up as little as one hundred dollars for a thousand dollars worth of stock. The brokerage houses loaned investors the balance at nine percent interest, then turned to Enterprise Bank to borrow at four percent the money necessary to cover the loans. Speculators continued to snap up BE stock at a dizzying rate, driving its price even higher. Soon BE's original "purchase" had doubled in value to forty million dollars. The time then was ripe for BE Securities to sell at forty dollars a share the same stock it had purchased at twenty dollars a share. The resulting profit was used to cover the brokerage loans to investors, and the brokers in turn paid off the interest owed to Enterprise Bank. And the ride into the wild blue yonder was far from over.

In three months, the original two million shares had been sold along with a subsequent issue of another million shares to satisfy the market's insatiable demand. By this time, the price had nearly doubled again, and the directors of BE Inc. sought new possibilities in market manipulation. Charles went over the details again and again. It was foolproof; every move worked just as he anticipated it would. He had grown rich. Every member of the board had grown rich. Private speculators had grown rich. And the Bachelor Foundation had grown rich. Barron was a happy man, spreading his good works throughout a grateful world. Pessimists might warn of storm clouds on the horizon, but Charles basked in the glow of success.

A cloud or two did appear occasionally. On this day, for instance, BE plunged during the second hour of trading. Charles had coffee brought in at nine and nervously continued running the tape through his fingers. By ten o'clock, the coffee was twisting his stomach into knots and his palms were sweaty. The telephone rang.

"What's happening, Charles?"

"Nothing extraordinary, Barron, a technical correction, nothing more. The economy remains strong. We remain strong. We should have nothing to fear."

"*Should* have?"

"We *have* nothing to fear. Trust me."

"I was going down to see a vessel off, but I think I'll wait here at the office. I'll call you later."

"I'll be here."

Charles went back to the tape and ran yards of it through his fingers. The volume was extraordinarily heavy. The tape was running nearly an hour behind trading in a wave of selling. Prices were plummeting. He called his personal broker and put in a buy order for one hundred thousand dollars.

"That should help, Mr. Cullen. It's a bargain day on Wall Street."

"Get that order in quickly," Charles ordered. "Get all your buy orders in quickly. It's not too late to turn this around."

"There are no other buy orders," said the broker.

"Just do as I say," he said, hanging up the receiver. Someone must buy, he thought. Prices are going to hell. It's bargain day, all right. What will it take to shake loose a little cash, he wondered? The market was awash with BE stock. Where were the big-time speculators when you needed them?

At eleven, Barron called again.

"It's still dropping," Charles reported. "Can you do anything?"

"I can buy."

"Then do it, please. I've already placed an order for one hundred thousand."

"That much? You're not getting panicky, are you?"

"I'm concerned," said Charles. "Nobody, absolutely nobody is buying. If you could match my purchase—"

"Of course, if you think it will do any good. If you want my personal opinion, I think this is a major correction. Prices are finally coming into line with earnings. Now if we could just get rid of those margin accounts—"

"We're trying," Charles conceded glumly. "Tens of thousands of investors are being wiped out—our investors. Margin calls are going out all over the system, but few investors have the cash to cover them."

"We were too generous with them," said Barron. "No more credit. It's the only way."

"That means many more thousands will be wiped out. We need cash and we need it quickly."

"I heard on the radio that the New York bankers are meeting to discuss shoring up the market. Enterprise representatives are sitting with them. We'll do our share to help stem the tide."

"I doubt if Enterprise will be able to help much," said Charles. "We're holding vaults full of paper that is growing more worthless by the minute. What we need is cash, lots of it. Call your broker and do what you can. Call your friends. Tell them it's their chance to get stock in quality companies at bargain prices. Tell them that the market needs them if it's to survive. They must buy, buy, buy!"

Charles called in another buy order, this time for one hundred thousand dollars. It gave him the hopeless feeling that he was throwing a bucket of water on the fires of hell.

By noon, New York time, the plunge halted and the market leveled off far on the downside. It had sustained major losses, losses in the hundreds of millions, but on the floor of the exchange, the consensus was that the worst was over. Unfortunately, that was not the impression that the overburdened tickertape was distributing belatedly to brokerage houses around the nation. As it lagged farther and farther behind trading, the tape spread the tale of the morning's disaster slowly, one click at a time. Throughout the hinterland, the mad scramble to sell turned to panic. Margin calls continued throughout the day, and thousands of investors, hopelessly overextended, found it impossible to respond with cash. Their securities were thrown into the whirlpool for whatever they might bring. More often than not, they brought nothing.

Next morning the pressure eased, suggesting that the worst might be over. In the back rooms of Wall Street and in boardrooms across the county, business leaders totaled their losses and charted programs of retrenchment. The slide, less precipitous now, continued in heavy trading throughout the day Friday, and into a brief Saturday session. Charles met late Saturday afternoon with BE directors, who concluded that the corporation had been badly damaged and there was little or nothing they could do about it. They were at the mercy of a market that had taken on a life of its own, and they could only wait and see what happened next.

"We have a day of respite ahead of us, gentlemen," Charles said. "I don't know what you're going to do, but I intend to gather my family around me, take them to church and pray like I've never prayed before."

*   *   *

Charles led the family procession into Grace Cathedral. Behind him came his grandson, Cullen St. Martin Bachelor, called Marty by his classmates. At ten years of age, Marty was tall and handsome in the uniform of Larkspur Academy. His mother followed, wearing a stylish dress of blue silk with a low waistline and long sleeves, a mink-trimmed hat and matching stole. Barron, as always, clad in a black suit and tie, followed his family down the aisle and into their pew. Together the family knelt in prayer. Charles was the last to rise from the kneeler.

After the service, they ran into Allie Wheatley in the vestibule.

"Allie!" Teddy exclaimed. "You look wonderful! Where have you been keeping yourself? You must come and have dinner with us. It's been ages since we've talked."

"I'd love to, Teddy. What a handsome boy you have, and so tall!"

"Thank goodness you're here," Teddy whispered as they headed for the car. "At last someone to talk to. If I have to listen to another word about the stock market I'll die."

After dinner, they left the men at the table and escaped to the patio to talk. Marty followed them.

"He's such a bright boy," said Allie. "You must be very proud."

"We both are," Teddy admitted. "But I can't take credit for his intelligence. He must get that from his father."

"You're much too modest, my dear. He is beginning to look a lot like Barron," Allie said innocently.

"I don't look at all like father," Marty said.

"At times you do," said Teddy, thinking how much he really resembled the young Tom Quinn.

"Daddy's hair is white," said the boy. "Mine is black."

"I remember your father when his hair was blond," said Allie. "That was many years ago when your mother and I were in school. You look very handsome in your uniform, Marty. How do you like school?"

"I like it a lot," he said. "It's very exclusive, you know. All the boys come from the very best families."

"Really, Marty!" his mother exclaimed. "I hope that isn't how you evaluate your friends. We sent you to Larkspur because of its highly accredited academic program, not for its social advantages."

"I know, Mother, but they are the very best boys, don't you think? And all very wealthy, too."

"That sounds like snobbery to me, young man. If that's what you're learning at the academy, perhaps we ought to reconsider our decision."

"But you know it's true, Mother."

"I don't know that at all! What makes you think they're any better than anyone else?"

"Because they have more money, of course. That makes all the difference, don't you think, Miss Wheatley?"

209

"Why, I never thought about it, Marty," Allie stammered. "I think nice people are just nice people. Money has nothing to do with it."

"I certainly agree," said Teddy. "Some very nice people are completely unselfish. Look at your father, for example. His job is to give his money away to help others."

"Yes, and that's peculiar," said Marty precociously. "All my friends say so. Their fathers seem to like making all sorts of money."

"There are more important things in life than money," Allie said.

"That's not what Grandpa thinks," said the lad. "He lost a lot of money, and he's very upset about it."

Charles came out onto the patio at that moment. He walked slowly, as if he were very tired. His face seemed drawn, his eyes heavy-lidded and darkly encircled. He paused at the fishpond where Marty sat idly watching the gold fish swim about. He put his hand on the boy's shoulder and smiled fondly down at him.

"Hi, Grandpa, let's walk to the park and feed the pigeons."

"I'd like nothing better, my boy, but I have some work I must attend to this afternoon."

"Then will you come back for supper? The cook's going to make Welch rarebit, and we'll have ice cream."

"That sounds very tempting indeed. But I must go now. I just came to say good-bye, and thank you, Teddy, for a delightful dinner."

Marty stood up and gave his grandfather a hug, and Charles held him tightly for a moment.

"You're letting all this stock market business trouble you, Father," said Teddy. "I wish you wouldn't worry so. I wish you'd never gotten involved in the corporation."

"Nonsense," Charles said. "This will pass. It's a technical correction. We'll ride it out." He hugged her, then held her at arms's length and gazed at her with sadness in his eyes. "Good-bye, my dear. And good-bye to you, Allie. It does an old man's heart good to see you two old friends together again."

"Come along, Charles. The car is waiting," Barron called from the doorway.

"Can I go too?" Marty asked.

"No, my boy. Your grandfather and I have things we must discuss," Barron said.

"I know," the boy said sagely. "You're going to talk about money."

"Perhaps we will," said his grandfather, brushing a curly lock of hair from his forehead. "Perhaps we will."

*   *   *

Monday was another horrendous day on the market. The volume of trade was still heavy, the losses severe. Again the tickertape lagged behind the action on the floor of the exchange, so that the news that arrived in San Francisco was unreservedly bad. By ten o'clock, Charles had thrown everything he had into the sinking market, and nothing seemed to buoy it. At ten-thirty, his agent at the exchange telephoned to report that several of the New York bankers were meeting again and that a ray of hope was spreading across the trading floor. Charles went back to the tape and noticed that steel was staging a modest rally on that than bit of news. But still the dismal reports continued and in the final hour of trade, more than three million shares went begging. Tomorrow's opening could be nothing but disastrous. Of that he was certain. He knew that the end had come.

It was late afternoon when his telephone ran, arousing him from a veritable stupor.

"Are you all right, Father?"

"Yes, yes, Teddy. I guess I just dozed off."

"I've had the radio on. It sounds terrible. What's happening?"

"It is terrible, but you mustn't worry. Promise me you won't."

"I'm only worried about you," she said. "I don't care about the money."

Charles was silent for a long time.

"You know, you're right, Teddy. The money isn't important. How's Marty?"

"Fine. I took him to the ferry this morning. He's back in school. He talked about the stock market all the way down to the slip. I'm afraid he's inherited your fascination with it. I do hope you'll see to it that he keeps it all in perspective."

"Of course, my dear."

"Can I bring you anything? Did you have lunch?"

"I had coffee and a roll brought in a while ago. I'm fine. I'll just get this mess on my desk straightened out and then I'll drop by Tadich's for supper. I dare say the place will be abuzz."

"All right, but don't work too hard. You need some rest."

"Yes, my dear. Good-bye."

The fog of an October evening had enveloped the Bachelor building by the time Charles put the last piece of paper in its proper place and turned to take one final look about the office. Then he rode the elevator down to the lobby, where he paused to adjust his fedora, pull on his gloves, and buff the silver head of his walking stick against his topcoat. The doorman, accustomed to his irregular hours, unlocked the door for him, and Charles walked out onto Montgomery and headed for Market Street. There he turned toward the Ferry Building and was suddenly transported to another time, a time when the city lay in ruins all around him and the fetid odor of smoke and ashes filled the air. In his mind's eye, he saw again the gutted, smoldering shell of the Palace Hotel and the full impact of the devastation rushed in upon him. His knees buckled, and he had to brace himself with his stick. Then he began shuffling slowly toward the wharves. Out on the pier, he paused to look back upon everything he had held dear and saw that it had vanished as if in a cloud of smoke. From his pocket he withdrew a fifty-cent piece for the boatman. It seemed a modest price to escape such a tragedy. In the dark of evening, the bay stretched before him, cold and forbidding. But somewhere across the water lay the promise of a better tomorrow.

*   *   *

On Tuesday, October 29, the bottom fell out, just as Charles knew it would. Huge blocks of the American dream were thrown into the vortex only to swirl away like water down a drain. By noon San Francisco time, it was all over. The battered economy, on its knees for days, finally collapsed in a heap of worthless gilt-edged paper.

Barron, who had been following the news on the radio, telephoned Charles's office to see if anything could be done. When his ring went unanswered, he headed immediately for Montgomery

Street. He found the office in perfect order, except for the pile of tickertape that had accumulated on the floor beneath the machine. Strange, he thought, that Charles had forgotten to turn it off. On the desk he discovered a letter addressed to "Barron, Teddy, and Marty." A cold chill passed over him as he reached for a letter opener. The telephone rang before he could insert the blade. It was the police.

"No, he's not in. This is Barron Bachelor speaking. I'm his son-in-law. Yes, of course. We'll be down within the hour. Thank you."

The police commissioner himself received Barron and Teddy in his office. He was solemn, but direct.

"We have reason to believe your father is dead, Mrs. Bachelor. We're pretty certain the body we removed from the bay is that of Charles Cullen, but a family member should make the official identification."

"I'll view the body," said Barron. "My wife—"

"I'll accompany him," said Teddy.

"All right, but first let me give you these things. They were found on Pier 23. A private patrolman for Bachelor Lines discovered them and gave us a call."

The commissioner laid upon his desk a fedora, a pair of gloves and a silver-headed walking stick. Teddy shuddered.

"And these were found on the body," the commissioner added, dumping some items from a small sack and sorting them out. There was a pocket watch that had stopped shortly past seven o'clock, a wedding ring, a wallet, and some keys. Teddy reached out tentatively, her fingers touching the wedding ring. There were tears in her eyes. "Oh, and this was in his hand," said the commissioner.

He handed her a fifty-cent piece.

213

20

Barron survived the crash with sufficient assets to make his presence felt at stockholders' meetings and his business reputation still intact. Whereas he had remained aloof from the day-to-day operation of BE Inc., he was determined not to let a board of strangers direct a corporation that had carried his family name for nearly three-quarters of a century. As The Bachelor Foundation foundered for lack of funds, he threw himself doggedly into the effort to save BE. First elected to the board in 1930, he quickly became its president and instituted a program of retrenchment. It began with the liquidation of the Enterprise Bank system, a move that further depleted BE's assets, for Barron insisted on making every effort to pay off depositors to avoid a panic. Next came the wholesale closing of failing affiliated businesses and the sale of marginal operations wherever buyers could be found. That left the corporation's emphasis on the historically most reliable producer, Bachelor Steamship Lines and its world trade network.

The closing of the Enterprise Bank in the summer of 1932 averted the chaos that was soon to overwhelm the rest of the nation's financial institutions. Teetering on the edge of an economic void, unable to balance its burden of unsecured debts, the nation's entire banking system seemed doomed to failure. Then, on March 4, 1933, Democrat Franklin Delano Roosevelt took the oath of office as president. The next day he issued an edict that halted transactions in gold to preserve the underpinnings of the currency and declared a bank holiday to halt the stampede by depositors seeking to withdraw their savings. FDR's action raised Barron's spirits, even though it came too late to save many of BE's business ventures. As more and more companies went under and the unemployment rate soared, it became clear to him that the only hope of saving what remained of Bachlor Enterprises was an infusion of capital. And there was no capital.

Barron's retrenchment efforts demanded month after month of eighteen-hour days, constant travel, and incessant demands on his time, talent, and expertise, all of which took a terrible toll. Only a few scant months after he finally was satisfied that he had done all he could to stem the flow of red ink, he was stricken by a mild heart attack. No one knew better than Barron himself that his years of youthful indulgence had weakened him irrevocably. There had been moments during his struggle against addiction when he thought he could feel the viselike grip of drugs upon his heart. And now, when he most needed his strength, his heart was tired and worn out, and it was failing him. Although he remained mentally alert, the attack turned him into a virtual invalid. Bedridden much of the time on his doctor's orders, he only occasionally felt strong enough to sit up in a wheelchair for an hour or so at a time. He had no choice but to relinquish the operation of BE to its board of directors. What little vitality he could muster he spent on his effort to keep the foundation alive.

"I trust the board now," he told Teddy, "I've taught them as best I could. But I felt pressured to close the foundation, so we reached a compromise. We voted to sever relations with the foundation. I'll keep it alive somehow with our personal funds. I must . . . it's a promise I made during the war and a promise I intend to keep, particularly in this day of bread lines and shantytowns. Charitable organizations are going to need our help, and that need can only become greater as the months pass. I know that someday we'll be in a position to play a major role again."

"What can I do to help?" she asked.

"You're doing all you can. You've cut household costs to the bone. We have virtually no social life. And most important, you don't complain."

"We could send Marty to public school."

"It may come to that," Barron conceded. "But only if we have no other recourse. He's making contacts at school that will be invaluable once the economy is on its feet again. We must try to give him every opportunity."

"Why not put the hacienda up for sale?"

"Who could afford to buy it? No, I've always thought I'd like to retire there someday when all this is over. It has great sentimental value, you know," he said, taking her hand in his.

"Oh, I feel so useless," Teddy said in exasperation. "There must be something more I could do."

"You seem to forget all you're doing to get me back on my feet again. No man ever had a better nurse or a more unselfish companion."

"No *man*, perhaps," she reminded him, "but I recall a woman who was nursed back to health, physically and emotionally, by a very unselfish husband. She owes him a debt she can never fully repay." She leaned over the bed and kissed him tenderly. The years had mellowed their relationship. There was no doubt in her mind that she had grown to love the husband who had taken back a faithless wife, who had accepted her son as his own, who had made a comfortable home for them, never asking anything for himself. "But if there is anything more I can do—"

"There's nothing more, Teddy, unless you happen to find a pot of gold."

There was no pot of gold, of course. She was even donating most of her household allowance to the Market Street soup kitchen where she spent two hours every Monday, Wednesday, and Friday helping to feed the hungry. At first she shared the embarrassment of those in the soup line, avoiding their eyes as they shuffled by with their bowls. But inevitably it brought to mind the experience of 1906, when as a schoolgirl, she had volunteered her time in the refugee camp. The current calamity might not be as devastating as the earthquake and fire, but its ultimate effect was similar. The depression had a way of erasing social barriers that had kept people apart. It instilled a deepening sense of interdependence. It brought people together. In no time at all, Teddy's embarrassment faded. She was offering a smile, a kind word, a nod of encouragement to those who came through the line. In her own way she was saying, "I understand. We all have suffered to some extent. We all have lost something. This is the time for us to pull together, to help one another. We can get through this with a little courage and determination. Don't give up hope."

Her teenage son had a very different view of the economic crisis. Marty was humiliated to find that she worked at a soup kitchen. He had returned from his first year in prep school a bitter young man, frustrated by the financial restrictions his father had placed on him. He resented being on a budget. He needed check-writing privileges in order to keep up with his classmates, he argued, trying to enlist his mother's support.

"They're old money, Mother. They're from the best families in the country, people who only know there's a depression because they read about it in newspapers. It seems to me that it's only the nouveau riche who are suffering, and it's their own fault for dabbling in the stock market."

"How dare you say that!" Teddy bristled. "There's not a family in America that hasn't been hurt to one extent or another by the crash. You would know that if you didn't choose your friends by the size of their fortunes. Perhaps you'll understand when we have to send you to public school."

"Nonsense," Marty said haughtily. "You wrote that father was working hard to save the corporation. I can't believe he's failed."

"He hasn't failed, but at what price? He's sacrificed his health. Why? Because he was thinking of our future. And all he asked was that you cut back on your spending."

"But I have to put up a good front, Mother," the boy insisted. "They know BE was Father's corporation. I've had to tell them he's giving all his money away through the foundation. They think it's terribly gallant, of course, but really, Mother, don't we come first?"

"If they consider it gallant to share with others, they ought to be quite impressed if you told them we're down to our last dollar."

"That's not funny, Mother."

"Indeed it's not. Your father has worked himself into a sickbed over it. I hope he never finds out how cavalier you are about his sacrifice. No telling what it would do to him. You're to say nothing to him about this, do you understand?"

"Oh, all right. But really, it's only money."

"Yes, it's only money. But don't underestimate the power of money. It was money that drove your grandfather Bachelor mad. It was money that caused your grandfather Cullen to take his own life. And it was money that nearly killed your father. I want you to go upstairs now and talk to him. And I warn you, don't ask him for more money; ask him what more you can do to help."

*   *   *

Barron's mention of a pot of gold stuck in Teddy's mind, but she was at a loss to make it a reality. Then one day in the early spring of 1934, an idea came knocking at her door in the person of Antonio Lazarro and his wife, Giovanna.

"We don't want to bother you, Mrs. Bachelor," Tony said shyly. "Maybe we shouldn't come. Vanna said no, we shouldn't come, but—"

A shudder went through her. Could it be they had bad news of Tom Quinn?

"Why, Mr. and Mrs. Lazarro, how wonderful to see you again. Please, won't you come in?"

"*Grazie*," Tony said with a nervous smile. "Come along, Mama." Giovanna Lazarro, her face frozen in a frown, her hands folded primly in front of her, followed Teddy into the parlor, where Tom's first portrait of his golden girl looked down from above the fireplace.

"Please, sit down," said Teddy. "May I bring you a cup of tea?"

"No, no, we don't want to put you to any trouble," said Tony.

"It would be no trouble. Tell me, how is the restaurant business? We haven't been out to dinner in ages. Barron has been ill, you know. Is everything going well with you?"

"No more restaurant," said Tony. "It's been divided. It's a garage now on one side where the kitchen used to be, and a small apartment on the other. Nobody had money to eat at *Vanna's* anymore, so now we keep our Ford there."

"We also remodeled Tom's studio," Vanna announced, prodding Tony.

"Yes, yes," Tony said, following her head. "It's a big apartment now. We rent it to a nice Italian family. They have four children. He's a fisherman, just like I was."

"Yes," Vanna said. "And Andrea, you remember Andrea. She and her husband live in the apartment next to the garage. He got laid off and they had no place else to go. So tell her why we came here, Tony. Tell her."

"Yes, we came across some of Tom's things. We thought you might want them."

"You mean in the studio," Teddy said by way of encouraging him to go on. She could see it all again as if it were yesterday—the cluttered room, the light pouring in through the front window, the easel with his latest canvas, the smell of oil and pigment, the lean, muscular arms that held her close. Yes, she remembered often.

"We found two paintings," Tony continued. "In the back closet, wrapped in a sheet. Maybe he forgot them. They've been there for a long time."

"Why, that's marvelous!" Teddy exclaimed. "Dr. Hobart will be thrilled."

"Maybe yes, maybe no," said Vanna disdainfully.

"Maybe you don't want nobody to see," Tony stammered. "Maybe you ought to look first. They're out in the Ford."

"You've brought them with you! Wonderful! I'm dying to see them."

Vanna stood up quickly, as if she couldn't get out of the house fast enough. Teddy followed them to the door and into the street, where Tony reached into the rumble seat and withdrew the paintings. He braced them against the steps and carefully lifted the dusty sheet that covered them. Teddy gasped in surprise at the sight of Tom's haunting painting of his mother, her ravaged beauty, the fear and weariness in her eyes as she trudged up the darkened stairway, the ghostly image of her night's companion lurking in the background. It was a masterpiece of moody introspection, one of Tom's earliest and very best works.

"It's beautiful!" Teddy said. "It's his mother, you know. I remember it well. And the other one?"

"Maybe you want to take it inside," Tony said nervously. "Maybe you don't want no one to see."

"Nonsense," said Teddy, as she gingerly tilted the first picture forward to reveal the second. It was the painting of her asleep amid a jumble of bedclothes, the golden light of early morning falling full upon her naked body. She quickly covered the canvases.

"I told you we shouldn't come," said Vanna disapprovingly.

"But it's Mrs. Bachelor's picture. She should have it," Tony said.

"Thank you, Mr. Lazarro," said Teddy, recovering from her shock. "I appreciate your consideration. But I can't accept them. They're rightfully yours. I'm sure Tom would want you to have them."

"We don't want them," Vanna insisted curtly. "You take them."

"I shouldn't," Teddy protested. "They're very important and valuable paintings. You should give them to the museum. Dr. Hobart would be delighted to have them. You could donate them." Then it struck her. "Or he might pay for them."

"No, no, no," Tony insisted. "They're not ours. They're Tom's, or yours. You give them to the museum. They don't belong to us."

"They certainly don't," Vanna agreed. "Good day, Mrs. Bachelor."

*   *   *

"Extraordinary," Hobart said. "Absolutely extraordinary. One of his very earliest works you, say. It borders on the surreal. It's excellent. His mother a Barbary Coast prostitute? I can't believe it! It's so intensely personal. Do you realize what a collector might pay for this?"

"There's another one in the closest downstairs. I didn't want Marty to see it."

"Good heavens, it must be really something! Let's have a look."

Teddy led him down the stairs and retrieved the painting from its hiding place. Hobart gasped when he saw it.

"Astonishing!" he exclaimed. "It's an entirely new direction for Quinn. It's unlike any of his other work. When was it done? It's so romantic, so intensely erotic. I never realized the scope of his . . . well, his interest in you. The more I learn about Quinn, the more impressed I am. He was an extraordinary young man. When was it done?"

"In 1917," Teddy said. "It was among the last paintings he did before the war."

"I thought what little work he produced in that period went up in smoke."

"This was done before he moved to the hacienda," Teddy explained guardedly. "It was painted in his apartment on Green Street and has been there ever since. The Lazarros found it when they went to renovate Tom's old quarters. It's been hidden away there for seventeen years."

"It's a beautiful work, Teddy. But then he could do no wrong with such a beautiful model. It's so sensuous, so provocative. It's reminiscent of Goya's *La maja desnuda*. And you, Teddy, you were his Duchess of Alba, his naked maja! Incredible! This could well become the art story of the century."

"I was afraid you'd say something like that," she said. "That's why I hid it. Can you imagine what Marty would say, or Barron? It must never be seen in public. Perhaps a private sale—"

"That's absolute nonsense, Teddy. It's a brilliant work. It must be shown. It's a Quinn such a we've never seen before. If this is the

220

caliber of the work he was doing just before he died, then his loss becomes all the more tragic. He had embarked on an entirely new phase, a romantic period, and apparently we have you to thank for that. The tenderness, the eroticism, the delicacy. This isn't the muscular dash of his blue-collar period; this is the deft touch of an artist enamored of his model. This will cause a stir in the art world such as we have never experienced. And we mustn't allow the modesty of his model to keep it from public view."

"Some things are more important," Teddy said quietly.

"I understand how you must feel. You may be right about your son. Young people can be very sensitive about such things, but certainly not Barron. He is a man of the world, after all. He will be proud of you! I remember those unhappy days when we all believed that Barron was dead. Why would he, why would anyone blame you for posing? How could he look upon this painting and not see it for what it is, a masterpiece."

"You think it may have some value?" she asked hesitantly.

"Artistically speaking, it's priceless. Commercially speaking, I dare say it would run into six figures."

"What about the painting of his mother or my portrait in the parlor of *The Blue Parrot* in the front hall?"

"Altogether? Worth a fortune, I'd say. I wouldn't be surprised if the right bidder offered a million dollars for the lot of them. Of course, you'd never sell—"

"Where would that kind of money be available today?" she asked skeptically.

"It's out there," Hobart said confidently. "In times like these, great art is one of the few things in the world that retains its value. You'd be surprised to learn how much of the money withdrawn from commerce has found its way into the art world. An auction in Paris last month attracted some of the largest bids in history. Oh, there's money in the world, my dear, money seeking safe haven in troubled economic times. Think of the oil princes, the arms manufacturers, the maharajas of the Near East, the royal houses of Europe, or what's left of them. There's a market for Tom's work, never doubt it."

"I see," Teddy said pensively. "In that case, I have an idea. Can you drive a truck?"

"A truck?" he asked in surprise. "No, of course not. What did you have in mind?"

"A little ride into the country," she replied mysteriously. "How about tomorrow? We'll take the old roadster. It should be big enough."

*   *   *

Hobart stood in the lantern light deep in the hacienda's musty cellar, surrounded by twenty or more paintings. In the cool atmosphere, his voice resounded off the earthen walls and echoed up through the open trap door into the kitchen, where Teddy sat alone at the table remembering. It was their last night together, and they had quarreled about time, unaware that they had so little of it. If only she had known then how precious time was. As the stale odor of smoke drifted off the paintings and out of the cellar, the terror of their last moments together came back to her over the years. She unbuttoned a cuff and turned back the sleeve to look at her scarred forearms. It had been worth it, she thought. Every moment of pain she had suffered over the years had been worth it. The greatest trauma of her life had vanished at last and in its place there was a ray of hope.

"Incredible," Hobart puffed as he struggled up the wooden stairs. "Teddy, how could you remain silent about this treasure all these years? These are works of genius! And so many! I counted twenty-three paintings, only one of them unfinished. Prodigious! And such intimacy! Such rapture! They will make a remarkable exhibit, a stunning show. It will revitalize the museum. 'Tom Quinn: The Romantic Period.' It will attract art lovers, critics, collectors from all over the world. It will be the exhibit to end all exhibits. And the love story! My God, Teddy, it will touch the hearts of millions! People who don't know a palette from an easel will weep at the tale of the tragic young artist obsessed with his beautiful but unattainable patroness. They'll write books about it, there'll be a moving picture—"

"Stop it! Please stop it!" Teddy screamed, tears rolling down her cheeks. Hobart staggered back in shock.

"My dear Teddy," he exclaimed. "I'm so sorry. I've been completely insensitive. This must be very difficult for you—the memories, the heartache you must have endured. Please, please forgive me." She had slumped forward on the table, her head resting on her arms,

222

her shoulders shaking with every sob, her tears dampening the ugly scar tissue that she had hidden for so many years. He laid his hand gently on her head and repeated, "I'm very, very sorry."

Teddy looked up and sat erect in her chair.

"No, don't be," she said, regaining control of her emotions. "It was just all too much. I was overwhelmed. Forgive me."

"Would it help to talk about it?" he asked.

"I remember the last time I saw Tom," she said. "We quarreled. He got very drunk, and a fire broke out in his studio. He was bitter. He didn't care if the paintings burned. He wanted them to burn. I sent him away for help and tried to save them. I thought he would be sorry later if they had been lost. I hid them away in the cellar so no one else would ever see them. They were ours. They were private."

"But you can't leave them there, Teddy," Hobart said gently. "They no longer belong to you or to Tom. They belong to the world."

"I understand," she whispered. "But it will be very difficult."

"For one with your courage? I think not. You risked your life to save these paintings. Could there be any greater risk?"

She looked at him steadily through tear-brimmed eyes.

"Yes," she said. "I risk my privacy, my reputation, my marriage. I risk the love of my son. I risk all that is left of my life."

"But you must think of Tom," he said earnestly. "Through these paintings he will live again. You owe him that, Teddy."

She stared evenly at the old man for a moment, then arose and went to the window and looked out at the charred ruins of the old barn across the way. They were overgrown now, the rubble entwined with wild morning glories and bordered by a golden phalanx of wild poppies. She could see the studio as it once was, see the handsome young artist smiling down from the window above, vigorous and full of life. A strange calm came over her, a feeling of happiness such as she had not known for many years.

"What makes you so sure that he's dead?" she asked.

*　　*　　*

One of the first victims of the stock market crash was trade unionism. After a decade of trying to overcome the stigma of radicalism, after years of painful struggle to unite the workers of America

223

and earn a modicum of respectability, the gains made by labor flew out the window to as shops and factories went dark, one by one, across the nation. It did a worker no good to belong to a union when there were no jobs. The impact was felt severely on the docks, where the struggle to organize had been the most difficult and largely ineffective. Favoritism was still the rule. Jobs went to the most passive, the most docile. Union members and their supporters were considered troublemakers and were routinely discriminated against in hiring. Tom Allmen was one of them. He was known to speak for many of his fellow workers, although he refused to divulge their names. He came regularly to the hiring office in San Pedro to plead their cause.

"There are no jobs, Mr. Allmen," said the man with the big cigar who sat behind a desk. "Get out of here."

"We could shut you down," Tom pointed out. "Our picket line could tie up your ships for weeks."

"Then we would kick ass and take names," said the man in his menacing monotone. "You and your rabble-rousers would never work on these docks again. Now get out of here."

"The president of the United States himself said that if he were a worker, he would join a union," Tom argued.

"Then we wouldn't hire Mr. Roosevelt," said the man with the big cigar. "Get out, Mr. Allmen. You're beginning to annoy me."

"There's a freighter sailing tomorrow," Tom pointed out.

"It's nearly loaded, Mr. Allmen. I don't want to ask you again. You're not only half-blind, you're apparently totally deaf. Get out." His voice was low and calm and ominous. Two burly men seated at the side of the room stirred restlessly.

"That ship is being loaded by scabs." said Tom.

"My patience has run out, Mr. Allmen. You don't seem to realize a very simple fact—we do not recognize your union. Do you understand?" He looked up at Tom and blew a thin ribbon of smoke at him.

"We'll see about that," Tom began, but the man's huge fist slammed down suddenly on the desk top with such force that his ashtray danced wildly, scattering cigar ash this way and that. The two goons rushed Tom and hustled him out the door. They paused at the top of the stairs that led down to the pier and looked back for instructions.

"I don't want to see you on these docks again," boomed the voice from behind the desk. "And tell your union people they are not welcome here. If they form a picket line, we will take their pictures, we will take their names, we will crack their skulls, we will see that they never work again. You tell them that, Mr. Allmen."

At that he gave a nod and the two goons flung Tom down the stairs. He bounced several times against the wooden steps, and his glasses went flying. Landing in a heap at the foot of the stairway, he struggled to his knees, grasping his right arm that dangled limply, painfully at his side. He peered about for his glasses.

"Over here, you blind bastard," said one of the goons who had followed him down the stairs. Tom crawled toward the man and saw that his glasses lay at his feet. As he reached for them, the goon's boot stomped on the lenses, crushing them. Tom tried to pick up the bent frames, but the goon kicked him in the ribs, collapsing him in a heap. He kicked him again and again. The toe of his boot split the skin of Tom's forehead, bruised his ribs, and drove the air from his lungs.

"Don't kill the son of a bitch," said a voice from the top of the stairs. "We need him to spread the word to the rest of them goddamned commies. Drag him out the gate and throw him in the gutter where he belongs. The rest of 'em will get the picture."

His friends found him on the street later, unconscious. They came forward furtively, gathered him up, and carried him away to his dingy apartment. When he came to his senses at last, he thanked those who had saved him.

"It's no use, boys," he told them. "We've come on hard times, and there's not much we can do but wait them out. I'm too beat up to be much use for a while. And the rent's overdue, so I think I'll have to move on. Good luck, and keep gathering those signature cards. The union's day will come. You can count on it. Don't give up hope."

During the dark days that followed, Tom could find only an occasional odd job. More than once, he was reduced to panhandling for a cup of coffee and a sinker. The only steady employment he found was on a work gang—thirty days on a vagrancy count. In his wanderings from rescue missions to hobo jungles, he often thought of returning to the docks, but there were no jobs for a union man, and he knew it. He was growing old, he told himself. He was no longer fit to lead the rough and tumble life he had lived since the war. It was time to step aside, time to turn over the labor battles to younger men, men with harder skulls and thicker skins, men whose idealism was fresh with hope and unburdened by the radical baggage of the past. He did see one ray of hope in his otherwise darkening world. He read in the newspaper that the struggle "up north" had moved to the streets. Longshoremen in San Francisco had hit the bricks, and among their organizers was a familiar name: John Loski, his benefactor from his IWW days in New York City. *Old Loski must have ten years on me*, Tom marveled, yet there he was still in the thick of it.

Hell, I can still carry a picket sign, he thought, *and it's been a long time since I've seen San Francisco.* His thoughts returned, as they so often did, to his beautiful Teddy, the only woman he had ever loved. *Maybe I'll see if old John could use a hand.*

21

"Move it a bit to the left into the light," Barron directed from his bed. Teddy stepped closer to the window and tilted the painting to catch the sun. He studied the work intently, at last shaking his head and sighing.

"You don't like it," she said.

"On the contrary, it's mesmerizing. How could it be otherwise?"

"It was just after you sailed aboard the *Maui Maiden*," she said by way of explanation.

"The first of a series of portraits, you say?"

"More than twenty others—at the hacienda."

"Then this one must have been done just *before* I sailed," he corrected her. "We had quarreled at the restaurant. You went away angry. Like a fool, I let you go. I telephoned you at home several times that night, but there was no answer." Teddy laid the portrait aside, turning it toward the wall. "Why, I do believe you're blushing," he said. "That's not very professional, is it? I see no reason to be embarrassed. It's a wonderful painting and a perfect likeness. Would that every artist had a model as beautiful as you."

"Barron, please—"

"I'm serious, Teddy. You're still as attractive as you were then. I don't blame Tom for falling in love with you or you with him. He was a very handsome young fellow."

She came to his bed and sat beside it, taking his hand in hers. She kept her face turned away, for the tears were coming, and she knew she couldn't stop them. With his free hand, he caressed her hair, evoking a sudden gasp from her, a suppressed cry.

"You mustn't weep," he said. "It's I who should weep, thinking of all the years I wasted, years I should have devoted to you. But we've no right to weep over lost time, because the time we've shared has been so precious. I'm not jealous, Teddy; I'm delighted that your beauty has been immortalized. I'm excited about the discovery. I don't care how many portraits there are, if they are good, then exhibit them with my blessing. I have no room in my heart for anger or jealousy."

"Oh, my darling, I'm so sorry. There'll be talk—"

"Don't worry about what people might say. If they are honest, they will say how beautiful you are and how fortunate I am to have you as my wife. They'll say what a wonderful relationship we have. And most important of all they'll say that Tom Quinn was a genius."

She leaned over and kissed him fervently.

"I don't deserve you," she said.

"I do have one concern," he said. "The exhibit, the publicity, it could lure Quinn back into our lives. If he is alive, he'd have every right to come forward to claim the accolades he so richly deserves. Inevitably that would bring you two together again."

"Certainly you don't believe—"

"I love you, Teddy, and I fear anything that might separate us. Not a day passes that I don't think about it, wonder if he's still alive, wonder if he'll show up some day."

"Then you think there's a chance—"

"Only a chance," he said. "I told you many years ago that I would do everything in my power to find Tom. You already know what my investigators found. Tom enlisted, was sent to France, was reported missing in action. It's the last we knew of him."

"And that was the end of it," Teddy said, an uneasy feeling coming over her. "Wasn't it?"

"Some things remain unexplained," Barron went on. "Tom Quinn was never heard from again. But examination of his regiment's records revealed a curiosity, a released prisoner of war for whom there was no previous record. It could have been a clerical error. It could have been Tom, perhaps, shell-shocked or suffering from amnesia. We'll never know."

"War can do many strange and terrible things," Teddy observed. "So you mean that Tom could still be alive."

"It's possible, but I'm far from convinced. My investigation had the man's name. They located him, followed him for several years. They found nothing to link him to art, to San Francisco, to you. He lived in a very different world. He bore no resemblance to the Tom we knew. The only thing they had in common was their given name. It's all in the dossier in the bottom drawer of my desk—the veteran's name, his movements, jobs he held, scrapes he got into. After a time, I halted the investigation, convinced it could not be our Tom. You may recall we discussed it at the time."

"So you think he's dead. How can you be so sure?"

"Because I know that he loved you, Teddy. Seeing his painting only reinforces that belief. If Tom had survived the war, he would have come to you. How could he stay away when—"

"He didn't know! He will never know!"

"Nevertheless the day may come when you'll want Marty to know. That's why I kept the dossier. With the discovery of these portraits, it is more likely that Marty will want to know about Tom, *all* about Tom."

"Never!" Teddy cried in outrage. "Marty has only one father, and that's you! I don't want to know what's in that file of yours, and I don't want him to know. It represents a part of my life that is over."

Barron smiled benignly and reached out for her hand. His face, more heavily lined since his heart attack, was the face of a man at peace with the world. Teddy's eyes lost their fire, and she laid her cheek against his breast and whispered, "I love you."

She felt a spasm run through him and looked up to find him staring at her with fear in his eyes. She rushed to the telephone.

＊　　＊　　＊

Barron had suffered another stroke and now was confined to his bed and required around-the-clock medical attention. A nurse was hired, and Teddy at last was able to convince her son that the family's fortunes were indeed desperate enough to require some sacrifice. Marty reluctantly agreed that he should withdraw from prep school, at least for his junior year, and attend public high school in the city. But he was adamantly opposed to exhibiting nude paintings of his mother as a means of raising money. The museum and the name Tom Quinn had been a part of his life for as long as he could remember. He had grown up with the *Portrait of Teddy* in the in the parlor and *The Blue Parrot* in the hallway. But the sheer eroticism of the painting now before him and the knowledge that his mother posed not once but many, many times for the artist, that was quite another story, and one that might not bear telling, not in the circles in which he moved. Marty shifted uncomfortably in his chair as Teddy paced the veranda.

"I was very young, of course," she explained. "I was adventurous and headstrong. Tom Quinn, well, Tom was like a family friend. He did the parlor portrait after dining with us one evening. I was flattered, as you might imagine. Later he wanted to do more studies of me."

"It seems he did a whole lot more," Marty observed coolly. "There you are stark naked in bed. My God, Mother, can't you just imagine what my friends would say?"

Teddy bristled.

"Artists' models can be women of virtue and high moral character," she said in a tightly controlled voice.

"I suppose they can be," Marty conceded. "I didn't mean to suggest . . ."

"You must remember that in those days your father was away much of the time. I didn't like being idle. I found it amusing, even flattering, that a famous artist wanted me to pose for him."

"You said some portraits had been discovered. Why not exhibit them and put this one away someplace?"

"That's just not possible. Dr. Hobart considers this a very important work. Besides, the others are nudes, too."

"All nudes!"

"All of them."

"What in the world were you thinking of?" he asked angrily.

"What I was thinking of more than fifteen years ago should be of no concern to you. What is important, and I cannot stress this strongly enough, is that the portraits are believed to be worth a great deal of money. I have been told on good authority that they might bring enough at auction to save The Bachelor Foundation. And that, my son, might be enough to save your father's life. In his condition, the collapse of the foundation could be devastating. I don't see that we have any choice but to go ahead with it."

"No matter what the cost?" the boy asked bitterly.

"I don't think the cost will be as great as you seem to imagine. These are not pornographic pictures, Marty, they are works of art. Dr. Hobart is preparing them now for exhibition. They needed cleaning and framing."

Marty arose and came to inspect the painting more closely. "I hope the others are more discreet than this one," he said. "It's obscene."

She could see his eyes going over every detail, the texture of her skin, the tousled hair, the rumpled sheets, and the eyes, the eyes of a woman aroused from a deep, untroubled sleep, and over all, the morning light flooding the scene with an erotic glow. She could almost see the struggle going on in his mind, the shock and outrage on one hand, the fascination, even titillation, on the other.

"What in God's name are people going to say?" her son mused. "They're going to think that my mother is a common—"

"Dr. Hobart estimates that painting to be worth half a million dollars."

Marty looked at her incredulously, then walked to the wall and stared down at the surf. He was silent for a long time. Then he turned to confront her, a sullen expression on his handsome young face.

"When will the exhibit open?" he asked quietly.

* * *

Hobart's column appeared in the Sunday paper. Its emphasis was on the discovery of a previously unknown body of work by an artist long lost to history. It was work, the critic said, that revealed a new dimension in the career of the man whose artistic genius had led to the founding of the San Francisco Museum of Contemporary Art and whose talent had inspired a generation of young artists. He discussed several of the paintings at length, and only in passing did the critic mention that the artist's model was none other than his patroness, Theodora Cullen Bachelor, wife of the famous philanthropist Barron Bachelor. The column was accompanied by a photograph taken years earlier at the Palace of Fine Arts during the Panama-Pacific International Exposition of 1915. It showed the artist, Tom Quinn, at the opening of that pavilion. Also pictured were the board of directors of the newly established museum, the late Charles Cullen, Barron Bachelor and his beautiful young wife, and Hobart himself. The column ended with the announcement that an exhibition of the portraits was to be held at the museum beginning in late June.

It didn't take much imagination to conclude that the story presented so objectively, so dispassionately, by the city's premier art critic would soon find its way onto the front page of the city's newspapers, despite the screaming headlines of labor strife that then engulfed the waterfront. The telephones soon began to ring at the city's newspaper offices, at the museum, at the Bachelor home, and Dr. Hobart's flat. The doctor solved his problem by attacking the telephone cord with his pruning shears. Teddy simply left her receiver off the hook until the telephone company could issue her an unlisted number. The museum ordered a battery of temporary phones installed and hired a dozen operators to take orders for tickets to the exhibition. And the newspapers assigned rewrite men to take calls that soon were pouring in from all over the country. They also sent reporters to the library and to the museum to research the career of the artist and the life of his beautiful model. Other reporters were dispatched to interview Teddy and photographers to take her picture and copy boys to pilfer family snapshots that might prove useful. Teddy handled them all with aplomb. Although she put on her best matronly manner to remind them of her station, she spoke willingly, even eagerly, of Tom and his work. But any questions suggesting that something more than a strictly professional relationship existed between artist and model were met with an icy silence and a disdainful glare. The reporters were left with harmless threads of fact from which to weave a romance with needles of innuendo and artful insinuation. And weave they did.

By Tuesday morning, "The Love Story of the Century," was spread across the front page, crowding out even a report of the pitched battles being waged between the police and striking longshoremen on the waterfront. The streets would run red with blood before the depression-weary public tired of reading about the illicit affair between a famous artist and a woman who was now the highly respected leader of San Francisco society. Soon the story, a mingling of fact and fiction, had reached into the art centers of the world via teletype. Its spread translated into millions of dollars' worth of free publicity for the Quinn exhibit. Dr. Hobart was ecstatic.

"Even the mayor recognizes its value," he boasted. "He called today to ask that we do our part to help defuse the strike situation. He suggested an exclusive showing for the working public with the emphasis on Quinn's blue-collar period, with no admittance fee as a good-will gesture on the part of the city and the museum. He thought it might help get workers off the streets and back to the bargaining table."

"I can't imagine there'd be much interest among the general public," Teddy observed.

"They'll be interested, all right," Marty observed angrily. "But their interest will have nothing to do with art. I can see it now, the museum crowded with those filthy communists drooling over paintings of a naked woman, laughing over the lurid tales the newspapers are printing. It's insufferable. I don't think I'll ever live it down."

"You'll survive," Teddy said. "I think you'll have a change of heart once the auction begins."

"That's crass, Mother."

"We'll see. At this point, I'd shake hands with the devil himself if it would hasten your father's recovery. Stop worrying about your reputation and take his dinner up to him. You haven't even looked in on him this afternoon."

"I was afraid to, afraid he'd ask questions that I wouldn't know how to answer without hurting him. I can't believe he'd go along with all this. I wouldn't know what to say to him."

"You might start by telling him you love him and that you hope he'll be well soon. You don't have to talk about the exhibition."

Hobart had turned away from them in embarrassment, but after Marty left, he came to her, put his arm around her and spoke softly.

"I'm sorry he's taking it so badly, Teddy. You were right; you saw it coming. I should have listened to you."

"That's utter nonsense," she said defiantly. "If he can't take a more sophisticated view of things, that's his problem. I'm afraid of his holier-than-thou attitude. He's a young man, yet he's acting like a petulant child."

"He's a teenager, Teddy. It's a difficult age," Hobart said. "This is a lot for sensitive young man to endure. Young people worry about how others perceive them. I can recall—"

"Mother!" Marty called, his voice tinged with panic. "Come quickly. The nurse thinks Father has had another stroke."

*　　*　　*

The Southern Pacific freight rolled into the San Francisco yards in the dead of night. As soon as the train began to slow, Tom leaped out of the boxcar. It was a difficult feat in daylight for a man with clear vision. In the dark for a man blind in one eye and only limited vision in the other, it bordered on suicidal. He hadn't seen the switchbox and landed hard on it just at the rail junction. His left arm, sore and swollen since his tumble down the stairs at the San Pedro pier, bore the brunt of his landing, which also sent his duffel bag flying. He lay very stiff as the cars clattered rhythmically by him. He was stunned and couldn't move his injured arm, but as his head cleared, he realized that his whole body ached, a sign he'd live to see another day. Not dead yet, he thought. Strange how things got more difficult as he grew older. A few years ago, he would have been up and running by now. As it was, his body protested painfully as he struggled to his feet and went in search of his bag. Finding it at last, he limped away from the rail yards toward the waterfront. At The Embarcadero, a voice whispered from the shadows.

"I wouldn't go that way, friend," it said. "The cops are patrolling the docks, and they get trigger happy in the dark."

"Thanks," said Tom. "Can you tell me where the strike office is?"

"Steuart Street," he said. "I'm going that way myself, if you'd care to tag along. We can watch each other's backs."

"Is it that tight?"

"It's a war zone."

"Seems quiet enough," Tom observed.

"The fightin' doesn't start 'til eight in the morning. It'll be plenty noisy then. You'll see."

His IWW card was enough to get him into the building, where he found John Loski seated at a table with several other men, hovering over a map. The little bull of a man with the bandy legs had aged a lot since their last meeting, but there was no mistaking the massive shoulders, the gnarled hands, and the scarred face. He spotted Tom in the doorway and raised his hand to shield his eyes from the glare of the overhead bulb.

"I'll be a son of a bitch," he muttered. "Is that who I think it is? Come in here, brother."

"I've come to pay a debt," said Tom. "I owe you one from the old days, and I'd like to lend a hand."

"You got a long memory, brother. I can't put a name on you, but I never forget a face."

"New York," said Tom, "just after the war. You signed me up." He reached into pocket for the tattered IWW card. "We were Wobblies together, but not for long. Got rousted, as I recall."

"They really put the run on us in the old days," said Loski, extending a brawny hand. "Well, we're really showin' them what we're made of these days. Welcome to the fight, brother."

"Allmen, Tom Allmen," he said to refresh the old fellow's memory. "I saw your name in the paper and said to myself, I owe old John a good turn. So here I am, fresh off a freight."

"We can use you, Tom. There'll be heads to crack tomorrow, count on it. Have you got a place to bed down?"

"Any safe alley will do," said Tom.

"If you got two bits I'll scribble you a note. Take it to the Seaboard Hotel and get yourself a bed. The boys there will take care of you. They're all good union men. And Tom, it's mighty good of you to remember the old days. A lot of hard years have gone by."

"And here I am running up a debt again," said Tom, taking the note.

"Lots of ways to pay it off," said Loski. "You'll see, come morning." The other men around the table squirmed impatiently, and Tom could see they were anxious to get on with the strategy session, so he shook Loski's hand again and made his way into the crowded hallway and out into the night. At the Seaboard Hotel, he presented Loski's note, but the desk clerk shook his head.

"We're jammed to the rafters, brother. I can give you a bed, but you'll have to share it with a guy who's on patrol. He'll be turning you out at daybreak."

"A couple of hours of sleep would be welcome," Tom said.

"That'll be twenty-five cents," said the clerk. "No need to sign in. We don't want any names written down, if you get my drift."

"Mind if I take this?" Tom asked, picking up a newspaper.

"Help yourself. It's yesterday's paper."

It was the banner headlines that had caught Tom's eye: "The Love Story of the Century," it said.

22

The opening of the exhibition rivaled a Hollywood premiere in its glamour and the size of the crowd that gathered outside the museum. Even the dock strike and the violence it precipitated failed to dampen the enthusiasm of a public desperate for diversion during the hard times. They came by the thousands to ogle the rich and the famous, and they were not disappointed. Publicity surrounding the show, which Hobart entitled "The Bachelor Portraits," had done its job well. Movie stars were there as were captains of industry. Potentates and magnates appeared, just as Hobart predicted. All about them was the aura of wealth, the smell of money. And an important number of them had come with open checkbooks, drawn by the opportunity to invest in one of the few commodities reasonably certain to increase in value over time. But the real lure to many was the chance to meet Theodora Cullen Bachelor, the beautiful and enigmatic Teddy, whose story had been told and retold in the press and periodicals for many weeks, growing more romantic and compelling with each telling.

Opening night was also a gathering of a few old friends. Teddy and Dr. Hobart were on hand to greet Gilbert Nance, the poet-turned-novelist and Literary Prize nominee, and his wife, Janice Kirk, recipient of the National Poetry Award in 1932. Film star Lucille Lowe, wealthy beyond all imagination after a succession of brief marriages, arrived in a black limousine accompanied by a matched pair of thoroughbred Afghan hounds and her latest paramour, a maharajah of somewhat more dubious pedigree. The petite actress, whose career on the silver screen faded with the advent of talkies, spoke glowingly of the late artist, hinting broadly that he had been her lover many years before when she was queen bee of an artist colony at Castle Cairn. Even the Lazarros were there, the innocents whose discovery had led to the unearthing of the now-famous Bachelor portraits. The Lazarros donated the eerie painting of the artist's mother to the museum and were guests of honor, introduced by the mayor himself.

Tom read of the glittering events between shifts on the picket line. The drama seemed unreal to him, so long had he been divorced from the world in which the story unfolded. It took a stretch of memory to recall the paintings around which the drama revolved. Only the beautiful Teddy Bachelor lived vibrantly in his mind's eye, so real and so wonderful that he found himself eagerly searching each new edition for photographs of her, while knowing full well that he could never approach her. Too much time had passed; too much water had gone over the dam. There was nothing there for him now, nothing but his memories. She had a nearly grown son, an ailing husband, a life so far removed from him that nothing could ever bridge the gap between them.

Tom drew a graveyard shift on the picket line, midnight to eight. So far that had kept him out of most of the skirmishes with the police, who were getting more vicious as the stalemate dragged on. It also gave him free time in the warm and quiet afternoons when he could find a park bench and sit in the sun and read whatever he could find that dealt with the exhibition. Every daily newspaper devoted a column to it; all the major national magazines followed it weekly. It seemed to him that everyone in the country was eager to clasp to its bosom the ill-fated young couple torn apart by the Great War, a couple whose love was now preserved forever in the work of the doomed artist. Tom soon got used to the idea that they were writing about him, and he rather liked it. For a man whose only romance was a memory, a have-not who was used to living in conflict with the haves, alone and unloved for years on end. He found it touching and rather gratifying. It was like attending his own funeral and hearing all the nice things people said, even though they didn't know what they were talking about. He spent hours poring over articles in his odd fashion, head cocked to give his good eye every advantage, while holding the printed page only a few inches away from his face. The periodicals included photo essays, several of which gave him the first glimpse he'd had in years of his own paintings. One magazine's cover pictured the beautiful and elegantly clad Mrs. Barron Bachelor admiring an unfinished portrait, with the model posed in the window of the artist's studio at the hacienda, her nakedness only partially hidden in folds of drapery, her velvety skin bathed in the brilliance of the morning sun. It brought tears to his eyes. He hadn't thought about it for a long, long time, but dimly across the years he could now remember that last morning when he stood before his easel, brush in hand, trying to capture all the emotion he felt for her and never quite succeeding. It seemed strange and inconceivably distant as if it all had happened in another lifetime to another man. The Tom Quinn he read about was a highly romanticized version of reality. How could this scarred, half-blind old roustabout once have been the handsome, talented young artist of the currently popular fairy tale? He looked at the callused hands and the gnarled fingers and the badly swollen arm and marveled that they had ever wielded a paintbrush that created works of art. He understood then how the aged soldier must feel as he pondered the heroic feats of his youth, or the white-haired athlete as he read news clippings from his college days. He peered into the mirror in his dingy room, looked into the rheumy eyes exaggerated grotesquely behind thick lenses, examined the face distorted by scar tissue and reshaped by long, hard years. He felt the wispy, gray hair and the black stubble of beard and wondered how these two could be one in the same.

They were not, he concluded. The Tom Quinn of the modern fable had vanished in the stinging mists of the Meuse-Argonne. The young artist had faded into history just as his eyesight had faded in the pain and horror of war. The innocent prodigy had been cast into the crucible of the twentieth century, and his naïve idealism, his vulnerable optimism, all his youthful impurities had been burned out of him, leaving him strong and lean and flexible, steeled for the punishing years of his maturity. They had been tough years, years that saw stubbornness and determination take the place of idealism, when cynicism served to shield him from the agonies of disappointment and failure. Tom Allmen was not an artist, he was a trade unionist, an organizer, a champion of the working man. He had dedicated his life to the struggle for human rights and the dignity of honest labor. All this in an age that demanded obedience from the silent, faceless drones who turned the wheels of industry, uncomplaining and poorly rewarded. He had made it his duty to teach them to complain, to demand the rewards they deserved. If his labor had not brought him riches, it had brought him peace of mind. But it also had left him old before his time, old and increasingly lonely.

It was the loneliness more than anything else that drew him inexorably to the museum, as a moth to a flame. He was desperate to know more about Teddy, who had been so circumspect in the interviews he had read. Was she really still as beautiful as she appeared in the magazine photographs? What a pleasure it would be to look again upon the face that he adored, hear again her voice and revel in her innocent and provocative sexuality, stand again in awe of her classic beauty. But would he dare approach her, would he have the courage?

He was curious about the paintings, too. He wanted to examine them, to try to understand why anyone would place great value on works of such an intimate nature. He hadn't painted them for others; he had painted them for himself and for her. No one must know he existed. No one must even suspect. A live Tom Quinn would be vilified for bursting the bubble of romance that had enveloped this event. No, the artist was dead and must remain so forever. Tom Allmen, on the other hand, was very much alive. What's more, he still had one clean shirt in his bag and a razor in his kit. Surely it could do no harm. . . .

*　　*　　*

Marty dreaded opening night. He was ashamed of the stories being spread about his mother, all the more so because she seemed to take a perverse pleasure in it all. In a measure of his own perversity, Marty was glad that his father, in a comatose state since his last stroke, would be spared the shame the boy saw descending upon the family.

"If he really knew what was going on, I would feel sorry for him," the youth told his mother.

"He doesn't need your pity," Teddy scolded him. "He needs your prayers. And if he did know what was going on, he is far too intelligent to confuse fact with fiction. He is sophisticated enough to regard these developments with some amusement and shrewd enough to realize they might mean the salvation of The Bachelor Foundation."

"But the idea of strangers reading all these stories about his wife and her lover while ogling pictures of her naked! What price do you think he would be willing to pay?"

"Your problem is that you believe everything you read," she said.

"But you've never denied any of it!"

"Let them think what they will of me. Thousands of people who never before heard of Tom Quinn now know that he is an important artist. Opening night is sold out. The first two weeks of the show are sold out. Six-figure bids had been offered for some of the paintings that haven't even been displayed yet. If the price of all this is a little embarrassment, then I'm happy to pay that price."

"It's mortifying," Marty moaned. "I'll never be able to face my friends again."

"You could if only you'd develop a sense of humor about it. Can't you see that people are making fools of themselves over this? They are the ones being manipulated by events, not I."

If he was slow at first to understand his mother's reasoning, he began to see the light as the museum filled to overflowing with celebrities at the premiere. A chamber quartet filled the museum with the strains of Bach partitas to keep the viewers moving at a brisk pace, while a dozen waiters cruised the crowd with flutes of champagne and trays of hors d'oeuvres. His mother, never more beautiful, accepted the adulation of her many admirers with queenly dignity while Hobart huddled with prospective buyers in whispered bargaining sessions.

Hobart's genuis for organization was apparent in every phase of the exhibit. The main gallery was hung with a sampling of Tom's early work, from street scenes of North Beach to his reminiscences of the Barbary Coast of his boyhood, including the haunting *Barbary Nights,* the only painting of his mother. Also on display were his dramatic remembrances of the great earthquake and fire, including the surrealistic *The Blue Parrot,* on loan from the Bachelor family. An entire room was devoted to the artist's blue-collar period, including a dozen paintings from the San Francisco waterfront of the prewar era.

At the archway that led into the newly renamed Bachelor Gallery was the transitional *Portrait of Teddy*, the artist's first effort to capture the beauty of his patroness, the work that had hung for years over the fireplace in the Bachelor parlor. The collection within the gallery, the newly discovered Quinns from his previously unknown romantic period, was the major attraction of the exhibit. It was

240

crowded all evening with a succession of admiring observers, connoisseurs and amateurs alike, all agog at the beauty and the rare intimacy of the nudes. In the center of the gallery on a slowly rotating platform was displayed the erotic *Teddy in Morning Light,* while the surrounding walls were hung with the other portraits, culminating with the unfinished *Last Portrait of Teddy.*

Marty, looking quite mature and handsome in his tuxedo, not only was impressed by the patrons of the arts, but awed by the adulations they heaped upon his mother. "You've grown more beautiful with the years," was an exclamation he heard often, and "What a great honor to meet you, Mrs. Bachelor. How wonderful it must be to have been immortalized by such a fine artist." If the guests were effusive, they also served to put Marty's mind at ease. Perhaps, he thought, the notoriety would vanish before fall semester. After all, it was not yet July. As for the lad himself, he spent most of the evening meeting old friends and associates of his father, and to each explained that, yes, Barron had suffered a series of heart attacks and yes, there still was hope for full recovery. And yes, he would be unable to attend the exhibition, although he had given it his blessing.

It may have been the elegance of the surroundings, or the general civility of the patrons, or the music or even the heady effects of the champagne, but the result was that Marty found himself slowly losing his reservations about the exhibit and its purpose. It obviously wasn't going to tarnish the reputation of his mother, who presided over all with regal calm and inimitable grace. Even he might survive the night. He became convinced of this when Dr. Hobart confided that the initial bids indicated the show was already an astounding financial success.

"We've received bids on several works," he whispered, "and since the asking prices begin at fifty thousand dollars, you can imagine what that means."

"It'll be too bad to see them go," Marty commented.

"Not many of them will go," said Hobart. "Unless I miss my guess, most of the purchasers will donate the works to the museum for permanent display."

"Why would they buy them and then leave them here?"

"Prestige, my boy, prestige. They'll attach a plaque with their name on it for all to see. Such pride of ownership will last forever, or until they sell the painting."

Late in the evening, Hobart strolled out for a breath of fresh air. The crowd that had gathered to gawk at the arriving celebrities had thinned out considerably. One passerby, a remarkably unprepossessing fellow, Hobart thought, had paused to study a reproduction of *The Blue Parrot* encased near the entry.

"A fine work, don't you agree?" Hobart called out cheerily.

"Yes, for a reproduction," answered the man as he turned to squint at Hobart through his thick lenses.

"So, you know your art, do you. Well, the original hangs inside. It is priceless."

"I would like very much to see it."

"Then come back on the Fourth of July. The exhibit will be open free to the public in honor of the holiday. Come, and invite your friends. You'll particularly enjoy the paintings in the main gallery. Most are from the artist's blue-collar period, pictures that glorify the working man."

"It took no artist to glorify the working man, brother. His toil itself brought him glory," the man said with a wry smile. "Too bad that's being overlooked in the streets of the city these days."

"What? What's that you said?" sputtered Hobart, aghast at the man's effrontery. But the fellow had turned away and vanished quickly down the fog-shrouded street. "Well, I'll be!" Hobart exclaimed. "I swear I've heard that voice before, and spouting the words of John Manchester! But no, it couldn't be."

*   *   *

The exhibit drew a huge crowd on the Fourth of July, mostly working people and the unemployed, lured by the free admission and the invitation of the mayor himself. It was the perfect diversion for many, a cultural event sandwiched between a picnic in Golden Gate Park and a late night fireworks display on Marina Green. But Marty was certain it was not an appreciation of the arts that boosted the turnout; it was the weeks of publicity and the interest in the private lives of the artist and his model that it aroused.

"Filthy working stiffs and gossiping housewives dragging their snotty-nosed brats," he muttered. "Dirty minds and nothing more. I'd like to throw the lot of them back into the street where they belong."

"I would remind you that they are here at the mayor's invitation," said Dr. Hobart. "The city is paying the bill, and they are the city's guests. I hope they will find the display elevating. At the very least, it keeps them off the streets, which was the mayor's intention. So long as they remain behind the ropes and keep their hands off the paintings, we must treat them with the same respect we'd show prospective buyers."

"That's a laugh! There isn't the price of a ticket among them, let alone a painting."

"I wasn't discussing economics, my boy. I was referring to attitude. Ours must be scrupulously democratic. This gesture is meant to soften the image of officialdom, to counter the repressive measures being used in the streets. We are obliged to be even-handed."

"I'll be evenhanded, all right. If I catch any of them stepping out of line I'll—look! Look there! What did I tell you! I knew they couldn't be trusted to follow instructions. Look at that one, would you! Hey, you can't you read the signs?"

Marty charged toward a balding man in thick glasses who had slipped under the rope to inspect *Portrait of Teddy*, his face only inches from the canvas.

"Wait! Wait!" Hobart called after the youth, but it was too late. Marty had collared the hapless visitor and was giving him the bum's rush. He shoved him past the guards and out the door and flung him into the street. Hobart, seconds too late to intervene, looked on helplessly as the man groped about for his glasses. He hurried into the street, retrieved the spectacles and tried to help the man to his feet. As the poor fellow fumbled with his glasses and the surrounding crowd laughed and jeered, Hobart got a good look at his face. It was the same man he had seen on the sidewalk on opening night, the man he had invited to return to the exhibit on this very day. Then came the shock of recognition.

"Quinn!"

"I meant no harm," said the man as the guards pushed their way toward him. Then he broke free and disappeared into the crowd.

"Let him go," Hobart told the guards. "It was a misunderstanding. It's best just to let him go."

*   *   *

Bloody Thursday exploded across the pages of San Francisco

history at precisely eight o'clock in the morning. The opposing forces had eyed one another warily across The Embarcadero for the several hours since daylight, but neither had made a move. At eight, the police let loose a hail of tear-gas bombs and charged the picket line with riot clubs flailing. Tom, yet to be relieved at the end of his shift, quickly tied a red handkerchief over his face to protect himself from the gas and braced for the assault. The strikers stood their ground, meeting clubs with picket signs and stumbling over the bodies of their fallen comrades as the attack intensified. Soon the weight of numbers forced the pickets to retreat into the littered alleyways off The Embarcadero and finally to Rincon Hill where they regrouped for a counterattack. Tom joined the first countercharge, armed with a piece of broken brick in each hand, holding his fire until he had closed the distance to the line of uniformed officers. As he reared back to toss his first missile he heard *pop-pop-pop,* a familiar sound that sent a chill through him. A scream to his right distracted him, and he saw a youth pitch forward grasping his chest.

"They're firing live ammo!" Tom yelled. "They'll murder us!"

The lead elements already were engaged in hand-to-hand combat amid the explosion of tear gas bombs, the blast of riot guns, and the crackle of small arms fire. Suddenly the street was littered with casualties, wounded men on hands and knees crawling for whatever safety they could find, the unconscious lying in pools of their own blood, the blinded staggering back to the safety of Rincon Hill. Tom paused to help a wounded striker just as a gas-masked policeman, looking like a monster from Mars, emerged from a cloud of poisonous mist.

"Look out!" cried the striker as a riot club hissed through the air. Tom raised his hand to ward off the blow and the bat smashed his injured forearm, missing his head by a fraction of an inch. The cop reared back to strike him again, and Tom let go of his injured comrade and turned to flee. But it was too late. The second blow caught him at the base of his skull and sent him sprawling into the gutter. He lay there unconscious as the battle surged back and forth around him until at last there was a break in the action and he was gathered up and carried to safety behind friendly lines. It was dark when he awoke, groggy and aching from the blow to his head. His left arm was numb and feeling it gently he realized bones were broken. All about him strikers were huddled in small groups around fires, nibbling on scanty rations and plotting the next day's battle. He fashioned a sling from his belt to cradle his broken arm and made his way among his comrades, offering words of encouragement.

"We'll beat 'em yet, boys," he said. "We'll come back strong in the morning. We've got right on our side. We'll win in the end."

But for all his bravado, he knew his fighting days were over. His left forearm was severely swollen, the hand purple and puffed up to the size of a grapefruit, the fingers so fat they could not move one against the other. His head ached so that it blurred the vision in his one good eye. All of the fight had been beaten out of him. There was nothing left but to slink away to lick his wounds. On shaky legs, he edged toward the perimeter of the encampment, and slipped into the shadows and down a dark street toward the railroad yards.

*   *   *

Headlines set in block type told the story the next morning.

3 KILLED, 106 INJURED
IN BLOODY DOCK RIOTS
S.F. Waterfront Rocked by Pitched Battles
Governor calls out National Guard

Alone in the semidarkness of his office at the *Chronicle*, the leading art critic and cultural arbiter of the city some called the Paris of the West, shook his head in disbelief. For hours he'd sat at his typewriter, glancing occasionally at the blank paper that defied his creative powers. With all the success of the exhibition, nothing came to mind but the ravaged visage of the man that thousands had come to venerate. Idly he allowed his memory to drift to scenes of the past: The handsome young artist in his plain clothing sitting silently, awkwardly at the dinner table, obviously charmed by his beautiful hostess. The enchanted young couple strolling arm in arm down the brilliantly lighted Avenue of the Palms at the Panama-Pacific Exposition. It was those memories that brought the true meaning of the Bachelor portraits into focus. The stories weren't exaggerated at all; it *had* been a bittersweet love affair. And in the end, the poor devil was thrown out of the exhibition of his own paintings. The enormity of such an injustice drove all other thoughts from his mind.

245

"You okay, Doc?" asked the copy boy.

"Yes, yes, Jerry. I'm fine. Writer's block, that's all. What's the latest?"

"Death toll's been revised," said the boy with a cool cynicism. "Just two dead."

"But they appear to have three bodies."

"One of 'em doesn't count, the one they found in the rail yard. Cops figure he's just a bum who grabbed for a freight and missed."

"Any I.D.?"

"He had an IWW card with his name on it. Another one of them commies, maybe come here to join the fight. Need any coffee, Doc?"

"No, thank you, Jerry."

"Well, I hope you can think of something to write about."

"Thanks, Jerry. I'm sure something will come to me."

*   *   *

At the other end of town, in a mansion overlooking the sea, Teddy sat alone in the parlor, reading the news reports of the rioting, horrified by the violence. Across the room, Marty sat clipping out stories of the exhibition for a scrapbook he had begun.

"It's dreadful," Teddy sighed, "all this bloodshed."

"The governor should have called out the guard first thing," the youth observed. "The editorials are right; a strong show of force would have prevented this rioting. I read that some policemen were injured."

"And three strikers were killed!" Teddy exclaimed. "And for what? A few dollars a day and decent working conditions. I can't believe it."

"It wasn't about money," said her son. "Those hoodlums were out to overthrow the government."

"Nonsense!"

"All right, just read the paragraph about the victims."

She ran her finger down the column and then read aloud: "Howard Sperry, a member of the ILA; Nicholas Bordoise, a member of the Cooks Union and the Communist Party, and Tom Allmen, a member of the Industrial Workers of the World."

"There, you see? They were communists and Wobblies, riffraff and rabble-rousers, just like the newspaper said. If you ask me, they got what they deserved. I have no sympathy for them, not a bit."

Exasperated, Teddy collapsed the newspaper into her lap.

"Haven't you got a tennis match this morning?" she asked. "You ought to be getting to bed."

"I am a little tired. I can finish this tomorrow."

He came to her, bent down, and kissed her on the cheek. She held him a moment, looking into his face. How much he looks like him, she thought, and yet—

"Goodnight, Mother," he said.

She nodded, and as he walked away, she could think of nothing but the handsome young hero of her childhood dreams, and the thought brought a feeling of emptiness, a deep longing, deeper than she had ever felt before. I'm growing old, she thought, old and lonely. Then as she dozed in the comfort of her chair, her mind wandered over the rich fields of memory. It was good to be with him again beside a mountain stream, laughing and happy, warm in his arms. She awakened when the clock struck midnight, laid the newspaper aside, and went slowly up the stairs. She paused at Barron's door, but did not go in. There was nothing she could do for him now, nothing anyone could do. Tom was all she could think of now. Later as she pressed a warm, damp cloth to her face, he appeared behind her. She could see him in her mirror, fresh and glowing in his youth.

"Oh, I've missed you so, Tom," she sighed. "How I wish we could have shared these past few weeks together. I've been so very, very proud of you."

But his image quickly vanished and she was alone. On her way to bed she stopped to take the dossier from Barron's desk drawer. "It can do no harm to read it now," she murmured, "and it has been such a long time."

*　　*　　*

Next morning the dailies agreed on a death toll of two, Sperry and Bordoise, who already had been anointed union martyrs. That afternoon a veiled woman appeared at the county morgue on the arm of a mortician to claim the body of the third man. On the first Monday of September, only a week after the death of Barron Bachelor, the caretaker at the hacienda saw Mrs. Bachelor's limousine arrived unannounced. The chauffeur opened the passenger door, and a veiled occupant emerged, clutching a funeral urn. She stood for a moment at the site of the old barn, her head bowed. Then she opened the urn and scattered its contents over the charred ruins. The caretaker assumed they were the remains of her husband and left the widow alone in her grief.